FLAMES
AND EMBERS
OF COAL

BY ELLIS ROBERTS

Anthracite History
The Breaker Whistle Blows

Ethnic History
Journey through Welsh Hills and American Valley

Poetry
Along the Susquehanna

FLAMES
AND EMBERS
OF COAL

A Historical Novel
of the Anthracite Region

ELLIS WYNNE ROBERTS

National Welsh-American Foundation
Washington, D.C.   *1990*

Second printing, with corrections, February 1991

Designed and composed by The Bookmakers, Incorporated, Wilkes-Barre, Pennsylvania

Printed and bound by the Haddon Craftsmen, Scranton and Bloomsburg, Pennsylvania

Manufactured in the United States of America

ISBN: 0–9616411–1–8

FOR

GAIL AND ELLEN

＆

CONTENTS

FLAMES
AND EMBERS
OF COAL

CHAPTER I

A PRISTINE VALLEY

Owen Roderick, twelve years of age, stood fishing on the shore of a small island in the Susquehanna River. The river was full of trout, bass, perch and shad. Owen was enjoying this late-summer Saturday, relaxing in the sportive experience. Earlier that day, he had gathered wild grapes and plums along the Plymouth Flats. Now he surveyed the meadows north of him and the high Tilbury Knob of West Nanticoke to the southwest and thought again as he often had: What a beautiful valley!

The pristine valley, called Wyoming, is about three miles wide and fifteen miles long. Holding the valley in its arms as they range from east to west are the Blue Ridge Mountains, part of the Appalachians in Northeast Pennsylvania. Passing through the heart of the valley is the Susquehanna River, following a serpentine route from Lake Otsego in New York State. The valley begins where the Susquehanna reaches the Lackawanna Gap in West Pittston near Campbell's Ledge and ends at the Nanticoke Gap where the river flows past Tilbury's Knob.

The beautiful valley was once the home of the Susquehannock Indians. Like other tribes, they were named by the white man after the river near their settlements. The French called the Susquehannocks the Andastes and Gandastogues.

The latter name sounded to the English like Conestoga, as they were sometimes called. The Susquehannocks, or Conestogas, were related by language and nature to the warlike and politically astute Iroquois.

Once the white man arrived, the same bountiful valley became a prize sought by both Connecticut and Pennsylvania colonists who spilled blood over the fertile valley as they fought for its possession. The value of the Wyoming Valley was not lost on the "Susquehannah Company," as the Connecticut squatters called themselves. They claimed the land under a grant from King Charles II of England. Charles then carelessly gave the same land to William Penn in 1681. A moral and fastidious Quaker, Penn refused to acknowledge his grant as clear title and insisted on buying it from the Indians who lived there as well, signing treaties for the same land. The Connecticut settlers advanced equal claims—they too had a grant from Charles II and a purchase from the Indians (although they mistakenly bought the land from Indians who had no claim to it). More to the point, they risked their lives pushing westward over a treacherous obstacle-course of mountains, streams, and rivers to establish a settlement. Once they were in the valley, the Pennsylvanians sent troops four times to try to dislodge them.

By 1867, the valley was at relative peace. The Yankee–Pennamite Wars, as the Connecticut and Pennsylvania conflicts had been called, were long over. The Wyoming Massacre, an ignominious rout endured by valley settlers at the hands of the English and Indians during the Revolutionary War, had long passed into history. The War between the States had just ended. Through it all, Wyoming Valley had kept its primeval radiance.

That late summer day of September 1867, outdoors was a tonic for Owen Roderick because most of his days were spent separating coal from rock inside a dusty, high, black building called a coal breaker. The work gave him the seriousness of a man, even though he was a boy.

As he fished, he spotted a beautiful golden trout, floating downstream—dead. It was the first time he had ever seen such a thing. Strange, he thought, I'll have to tell Taid. His Welsh grandfather, Taid, was an expert in fishing. He had fished the Dee and the Wye in Wales, and he was versed in the ways of trout. He would know why a large, fat trout would die in the clear water of the Susquehanna.

Taid would explain it all to him, and he would explain it in Welsh, for Taid thought, dreamed, and spoke in the Welsh language. Owen's parents also spoke Welsh exclusively to each other and to him, but Owen always replied in English. He was slowly losing his Welsh at his work in the coal breaker. Fortunately, all the Welsh were bilingual; consequently, communication was never a problem.

Owen gathered his catch and pushed off from the island in his little homemade boat, like a Welsh coracle with space for only one fisherman, to set out for home.

As he entered the kitchen, his mother greeted him in Welsh, "Well, my boy, are we going to have a nice fish supper?"

"Yes, a full one too, Mam," he replied in English. Proudly he held up his catch—three trout and two river bass. "We'll have a feast."

"Wonderful, call your Dada. He's under the arbor with Taid. He can clean these in no time. I'll have the frying pan ready."

Owen ran out joyously, shouting of his catch. His father

patted his head and accepted the fish. Knowing that cleaning them was his task, he entered the house.

Turning to his grandfather, Owen said, "You know, Taid, I saw a beautiful dead trout floating in the river. Why, I wonder?"

"Oh, I don't know really. It could be one of many things."

"But I've never seen one dead before."

"Well, I'll tell you what we'll do. Tomorrow, after church and before dinner, you and I will take a little walk. Your mother and Mr. Harris, the preacher, wouldn't like us fishing on Sunday, but just a little walk, you know," he said, winking, "and maybe we can find an answer."

The next day, Owen and his grandfather walked along the western shoreline of the Susquehanna for about one hundred fifty yards without seeing any trace of a dead fish. But when they had gone another fifty yards, they found a little inlet, murky and muddy. There, half in the water and half on the bank, was a large, dead river bass.

"What's this!" Taid exclaimed, walking around the inlet to pick it up.

"Could the muddy water kill it?" Owen asked.

Taid, now on one knee examining the bass, said, "This is not mud."

"What is it, Taid?"

"I'm afraid it's from the Avondale Breaker. It's mine water, full of poisons."

"How could it get down here? The breaker is up there on top of the hill," Owen puzzled aloud.

"Let's look," his grandfather said. "Maybe we can trace it back from this little pool."

"But I don't see any mine water."

"It's seeping in underground, but let's walk up the hill. Maybe it's running on the surface somewhere."

They looked up toward the breaker, standing four or five stories high, a black step-like structure, about two hundred yards above the river's edge. It was quiet on this Sabbath. Six days every week, it rattled and moaned as it cleaned and sized the coal, cutting the huge chunks of coal mined earlier and delivered from the mine to the coal breaker on the surface.

Owen and the other boys sat on small planks straddling iron coal chutes as the coal and all its impurities passed beneath them. Owen and the other boys had a job called "picking slate," removing the stone and slate as it passed so that only coal would reach the market. It was a gruesome, tiring job, seven in the morning until five in the afternoon. In winter, the boys seldom saw sunshine. It was dawn-to-dusk, monotonous work.

Walking with eyes glued to the ground as they sought a dribbling stream, Taid and Owen suddenly found themselves staring at the shoes of Bill Jones Three, the Avondale watchman who protected the land as well as the breaker. He was especially vigilant against poachers who entered the yard around the breaker to steal coal. Like every other Bill Jones, he had acquired a nickname because the small borough of Plymouth had at least a dozen Bill Joneses. He was Bill Jones Three because, having been widowed twice, he was now in his third marriage.

"You're on coal company property," he said sternly.

"Just a Sunday afternoon walk," Taid said, "no harm done."

"You know better, Mr. Roderick. Take the boy and go."

"Aye, no harm done." Taid turned, took Owen's hand, and started back down toward the river.

Halfway down, Taid touched Owen and rolled his eyes up the hill. "Is he gone?" he asked quietly as they continued to walk.

Owen turned and Bill Jones Three was still staring down at them. "He's up there," he whispered.

Then Taid turned and in his sweetest voice said, "Sorry, Bill, the boy has to have a tŷ-bach. Can he go by there?" He pointed to bushes to his right.

"Hurry then," said Bill.

They walked to the bushes and Owen said, "Taid, I don't have to go."

"Go!"

Owen understood.

Taid pretended to wait impatiently, all the while keeping his eyes on the ground. Spotting what he was looking for, he spoke urgently to Owen, "Brysia."

Owen hurriedly finished his forced outpouring, and they resumed their walk down the hill. They looked back yet again and saw Bill Jones Three standing in the shadow of Avondale Breaker.

When they got back down to the flats, Taid finally spoke. "Owen," he said, "I saw some breaker water, just a cupful, but I wanted to get a better look at it. That's when I thought 'tŷ-bach.' While you were in the bush, I looked and saw the tiniest ripple of rusty water. Coming to the surface it was, and exactly the color of breaker water. That's what's poisoning the fish."

"What can we do?" Owen asked. "How can we stop it?"

"Nothing."

Taid hurried along impatiently. Owen knew he had not heard the last of the dead fish and the poisoned water. When he got into the house, his parents were having a cup of tea, which, as Welsh, they might be doing almost any time of the night or day. Taid promptly flew into a torrent of Welsh about the breaker-water killing the fish. Owen's father picked it up with another protest.

"Don't get so excited," Mam said to both of them. "Do you think a few little fish bother anyone in mining? Two good men killed last week and three last month. What's a few fish anyway?"

Dada cooled a bit. "But it is so easy to stop," he said. "Dig a cesspool by the breaker, pump it up the hillside to the top. Send it down the other side, away from the river. Now as far as killing and maiming men, that's another matter. Protecting men costs too much. This little Avondale Colliery cannot afford more expense, at least that's what the fire bosses and section bosses say. But they could spend a little on a few pumps to keep the river clean."

"Why don't we tell them and ask for pumps?" Owen asked.

With the same negative tone, Taid said, "We can't. No, Owen bach, it's nothing we'll say, or it will be the sack for Dada and me and we can't have that, can we now?"

"That's the point you must remember," Mam added. "Whenever you make a suggestion that might be helpful to everyone, you must hold back because the section foremen are afraid of the mine foreman, and he is afraid of the colliery superintendent, the superintendent is afraid of the general superintendent, and he is most afraid of the board and owners.

No one wants to make a suggestion or recommendation. It might be turned down, and then he'll be a marked man. Everyone would rather keep quiet, act pleasant, and put on airs as a silent admirer of the company."

"So, for now," Dada said with finality, "Owen, you can still fish upstream and there will be plenty of fish for years. Let's eat the rest of those you caught yesterday and have a good supper."

Like most Welsh families, they preferred good food to idle talk, and so they had their meal. As they sat finishing with tea, Owen was still uncomfortable about the fish. To him, good fishing was not just idle talk. He asked, "Dada, do you think the time will ever come when the fish will not be able to live in this river?"

"No, Owen, not in your lifetime. Of course, it all depends, now doesn't it, on how much coal and how many coal breakers you will see emptying into the river. If the valley has as many rich veins of coal as they say, you can be sure they will be mined. And the coal should be. The people must have coal. So, if the new breakers and water runoffs empty into the river, there might come a day when the fish would all die."

As Dada was talking, Mam looked out the window. "Look who's coming across the way. I do believe he's calling on us."

"Who?" asked Taid.

"Mr. Daniel Daniels. Yes," said Mam, "the Old Pain himself."

As she spoke, Mr. Daniels knocked on the door. Dada opened it and said, "Come in, Mr. Daniels. What can I do for you?"

"Well, it's not a pleasant word I have for you Mr. John

Roderick," he said, fumbling and hesitating as he edged into the house.

"Have a seat anyway," said Mam, knowing whatever Mr. Daniels had to say would take some time. Even casual weather comments from Mr. Daniels became exercises in ifs, ands, and buts. Mr. Daniels was employed by the Avondale Colliery to do various bookkeeping chores both at the breaker and at the company store. As a Methodist deacon, he had assumed an unctuous manner, thick as fudge.

Mr. Daniels sat down and fumbled with his hat. "Mr. Roderick," he said, "an hour or so ago, Mr. Jones was good enough to come to my home to report that your boy Owen and his grandfather were on coal company property when they should not have been. You know, Mr. Jones is under my supervision so he has to tell me. Mr. Roderick, I'm sorry, but I must report this to Mr. Superintendent Brown."

"What do you have to report?" Dada interrupted.

"Well, you know . . ."

"They were merely walking, Mr. Daniels, they were not stealing coal on the property."

"That is true, Mr. Roderick, but you see rules are rules, and Mr. Brown does not like trespassers because sooner or later . . . well . . . sooner or later the property will be overrun with poachers. The rules are rules. Just as they are at the company store. If a man earns a living at the mine, he is expected to buy his food and supplies for work at the store. And while I'm here . . ."

"I see, I see," said Dada. "What you are really here for is to remind me again that I am not patronizing the store."

"Well, that *and* the trespassing. But I'll explain to Mr.

Brown it was just a harmless Sunday afternoon walk. The store, now that's far more important, Mr. Roderick. I told you last month, the company must have your business or you won't be entitled to work at Avondale, will you now?"

"I told you last month, Mr. Daniels, that we buy most of our groceries at the store and all my powder for the mine as well."

"Yes, Mr. Roderick, but I noted your account last Friday. You have not bought a pound of tea at the store in over three months, and only two pounds of butter in six weeks. Your wife has not bought any dry goods in over a year."

Dada was embarrassed. He had underestimated Daniels the Pain's addiction to scrutinizing the company store's accounts. He remembered too well that Sam Stevens had been fired because of his store account.

"Very well, Mr. Daniels, I see your point. My wife has meant no harm. She was very excited about some new patterns in cloth up at Mr. O'Brien's store, and she may have picked up a few pieces, but you can be sure we never will again."

"Thank you, thank you, Mr. Roderick. We need your business . . . we want your business . . . we want all of the employees at Avondale to know it." The Old Pain finally rose and too ceremoniously took his leave. Departing, he continued to utter repetitious thanks.

Daniels was scarcely out of earshot before Mam lost her temper. "That old pain, the nerve of him, checking on my dry goods."

"Not only dry goods, Blodwen, your larder, as well."

"They'll soon be counting our cups of tea," she said. But she knew as well as her husband that his job was at stake.

She agreed that his capitulation was only logical, and when she cooled a little, she added, "Why in God's name do they deny a man like Mr. O'Brien a little business. He has a fine family and he's what I call an Irish gentleman."

Taid had not uttered a word since before supper, but now he could not resist interjecting, ". . . who always has the best dry goods in northeast Pennsylvania."

"Oh, go on with you. Be serious now."

"I am," Taid said, "we've had a good day. We can't walk on the company's coal land. We can't stop the company from killing the fish. We can't buy goods from anyone but the company, even if someone else can sell us cheaper or prettier. But why make a fuss? We knew it all the time."

"Taid, was it like this in Wales?" Owen asked his grandfather.

"Yes, my boy," he answered, "and a long time ago, much worse, much worse! When I was just ten, a little younger than you are now, I worked in the mine, opening and closing doors to control the air. Women worked deep in the mines along with men for ten and twelve hours a day. Before that, it was worse still, or so my father said. The mine was hardly a mine at all. There were perpendicular holes in the ground. The entrance was just big enough for a bucket holding a few women and children to descend. The bucket was connected with a rope and controlled winch and dropped down to a coal vein. Working in those holes, they were like groundhogs. My father—your great-grandfather—worked in a more developed mine, as they called it, when he was older. He told me he dragged coal from the face to the main road. There were no wheels on the cart, but he had to drag the coal for sixty yards.

Most times he came home from work with hands bleeding."

"As for myself, before I came to the United States, I did it too. I remember many a settling-up Saturday, like our pay-day here. I remember after a whole month of work that I had next to nothing left. They took out stoppages, as they called them, against the cost of powder and of sharpening augers and candles. Yes, we worked with candles to give light. But bad as I had it, my father had it worse. Week after week, I saw him go down the old shaft to kill himself. And every morning at six, before he went down, there was a prayer meeting on the surface where he gave thanks to God for keeping his children from starvation."

A single teardrop escaped from Owen's eyes as he listened, and he quickly ran to the pantry as though to get a drink of water. He didn't want them to see how terrible the story made him feel.

"Well," said Dada, "those reminders make The Pain seem like just a pest."

A very few minutes later, Owen's mother reminded him it was bedtime. "Time now, Owen. It's up at six you'll be— and too sleepy to say good morning."

Owen did not argue tonight. He knew the breaker would be running at full capacity in the morning. He hated it. Especially did he hate the breaker whistle. The breaker whistle blowing in the winter wind or in the calm of summer was a shrieking cry, a morning call that roused the town and country-side. Tonight, in the comfort of his bed, he would forget it and put himself to sleep with only the most beautiful thoughts. And this night, as every night, they were of Miss Rhondda Hall.

è& è& è&

Rhondda was pronounced correctly "Rontha" by the Welsh people of Avondale and Plymouth, who knew that a dd in Welsh was equivalent to an English th, pronounced as in mother. All others called her Rhondda, but at least they spelled it correctly. To Owen and her students, she was their inspiration. They, of course, called her Miss Hall.

When Owen had to leave school to work in the coal breaker, he was very unhappy. Only a year earlier, he had been captivated by his sixth-grade teacher. The auburn-haired Miss Hall was fresh from the Friends Academy in Philadelphia and she came with missionary zeal to teach the children of coal miners in a one-room schoolhouse. She was seventeen years old. Unlike the other two teachers he had had in the first five grades, Miss Hall never impatiently slammed her ruler on the desk. Instead, she moved among small groups of three or four, designated as grades, and gave each student a moment of attention, testing some, encouraging others, chiding, urging, usually pleasant, even smiling. The boys worshipped her; the girls imitated her. And Owen loved her. This night, as he lay in bed, he recalled the beginning of his adoration when he was in her class and she in her first term of teaching.

On the first cold day of autumn, when Owen anticipated the potbelly stove should be fired up, he was at the school door when Miss Hall arrived.

"Good morning, Owen, what brings you out so early?" she greeted him.

Owen hesitatingly said, "Miss Brown, our old teacher, I

mean our last teacher, had me start the stove. I thought it might be cold enough. Would you like me to start it?"

"Well, thank you Owen. I think that would be fine. They showed me the woodpile behind the school, but if you would bring some wood in, I'd be obliged to you."

In minutes, Owen had the wood in and the fire started. From that day until the day he left, he was in charge of the stove. Those wonderful early mornings alone with Miss Hall he would never forget. He shared his family's joys and problems with her. She in turn told him about life with her father and mother in Philadelphia.

Her father was a Welsh Quaker who owned a small iron foundry in Philadelphia. He used anthracite to fuel his iron furnaces and that was how she knew about Wyoming Valley. Her father was a friend of Asa Packer of Mauch Chunk, an energetic canal and railroad builder. Packer had encouraged Hall to send his daughter to the anthracite area where the children of miners needed to be taught.

Rhondda Hall's mother was also a Quaker; her ancestors had come to America from Bala in North Wales more than a century and a half earlier. Owen was quite pleased to hear that.

"And could your mother speak Welsh to you?" he had asked her one morning as she was telling him about her mother.

"No, I'm afraid not. In a hundred and fifty years, the Welsh language had disappeared."

Eager to establish a closer bond, Owen persisted, "But you do know a few words, don't you?"

"I'm sorry, Owen. I know it would help me here, with so many Welsh in Plymouth, but the Welsh of my ancestors was gone by the time of the American Revolution."

Owen was disappointed.

"As a matter of fact," Rhondda added, "many of them lost their pacifistic principles as well. When the Revolutionary War began, they got so excited about independence that they forgot their stance against war."

"Are you still a Quaker?" Owen asked.

"Yes, I think of myself as a Quaker. But there are no meeting houses here, so I attend the Episcopal Church in Plymouth. However, whenever I can, I worship as a Quaker."

"Are there many differences between Quakers and Episcopalians?" Owen asked.

And then, as she always did, Miss Hall detailed some of the differences and similarities, always trying to level her answers to Owen's intelligence and curiosity. Owen's strength was his curiosity, overcoming his limited exposure to books, a curiosity that enabled him to learn from family members, from his pastor and friends in the church, and from Miss Hall most of all.

Like all great teachers, Rhondda Hall taught her students by learning about them and using their own experiences as a source of knowledge. Avondale in Plymouth had a rich heritage as a small anthracite town and she wanted her students to know it. To an outsider, Avondale looked like a rather squalid village of company houses. To her children, it was an exciting, friendly place to live, swimming and fishing in the Susquehanna, picking huckleberries on the mountainside above the Avondale Breaker, hiking up to Tilbury Knob, ice skating in winter on the old North Branch Canal, sleigh riding on every hill.

Miss Hall wanted them to know that Plymouth was not just another coal borough, it was the anthracite borough from which Abijah Smith and his brother John, in 1806, shipped their first ark-load of coal, fifty-five tons to be exact, down the Susquehanna River to Columbia, near Lancaster. This was one of the first, if not the first, attempts to market the shiny, hard stone coal. Unfortunately, the first attempt of the Smith brothers failed, and they hauled the fifty-five tons back to Plymouth, unsold.

Accenting this failure and adding a moral story to an interesting historical one, Miss Hall excited her students with the vivid account of Judge Jesse Fell's success in burning anthracite coal in an open grate without applying a forced draft. This discovery excited the Smith brothers especially, because now they could show people how well anthracite would heat a home. She told her students that other men, especially one Oliver Evans, had also burned anthracite successfully; but Judge Fell's success in Wilkes-Barre, so close to home, really stimulated the demand for coal in Wyoming Valley.

Miss Hall found the students in rapt attention as she read the letter Judge Fell sent to his cousin explaining the discovery:

Esteemed Cousin:

When I saw thee last I believe I promised to write thee and give some data about the first discovery and use of stone coal in our valley. . . . Accordingly, in the month of February,

1808, I procured a grate made of small iron rods ten inches in height and set it up in my common fireplace and of first lighting I found it to burn excellently well. This was the first successful attempt to burn our stone-coal in a grate, so far as my knowledge extends. On its being put in operation, my neighbors flocked to see the novelty but many would not believe the fact until convinced by ocular demonstration. Such was the effect of this pleasing discovery that after a few days there were a number of grates put in operation. This brought the stone-coal into popular notice.

As soon as the Smith brothers heard of Judge Fell's success in burning anthracite, they decided to send the ark-loads of coal back down to Columbia once again. On this trip, they also sent masons along to build fireplaces and show people that this "stone coal" could be burned. They sold their coal for ten dollars a ton and proved that it produced more heat than two and one-half cords of good wood. Furthermore, it was cleaner, it required less labor and attention, and it burned longer. The Smith brothers became the first successful dealers in anthracite. They next shipped coal to New York City, to a company that belonged to Price and Waterbury, who became the first retailers of coal in America, selling it for $16.67 for two thousand pounds, or one short ton.

Owen found Miss Hall's history fascinating, as did most of her students, who took the story of early anthracite home to their parents. Like the other children, Owen found the reaction of his parents puzzling. They seemed to have many negative thoughts about coal mining. It was not a romantic history of discovery and profit for them. They seemed to get a sad, skeptical look on their faces when the topic of coal mining came up.

The morning visits with Miss Hall were now a thing of the past. Sometimes Owen might not see her for six full days, an interminable time, until he could call to see her at the home of a widow, Mrs. Llewellyn Williams, who provided accommodations for boarding. Inevitably, he would call on Saturday afternoon about one o'clock, telling his mother as he left the house that he was going to O'Brien's Store with Miss Hall to help her with her groceries. And he did this. Miss Hall was eager to see her inquisitive and bright young friend and to receive his help any Saturday.

But she was especially eager to impress upon him the need for more reading and education. She gave him books of short stories and biographies and much history, which he devoured. She also gave him advanced math books that lay dormant on his table for weeks. He had average math ability, but once he got stuck and had no one to ask for help, he quickly dropped the math and immersed himself in the other books.

In the year since he had left school, Owen had not felt any interruption in his education. From his mother and father, from Taid, and especially from Miss Hall, his knowledge and maturity had seasoned. Through it all, his admiration for, his attachment to, and his enchantment by his teacher had grown.

And so Owen drifted to sleep as he did every night, not thinking of the events of the day, like today's incident of Jones Three, the dead fish, and the pollution of the Susquehanna, nor of his pleasant talks with his dear Taid, nor of the unpleasant visit of Daniel Daniels, but only of Miss Hall.

CHAPTER 2

ॐ

FLAMES OF COAL

Next morning, Owen and his grandfather took their breakfast together. Dada stayed in bed because he could not move to a new mining breast until a gangway was driven. He had been promised it would be ready by the next day.

While eating their uwd, as they called oatmeal, and drinking their tea, they made sparse conversation in the early morning hour. They left the house together with a warm "ta ta" to Mam and started their quarter-mile walk up the fields to the breaker and colliery.

Too old for active mining or laboring, Taid was employed as a road-cleaner, keeping the gangways clear of large boulders of rock or coal, which might interfere with the mules and cars as they hauled coal from the workplace to the foot of the shaft, before the coal was lifted to the breaker. The new Avondale Breaker stood right above the shaft as an efficiency measure, shortening the distance between the colliery and breaker.

The two walked the hill together, and they talked again of the polluted water running from the breaker into the Susquehanna. They recalled some of their fishing expeditions of the summer, and ended as they usually did, with Taid describing to Owen the challenges of fishing in the falling waters of the River Dee in Wales.

When they reached the coal breaker, Taid gave Owen a shoulder hug and sent him climbing up to the breaker. Taid continued a few steps and joined a group of six or seven miners and laborers, and in seconds they were in the cage dropping underground. Owen, who paused to watch the cage descend, called out as he always did, "Ta, Taid."

By the time Owen arrived at his workplace, the Avondale Breaker was just struggling to get itself started. The young breaker boys had taken their places over their chutes, but coal was not coming through yet, so they lounged half asleep on their little plank seats. At twelve, Owen was one of the older boys, and he preferred to stand looking through a small opening in a broken pane of glass, gazing across the Susquehanna toward Hanover Green and Nanticoke.

Gazing down to the mine yard, he saw Pat Riley carrying a load of hay toward the cage in the mine shaft. "They sure take good care of the mules down there," Owen thought to himself. The machinery of the breaker groaned and sputtered, then suddenly, like a junk yard in an earthquake, began a thunderous orchestration of dissonance, a deafening slapping and banging of gears, belts, pipes, and boilers. The breaker had started up. The noise was deafening.

Owen started quickly for his chute, but old Shadow Morgan, the breaker boss, screamed over the noise, "Wait a minute, Owen. Run down to the supply shanty and ask Joe Butts for a can of heavy grease. The goddam gears are all but frozen tight."

Owen was happy to run the ten minute errand; any relief from the chute was welcome. As he crossed the yard, he saw

Pat Riley going down with another load of hay. He took the grease from Joe Butts in the supply shanty and started back to the breaker.

Walking with the grease for Shadow Morgan, he looked up at the breaker and wished that somehow he could avoid going back in. Suddenly, a spurt of flame shot up from the shaft to the top of the breaker. One moment it was a drab Monday like any other; the next the flames gushed out of the shaft and shot high through to the top of the breaker. It happened in an instant. Like an oil gusher made of fire, the flames seared the whole mine yard.

Within seconds, the breaker was an inferno, the mine yard a hellish chaos. Old Alex Wier, the surface engineer, pulled the breaker whistle and tried to blow it continuously, but in a few minutes the heat became too much for him and he had to escape. By then, the flames and the whistle had aroused the town and brought the entire community to the site. The flaming, fiery breaker sitting on top of the mine shaft sealed the only mine opening. There were a hundred or more men working down there and they were trapped.

The minute he saw what was happening, Owen screamed and ran back toward the shanty and the colliery office, tears already streaming down his face. "Help them! Help them!" he cried. "The boys are up there! Oh my God! Help, help! Taid, Taid!" No one paid any attention to the breaker boy, and Owen turned and ran, and kept running, out of the yard, down the hill, to his home. His father and mother had heard the breaker whistle. They were running up the field where they met him. He fell into his father's arms—sobbing, shaking, half delirious. Dada picked him up and carried him into the house, still crying, "It's a fire, a fire in the mine . . . the men, the boys, will all be burned . . . I wasn't there. I was going for oil . . . Oh, Dada, save them, please, please!"

"That's all right now, Owen. They'll have the fire put out in no time at all. Just calm down, calm down." They both tried to calm him and his mother, in a litany of endearments, cooled his brow, still sweating after his crazed run from the colliery yard.

"Take care of him," Dada said, and hurried to the colliery himself.

There he saw men and women milling about and watching. Although they were trying to express concern, they were actually interfering with the attempts to put out the fire. The frantic cries of the wailing women and the impatient curses of the frustrated firefighters split the air. Firemen from Kingston and Luzerne had arrived. They were persuading, entreating the mass of people to move. But the frantic crowd of men, women, and children were looking for one thing—a sign, a word, some hope that a father or brother was safe.

The Bloomsburg and Lackawanna Railroad tracks ran beside the Susquehanna. Soon they were bringing men and machinery from points as far away as Scranton. By one o'clock, the train had brought in the Nay Aug Steamer from Scranton. Since they were unable to clear the yard of the frenzied crowd any other way, the firefighters turned the hoses on the human melee. It was pitiful but it worked and it finally enabled the hose companies to concentrate on the fire.

To save the trapped men, the rescue workers decided to

pump air down into the mine although they knew it would intensify the fire. They hoped that the men in the mine had somehow sealed themselves off safely in some corner. Ultimately, all the above-ground structure – the cage, the breaker, everything – was destroyed.

Rhondda Hall moved about among the mass of individuals standing out of harm's way in the rear of the mine yard. She was surprised at how worried she was about Owen. She did her best to reassure those in anguish but her compassion mostly fell on deaf ears. Her pupils clung to parents or other family members, trembling and in fear. When she saw Owen's father she ran toward him.

"Where is Owen? Did he get out?"

"Yes, yes. He's at the house. He needs you. Can you go down there?"

At once she turned and ran down through the field in a race of joy, and into the house. "Where is he?" she asked.

Mam held her fingers to her lips, "I've given him a little paregoric, he might be dozing."

"I must see him," she said, and Mam took her to the small parlor where he lay. He opened his eyes as he heard them.

"Oh, Miss Hall! Taid is in the mine! I must find him."

"No, no, Owen. There's nothing you can do. There are hundreds of men taking care of everything." She took him in her arms, nearly crushing him, and for the first time kissed him fervently.

"My Taid, Taid. I know he's killed!" He began to sob.

His teacher continued to hold him tightly. Once his sobbing diminished, they cried quietly together.

☙   ☙   ☙

Dada did not know where to begin to help. He saw Red Williams, an inside assistant foreman, directing five men clearing debris from the shaft area.

"Red, where can I help?"

"We've got another big job to do. Go talk to Dan Evans. He wants someone to put a crew together to build a rigging. We've got to get down inside."

Dada found Evans standing near the mine lost in thought. "Dan, tell me just what you need. I'll talk to the best of the union men; they're the most skilled and most reliable."

"Fine. You figure out what we need. Anything to substitute for the cage and shaft. We've got to get down. We still don't know how many are alive down there. We don't know if it's safe to go down. We don't know how much gas is down there."

"Hurry and get your men started," Dan ordered.

As the fire had subsided and the flames fell to flickers, the hysteria turned into deadness. Fear and grief silenced the onlookers.

By five o'clock, four hundred feet of Nay Aug hose was dropped through an air tunnel so that water could be poured into the base of the shaft. By this time, the fire had been extinguished above ground and work had already started to clear the charred timbers from the shaft area.

It took Dada and his crew two days to jury rig a derrick and a system for re-entering the mine. Once they had it running, they sent a caged dog down first to test for gas. The dog survived. Then Joe Virtue volunteered to go next. Halfway

down, burned timbers obstructed his passageway. Charlie
Jones and Stephen Evans also descended to clear the obstruc-
tions. Seventy yards down into the mine, they found a door
barring their way. Afraid there might be poisonous gas behind
the door, they came back to the surface.

The next two men to go down were Tom Williams and
Dave Jones. The gas killed them both.

It took two days to clear the mine of gas. Then a crew of
six, led by Jim Fowler and Dada, finally entered the mine,
where they found the terrible answers to all the terrible questions of the past three days. They found seventy men huddled
dead behind an incomplete barrier they had constructed to
seal themselves from the gas.

They looked at the victims in complete silence for a minute or so. Suddenly Dada gasped. "Look there," he said, "It's
my father."

Jim Fowler grabbed him. "Hold on now," he said, expecting Dada to collapse.

Dada stood hunched over for a moment. Then he stood
up straight. "It's all right, just let me touch him," he said.

He had no difficulty reaching his father's body—half kneeling, half lying among the other dead. At his feet was the small,
worn and coal-black New Testament he always carried in his
back pocket. Dada picked up the little Bible, stuffed it into
his pocket, and lowered his father's head to the ground so
that he was in a resting position. Then he turned away.

"Let's get to the surface," he said. "We must get these
bodies out."

When the crew got to the surface, they reported the find-
ings to the coroners, Wadham and Eno. Later in the day,

another crew found the bodies of forty more men and boys. In all, a hundred and ten men and boys had lost their lives.

The coroners were charged with identifying and counting the bodies as they came to the surface. It took three days. Myron Kingsley was in charge of the long, tedious task. He used his own horse, windlass, block, ropes, and tackles, but he also relied on the mechanism constructed by Dada and the men. It was a time-consuming job; the cage held only one or two bodies in one ascent and the horse pulling the cable traveled in a circle for more than 5500 feet—more than a mile. Every trip took eight minutes or more.

The Scranton newspaper printed a diary of the procedure:

> . . . 2:40 P.M. The twenty-fourth corpse is William Reese, Coal Street, Plymouth. Wife in old country, arms raised as though boxing, hands clenched, died in agony. . . . The twenty-sixth body is that of William N. Williams, Turkey Hill, Plymouth. Wife and three children, face bloody. Wife in crowd, screaming. The fifty-second and fifty-third bodies, man with son in his arms. The saddest sight of today, John Butch, left arm clasped around boy, John Jr.

On the last day Dada brought out the body of his father. Miss Hall, who worked indefatigably to comfort and aid the widows and children, now stood mutely by, waiting with them. The silence of the mourning group was broken only by the shrill cry or moan of a widow recognizing the body of her husband, or a mother recognizing a son.

When Miss Hall saw Dada and his friend Red Williams removing Taid's body from the cage, she quickly went to a pile of canvas pieces, extracted one, and ran with it to Dada. The canvases, used to control air in the mines, were now stacked high, ready to provide some dignity to the victims.

Dada and Red enclosed Taid's body in the canvas and prepared to take it down the field to the house.

"Go before us Rhondda, if you will," Dada said. "We'll give you time to get Owen and bring him up by the old township path, so he won't see us. Keep him with you most of the day. It's time that he see the full devastation of this awful thing. Put him to work, and if you can, keep him overnight."

Rhondda responded quickly. She picked Owen up at his house and led him through Avondale scenes that were to mark his conscience forever. Among the affected families, he saw suffocating silences, heard harrowing cries, wailing, self-castigation, accusations. Most of all, an exhausting, wearying, interminable search for reasons. Why? Why? Why? He poured endless cups of tea and coffee, served countless sandwiches, ran innumerable errands, carried groceries to small homes, some no more than hovels.

Late in the afternoon, Miss Hall took him to the neat home of Mrs. William Evans. Perhaps she wanted to give Owen some perspective, some one thing to mitigate his grief for Taid. The preoccupation with service had helped. Now she took him to the Evans home where William Evans lay with his three sons, Lewis, William, and Methuselah, in separate coffins. As they approached the house, they heard Mrs. Evans crying. Once inside, they saw her obsessively turning from one casket to another, calling out, brushing a forehead, touching a hand, smoothing a hair, kissing a cheek, crying in her pain. She had no one left but a six-year-old daughter.

Until late in the night, Rhondda and Owen visited home

after home of the bereaved. At ten thirty, they returned to Miss Hall's boarding house where she gave Owen her bed and collapsed on a couch. She had fulfilled Dada's plan for Owen. As Owen fell asleep, he was not aware that Taid's body had been prepared for burial and was lying at home, being mourned exactly as the victims he and Miss Hall had called on.

When Owen awakened the next morning, he felt rested but strange. He felt stronger but he also felt older. He would not be able to put his feelings into words for some years, but activities of the previous day had matured him. He had started the day as an emotionally drained twelve-year-old and awakened the next morning a young man with a calming, broadened vision. He accepted the word of Miss Hall that today, Sunday, was the day of his grandfather's funeral.

After a good breakfast, he and Miss Hall walked to his home. Dada and Mam took him into the parlor where his Taid lay clean and composed in the casket. Owen's eyes filled, but at the same time, he felt consoled. For hours after the tragedy, he had pictured his grandfather lying underground, mangled, or surviving under tons of debris in excruciating pain. Now seeing him resting as though sleeping, Owen felt somehow soothed and reconciled.

The afternoon of that exhilarating September Sunday, the graveside funeral was held high on the Plymouth mountainside. Owen hardly heard the remarks and prayers. He scanned the Susquehanna and the Wyoming Valley. He could view the entire east side, the hills of Plains, Wilkes-Barre itself, Hanover Township, Nanticoke, and the running mountains. The sight enveloped him.

After the funeral, Owen joined his mother, father, Miss

Hall, and several hundred other people, gathered on another hillside just to the left of the Avondale ruins. They had come to hear John Siney of St. Clair, Pennsylvania, a small coal town outside Pottsville. Siney was the organizer and president of the Workmen's Benevolent Association. Born in Ireland but unionized by his work in the cotton mills of Lancashire, England, he was well known in the anthracite region. He had led the strike that closed Avondale only a month earlier. He was admired because he had been able to get miners an increase in pay by tying their wages to an increase in the price of coal.

Siney spoke to the audience of miners and their families. Many of them had come from as far away as Carbondale.

With Dada and Mam on one side and Miss Hall on the other, Owen strained to see the speaker. He listened carefully as Siney warmed to his subject: "You can do nothing to win these dead back to life, but you can help me win fair treatment and justice for living men who risk life and health in daily toil."

Miss Hall squeezed Owen's hand as she heard these words. Siney was much under the influence of another Englishman, William Weaver, and he threw his challenge to the miners and their families by quoting his hero: "Union is the great fundamental principle by which every object of importance is accomplished. Man is a social being, and, if left to himself, in an isolated condition, would be one of the weakest creatures, but associated with other men, he works wonders. We know this is true because we see it as men join to build cities, improve sanitation, provide water and coal for each other. Our armies, our railroads, our banking are created when men work together cooperatively. Why then should the miners be antagonistic and individualistic. The union of minds and hands among miners is just as creative. We gain warmth and earnestness through union with each other."

The audience was captivated as Siney continued, "Does it not behoove us as miners to use every means to elevate our positions, by reforming our character, wiping out our personal animosities and frivolous nationalities, abandoning our pernicious habits and degrading pursuits? Our unity and voices will then be heard in the legislative halls.

"There must be an organization of Labor. One of America's immortals has written: 'There is no East, no West, no North, no South.' Unite for the emancipation of our labor and the regeneration of our moral species."

And then, his final plea rang out in verse:

"All men are brethren—how the watchword runs! And when men act as such, is justice won."

The applause rang over the hillside. Appreciation and gratitude lifted those in the midst of grief and pain, not so much the call for union since these Welsh had already brought their solidarity from the chapels, quarries, and mines of Wales, but the moral tone of Siney's address echoed another sermon delivered on a mountain. The listeners were both assured and inspired.

& & &

Sixty-one of the victims remained unburied. They lay in the mine yard in their crude coffins awaiting their families. These sixty-one had originally been residents of Scranton.

Like Mrs. Evans who had lost her husband and three sons, many of them had only recently moved to Plymouth. Their family grave sites were in Scranton.

The Scranton *Republican* announced that a free train ride would be available for persons traveling from Scranton to Avondale to return with the bodies. When the special train left Scranton, it included ten box cars, nine open cars, and one passenger car. All were filled with people. As the train pulled into Pittston, hundreds more waiting there could not board. Later in the day, another train with seventeen flat cars arrived at Avondale.

Once the coffins were loaded on the train for the journey to Scranton, another hundred or more passengers, including Dada, Owen and Miss Hall, jammed into what space they could find to stand for the eighteen-mile journey. So many of the dead had been close union friends of Dada that he had joined the others to attend their funerals. Owen pleaded to go along, and Mam gave permission when Miss Hall offered to accompany them to keep a special eye on him.

When the train reached Scranton, the first contingent of the funeral procession went immediately to the cemetery where open graves were waiting. They had been dug earlier in the morning by seventy volunteer laborers from Scranton. The religious services were in charge of the Reverend M. A. Ellis and the Reverend William Roberts, D.D. Dr. Roberts proclaimed the tragedy, ". . . A sad calamity! A dreadful catastrophe! Death lurking in fire, smoke and sulphur, suffocating and extinguishing the spark of life. Death, insatiable monster . . ." Although he went on in this vein for the better part of an hour, the last bodies did not arrive from the train until seven o'clock, long after the funeral services were over.

Dada, Owen, and Miss Hall stayed overnight in the home of Dada's cousins in Hyde Park. The area was called Patagonia and undoubtedly owed its name to Patagonia in southern Argentina, where a number of Welsh had established a South American colony.

After te bach, the cousins relaxed together. They all shared the news in the Scranton *Republican*. Mayor Martin Kalbfleisch of Brooklyn and Mayor Oakley Hall of New York City had both sent resolutions of sympathy. The paper quoted the extensive coverage of the *Philadelphia Inquirer* and *Harper's Weekly*. *Harper's* had even sent photographers and artists to depict scenes of the tragedy and its aftermath. Soon, their stomachs and their minds both too full, Owen and Miss Hall retired.

Dada sat up late, however, talking with his cousin Evan, whose mother had been a sister to Taid. Evan spoke fondly of his Uncle David, as he knew him, and offered his cousin what comfort he could.

"John," he said, "you've suffered through the most tragic year in your life. You've not only lost friends and work companions and neighbors, but in the midst of it all you've lost your father too. Your son is devastated by the death of his Taid. I want to do anything I can to help you. Is there anything you need?"

"No," Dada answered. "Your offer is kind. Your croeso has been of the warmest. I'm eager to restore some order and routine to our lives. This is the way, I think the best way, to conquer grief. Don't you agree? We'll have each other at home. Our supplies are fair at hand, and our needs are a home, food, and a few comforts. We have those. But for how long I do not know. The Avondale colliery . . ."

"Yes, the colliery," Evan interrupted, "will it open soon?"

"I doubt it. The colliery is wrecked inside and out."

"What will you do for work?" Evan asked.

"Well, I was hoping to get on a laboring crew repairing, but I heard yesterday that union miners will find it hard to get that kind of work."

"Oh, that antagonism again rearing its head?"

"That's right," said Dada. "There's resentment that we won too much last summer. Too much. We won ten cents a car more. But we did get them to promise not to cut our wages without giving us thirty days notice. More than that, John Siney is convincing more and more miners to join."

"Same here," said Evan. "I believe there are at least four new locals in Scranton."

"Well, the company . . . if they can keep the union people out of the jobs rebuilding the colliery . . . if they can do that, they will."

"If you don't get work there, what next?" Evan asked.

"I may have to go down to Carbon or Schuylkill. Or maybe to Danville to the iron works."

"No, John, I have a better idea. Join me here at Briggs Shaft. I have a good place. Plenty of coal, a rich vein, four feet thick. You can stay with me, board here for a couple of weeks. Then, if it works out, you can bring Blodwen and Owen here and get your own home."

Dada wanted to stay in Plymouth. He gazed at his cousin for a few moments in thoughtful silence, weighing his alternatives. "Thank you, Evan, thank you very much," he said. "Let me talk it over with Blodwen. She loves her little home in Plymouth."

"I know," Evan said, "but remember that a family cannot survive very long without the man in the house bringing home a pay envelope. You know you're welcome here."

Both men fell silent, each thinking his own thoughts. Evan yawned and stretched; then a question that had been chewing at the back of his mind for days came forward again. "John, have they found out how the fire started?" he asked.

"Not exactly, but they guess now that some of the hay that Pat Riley took down every morning for the mules somehow caught fire from the ventilating furnace at the bottom of the shaft. You know how the furnace heats the air so it will rise out of the shaft and pull new air into the mine. But I know Pat Riley. He's not a careless man, so I'm sure it was not his fault. Maybe the furnace overheated. Maybe it exploded. I don't want to think about it now."

"I understand," said Evan. "It's been a very long day. Gwely is beginning to sound good to me."

And with no further conversation, the cousins retired.

The next morning at five o'clock, Dada, Owen, and Miss Hall joined about twenty more who had stayed in Scranton overnight for the trip back to Plymouth. The DL&W train, which usually carried only empty cars and laborers to Avondale, today had only these few passengers and a load of timber and other supplies for the reconstruction of Avondale.

CHAPTER 3

EMBERS

For the next ten days, John Roderick tried repeatedly to join the rehabilitation crew, but the answer was always, "Not right now, John." No one ever mentioned the union. But a few additional workers were hired every day, men he knew to be less experienced and less skilled, so John knew what was keeping him from a job. Even though he had never been a spokesman for the union, merely one who believed in the union as he believed in the church, he was marked as a union man.

In Wales, the mines and quarries had spawned a breed of men whose lives were directed by the whirlwind Methodist revival of the nineteenth century. Economic justice was the goal for both leaders and followers. These leaders, these men of mines and quarries, argued, informed, and persuaded each other that the kingdom of God included their land, their homes, their country, as well as their heavenly objective. A labor leader was likely to be a clergyman as well, driven by his own interpretations of the gospels to work for economic justice.

John was one of those men to whom religion in his work and in his home was always the same. He was not a rabble rouser or a leader, but everyone knew he was a man of integrity—and everyone knew he supported the unions.

As the days went by and work continued to be denied him, John began to think that the only thing he could do was accept Evan's offer and go off to work with him at Briggs Shaft in Scranton. And yet he knew that Blodwen and Owen might not be ready. He hesitated to suggest the move to Scranton even as he began to believe it was becoming inevitable.

He knew Owen would be unhappy. Owen had returned to work at O'Brien's. True, he was making only thirty-fiye cents a day, less than half of what he had earned in the breaker, but he liked the work. It was far less monotonous and back-breaking, and often very rewarding. Owen had graduated from being a delivery boy to being a clerk. He enjoyed the con-tacts, the conversation, and the news. Of course, the usual bantering and pleasantries were no longer suitable small talk. The disaster had stamped the town with a melancholy that would take months to dissipate. For Owen, the store work was enlightening. When he carried groceries, the nip of the autumn days, the light touch of color on the late September trees were experiences he had missed as a breaker boy. Once, after he delivered an order to Mrs. Eno down on the flats, he ran down to the river. It was the first time he had visited it since that last Sunday with Taid. He picked up a few stones and skimmed them; there in the autumn sun, he was not unhappy.

Rhondda Hall had a far more challenging task. Every child in the one-room school had been affected by the disaster. Many children had lost fathers and brothers; others had lost uncles or cousins. When they came back to school, Miss Hall picked up where the class had been when the Avondale Breaker whis-tle pierced the town with its horrible scream. But, as she worked with one or two as she usually did, she could see that the others couldn't work on their lessons. They were numb and passive, uninterested, mourning.

For the next several days, therefore, she abandoned her older techniques. She taught them as a group, really not teaching but ministering to them with poetry, literature, and music. She read of tragedy, of new hope, the future, and of overcoming evil with good. She opened discussions and encouraged the students to speak of their loss, of their feelings, of helping others overcome grief. The children shared their families' fears of poverty, their frustrations in trying to understand the fire. That one unanswerable question echoed throughout all their other questions. Why?

As the weeks went by, their attitudes began to brighten, their curiosity to return. Here and there a smile broke, seeped through. In time, classes resumed their normal structure.

In the second week of October, when the gold and red of autumn blazed their brightest, when Plymouth's maples, oaks, and poplars shone, the Reverend Glyn Williams organized a Sunday afternoon memorial prayer meeting. Since there was not a church or any other building large enough to hold the group, the meeting took place in the field where John Siney had spoken. The prayer part of the meeting ended after one hour. The closing hymn, *Hyfrydol*, echoed over the countryside as two hundred Welsh voices rose in four-part harmony (for it would never have occurred to them to sing in any other way). Almost at once they went on to *Llangloffan, Llanllyfni*, and then for another hour more and more songs of worship and prayer.

When the session finally ended, Dada, Mam, and Owen

met Miss Hall and invited her back to the house for tea. By the time they got there, John had made a decision. In the presence of the three closest to him, he would announce he was going to Scranton to work. He felt that Miss Hall's presence would keep Owen and Mam on an even keel.

As they finished their tea, he said, "Let us take a moment or two together to share some thoughts."

They could see Dada was serious and had something important to say. They gave him their attention, and listened, and the sudden quiet unnerved him a little. After a few false starts, he began: "As you know, I have not been able to get on the crew of men reconstructing the mine. We cannot afford to be without a pay envelope much longer, so, I'm sorry to say, I've made a decision to go to Scranton to work with my cousin Evan at the Briggs Shaft Mine. I know we are happy here in the home, but a home does not last long without a pay coming in."

Mam had been expecting this decision. Her face reflected the pain of it. "When shall we move?"

"Not right away. I think I should board with Evan for a fortnight or so. In the meantime, I shall be making some inquiries there about a new house—one I hope will be near Evan and Ann." Then turning to his son, he said, "Owen, you will be man of the house while I'm in Scranton. Follow your mother's orders. Take care of her and the house. You can still work for Mr. O'Brien, but there are many ways you must be extra helpful to your mother when I'm away."

Miss Hall felt the atmosphere becoming uncomfortable. She did her best to interject a positive note, "I know, Mrs. Roderick, this is a lovely home, but you will not be giving it up. You will take your furniture and your pictures. Perhaps in Scranton they will be even more attractive, perhaps you'll find a nicer house. It may be only for a year or two. I'm told that within five years we may have a half dozen new breakers working in Plymouth. The demands for coal are growing every month. But then again, you may be happy in Scranton. You may not choose to come back. Anyway, I'm sure everything will work out." Seeing Owen's dismay, Rhondda spoke directly to him. "Come, Owen, walk me a little way home."

Without changing his expression, Owen left the house with her and walked up the field to the street. Then he turned, abruptly said good night, and ran back toward the house. He did not enter but kept running down to the river. In the last daylight minutes of that October evening, he sat at the river's edge crying softly. "I am leaving my home, and I shall never again have my Taid, my fishing, and my Miss Hall." The tears gushed from his eyes.

CHAPTER 4

෪

A NEW HOME

W hen John Roderick found a house to rent, he brought
his wife and son to the Hyde Park section of Scranton.
The city of Scranton as a united municipality had come into
existence just three years earlier, created out of the boroughs
of Hyde Park, Scranton and Providence. As the iron foundry
started there by the Scrantons grew into one of the largest
and richest companies in the country, the growing town had
quite simply engulfed its neighbors except for Dunmore, a fief-
dom of the Pennsylvania Coal Company, which clung to its
independence. Providence, a reluctant borough in the merger,
tried to secede from the consolidation, claiming "powerful interests" had included the borough in the merger, contrary to
the wishes of its citizenry. This bid for secession failed, and
the city of Scranton, incorporated by the Pennsylvania Legislature in 1866, emerged intact with a population of about
25,000.

When the Civil War started, the three boroughs had a
population of only 18,000. About ten years later, when the
Roderick family moved there, the population had already
climbed to 35,000. Coal and iron were indispensable to the
burgeoning nation and the demand for workers in the mines
and foundries was insatiable.

The Roderick family arrived in Scranton at Thanksgiving time in 1869, just as Owen was turning thirteen. Using his experience at O'Brien's store as a wedge, he got a job at Miller's grocery in his new neighborhood. John worked with cousin Evan, and the first year went by quickly. Mam became quite content in Hyde Park. Except for its floor plan, which was somewhat different, her new home became a duplicate of her home in Plymouth.

Hyde Park in 1870 was a virtual Welsh village, and Mam revelled in its culture. As in Avondale, there was a Welsh sermon every Sunday morning in her church. There was also a Welsh newspaper, *The Baner America*, published weekly in Scranton to report news of the large Welsh populations in Pennsylvania and upper New York State, especially the Utica, Waterville, and Remson areas. The Hyde Park Welsh Philosophic Society met in the building where *The Baner* was published. It opened doors for young people interested in literary and musical achievements.

There were other influences, too, broadening their perceptions of America. More and more, Irish, Scots, and English families were migrating into the coal regions. While they tended to live in isolated patches, a few were scattered throughout the Welsh population of Hyde Park. Three doors from the Rodericks, the O'Neill family, recently from Ireland, became warm friends of Mam and the other Rodericks. The O'Neill boys learned to play baseball from Owen, who had learned it from the Avondale breaker boys; soon they were more proficient than he in catching and batting.

Most of all, Owen found Rhiannon, his second cousin,

daughter of Evan. She was a delightful companion and together they enjoyed the same coming-of-age adolescent interests. In the little Welsh church, they led the young people, under the guidance of the Reverend Mr. Williams. Whenever they could, they attended Cymanfaoedd and Eisteddfodau together. They would not miss the Bethania Church Eisteddfod, held every Christmas Day.

As Owen and his family were becoming Scrantonians, Rhondda Hall spent the first year after the Avondale fire in Plymouth doing as much social work among the families of her students as she did teaching. The trauma still pervaded the town. Every day she returned home from school at about four o'clock, took a short nap, prepared her supper, and then visited two or three different families. Sometimes, she would sit with several children, permitting a widow to visit with a neighbor or attend a mid-week prayer meeting or church social.

The tragedy of Avondale brought her own family closer and bonded her to them as never before. She began to write more letters to her parents in Philadelphia. She knew that her father's iron-producing plant depended on anthracite coal as the fuel for firing his iron furnaces so she sent him news she was certain he would appreciate – her personal account of labor and production problems in the coal industry. He, in turn, answered her questions about the history of iron-making, especially the discovery of the way to use anthracite as a smelting fuel. He gave his daughter so much material that she could incorporate the story into a lesson plan for the older students. He told her the story of David Thomas, who learned iron-making in Scotland and Wales and built the first anthracite-fueled iron furnace in Ynescedwin, Wales. Thomas was induced to come to Pennsylvania by the owners of the Lehigh

Coal and Navigation Company to build their first large furnaces in Catasauqua and Danville. The production of anthracite went up sharply to meet the new iron-industry demands. Her father had struck up a friendship with David Thomas when the latter helped him start the new Philadelphia business. When Thomas heard that his daughter's friends had moved to Scranton, he pressed her for information about the Scranton family. He knew just a little about their initiative and daring entrepreneurship. He admired their venturesome spirit and saw them as models for the expansion of the United States and its rise as the democratic leader in the world.

Stimulated by her father, Rhondda devoured all she could read. She subscribed to the Scranton *Republican* and read it every day. It came to Avondale over a branch of the Scranton's own railroad, the Delaware, Lackawanna and Western. The years passed swiftly as she labored tirelessly, teaching and serving Avondale.

❧   ❧   ❧

By 1871, the Rodericks had become to feel completely at home in Hyde Park. As Owen reached fifteen, his father and mother, like most parents, suddenly began to realize how much their boy had changed. The boy of twelve was now a youth of fourteen, a head taller than his mother, almost as tall as his father.

"And he'll be taller than you in another year," Mam observed one day.

"I believe he will," John answered, "but I hope he'll fill out a bit. He needs some flesh and muscle."

"Muscle indeed. And what for?" Mam asked.

"Well, he can't be a grocery errand boy all his life."

"There is plenty of time. He'll be working hard all his life. A few years as an errand boy won't hurt."

"Well, I must tell you, Blodwen, I think we will need his help sooner than you think. I have been earning fairly well, but I worked only a hundred and sixty days last year. As it is, that is enough. We can manage very well on that. No horse and buggy, to be sure. But enough."

"Well, let's be satisfied then. Give Owen a chance to become a man before you ask something more from him," his wife said. "Can't you see how well he manages himself, how he loves to read. I believe he's read every book in Reverend Williams's library. If he worked harder, he would be too tired to read at night."

"I'm very, very pleased about that," said John. "I wish he could go on working at the store. But I must tell you, this year—before it's over—may be a hard one indeed . . ."

"Not another strike, I hope." Mam had weathered enough strikes to know first-hand the deprivation they caused. She had lived through them in both Wales and America.

John paused and then said thoughtfully, "I don't know about a strike. Perhaps we will be forced into one. What I do hear is that the company is planning to cut our wages. If it does, we will need more help from Owen. If the rates go down, I will need help to get more cars of coal out. Owen is old enough now to go down with me."

"Not yet, John, please. Give him time," Mam said.

"I'd like to. I'll not hurry it. But, if I have to, well then . . . there are many young boys, younger than Owen, at Briggs. Of course, they lied about their age, but they're there.

Most of them are patchers, running and helping the mule drivers, opening and closing doors, and running errands inside the mine as the coal is carried out. I'll not have Owen do that. I'll use him to help me. That way, I can keep an eye on him, guard him . . . teach him, too, to be a good miner."

Mam was not reassured. "He needs more time. He may be tall, but he is not that strong." She paused, and then on an impulse shared a dream she had been keeping from her husband for some time. She spoke slowly and as gently as she could. "I was hoping he might go from the store into a bank or into a more responsible job in some larger store—anything but those old mines."

"Well, that's why we came here," John said. "We're coal miners."

"So you are," Mam replied. "I was hoping Owen would not be. It's hard enough watching you go in the morning, not knowing what foul thing will break your arm or leg or suffocate you. Seeing you both go would be too much for me."

John did not reply immediately. He knew her feelings and he knew the daily agony of most mothers who had husbands and sons in mining. He tried to assuage her feelings. "Well, maybe I am too edgy about what I've been hearing. I'll know better about it after the union meeting tonight. The local has had a letter from John Siney. We'll hear it tonight."

❧   ❧   ❧

That night, the locals of Scranton gathered on the South Side in the hall of the Workingmen's Benevolent Association on Cedar Avenue.

Zingo Parks, a young organizer for John Siney's union, stood up to read Siney's letter. He spoke loudly for all the men to hear.

> *Dear Brothers:*
>
> *All of us abhor strikes. They should be used only as a last resort, only after discussion, compromise, and justice have failed.*
>
> *We today face an attack upon our union and our families. The gains we won in 1869 are to be repealed. More important, the coal companies threaten us with a thirty-three percent reduction in wages.*
>
> *In November 1870, when prosperity appeared to prevail, a small cloud appeared on the horizon. It was a decree from the Delaware and Hudson Coal Company with offices in New York that "from and after December 1st next following, the miners would be paid eighty-six cents per diamond car in place of one dollar and thirty-one cents."*

At this, the men gasped audibly and broke into an angry babble of protest. It took the chairman several minutes to restore order. At length Parks was able to continue:

> *What an outrage! At a single strike of a pen: One-third less pay. At once, the DL&W and the Pennsylvania Coal Company joined to make the decree a concerted one.*
>
> *Therefore, I recommend to you that as of December 1, 1870, the day that this infamous new rate is to take effect, not one miner of the Workingmen's Benevolent Association enter*

into this enslavement rate system and that we join hands together
to retain an equitable and just compensation for our labor.

Fraternally yours,
John Siney
President

The end of the letter brought a torrent of conversation
and disorder. Quiet was not restored until the chairman managed to get it across that Zingo Parks had further word from
John Siney.

Dropping the letter to his side, Parks began to speak again,
bringing a further message from Siney.

"I came here tonight to answer any questions you have.
John Siney cannot believe that these corporations could be so
reckless as to endanger the economic stability of anthracite
coal. Yet they have done it. Before the chairman calls for a
vote to act on President Siney's recommendation, I will try to
answer questions."

A confused chorus of protest came from the angry group.
It amounted to a single simple question: "What the hell are
they trying to do?"

"I'll try to answer that," said Parks. "There are more and
more men coming into the area. The company thinks it can
get men to work for whatever they'll pay. They think men
coming from the old country will work for much less than
they're paying now."

John raised his hand, and when the chairman recognized
him, he began to speak. The men calmed down. "I don't know

whether they can get men or not, but I know we can't work
for this rate. Here, let me give you some facts, and every one
of you here can testify to the truth of these facts."

"I can cut six diamond cars of coal a day. Most of you can
too. . . . Six cars at a dollar thirty brings me seven eighty-six
a day. Out of this I pay my laborer two dollars. My oil and
powder cost eighty-one cents. Dockage and tools cost me
another forty. Subtract the costs and I take home four dollars
and sixty-five cents a day. If they take this down to eighty-six
cents a car, I will end up getting two forty-five a day. What in
heaven's name are the owners thinking about? And don't forget
we only work three days a week. Even the congressman from
my old home in Plymouth calls this a 'clap of thunder in the
sky!' I read in the *New York World* that congressman Hendrick
Wright places the odium on incorporated capital, and he is
absolutely on the mark."

Another speaker, Bobby Campbell, a rational Scotsman,
asked calmly, "Has their production gone down, are they losing
money?"

Zingo Parks answered him, "They've sold over 16 million
tons this year. In ten years, they hope for 30 million tons a
year. No, as a matter of fact, we know that their profits go up
every year." He consulted a sheet of paper, which he kept shift-
ing from one hand to the other. "Here is the dollar figure passed
out to its stockholders. Between 1866 and 1870, the
Lackawanna Iron and Coal Company had profits more than
four million dollars—four straight years of money-making!"

The reasonable questions were suddenly over. Trevor
James, a squat former rugby player from Swansea, who had
mined stone coal in Wales, rose to his feet: "I know those bas-

tards," he cried. "They'll bring a lot of their 'blacklegs' in here to go to work and take our jobs! There's not a goddam miner here will go to work for that money! I say stop the talking. Tell Siney the battle is on!"

A roar of approval erupted. The chairman banged and shouted for order to no avail. In desperation, he tried to shout the parliamentary procedure. For two minutes, the miners raged. Finally, with no one listening, he leaned over and muttered into the recording secretary's ear, "We accept the recommendation of John Siney."

The fury of Trevor James had ignited even the most passive.

❧   ❧   ❧

In the midst of the heated discussion, Alan Moses and Sean O'Donnell, who had not come to the meeting, having had more important business hanging around the Lackawanna Station collecting gossip, came rushing in looking for Trevor James.

"Listen to this, Trev," Sean shouted. "The telegraph operator down at the station just got a message that a mob of miners blasted a boarding house down at Mt. Carmel. I think there were twenty-nine blacklegs in the building. I don't know where the company got them scabs, but they were there, with blasting powder and all, ready to go to work. Some of the miners spotted the powder inside. They sent some gunshot into the house and exploded the whole damned place. The mob went crazy."

The news buzzed through the crowd. Many of the men

wanted to go out and blow something up as a gesture of solidarity. Between them, Zingo Parks and the chairman managed
to restore something faintly like order. Parks began to speak
again, in his powerful voice. "Listen men, this kind of thing at
Mt. Carmel can do us more harm than good. Some will say
this was done by the Molly Maguires and that our union is
filled with them. We'll be condemned by every newspaper in
Pennsylvania. Do you hear what I'm saying?"

He paused and stared at the men. John Roderick felt that
the last thing he wanted to do was call attention to himself,
but he believed he had a duty. Once more he raised his hand.
"For all we know, Gowen, the company boss down that way
may have hired someone to do the shooting himself, just to
hang it on us. So please—we can only win by peaceful means.
I know Mr. Siney feels the same way. Zingo Parks will verify
it. Wait and see. By tomorrow, John Siney will have a reward
out for the culprit who fired that shot. Remember, none of that
tomorrow."

The miners listened attentively to John but fell into buzzing groups when he finished. It was obvious that they had
mixed feelings about the news from Mt. Carmel. Involved in
exactly the same fight, they were inclined to shout a triumphant hurrah. What John said cooled them down and gave
them thoughts to ponder and argue. But there were many
who revelled in the Mt. Carmel boarding house blast of the
blacklegs.

The strike started January 6, 1871, and spread quickly.
The Workingmen's Benevolent Association closed down the
mines in Wyoming Valley, Scranton, and Schuylkill County.

For three months, the miners held out. The coal companies, with a good stockpile, felt no pressure. By April, many of the miners could not go on any longer. Their credit gone, their savings used, they started to drift back to work. In doing this, they took their lives in their own hands because the stronger, more dedicated unionists would not let them go to work. Violence broke out around several collieries.

CHAPTER 5

ଛ

THE BATTLE OF BRIGGS SHAFT

On Good Friday, April 5, 1871, a riot broke out in Scranton between factions of miners. A thousand union men, insistent on continuing the strike, kept defectors from going to work. The mob was too large for the police to handle. Mayor Monie of Scranton pleaded with Governor Geary for help. The governor called the Pennsylvania National Guard into service to keep the peace.

John Roderick and the other miners at Briggs Shaft were not intimidated by the soldiers and were loyal to their cause. For five more weeks, they kept Briggs shut down. William Scranton, young son of Joe Scranton, was incensed with what he considered to be an invasion of his privacy. He publicly announced that he, William Scranton, the Superintendent of the Lackawanna Iron and Coal Company, would guarantee protection to any men who wanted to return to work at Briggs. He himself would accompany them to work, and the soldiers would protect them.

William Scranton could not understand the union mind. He believed in a free land, where work was available, no one but the owner of an industry or business should make decisions about wages. He firmly believed that for a group of self-appointed agitators to keep men from working in order to get wages to which they were not entitled was un-American. He

was determined that America would not collapse before ter-
roristic ideas like syndicalism, anarchism, and communism,
which were now sweeping over Europe. The French Commune of 1870 must never come to the United States.

&   *&*   *&*

On the other hand, miners—who risked life and limb every
day, who had fought for their contract in 1869—were not
about to surrender their achievements, were not about to
work for one-third less money when the Lackawanna Coal
and Iron Company was making huge profits and when men
like William Scranton were prospering.

Consequently, when William Scranton offered safe conduct to scabs, John Roderick, with Christian patience, and
Trevor James, with rugby aggressiveness, led the effort to
prevent the blacklegs from stealing their jobs. On a mild May
evening, the miners met in a large field, a mile above Fellows
Square. John made his plea for unity and firmness without
violence. "What we need, men," he said, "are numbers to
keep the others from going back. Let's remember, those going back are our friends. We worked with them day after day,
and we will again. Don't blame them too much for giving in.
I'm sure there'll be no more than forty going back with Mr.
Scranton. And remember, they're going back because they
can't take it any longer. Their credit is gone. The company
stores are on their backs. Some of them are in debt to the First
National Bank, the Scrantons' bank. Their children are hungry
and their wives are frightened. So the best way to handle this
is to get out big numbers and just stand peacefully in their

way. And don't let the soldiers or Scranton himself provoke you." He paused. "Trevor," he asked, "do you agree?"

Trevor arose from the grass where he had been listening and lounging. "With all due respect, Roderick," he said, "I don't think it will work. In the first place, if it's a nice May morning, as I expect it will be, most of the men will be planting their gardens or out picking coal off the coal banks. We'll have a hard time getting as many tomorrow as we have here tonight. So, I think we have to let those going with Mr. Scranton know that we hate what they are doing. You say their children are hungry. I don't think so. Not at this time of year. Now, January, yes, I'd agree, but not now. We must get them to hold out till September. By then the company's stock pile will be down. The company must get us working for the winter production or they'll go bankrupt."

After much further discussion and argument, the meeting broke up indecisively, except that the plea to be on hand in the morning was stressed.

However, the next morning, as Trevor predicted, there were far too few to keep forty men from getting into the mine.

By early afternoon, the word had raced through the colliery area that the blacklegs had started to work, and that the strike was all but lost. In the late afternoon the blacklegs returned home from work, again led by Scranton and followed by National Guardsmen. Several hundred striking miners, along with their wives and children, barred their way at Fellows Square. The pushing and shoving began, then a barrage of stones flew between the troops and blacklegs on one side, and the angry strikers on the other. One of the blacklegs had a rifle. He fired into the band of strikers, and Benjamin Davis and Daniel Jones fell dead.

Both Davis and Jones were highly respected members of the Hyde Park community. The killings tore the city of Scranton apart. The community conflict was exacerbated when the Scranton *Republican* carried headlines for days blaming the tragedy on the union. The *Republican* was published by Joseph A. Scranton, a half-brother to William Scranton. One of the first reporters described the shooting in the following manner:

> Accordingly, we made our way to Briggs shaft, with the intention of seeing the soldiers who accompanied the laborers from work, and also Mr. W. W. Scranton, and thus ascertain the truth. On arriving at the mine and stating the object of our visit, we were immediately introduced to Sergeant D. W. Holly, who commanded the detachment in question. The Sergeant, at our request, then called the men around him under his command at the time, that they might be witnesses to the correctness of his statement, or add any item of importance bearing upon the matter which might have escaped his notice. The following conversation then ensued between our reporter and Sergeant Holly:
>
> REPORTER: Sergeant, I understand that you were in command of the detail of soldiers who accompanied those laborers to their homes on Wednesday evening?
>
> SERGEANT: Yes, sir, I was.
>
> REPORTER: Will you be so good as to state how many men were under your command?
>
> SERGEANT: There were eight.

REPORTER: What position did you occupy in relation to the squad of laborers?

SERGEANT: We were in their rear.

REPORTER: You had, then, a good opportunity to observe all matters going on in front?

SERGEANT: I do not think that an incident in the whole affair transpired, which we did not see.

REPORTER: Now will you be kind enough to state, just as clearly as you can, everything that took place from the time you left this mine in company with the laborers until after the shooting?

SERGEANT: The real facts of the case are simply these: We left the mine at about five o'clock and proceeded along the railroad some distance until we came to—I do not know the name of the street—the place where we turned toward Hyde Park. As we were going along, crowds of men and women and children were assembled at different points along the road who, at every step of our progress, insulted us by calling us blacklegs and other more filthy names, pointing their fingers at us and trying to spit upon us. Some of the men had stones in their hands, and the women pulled up their sleeves and shook their fists at us, uttering the most filthy expressions. We proceeded, however, without further molestation than this until we came to what they call Fellows' Corner. At this point, a large crowd had assembled, of men, women and children, the children occupying the front, and crowding the road so that we could hardly get past.

REPORTER: How many do you think there were in the crowd?

SERGEANT: Well, there were at least four hundred. As we approached, I saw revolvers drawn on each side of the way and pointed across the line of march. I immediately apprehended a disturbance. But we passed on without saying a word but keeping a sharp look-out on each side. As we began to get into the crowd, a yell was made by the mob accompanied with a storm of hisses and epithets. I saw several with stones in their hands, and one was thrown among the men, but I did not see it strike anyone. We kept along, and I saw one of the men who was later shot standing a few yards from the road with a stone in his hand. Immediately behind him was the other man who was later killed, with his one hand resting upon the left shoulder of the man in front and as the other laborers passed, he put out the other hand over the right shoulder shouting, "Look at the G–d d––n blackleg s–n's of b––––s." At this moment the man who was in front jerked the stone which he held in his hand immediately into the air and I saw it strike Cairns upon the back. Cairns immediately halted, leveled his gun and fired. I saw the man who was shot put his hands upon his stomach, quiver for a few moments, turn nearly half way around and then fall. The other man made a step back, turned in the same manner and fell also. My men, at the moment the shot was fired, turned and made ready to fire. Mr. Scranton then shouted, "Don't fire, boys, that will do," and then he and I walked in front of the men and struck up their muskets. The crowd at once took flight, and I never saw such a scattering in so short a time. They tumbled right over the fences in the most terror-stricken manner. We paused for a few minutes and then Mr. Scranton gave the order to "march," and we followed, accompanying the laborers for a short distance. The laborers then said that they guessed we were far enough, that they could take care of themselves now. They asked us if we were afraid to go back and offered to escort us to the shaft if we wished. We told them we were not afraid, and we turned and reached the shaft without a word being said to us.

REPORTER: That is all that transpired?

SERGEANT: That is the whole of it and exactly how it happened.

REPORTER: You saw that the *Times* stated that they both were innocent men, one of them—Davis—being on an errand to obtain medicine for a sick child, and that he did not throw a stone at all.

SERGEANT: Yes, I saw that and it is a lie. *The man that threw the stone got shot*, and it does not make a bit of difference whether he was going for medicine or not—*he threw the stone and he got shot*.

REPORTER: Did Mr. Scranton order the men to fire—you saw the testimony of these men who swore that he did?

SERGEANT: He did not. I saw the testimony and it is a lie also.

Despite this report, the vast Welsh population of Hyde Park did not believe a word of it. The killing of their neighbors was unbelievable. Ben Davis left a widow and four children. Daniel Jones (nicknamed "Spurgeon" after the great English evangelist because he was a lay minister) left a widow. Their funerals were a massive expression of sorrow and unity. The Reverend M. A. Ellis, who had preached at the graveside service for the Avondale victims, conducted the services, attended by three thousand Brotherhood members and Ivorites and their families.

The Scranton *Republican* waxed eloquent over the funerals:

> From this [the funerals] an unintelligent individual would infer that they had been distinguished as public benefactors. It is an old injunction to 'speak no ill of the dead,' and we have no desire to violate it. But surely some distinction should be made at public funerals between the honor deserved by those who fall at the post of duty and the duo of individuals struck down in the act of inciting riot and bloodshed.

The voice of justice was heard momentarily when both William Scranton and the man who fired the shot were brought before Judge Dana at the Luzerne County seat in Wilkes-Barre. Identified as the gunman, not a national guardsman but one of the miners who had all carried rifles, was Fenian Cairns. William Scranton was released after two days in prison in Wilkes-Barre. Cairns was also absolved.

The *Republican* was unrelenting in its attacks on the union. The paper developed a technique of indirect attack, printing letters to the editor like this one, which purportedly came from a laborer in Pittston:

> When I worked in Hyde Park I was not only obliged to do my own work but the greater part of the miner that hired me. It

was John, or Tom, or Pat, or Jacob, or Hans, "give me the drill, the scraper, the needle, the hammer, the wedge, go get some tamping and then help me tamp the hole." This I was expected to do after drilling four out of five feet of a hole, while he was sitting down talking to some of his neighboring miners, while we poor devils innocently believed him to be preparing a cartridge to be put in the hole that we had to drill, and when there was enough coal cut, no matter how hard or how long the laborer had to work, Mr. Welshman put on his coat and went home to enjoy himself in the bosom of his family, cultivate his mind if he felt so disposed, or engage in any other amusement. And we get a nominal one-third of the sum total, whilst we are the men who considered it necessary to have T. M. Williams come to their aid one day last week. He had the impertinence to say "he had the cow by the horns and he would hold her there." He may remember when Mr. Parrish, of Wilkes-Barre, held him by the horns, or rather he held Mr. Parrish, as it was through him he rode into the mine inspectorship. Time was when Hyde Park miners paid very little respect to this modern Mokanna–this humbug–this gas bag, who cares as much for the miners or laborers of Hyde Park as his prototype, the rascally Siney, who while in Halifax, England, was a drunken rough and rowdy.

Pittston, May 10 1871.

The paper also gave prominence to a resolution adopted by Irish miners and laborers at the Bellevue Colliery:

> RESOLVED, That we do form ourselves into
> a society and never again mix or associate
> with the Welsh inhabitants of Luzerne
> County as in their late murderous outrages
> they have shown to us that they are a class
> of beings who should never be allowed to
> associate with peaceable and law-abiding
> citizens.

But all Irish were not so welcome to speak. Peter Quigley of Carbondale had clearly committed the unforgivable sin of joining the union:

> At the close of these remarks, Peter
> Quigley, of Carbondale, who had posted
> some of his men conveniently to call on
> him to speak was accordingly called upon,
> and was permitted to speak owing to the
> fact that the laborers did not wish to create
> any disturbance. It will not be safe for him,
> however, to try the same game again. If
> he has the regard for his empty head which
> we think he has, he will keep at a distance.
> Several times his crowd attempted to pro-
> duce discord in the meeting and draw the
> laborers away, but it was a total failure
> and showed that the laborers were not to
> be diverted from their purpose by any such
> miserable jack-a-napes as he, and that the
> influence of the leaders of the W.B.A. over
> the members is completely gone. After
> Quigley had got through with his gibberish,
> a resolution to the effect that work was to
> be resumed by the Irish, Germans, Scotch
> and English, on Monday at the rates offered
> by the companies, leaving the question of

> arbitration until afterwards, was passed unanimously. Some of Quigley's men, however, made a considerable howl, but all to no purpose. The meeting was adjourned.

Obviously every ethnic group was judged by its relationship to the Workmen's Benevolent Association. Quigley was attacked, but the Irish blacklegs could do no wrong in the eyes of the *Republican*:

> The orderly character of the men employed at those mines has been throughout the present struggle the most praiseworthy and Mr. Connell has therefore the most absolute confidence in their honor, and does not think that a man out of the 400 at work here would be guilty of such a wanton outrage. They are nearly all Irishmen and have been at work for the last three or four weeks; and this, no doubt, was the cause of the incendiarism, as the burning of the bridge severed all connection with the lines for transportation and, of course, necessitated for a time, the suspension of labor. There seems to be little doubt but that the fire is the work of some of the W.B.A. of Hyde Park, and adds another item to the catalogue of their villainous proceedings since suspension took place. Men may, on some occasions of great excitement, be tempted to commit certain acts of violence, of which in their soberer moments they would not be guilty; but a thing of this kind is the result of premeditation, and takes place according to a deliberate plan, and nothing but the basest

set of scoundrels could be employed to
perpetuate such a crime. But of these the
W.B.A. have an unlimited supply, and
there is no extent of villainy to which
under their present leaders, they may not
proceed.

William Scranton and Fenian Cairns spent two days in
jail for the murder of Davis and Jones. With their release, most
of the unionists realized that the strike had failed. More important, the pressure of businessmen and clergy to restore
some sense of prosperity and peace saturated the community.
The last holdouts were in debt, their resources wiped out by
four months of struggle. The miners of Schuylkill had already
capitulated. Rumors had begun to fly that John Siney was a
marked man.

Two years later, when the great depression of 1873 hit the
nation, it affected Northeastern Pennsylvania worst of all. In
its aftermath, John Siney and Zingo Parks were both indicted
under a Pennsylvania law for "conspiring for the purpose of
raising wages." Although Siney was acquitted, he died in 1876
in St. Clair, a broken man, much of his salary still unpaid.
Zingo Parks was convicted and sentenced to a year in prison,
but his sentence was suspended by Governor Hartranft.

❧

CHAPTER 6

THE QUESTION OF VIOLENCE

Like all other union miners, John returned to work, as did his cousin. Evan was sympathetic to union organization, but he was not articulate or expressive. He was often skeptical of John's outspokenness, but he was never critical. They continued a warm relationship as they shared their workplace and mined coal together. John saw the end of the strike as a temporary defeat. Blodwen was not so sure.

One of the immediate effects of the failed strike was an increase in violence, especially in Schuylkill and Carbon counties. The collapse of the union led to union vigilantism by small groups of men who tried to correct grievances with threats and fists—and sometimes with guns.

The violence was upsetting to Owen's mother. One Sunday morning after church, she referred to the Reverend R. J. Williams's sermon.

"You know," she said, "I do believe Reverend Williams was off the mark today."

"Off the mark? How?" John asked.

"He seemed to be approving of the violence we hear about in Shenandoah, Pottsville, and the coal regions down below here."

"Well, now," said John, "I don't believe he really said that . . ."

"What did he mean then when he said, 'the Molly Maguires, whoever they are, are not the only villains in the coal fields.' Sounds like an approval to me. And why he said, 'whoever they are' I'll never know. We all know who they are."

John thought about this for a moment. " 'Villains' covers a lot of ground, I'll admit, but he's right, you know. If you want to count villains in Pennsylvania, you'll have to name more than one group or one person."

"And what of 'whoever they are'?" Mam asked.

"I think 'whoever they are' is a good question. Are the Molly Maguires real or a figment of someone's imagination?"

"Now, John, be sensible. The papers are full of shootings by these Molly Maguires."

"That's the point Reverend Williams was trying to make. We have no proof that such an organization exists. Individuals yes, but are they really an organization?"

"Do you deny all the violence and killing?"

"No, but whose word do we have that there is an organization called the Molly Maguires? I believe the violence is there. Yes, it happens, and will happen again. I believe when men are denied a way to have justice, when their organizations are smashed, they lash out. If they cannot sit peacefully and get a company store to agree to fair prices, they will burn it down. It is not right. It is not sensible. But I can understand their anger. We felt some of it at Avondale."

"But we did not act like barbarians and burn down the store."

"No, we didn't," John agreed. "But I can understand the anger of a man wanting to do it if his children are hungry. If he works month in and month out and gets a due bill saying he has no pay coming, and that he owes more and more to the company each month."

"But even so, John, you would never commit an act like that."

"No, I suppose I wouldn't," John admitted.

"Well then, why?" Mam persisted.

"I've thought about that a great deal lately, and all I can say is that some men believe that if you cannot get a fair trial or hearing or if you are locked out and have no way of changing conditions that are strangling you, then as a last resort and in fury, you attack. Did you ever hear of the Rebeccas in Wales?"

"Yes, but all they ever tried to do was get rid of toll-gate taxes."

"Blodwen, who told you that?"

"My grandmother, Nain Jones, told me."

"Well, my girl, Nain Jones had a bad memory or she was spoofing her granddaughter."

"What do you know of the Rebeccas?"

"To begin with, Nain Jones was right in one sense. The toll gates were the problem. Landowners set up gates on their property, and all the poor Welsh farmers and travelers were held up for tolls. It was highway robbery, as they say. Pretty soon there were so many tolls that a poor farmer going to market was risking his entire profit to paying them. That's what got the Rebeccas started. But what your dear grandmother didn't tell you was that the Rebeccas destroyed people's property and even kidnapped many. They dressed as women and they burned homes and barns; they caused thousands of dollars of damage."

"Did the violence accomplish anything?" Mam asked.

"Yes, the tolls were gradually ended. But I'm not saying that violence always leads to reform or change. Violence often breeds nothing but more violence. It is amazing to me how many times stupid people or stupid governments, be they villages or countries or coal companies, will ignore problems until violence breaks out. They're like ostriches with their heads in the sand."

"But do you believe people should always get what they demand?" Blodwen asked.

"No, certainly not. But if the aggrieved can go with dignity and explain their grievance, if they feel they have been listened to, the chances of violence are lessened," John said.

Mam thought that through a bit and agreed.

"I believe to a degree you are right, but on the other hand, the world is filled with people who seem to want to destroy and kill. That's why we have murderers, rapists, and wars."

"True enough. Yes, there are such people. But I think most of the violence and killing is not premeditated. Governments . . . cities . . . companies . . . nations just drift into it because they have not taken steps to prevent it. We would still be a colony of England if the British hadn't been daft. The French monarchy was even more stupid. The Lackawanna Coal and Iron Company was just as *dwb* because they hated the union so much they would have nothing to do with it. Stubborn as mine mules they were. But someday . . ."

Owen came into the house and immediately took in the

seriousness of the discussion. "Who's preaching here today?" he asked.

"Careful, boyo, we're having a good discussion," his father cautioned.

"No harm," said Owen grinning, "just thought I heard a few echoes of Reverend Williams's sermon."

"You did, my boy," said his mother. "But we settled nothing, so we'll have a bite to eat. You're just in time. Where have you been since services ended?"

"With Reverend Williams," Owen said.

"I should have known. More books is it? Which one now?"

"Not one—two," Owen said enthusiastically.

"What are they?" Dada asked.

"One is a little one called *Walden*. The other is a book of poems."

"Poems? Fine! *Ardderchog!* Let me have a look."

Dada's face expressed disappointment as he leafed through.

"These poems are all by the same man, this William Cullen Bryant. I'm looking for Taliesin or Aneirin. Or William Williams' Pantycelyn or Ann Griffiths."

"Oh, I've read some of those, too. Mr. Williams sees that I get plenty of the Welsh."

"Who is this William Cullen Bryant?"

"He's a newspaper editor and a translator. And best of all, I think, a great poet of God and his earth."

"Hm. Sounds interesting. Leave it on the table. I'll have a go at it myself."

"And after dinner that will be," said Mam, "Say a word of thanks before we have this food."

Dada bowed his head to say grace. Then he looked up

and turned to Owen. "The grace you used to say as a small boy, the one Miss Hall taught you, that would be fine. After these last months—a good reminder. If you please, Owen."

Three heads bowed as Owen recited:

> *"Good for good is only fair*
> *Bad for bad soon brings despair*
> *Bad for good is vile and base*
> *Good for bad shows forth God's grace."*

After a short pause, he added:

"Bless us O Lord and these thy gifts which we are about to receive from thy bounty through Christ our Lord. Amen."

"Thank you, Owen bach, let us eat," said Mam. "But, tell us of those last lines of your prayer—I never heard that grace before. How did you know that?"

"Oh, that! That was Mr. O'Brien's prayer in the store at Avondale. I heard him say it so many times it stuck in my mind. Anytime he munched an apple or nibbled a piece of cheese, or even when someone surprised him by paying an overdue bill, he'd mumble that prayer half aloud, half to himself. I would catch only a few words of it until one day when there were no customers around I asked him to say it slowly and aloud. He did. From then on I'd hear different snatches of it, until finally every time he ate a snack the prayer went through my mind. I surprised him one day when he gave me my week's pay and I said "Thank you, Mr. O'Brien and Bless us, O Lord . . . and ran through it all. He laughed and said, 'Watch out Owen, we'll have you at St. Vincent's yet.'"

"Well, it was very lovely," said Mam.

"Not a bad combination at all," said Dada. "A Welsh Quaker prayer from Miss Hall and a fine Catholic prayer from Mr. O'Brien. We're saved all around—on every side." Smiling, he carved the roast lamb.

As they sat relaxed at the close of the meal, enjoying a final cup of tea, Owen said, "When I came in the house just before lunch, I couldn't help hearing you talking about the Rebeccas. What brought that on?"

"It came from Mr. Williams's sermon. Your mother was criticizing the Molly Maguires, and I was trying to say the Rebeccas might be a beam in Welsh eyes."

"I hope you are not suggesting that the Mollies are merely a small mote," said Owen.

"Not at all, just that we Welsh should realize we've had some violence in our own history."

"You know, Dada, there might be another way to explain . . . now I don't say to excuse . . . the Molly Maguires."

"Tell me, how is that?"

"Remember now, it is not my idea. It's just that last month, Mr. Williams gave me a book on the Civil War. The book blamed much of the killing, looting, and shooting on the returning soldiers. The Reverend Mr. Williams's sermon today came from that book. He told me he was going to preach on it."

"Beyond what Mr. Williams said, what did you learn from the book?" asked Dada.

"After the war it was—and still is—hard to get men to give up their guns. Everyone wanted to protect himself. All kinds

of disputes over land, property, hurt feelings, and petty rivalries ended in killing. The book says that much of the shooting
we hear about in the West comes from their war habits. The
book mentions the Molly Maguires, too, and says many of
the miners in Schuylkill County and the others in Carbon
County fought in the war."

"The only thing wrong with that theory, Owen, is that
during the war, people tell me, there were more miners opposing the war down there in Schuylkill County than were
fighting in it. They had a word for them, Copperheads I believe. The Copperheads opposed the draft and rioted against
it."

"Maybe so," said Owen, "but many Schuylkill miners were
part of the Pennsylvania Volunteeer Infantry too, and I
couldn't help see how war and violence stuck in their lives.
Over a hundred of these volunteers were hardcoal miners
and they were very important miners in the war."

"In what way?" Dada asked.

"Well, according to the book they almost won the big
battle of the Crater, but not quite. But that's not the point.
What the book says is that when these miners came back from
the war, they were rough, violent men. They worked in dangerous, violent times. It was natural for them to use guns and
dynamite to solve any problem."

"Hm, I see his point. But, Owen, you have struck my
curiosity. Where was this battle of the Crater, and what did
the coal miners do?"

"It's a long story. Are you sure you want to hear it?"

"If it's about coal miners, I most definitely do!"

"Yes, it's about miners. In fact, it starts with a coal min- .

ing engineer from Schuylkill, a lieutenant colonel named Henry Pleasants. He was only thirty-one. One day, Colonel Pleasants was walking along a trench where his Federal troops had been facing the Southerners for weeks. The Federals were dug in, closer than they had ever been before. The troops and officers were jumpy and frustrated. They were trying to capture St. Petersburg and then move on to Richmond. But they were making no progress at all. As a matter of fact, General Grant had been trying to break the defense of General Lee for months.

"As Colonel Pleasants walked along, he heard one of the soldiers, one of the Schuylkill miners, say as he looked beyond the trench to the Confederate fort: 'We could blow that damned fort out of existence if we could run a mine shaft under it.' Colonel Pleasants thought about it, then went to a bomb-proof ravine where the regimental officers lived and told them what he had heard.

"Apparently Colonel Pleasants agreed with the soldier. He said 'That damned fort is the only thing between us and Petersburg, and I know we can blow it up.' The officers agreed and they decided to approach General Burnside himself. Burnside liked what he heard too and took it up with General Meade. Meade was not so enthusiastic. Army engineers ridiculed the idea."

"Why did they do that?" Dada asked.

"I forget some of the details, even though I read the chapter about the Crater twice. I was spellbound by all this. It was so close to home. I think the reason was that they thought it was impossible to dig a tunnel five hundred feet long. The danger of it collapsing and the lack of ventilation were too risky.

Anyway, Meade didn't like the idea, but Grant was pushing him to do something, so to keep his troops busy, he gave a go-ahead without much hope.

"Colonel Pleasants got all the coal miners together, put a Welshman named Harry Reese in charge, and set them digging just as though they were back in Schuylkill mining coal. They worked in shifts around the clock. They dug a tunnel five feet high, four feet wide, and five hundred feet long."

Dada interrupted. "How did they shore it up? How did they keep the Rebels from finding out what they were doing?"

"Colonel Pleasants got the lumber. He had his men tear down an old railroad bridge, and then he found an old barn somewhere back of the trenches. Hiding their work from the Rebels was hard, especially piling the dirt in the rear under bushes where the Rebels couldn't see it. Doing this kept almost every soldier in the regiment working."

"How about the ventilation?" Dada asked.

"Somehow—it was too complicated for me to understand it completely—they built cross-shafts and wooden tubes. They built a fire to create a draft and pulled bad air out and clean air in. In three weeks they were under the fort. Pleasants had the men dig a seventy-five foot shaft at that point, like the top of a T, at the end of the tunnel."

"And the Rebels never heard that?"

"Up to that point, no, but finally they heard some noises and began digging shafts of their own. They didn't know exactly where Pleasants' tunnel was, and they missed it completely. Then Pleasants put three hundred and twenty kegs of powder, twenty-five pounds each, cross-shaft. That's four tons of powder. The fuses, just like the ones you use in Briggs, Dada, were run into the powder. Then they piled forty feet of dirt to protect the tunnel entrance from the explosion so that after the explosion the Union troops would have a clear road right into the fort.

"At the last minute Grant ordered a change in the attack plan. The first plan was to have a division of General Ferraro's pour into the shaft after the explosion. That was a problem for Grant, because Ferraro's troops were all Negroes. The use of Negro troops had caused great controversy and they had been used very little. Ferraro's soldiers were ready and eager; they'd been proudly waiting for some action. Meade and Grant were afraid they'd be criticized by the abolitionists, especially if they allowed these troops to be slaughtered in a dangerous and risky battle. So the Negro troops had to wait for a later command and another division replaced them.

"The order for the explosion came at three o'clock in the morning. Nothing happened. An hour went by. Grant and Meade got more and more impatient. Colonel Pleasants ordered Harry Reese to go into the tunnel to determine why the powder had not exploded. Reese found a typical mining problem. Where fuses had been joined together, the burning had ended. He replaced the fuse, lit it, and made a dash out of the tunnel.

"The fuses finally burned all the way to the powder. The earth rumbled and then erupted like a volcano. Some soldiers described the rounded hill rising like a great loaf and splitting apart, spouting flame and smoke.

"Troops waiting to charge were stunned—the mountain seemed to be falling toward them. They ran from it. Other

Federals, under Burnside and Meade, had specific battle plans to follow, but they were already disoriented by the explosion, and the Confederates almost immediately began to fire on them. A small contingent got through to the site of the fort, but there was nothing left but a huge crater, sixty feet long and thirty feet deep. The crater was full of timbers, guns, wreckage of every description, and human gore. There were legs and arms and other parts of Southern soldiers.

"The miners had done their work too well. They had blown out a clearing that any army could march through—five hundred yards of clearing. But the Federals were unprepared, really in disarray. Troops marched forward, right down into the crater, and it became so jammed with soldiers they couldn't move forward or backward. The Negro troops followed the first contingents. At first they were successful but then they found themselves packed into the Confederate trenches. The trenches were so full of Federal troops that they could hardly raise their guns to shoulder level. Then the Confederates counter-attacked and drove them back.

"All the Northern soldiers retreated. Many were massacred at close range, some surrendered, and others climbed back into the crater where they were helpless targets. It was a terrible defeat. The skillful work of the Schuylkill miners was planned to win a great victory, but General Grant finally called it, 'the saddest affair I have ever witnessed in war.' "

"How many of the miners were killed?" Dada asked.

"I believe—if I remember right—" said Owen, "that about one hundred miners got into the battle, and seventy of them were killed."

"My, my," Dada exclaimed, "and the writer of the book

believes . . . and Reverend Williams agrees with him . . . that the men returning from the war and such violence would . . . what?"

"Would value human life less and less," said Owen. "They saw gruesome death over and over. They got used to it. Settling quarrels, large and small, was done one way. Knives, powder, guns . . . they became everyday tools and weapons."

"I don't know whether I can accept that," Dada said. "I must think about it a little longer."

Filled with his reading and the sermons of Reverend Williams, Owen was more convinced. "I believe it, Dada. How else can you explain the Molly Maguires or whoever they are?"

When Owen went to his bedroom, where he did most of his reading, his father followed him with his eyes, feeling proud of his son. He knew that the minister had become an inspiration to the boy. Williams had mesmerized Owen with his passion for poetry, history, and biography. Owen was more than ready for the literary stimulation. His intellectual curiosity, nurtured by his parents and stimulated by Miss Hall, had begun to bloom under the tutelage of Mr. Williams.

CHAPTER 7

&

A VISION

One Saturday afternoon in the summer of 1873, four years after the Avondale tragedy, a rather short man with brown hair and a blond mustache knocked on the door of the Roderick family home.

"My name is Terence Powderly," he said when Mam opened the door. "Does Mr. John Roderick live here?"

As she wiped her hands on her apron, Blodwen noticed the clean and cultured appearance of the young man. "Yes, he does," she said. "Would you like to see him?"

"Indeed I would, if I may."

"Come in then, please."

Blodwen hurried to the back door and called to John, who was repairing a gate in the backyard fence. "There's someone here to see you," she called.

Gathering up a handful of tools, John placed them on the back porch and entered the house. Terence Powderly was standing in the living room.

"Good afternoon, Mr. Roderick. My name is Terence Powderly."

John introduced himself, wondering who in the world this man might be. The thought flashed that he might be a recruiter for a new lodge, or a salesman, though he doubted it. Perhaps he was a doctor. Only doctors looked this tidy and well dressed.

"Please sit down, Mr. Powderly."

"Thank you very much. I'd appreciate sitting. I'd like to talk to you—and maybe at some length if you have the time. Is it a convenient time for a visit? I thought Saturday afternoon might be."

Dada smiled and said, "That depends on what we shall talk about."

"Mr. Roderick, I am an officer of the Scranton chapter of the International Union of Machinists and Blacksmiths of the U.S.A. I know that you are a highly respected member of the miners' union. What I'd like to talk to you about is how working men and women in Northeastern Pennsylvania can protect themselves and improve their lives. May we talk?"

"For hours on end," John said. He did not relax completely, however. Powderly did not look like a laboring man. He could be one of those spies John had heard about infesting Schuylkill County. John needed considerable reassurance before he would be completely open with this man. "Tell me, Mr. Powderly," he asked, "where is your home?"

"Please, please call me Terence. I'm twenty-two years old and I was born in Carbondale."

"Just twenty-two! My, my, you're very young to be so serious about working people. Most twenty-two-year-olds are too busy courting or playing baseball."

Powderly laughed. "I do both, but I must admit I spend much more time on my work as a machinist, and of course, trying to increase our union membership."

"And your family?"

"My parents came from Ireland and first lived in Ogdensburg, New York; then they came here to this area, to Carbondale. And your family Mr. Roderick?"

"My wife and I were both born in Wales, as was my son who is now seventeen. We came from Wales to Plymouth. I worked at Avondale until the great fire there."

"Avondale!" exclaimed Powderly, "Avondale! What a horrible tragedy! Were you there in the . . .?"

"No," Roderick interrupted, "but my son was working in the breaker. Fortunately, he had been sent on an errand into the mine yard by the breaker boss. Unfortunately, my father, a road cleaner, was in the mine and perished with the others."

"I am so very sorry," said Powderly. "I know there's nothing to be said. I was there right after the fire for a day. Seeing those widows and children was too much for me. And yet, I'm glad I saw them. That day changed my life. You might say I would not be here if it hadn't been for that day, when I heard John Siney speak on the hillside."

"Well, we have shared an inspiring experience," said John. "We were there also to hear Mr. Siney."

"You were? Wonderful!" said Powderly. "But it was more than that for me. I realized for the first time that the death of those miners was a call to me and to the living to neglect no duty to our fellow men. I realized that day that there was more to win through labor than dollars and cents for yourself. I caught such an inspiration that I resolved to spend my life dedicated to working men and women."

John was moved by the young man's seriousness. He believed him. Just then he heard Owen's step at the back door. "Owen," he called, "come and meet our guest." Owen's gangling form appeared at the door.

"Mr. Powderly . . . Terence," John said—he was not comfortable addressing the young man as mister. "This is my son,

Owen. Owen, this is Terence Powderly of the Machinists'
Union. He just told me that he was at Avondale when John
Siney gave his wonderful speech. He was in the audience with
us that day."

Powderly stood and extended his hand. Owen, who was
at least four inches taller, shook his hand and sat down
immediately.

"I'd like my son to sit with us if you don't mind. He's very
interested in these matters and has read quite a bit about them.
He reads quite a bit about everything. Maybe you can tell us
why you went to Avondale in the first place. You must have
had some sympathies for laboring men?"

"Indeed I did. As one of twelve children, I went to work
when I was thirteen. My first job was with the D&H, as a
switch boy on the gravity railroad. I'm sure you know about
that railroad. I moved up the ladder to repairman, then brake-
man. When I was seventeen, about your son's age here, I was
very happy to get an apprenticeship under a man named James
Dickson who was the master mechanic of the D&H. In three
years, I was a full-fledged machinist. When work got slack on
the D&H, I moved to Scranton and became a machinist, first
with Pennsylvania Coal, then with the DL&W."

"And now, Terence, what do you do now?"

"I am still a machinist, still with the DL&W. In my spare
time, I am a union officer and organizer. That is why I am here
today to talk to you."

"What do you mean? I am a coal miner. You are a skilled
machinist. What do I have that you could need?"

"I do not want anything Mr. Roderick—except some of
your knowledge and insights into labor organization among

the miners. You see, I feel that all the violence of your last strike could have been avoided. The killing of Ben Davis and Daniel Jones was heartbreaking."

"More than the public will ever know," John said.

"Mr. Roderick, we are moving into a new era of understanding between capital and labor. I am president of my machinists' local, yet my relationship with Mr. Scranton and Mr. Dawson is friendly and cooperative. When they have need of good machinists, they depend on me and the union to help them find skilled men. Nevertheless, they know I am a union man through and through. My first point is that this kind of cooperation must be established in the coal mining industry."

"I don't know," Dada said. "I would be one hundred percent for it, but you know the misunderstandings and hard feelings that exist here. Where do we start?"

"Right here in Northeastern Pennsylvania. I think we can show the world how to bring peace and prosperity for both the owners and the workers in mines or factories or wherever men and women work."

Dada shook his head and said, "Too much. That's expecting too much."

"It's very ambitious, but I am convinced we can do it. First we must bring order and discipline into our labor ranks. We can use our record in the Machinist's Union to prove our good intentions."

"But we—the miners—have nothing in common with machinists. You have your union. We have ours."

"We both have the same hopes, the same vision. This brings me to the main reason for my visit today. My belief, Mr. Roderick, is that we must build one large union of working people, uniting miners, steel workers, factory workers, skilled carpenters, masons, machinists, bricklayers, construction workers, garment workers, silk mill workers, textile workers, excluding no occupation or industry."

Dada shook his head sadly, saying, "That's impossible."

"The union is already started, Mr. Roderick."

"Where? What is it called?"

"The Knights of Labor," said Powderly.

"I've never heard of it. When did it start? Where is it?"

"Not long ago. In fact, officially it started in 1869, the year of Avondale."

"Just getting started then, is it?"

"Exactly," said Powderly. "Do you think the miners will join?"

"I don't know, but I do know that Siney's union is going downhill. It's not his fault. The strike . . . the shootings . . . everything went wrong. So I don't think there will be much union talk for some time."

Powderly was not dismayed. "We need a union now more than ever. Not just a miners' union—a big union. Will you help me organize it?"

John Roderick remained thoughtfully silent for a long time before answering. He could sense that his answer was very important to Powderly. "I don't know. I don't know anything about the Knights of Labor."

"Let me tell you a few things briefly then," said Powderly. "The organization started with much secrecy, with secret rules and initiations. It was secret to protect members from threats and from being fired. But it always was a noble bond of brotherhood with Christian goals. Its secrecy, however, made it suspicious. The Catholic Church is especially suspicious of it. I know because I am Catholic and I have heard priests warn against it. I believe secrecy must now be abolished but that we must not lose our altruistic goals. We must make it open and we must make it democratic—we must make it a union in favor of conciliation and arbitration, a union that strongly opposes violence and strikes. A strike might be called only after every other cooperative means to settle disputes has been used. Above all else, we must be against violence. The shootings in Scranton hurt us badly."

As Powderly spoke, his eyes—behind their thick glasses—lit up with his fervor. Although he spoke quietly, Owen, who had been listening attentively, could imagine him delivering much the same speech to a group of workers. Now he asked, "What do you think of the Molly Maguires?"

"They are a menace to all working people. They have set back unionism many, many years," Powderly replied.

John and Owen were unsettled by the vehemence and directness of Powderly's reply.

"But don't you think they brought attention to the plight of miners and their families?" John asked.

"Perhaps in a way, yes," Powderly replied, "but their killings make us all easy targets. Even now, the W.B.A. and Knights of Labor are attacked as nests of Molly Maguires. The crazed individualism and secrecy of any group will not bring about justice for labor, Mr. Roderick. I do not want to dwell on the alleged Molly Maguires, but they are like any other secret organization—they will be opposed by the public. Such wild, disorganized fanaticism is no match for the large railroads now taking over the mines. The Reading Railroad has just bought forty thousand acres of prime land for ten million dollars. What can a small group of vengeful men do against that kind of financial power?"

"Don't misunderstand me, Terence. I agree with you. I have spoken out against fisticuffs and clubs at union gatherings . . ."

"I know you have. Mr. Scranton himself has told me that."

"You know Mr. Scranton intimately?" John asked.

"No, not at all. No, he is my employer, but as I said earlier, he does recognize our union. He recently granted us a ten percent increase in wages."

"I wish he would have respected ours," John said.

"I can't account for his actions at Briggs Shaft, Mr. Roderick. That was not at all like him. There must be some explanation, and someday we may get it. In the meantime, I feel that if the Knights of Labor were accepted by the miners — if we could only organize the miners between Carbondale and Pine Grove, miners from Scranton, Wilkes-Barre, Hazleton, Pottsville area—thousands of men. If we could form these men into a peaceful group, not making radical demands but asking for fair wages and safer working conditions, we would win the respect of the public and the coal operators themselves. We can prove to the operators that miners earning fair wages can bring them more profits."

"Well, Terence, when you put forty railroad cars behind a single engine, you can't get it over the Poconos. It's a tough haul. What you propose is a tougher one. You need more engines if you are to organize the miners."

Up to now very tense, Powderly smiled a little. "Yes, its

a tough haul and a long haul too, but we can get the engines. Respected men like you can do it. Think it over. If you believe in fairness, as I know you do, if you come to see that only by organizing working people from the factories and the mines – and any others we might invite – into one body, called the Knights of Labor, then we can work together."

"When you say others, you mean anyone?"

"Almost," said Powderly. "The by-laws of the knights do exempt some persons and groups."

"Who are they?"

"Brokers, lawyers, and saloon-keepers. None of them may be members."

John smiled in turn. "You said earlier that someday we may understand why Mr. Scranton accompanied the National Guard and escorted the blacklegs to and from work there. You know him indirectly. You work for him. You say he is not opposed to your machinists' union, but I don't believe the miners will ever forgive him for what happened at Briggs, do you?"

"No," said Powderly, "I don't think the average miner will understand. But I think we will. We will understand because we know that the operators are in business to make money. They have big investments. They take risks. They borrow money. They are under pressure from their banks."

"I know what you are saying, but remember, Terence, the average miner has his own problems. Seeing how the Scrantons live, seeing their wealth, their homes, their fine teams of horses, a miner sees wealthy people who do not have an ear for a miner's problems."

"But they do have many overwhelming difficulties,"

Powderly emphasized. "Consider the problems of the first Scrantons. William Henry, Seldon Scranton's father-in-law, took a big gamble in buying five hundred acres of land in Scranton, hoping to build a blast furnace. He bought the land but could not find the money to build the iron furnace until Seldon got his brother, Colonel George Scranton, to join in the venture. They soon found they had misjudged the amount of iron ore in Scranton and had to import ore. Other increased expenses compelled them to borrow money from outsiders, and they almost lost the business before getting it started. Joseph H. Scranton, a cousin from Georgia, invested in the venture and they were able to keep control in the Scranton family. They finally got started and produced nails. The nails were too brittle. The ore was low grade. Bankruptcy loomed. They forgot nails and decided to build rails for the burgeoning new railroads."

"So they turned it around, did they?"

"No, not so fast. It took time and circumstance. English companies had a monopoly on rails, but England could not meet the demands of Europe. So when the Erie Railroad could not import rails for a new line between Port Jervis and Binghamton, the Scrantons got a contract, even though they had never manufactured a single rail, nor did they have the capital to start to do so. Great salesmen, they convinced the Erie to advance them $90,000 to build a rolling mill to produce railroad tracks. Then they produced the rails, but were faced with the problem of getting them from Scranton to the line location. There was no water route, so they had to get many teams of horses to carry the rails through the wilds of northeastern Pennsylvania and southern New York state. They did it four days before the contract was up. Investors were happy and the Scrantons were admired. They broke the monopoly of the English. Nicholas Biddle, former President of the Bank of the United States, hailed them for releasing the nation from English dependence."

Powderly was now speaking with great admiration for the Scranton family.

"Remember, Mr. Roderick, the Scrantons had many smaller problems all along the line. Bad products like their nails made many enemies. Wilkes-Barreans looked down their noses at these New Jersey newcomers. They saw Wilkes-Barre as the center of the world, and it is the county seat of Luzerne County. So when the Scrantons tried to raise capital, there wasn't much to be had close to home. They had to rely on New York bankers and investors."

"Are you saying they needed more money?"

"Yes, for new ventures. In these associations with the Erie Railroad owners, they learned the importance of railroads. If their iron business were to grow, they needed connections with large cities. They planned first to connect with the Erie—no more teams of horses—so they built the Legget's Gap Railroad from Scranton to Great Bend, Pennsylvania, then officially called it the Lackawanna-Western. The railroad gave their business and the city of Scranton access to markets in New York state and Canada. And then they realized Scranton needed more.

"The Scranton Iron and Coal needed another connection just as much. They needed to get to the Delaware Water Gap to connect with Philadelphia and New York City. They got a charter for a railroad called Cobb's Gap Railroad, held a meeting in Stroudsburg, and sold 18,000 shares for $900,000. The Scranton interests bought a majority of the stock. The state of Pennsylvania recognized the two railroads out of the city of Scranton and approved a new name, the Delaware, Lackawanna and Western." Powderly kept John and Owen captivated as he continued.

"The new railroad line over the Poconos connected with the Central Railroad of New Jersey. The Scrantons now gave the city a great leap forward. Most of the other railroads, except the Reading, still connected with canals and rivers. Scranton was open to New York and Philadelphia ten years before Wilkes-Barre enjoyed the convenience. Scranton vaulted to become the anthracite coal capital of the world. So you see how the Scrantons boomed their adopted home. They pushed Scranton into phenomenal growth."

Owen, who had been sitting still, fascinated by the history, ventured to ask: "How many millions did they make producing their rails and building their railroads?"

"You mean these first Scrantons?" asked Powderly.

"Yes, these iron and coal and railroad-building Scrantons," said Owen. "How many millions did they make?"

"Well, let's see now," said Powderly, "none of them made much money. This is the point I was driving at all along trying to answer your father's misgivings about William Scranton. Why would he carry a gun and march his men to Briggs Shaft? He will have to answer that, but if you followed my story I think you will have an idea.

"Selden Scranton went bankrupt in 1844, and when George Scranton died he had no money. Does that answer your question, Owen? That's what I'm saying about William Scranton."

"Why did William Scranton act as he did at Briggs? Fear. Fear. He is frightened of bankruptcy and failure. The miners don't know it to this day, but William Scranton was merely the superintendent of the Scranton Iron and Coal. Joseph was president, but he could not make his son president. The New York investors took complete control of the company the year after the Briggs Shaft killings. During the strike, both William and his father knew what might be in the offing. William Scranton was under excruciating strain to keep the mining division of Scranton Iron and Coal not only solvent but profitable. He just could not let the Briggs be idle another week. It had not produced a ton of coal in months. The costs of controlling the water, gas, and air were mounting. The great profits of 1867 to 1870 were being wiped out. I believe William Scranton acted out of pressure and fear, but I believe he is a changed man. His father is dead now and he has greater responsibility than ever before. He has been influenced by the killings at Briggs Shaft."

"Has he really changed?" Dada asked, "or is it that he now needs you? He is managing a successful iron company. He needs skilled mechanics and machinists. You can find them for hire. Is he driven by profits or fair play? Did Briggs Shaft, the killings, his arrest, change his character? If he were so filled with fear, Terence, why didn't he sit down with us, explain his economic problem? Between us, we could have reached a compromise."

"Pride perhaps," Powderly answered. "You must understand, Mr. Roderick, operators and owners are influenced by their habits and history. They are individualists who take risks. They think they will make or break depending on their own work, their own planning and decisions. I am sure it will be a tremendous challenge for us to make these men believe that unions do not exist just to conquer them."

Turning to Owen, Terence Powderly said, "Owen, your father said you are a great reader, and I believe that reading gives us balanced judgments. You are well aware of the complexities of character, especially if you have read Shakespeare. Can you understand a man like William Scranton, a man who has done good things, but is driven to commit an act that led to the death of two men?"

"I have not read Shakespeare—yet," Owen said. "I'd like to. I think I can understand a man like Mr. Scranton. But, I have heard a third description of Mr. Scranton. I know him as the man who led the blacklegs. I have heard you describe him as a man about to lose his position and money, a man afraid. But I have also heard him described another way, as an athlete. The summer when he was home from Yale University, they say, he was a show-off, a braggart. Even now that he's nearly thirty I hear he is prone to display his strength, how much he can lift. When he led the blacklegs, they say, he acted as though he were still in college leading his team, so intent on winning that he forgot he is not a college hero kicking against Harvard but in a world of people trying to keep families alive."

Terence Powderly was surprised at Owen's picture of William Scranton, but having had more contact with him than either Owen or John, he was not dismayed. He rose and clearly realized he had stayed long enough. "All I can say is that I am convinced we can work with Mr. Scranton." Turning directly to John, he said, "I am glad we had this talk, Mr. Roderick, and I am glad that Owen joined us. I can see we have much, much more to talk about, so I hope you will permit me to come back a week today. I am more sure now than when I came in that you have the interest and vision to join with us. Owen, I am counting on you, too. In the next ten years, Scranton is going to become one of the most prosperous towns in the United States. It will be the anthracite capital of the world. It will be a great iron-producing center. Mr. Roderick, Owen, let me tell you what I mean. We have already mined over twenty-seven million tons of coal here since 1832. That was the year William and Maurice Wirts brought Welsh miners into my home town of Carbondale."

"Yes," Owen said, "I've read about those first Welsh miners. They arrived by boat in Philadelphia, and then it took them two weeks to get to Carbondale traveling by rivers and canals." He paused. "The first names given to Carbondale were strange – Ragged Island and Barrendale. Who named it Carbondale?"

"Washington Irving, the writer, he gets the credit," said Powderly. But many people are unconvinced about that. However that may be, the main point I am making is, that in the next *ten* years, we will mine twenty million more tons of coal. It can bring prosperity to thousands of us while it rewards its great capital investors. It can happen if we reduce labor strife with labor peace. We can talk more about this next week."

Powderly rose, shook hands warmly with both John and Owen. At the door, he again affirmed their next meeting.

When Powderly had gone, Mam was curious to know about the visitor and the purpose of his call. Dada responded with a detailed account of the dialogue.

"The Knights of Labor," she said aloud, "a very grand name, isn't it? I wonder if taking that uppity name will do anything to bring the men closer together."

"What do you mean?"

"Bring men from Scranton closer to men from Wilkes-Barre, and then bring those two groups closer to the men from Hazleton."

"I don't know," said Dada, "but we certainly know that is one of the hardest things to do."

"And the hardest of all is trying to get the miners of Scranton to act at the same time as the Schuylkill and Carbon men," said Mam. "They never seem to agree on when or why they should strike. Three years ago, the Scranton miners wouldn't go along with them. When we had the bad time at Briggs, they kept working. If Mr. Powderly's Knights of Labor want to do better, they shall have to get men to cooperate better than that."

Dada nodded his head. "One of the problems is that the smaller mine owners down in the lower counties are often willing to sit and talk to the miners. They see a willingness on the part of miners to tie their wages to a base system so that wages and prices of coal have some kind of standard."

Mam asked, "Would Mr. Powderly agree with that?"

"Oh yes, I believe he would, but the Lackawanna owners certainly would not. You see, here in Scranton, the mine owners are larger corporations, into iron as well as coal. They depend on bankers, financiers, and stockholders. Their attitude toward the miners is 'It's none of your business. If you behave yourself, we'll see that you have a job.'

"As for the owners in Schuylkill and Carbon, and for that matter in lower Luzerne county, the owners seem to be—and I'm not sure—but they seem to be more knowledgeable about mining, more interested in improving the whole industry. Of course, as I said, they are smaller and are closer to the men, too."

The conversation continued on about mining and how the conditions might be improved if they had unity among the miners.

Finally, Mam asked, "How did you leave it with Mr. Powderly?"

"He's coming back next week. I'm eager to talk with him further. He's a thoughtful man."

CHAPTER 8

ह

VISIONS DIMMED

T erence Powderly did not return to see the Rodericks. His vision of an all-encompassing union faded as he suffered personal disillusionment and the national economy went into a severe depression. The cause of it lay in the economy of the Civil War and its aftermath.

During the years of the Civil War, wages had increased rapidly. By 1866, the wages were sixty percent higher than they had been in 1860. However, in the same period, the rise in the cost of living had been ninety percent. Rents increased even more. Inflation had more than wiped out gains. In the 1870s, the national economy came under great stress through the manipulations of a few moguls—men like Jay Gould, Daniel Drew, Commodore Vanderbilt, and James Fisk. Their speculations in corporations, trusts, railroads, and precious metals filled the decade with panics, business failures, depression, and outright economic calamity. Their dealings not only drove the economy to near collapse, but polluted the political system as well. State and national legislators were participants in bribery scandals. One New York state senator, who received $100,000 from Gould and $75,000 from Vanderbilt, sold his vote to the higher payer.

Two weeks after the Avondale disaster, Jim Fisk attempted to corner the gold market. Only the United States

Treasury sales of four million dollars in gold prevented his doing so. On Black Friday, hundreds of banks and commercial companies went bankrupt. Thousands of businessmen lost their fortunes and their reputations. President Grant himself was accused of being implicated in Gould's transactions. Because so many of his advisors were involved, his administration was condemned forever. The panic of 1873 swept across the nation.

The whole next decade was marked by the creation of new business organizations, including syndicates and trusts designed to protect and increase industrial efficiency, power, and profits. In self-defense, laborers turned to those who would organize them for protection in the workplace. They turned to men like Terence Powderly.

When Powderly called on the Rodericks in the summer of 1873, he was already an acute observer of labor's visions. Less than a week later, the Panic of 1873 destroyed his hopes and took away his job. In 1873, three hundred iron manufacturers closed. Eighty nine railroads went bankrupt. Lackawanna Iron & Coal survived, but management's benevolent attitude toward Powderly and the other unionized employees changed drastically. Walter Dawson, his former friend, told him he would have to go because the company was afraid of the unions. Powderly realized he would have to leave Scranton to find work. Dawson had turned into a bitter anti-union boss who had Powderly blackballed wherever he could.

Even William Scranton could not save Powderly's job. As John Roderick had implied in his questioning of Powderly, William Scranton could cooperate with the machinists' union only as long as it was profitable to do so.

Now married, Powderly had to find employment. He became an itinerant machinist, working first in Windsor, Canada, then in Buffalo, walking most of the way there, then in Galion, Ohio. Everywhere he went, Walter Dawson found a way to let his employers know about his union activities and insure his dismissal. At last he moved on to Oil City, Pennsylvania, where he found steady work. His wife joined him there. He stayed in Oil City for nearly two years as a skilled machinist and a member of the union there.

His interest in unionism and his zeal won the attention of international leaders. These two years also gave him time to acquire other skills. At seventeen he had not been able to write. Now, at twenty-five, he wrote well, spoke fluently, and was a persuasive leader.

CHAPTER 9

❧

A DECISION

The Rodericks scarcely noticed that Terence Powderly failed to keep his appointment. They were too busy with their own problems. John found himself reduced to working two or three days a week at most and had to dig more coal to compensate for the lost days. He began to think that the only way he could make ends meet was to take Owen down under to labor beside him and Evan, but he knew how much heartbreak Mam would endure if he did this. He knew the danger to which he was exposing Owen. Most of all, he knew that working in the mines would end Owen's reading and education. After nine or ten hours spent loading six or eight cars of coal, Owen would be so exhausted that once he had washed, dressed, had his supper and relaxed for an hour or so, he would fall asleep, pull himself off the sofa, and go to bed until 5:30 the next morning. Dada remembered his own experience in the mines of Wales, and he had seen the young mine laborers in Avondale and Briggs. He knew well what would happen to Owen.

Mam had used every bit of logic and every ruse to keep Owen above ground, as she often put it, but to no avail. One of her persuasive measures was an invitation to Rhondda Hall to spend a weekend with them. Since she had seen the Rodericks only a half-dozen times in the four years since the

Avondale funerals, she was eager to visit. She had not seen them in a year.

Mam knew that Rhondda would be her greatest ally in trying to convince Dada not to take Owen into the mines.

Owen himself had mixed feelings. He enjoyed his work in Miller's store. Older and more experienced than he had been at O'Brien's, he was much more assured. He had lost his boyish enthusiasm, so appealing to the Avondale housewives, but his new touch of adolescent shyness substituted very well. Many of the latest Welsh immigrants bought from Mr. Miller because of "that Welsh boy who really understands every word of Welsh I speak to him."

Having worked in the coal breaker, Owen was well schooled in the atmosphere of mining. He knew many breaker boys who "had graduated" to become patchers and then mule drivers. He had talked to them and had heard them say "I'd rather work in the mines any day than in the breaker. That breaker is a killer; same thing over and over, drive you crazy, pick, pick, pick. And that Shadow Morgan is a pain in the ass, going around poking you in the ribs with that goddamn stick of his, that is when he isn't banging away at some clogged chute. No, give me the mines anyday. You get plenty of room and lots of different jobs to do. Best of all, you get a real good exercise. You can run, run, run. And a lot more talk. The goddamn breaker makes so much noise you can't hear yourself think. Down under you can talk plenty with drivers, miners, even some of the bosses. And those drivers, can they tell the stories! And they ain't Sunday School stuff, either."

Yes, most of the breaker boys looked forward to the greater freedom in the mines, the manhood it gave them, and of course, twice the pay. But the same enthusiastic breaker-boys-turned-patchers could freeze you with endless horror stories: how big Hunky Joe broke his leg; how "Harp" Pete Dougherty got his skull fractured. Every accident story identified the victim by his ethnic origin. None of it was malicious, just plain identification. If six men were caught under in a caving room, the conversation about the accident might sound like this:

"Who were they?"

"Geez, I didn't get their names, but three were cheese-eaters, two were krauts, one was a paddy, and one a hungarian."

The term hungarian was a blanket term for Slovaks, Poles, Russians, Lithuanians, Ukranians, or Ruthenians. Later, as their numbers increased, *hunky* became the general term used, usually—in self-defense—behind their backs.

The descriptions of accidents and deaths relayed by the boys were detailed and gruesome.

Owen's attitude toward going down the mines was mixed, therefore, because he had varying pictures in his mind. He knew how much economic pressure Dada was encountering, and he knew that laboring with his father would pay him double what he was earning at Miller's. He was not eager to go down, but if his father needed him, he would certainly go.

Miss Hall's visit did nothing to change the situation. Mam had a long talk with her about her dreams for Owen. Rhondda, in turn talked of Owen's abilities and intellectual curiosity, the quality she saw as his greatest gift—the quality, she said, that marked the real scholar, that inquisitiveness for fact and cause and results that leads to great satisfaction and rewards, to discovery, clarification and understanding, whether one be historian, scientist, lawyer, doctor, or businessman.

Between the two women, the hope for Owen's education and future tied them in a common anguish as they confronted the probability that he would have to work with his father and cousin.

When Miss Hall arrived, her encounter with Owen for the first time in a year was an awkward moment for them both. At sixteen, Owen was an inch or two taller than she, yet there was still within him a hint of the twelve-year-old who had lighted the school fire for her every morning. There was a hesitant moment when they met, but it disappeared as she ran to him, clasped both his hands, and shook them, saying, "Owen, you're growing too fast!"

He smiled and said, "It's Mam's cooking, I guess."

Saturday afternoon they took a long walk to Washburn Street Cemetery where they visited the grave-sites of the Avondale victims at the west end of the cemetery. Each grave was marked merely with a flat stone, five inches square, bearing only a number. There were no names. A cemetery worker explained that there was a list of identifications in the superintendent's office, but they both felt a pang of disappointment at these insignificant tombstones. They had known many of those buried here, known their families, and been part of their suffering. These markers were not enough.

"Someday," Miss Hall suggested, "there should be a large steel marker here. Better still perhaps, a huge, two-ton boulder of anthracite coal with a steel plate bearing every man's name. They were all fine men. They deserve something more. If the world doesn't know about them, the city of Scranton should. They are part of the history of this city. They should be remembered here, at least."

Beyond the cemetery, they hiked to the top of West

Mountain; where they sat they could look across to East Mountain, with the Lackawanna Valley and the city of Scranton spread out beneath them.

"What a beautiful view this is, Owen. It reminds me so much of the mountain above Avondale. It should, I guess; it's the very same range. Just eighteen miles or so north of Avondale."

"Have you ever walked up to Tilbury Knob in West Nanticoke?" Owen asked. "That's my favorite spot. The view of the Susquehanna is so beautiful. But the climb up to it is really hard."

"No, but I took the Lackawanna on a day's excursion one time to Wyalusing. They say it's the most spectacular view in Pennsylvania. Some of the men and women were brave enough to stand in the river on Wyalusing Rock. Too much for me! I was willing to feast my eyes on it from a bit farther back."

Their conversation drifted from these pleasantries to conditions in Avondale and Miss Hall's work.

"Oh, I'm still teaching every day. I don't visit families as much as I used to. Families are now back to their regular routines. Tragedies are not forgotten. They are still heavy on some hearts, but the people know they must get on with their own lives. And you Owen, I know that you are busy reading so much. Your mother told me that you have read almost every book in Reverend Williams's library."

"Not quite, but I have read many."

"What else have you been doing?"

"Oh, just playing a little baseball and helping a little around the house." He did not tell her he still did much daydreaming about her. And he still thought about her before going to sleep every night. Now that she was here only two or three feet away, she seemed the same as ever. He remembered her arms around him the day Taid was killed. He recalled the fleeting touches of her as he had helped her with groceries. He yearned now for some reason or accident that would free him to touch her, even hold her. His body and mind were in the age-old battle of all sixteen-year-old boys. Instinctively he wanted to devour her. His mind told him not to be preposterous. This was a grown woman, his teacher, so all his vagrant impulses were controlled, as he strained to keep the conversation interesting.

"Do you still go to the Episcopal Church?" he asked.

"Oh yes, almost every Sunday. You remember Mr. Burr, the minister there, I'm sure."

"Yes, I do," Owen said enthusiastically. "He distributed a lot of groceries after the fire. He helped most of the families."

"That's right. Well, Mr. Burr has been good enough to help me with a few chores around the house. One Saturday, he insisted on helping me with my groceries just as you did. And last week, he was good enough to take me to a play at the Academy of Music in Wilkes-Barre."

Owen's libido collapsed. Every bedtime fantasy, every daydream suddenly seemed ridiculous. He was embarrassed within himself. In his mind, the kindly Mr. Burr was an intruder.

Then Owen's common sense returned. I suppose, he thought, they will soon marry. That's the course of events. I'd better change the subject.

Miss Hall spoke before he did. "Owen," she asked, "how do you feel about becoming a coal miner?"

"Oh, all right, I guess."

"Are you afraid?"

"Everybody gets used to it. My father says he's still often afraid, so they—he and my cousin Evan—are very careful, very good miners."

"Do they think you're strong enough? Coal is heavier than groceries, you know."

"I know, but I can handle the coal."

They talked for half an hour more about the Briggs Shaft killings, about books, and about Miss Hall's family in Philadelphia. Finally she said, "I've had a lovely afternoon, Owen, but I think we'd better start down home."

"Where will you go to church tomorrow?" he asked as they started back.

"Oh, I'd like to go with you and your parents. I'd love to hear Reverend Williams. He's helped you so much."

"Don't you need to find an Episcopal Church?" Owen inquired.

"No, not at all. I will go with you. Someday I would like to visit the new St. Luke's Episcopal Church on Wyoming Avenue in Scranton. I have been to St. Stephen's in Wilkes-Barre and it was very nice.

"Not as grand as some of their parishioners," Owen said.

"What do you mean?"

"I heard Reverend Williams say that some of the Episcopalians attend services wearing tails and high silk hats."

"Really, well that would be nice to see."

"Mr. Williams said not. The church is no place to parade yourself," he said.

Miss Hall, half in jest, replied, "Maybe they believe that they are glorifying God by wearing their best."

"I agree with Mr. Williams, the church and people should be plain and simple."

"Owen, you talk like a Quaker."

"Don't you agree?" Owen asked.

"Not always. I believe the Quakers are right. Yet, at the same time I can admire the great cathedrals of Europe and believe they were built as a way to glorify God."

As they walked, Owen was filled with unasked questions about the Reverend Charles Burr. He dared not ask, but then he spluttered, "Mr. Burr, how does he feel about churches?"

"Mr. Burr? Owen, I really don't know. I don't believe he thinks much about it. I'm sure he doesn't care how people dress as long as they try to be good, honest people."

"Do you like him very much?"

"Yes, I'm very fond of him. He is a studious person—like you in many ways—and very compassionate as well."

Owen was very sorry to hear this, but he did not respond.

When they arrived at the house, John was clearly waiting for them. "Come in, come in," he said. "Evan is here. Let's all go to the parlor." Dada had predictably brought Evan and Miss Hall together to ease the strain of telling Mam and Owen that the day for a decision had arrived.

"As you know," he began when everyone was seated, "we have talked about Owen leaving Miller's store and joining Evan and me. I think the time has come. Last week Evan and I worked only two days. We got out only five cars each day without a helper. Our pays for last week were thirteen dollars and ten cents. We just cannot live on that. Even if our work week is increased to three or four days, we cannot make enough for food and rent and clothing. So—Owen has told me he is ready. And if he is, then he must give Mr. Miller one week's notice. According to my calendar, Owen should join us a week Monday—that is if there is work. Better to say the next workday after next Monday."

Everyone knew that every pro and con of Owen's joining Dada and Evan had been gone over and over. There was no point in opposing the decision. Life dictated it.

Mam had all but exhausted herself discussing it with Dada, but she too saw the inevitability. Her job now was to ease the tensions, and she did her best, saying, "A cup of tea, is it?"

Dada did, too, as he said to Evan, "Evan, tell Owen about Trigger Owens. He'll be running into him at the cage. Owen should recognize the tallest story-teller of the anthracite, and the biggest liar west of Cardiff."

🐌   🐌   🐌

On Sunday, Rhondda attended church services with the Rodericks and heard the Reverend R. J. Williams. She helped Mrs. Roderick with the Sunday dinner and planned to catch the work train early Monday morning to be at school by nine.

On Sunday evening, before retiring, she talked to Owen one last time. She could not hide her feelings about his new work. "I know your father and Evan will be with you, Owen, but do be careful. I hope times get better and you will not need to work with them very long."

"I hope so," Owen said. "I'd like to get work that I would enjoy doing all my life, a job that would give me a chance to learn and to grow, something that lets me help people the same way that you do."

"You will. I know you will, Owen. In the meantime, I'm going to come back in two weeks, just so that I can see how you are doing, just to hear what it's like. I want to be assured that you can do it and that you don't really hate the work."

"Well, even if I hate it, I'll do it. I want to help them at home. Even when I'm working at Briggs, I know I can keep reading and educating myself. Mr. Williams said there are great opportunities for self-educated men. He knows a man from Providence who studied and became a lawyer without one day of school. He's now a judge in Utica, New York. Maybe if I study, I can do something too, maybe be someone someday."

"Don't put it that way, Owen, you are someone already. I'm sure you mean you'd like your life to have some meaning, to have the satisfaction of doing some good in the world."

"Yes, that's what I mean. I enjoyed listening to Mr. Powderly so much. He said hearing Mr. Siney speak at Avondale changed his life. Avondale itself made a great impression on him. When he talked to Dada and me at our house, I felt that he really wanted to improve our lives, that he was almost like a missionary. I'd like to feel that way some day."

"I'm sure you will, Owen. I don't know very much about Welsh, Owen, but my mother never put me to bed when I was a child without saying 'nos da'. So I'll say my nos da, to you and see you in two weeks."

"Nos da," Owen said. Lying in bed, he found himself doing what he had done at bed-time since he was twelve. If anything, his imagination was more active than ever as he pictured himself five years older than Rhondda, not five years younger.

%

CHAPTER 10

THE EDUCATION OF
A COAL MINER

T he following Tuesday, Owen prepared to accompany
his father and cousin, whom he called uncle, on his first
day of work in the mines. When his mother called him, he
awoke to a dark, rainy morning. Arriving to work at Miller's
store had been easy in the early daylight morning hours. Now,
he was reminded of those dark mornings when, as a breaker
boy, he staggered to dress for the ordeal.

This morning, he was excited, fearful, inquisitive, and
just a little dejected. His job at the stores of O'Brien and Miller
had given him a taste of work that was not monotonous or
lonely, but pleasant in opportunities for human interaction
and communion. Best of all, the environment was stimulating
and the outdoors refreshing and wholesome.

He dressed in his work clothes, much the same as he had
worn in the breaker. These were new and larger for his growing
body. His work shoes, stronger than needed for the breaker,
were made of leather and very heavy—both soles and heels
were finished with hobnails. His cap had a hook above the
peak on which he would attach his lamp. The lamp was shaped
somewhat like a tobacco pipe. Inside the body and along the
stem, tightly wadded cotton dipped in kerosene or oil pro-

truded out of the stem as a wick. Lighted, the lamp was the only light that pierced the total blackness of the mine.

By the time Owen was dressed, his mother had prepared his breakfast and packed his dinner pail. The pail was filled with two cheese sandwiches and an apple. A special compartment on top was filled with tea. Usually, Dada left his home with a quick, warm "ta" to his wife. This morning, he was delayed as Mam hovered over Owen as though she were restraining him to the last minute. Then, with several hugs and kisses, she released him. And they were gone.

At the top of the shaft, Evan was waiting. Small groups of miners gathered near the cage entrance waiting their turns to go down. Owen and Dada joined Evan to wait.

The cage was the miner's elevator, carrying men and coal. In the morning, it got men into the mine. At quitting time, it brought them out. During the day, it made scores of trips bringing out the loaded cars of coal to be rolled to the breaker. Occasionally, when new mules were brought in to work, or mules were taken out for rest or rehabilitation, they rode the cage. Usually, however, the mules were stabled inside the mine and never saw daylight.

Owen waited impatiently. He hoped he would not become the butt of a cage story, one of the thousands told about that first cage ride of young recruits, vomiting, passing out, or falling under buckling knees. The stories, repeated at every funeral or wedding, had entertained him often when he was in the breaker. He vowed he would get between Dada and Evan to hide any reaction to his first ride. He hoped he would not be observed. That hope was short lived. Trigger Owens, the best hunter and story-teller in Hyde Park, spotted Dada, then Owen, and shouted for all to hear.

"Owen, where are your groceries? Good thing you left them at Miller's. You'd lose them this morning." And then, with a wink to his laborer, young Tim Farrell, he said, "Watch Owen, you don't lose your breakfast."

Twenty or thirty mining men turned to look at him, all with knowing grins.

The cage suddenly shot up from the mine, stopped with an up-down little jerk. A fence-like gate opened, and in seconds Owen was jammed in with ten others. Dada pushed him to the edge where a two-by-four plank ran horizontally across the side of the cage. A bell rang, and the cage plummeted three hundred feet into the mine. With open mouth, gasping for air, Owen grabbed the guard plank and involuntarily closed his eyes, sure the cable had broken and people would read: *Young Man Killed on First Working Day*. As the fall eased, his knees buckled so that he was almost sitting. Then with a jerk, the fall ended. Trigger and three or four others yelled: "OK, Owen, if you can walk, it's time to go to work." They all laughed.

Dada whispered, "Are you all right?"

Owen did not answer, just kept walking with the others away from the cage. The men divided as they approached three gangways, taking different directions from the bottom of the shaft.

A few steps away from the cage, they lit their lamps and started down the gangway to the coal breast where Dada and Evan had their workplace. The darkness was claustrophobic.

The naked little flame from his cap made scarcely an arm's length of light as it spit little sparks from the flaming cotton wick.

Hardly recovered from the cage ride and the darkness, Owen found the walking treacherous. Huge lumps of rock and coal made every step precarious. Dada and Evan, heads down, with their lights shining directly in front of every step, moved as though they were walking on a garden path. Slowly he tried to imitate their gaits, but he stumbled often, losing his balance on the ground's alternate cover of soft, wet, mushy silt and rocks varying in size from pebbles to boulders.

When they got to the breast, they found their picks, shovels, drills, augers, and other tools were all as they had been left on the last workday. This breast face, similar to the others, ran at a right angle about thirty feet from the main gangway. A short line of track had been laid so the empty coal cars could be run in and the filled cars pulled out.

"Look here, Owen," his father said, "and never forget to do this. Before we start to work, we test the roof." As he said it, he used his iron bar to poke overhead, checking for loose, threatening rock. He continued to bang the rod against the roof saying, "You can tell by the sound whether you have a solid roof. If you get a hollow ring, you know your cover is not solid. Of course, every minute of the day . . ." Just then Owen jumped and lost his balance. Two huge rats scampered between his hobnailed shoes. He had heard the exaggerated stories of large rats, but what he saw, he would later swear, were the size of small cats.

"You'll get used to them," his father said. "Every minute you'll be ready for the smell of gas. You'll know it. There's plenty of stench down here, with the decaying old wood props, the sulphur, bad air, but always be alert for gas."

In minutes, his father and Evan were preparing to set off an explosion to blast the coal from the walls of the breast. There was a flurry of picking, cleaning, hammering and then, finally, a long period of drilling holes into which they placed black powder. When the explosive powder was in place, they ran slow-burning squibs through the holes to the powder. His father and Evan did this work from a kneeling or a standing position. Later, he would see them move into a crawl-space just wide enough for them to crawl on their stomachs.

As they worked, Evan said, "Look here, Owen," after every step of the preparation. "You won't have to do this for a while, but it's better you get it right from the very beginning, no short cuts. Notice, safety all the way it is."

Trying to take in every bit of instruction he could get, Owen found his concentration broken by the noise of squeaking, swaying, ungreased coal cars, the cracking of a whip, and a string of expletives that would raise a mule from the dead.

"Get going, you bag-eared, thick-ass son of a bitch," came echoing from the gangway as the whip cracked to the words delivered with a rich Scottish brogue.

"That's Scotty McLauders, Jim's boy," Evan said.

Dada added, "Just arrived from Scotland two months ago. He's bringing us two empties. Evan, take Owen out to the gangway and show him the switch. Show him how we get the cars in here."

Evan hurried with Owen following and got to the switch just as Scotty reached it from the other direction.

"Hello, Evan," Scotty's burred, pleasant voice rang out.

"You have a new helper, aye?" Scotty, a moment before a raving maniac, was now composed and gentle.

"Yes, this is Owen, John's son. I'll show him how to disconnect your cars and to pull the switch and roll the cars to the breast."

As soon as Evan disconnected the cars, Scotty reined the mule and went straight ahead to pick up full cars somewhere down the gangway, walking behind the mule and calling back, "See you later, Owen."

Before Scotty and the mule had gone sixty feet, they came to a door that controlled the air. There, an elderly man, who had lost one arm in a mine accident, got up from his stool to open the door. He opened the door every time a trip went by. Usually, the draft would close the door, but sometimes the man would have to shut it as well.

Scotty's mule, which had stopped before the door, now refused to move on when the door opened. Scotty, with his whip in his right hand, became once more the raving, whip-lashing, cursing wild-man and disappeared down the gangway, shouting back to the door-keeper in his beautiful Scottish accent, "See you later, Frank, man."

Having switched the track and explained it to Owen, Evan with Owen's help, pushed the first car around the switch and part way into the breast. It was the first muscle work of the day and Owen enjoyed it.

They pushed the second car to the same area, where Owen's father had completed his drilling and was ready to light the squib.

Owen was slightly nervous watching the final stages. He hoped that the powder was well placed and that they would get a good charge with lots of coal. He knew enough from hearsay to wish for that. He hoped, too, that the squibs were not wet, so that once lit they would burn directly to the powder and set off the explosion. He had heard of so many miners being maimed or killed when they went back to investigate why a fuse or squib failed. The accident usually occurred because an impatient miner, thinking the fuse was extinguished, went back to light it again just as it fired or exploded. There were so many such accidents that some miners would not risk investigating a defective fuse. They would call it a shift and go home.

Evan went to light the squib, as Owen and John retreated behind the empty coal cars. Owen could see the sparkle of the squib as it started its journey to the powder. After lighting the squib, Evan hurried to join them. In a minute, as they huddled together, the explosion sent a cloud of choking coal dust and smoke through the chamber. Only after some of it cleared could they see they had extracted a good pile of coal and rock from the face.

When the smoke cleared, Owen's father showed him how to chop the larger pieces before loading the car. He told Owen to start with the smaller coal, shoveling that into the car first, using the shovel as long as possible, then hand-loading the larger pieces with a good topping. Loading was the main reason Owen had been required to work with his father and uncle. When the car was full, he looked at it and wondered how many he would load in the years to come.

His uncle showed him a metal tag, "Look, Owen, this is our car so we mark it to get credit. See how I attach it to the car. Up top they will record it."

Owen asked, "Couldn't someone take that off and substitute another one?"

"Oh, yes. That's been done," said Evan, "but anyone who does it is a fool. He's worse than a horse-thief, and when he's caught, his days of mining are over."

Evan, Owen, and his father then moved the full car back to the face. It took all their strength to move it. One turn of the wheels and the car moved easier. The second empty was set and loaded in the same way.

Once the second car was filled and tagged, Dada said, "Let's have a bite." And so, like most miners, they sat on the largest piece of coal at hand, ate half a sandwich and half an apple and drank some tea.

Between munches, Owen observed aloud to his father that Scotty certainly let out more swear words in one breath than he had ever heard.

"Well," Dada said, "I can't protect you from hearing them and perhaps others much worse. Remember, Owen, nothing you hear will change your speaking habits unless you start repeating the words. Swearing, or any other evil, cannot corrupt your character unless you yourself imitate it. Our good Lord said it well." And then in Welsh, Dada said, *"Nid oes dim sy'n mynd i mewn i ddyn o'r tu allan iddo yn gallu ei halogi; ond y pethau sy'n dod allan o ddyn sy'n halogi dyn. (There is nothing that goes into a man from the outside that can make him unclean; rather it is what comes out of a person that makes him unclean.")*

"Just remember, whether you work here in the mines or in a palace, you will encounter corruption—the mild sort like Scotty's language or major kinds like dishonesty or infidelity. When you do, you'd better remember that old Welsh verse."

"That doesn't help Scotty with his mule much," Owen observed. "I suppose getting him a more obedient mule would help him."

"A more obedient mule?" Evan howled and Dada joined in. "We'll tell you a little about mine mules when we have our lunch," Evan promised.

They finished their bite. "Let's see now," Dada said. "I think we should get ready to set off another charge. In the meantime, let's hope Scotty comes back and picks up these two full cars and leaves two empties here. And Owen, while I think of it, I know you've learned a few things already this morning, but there's one thing that is far more important than anything technical you might learn about mining, and if Scotty is not here within a half hour, you will have received a real lesson."

"More important than anything?"

"Yes, but I'll wait until Scotty gets here."

The drilling and other preparation for setting up the next explosive charge took Dada and Evan another forty-five minutes. Scotty had not yet arrived with the empties, so Dada and Evan sat down. In the meantime, they had shown Owen the necessity for checking all the props around the breast and again double-checking the roof. Owen then had walked to the gangway and practiced throwing the switch to bring in the cars.

In another five minutes, Scotty arrived with his recalcitrant mule, but without empties.

"Where are our empties?" Dada asked Scotty sternly.

"Weren't any at the bottom, Mr. Roderick." Using the formal address was his way of apologizing. He knew that when miners wanted empty cars he should be there with them. "I came to get your coal out and I'll be back first thing." While he talked, he was hitching his mule to the loaded cars. Owen set the switch at the end of the breast, and without another word Scotty was gone. He did not return with more empty cars for another half hour. When he did, he did not say a word but left hurriedly. Owen and Dada pushed the empties into the breast.

"Now, Owen, you've had an important lesson in mining. We've lost at least an hour today waiting for empty cars. One of the most difficult parts of mining is getting those empties when you need them. There have been more misunderstandings, violence, and retribution over getting empties than almost any other problem in the mines. Remember, always keep a good will with the foreman. If he knows you are serious and industrious, he will respect you. More important, treat drivers like Scotty with respect. Did you notice how businesslike Scotty was when he was late. We didn't yell or scream at him. We knew there was some reason he did not get here sooner. Some day he will tell us. Many miners are always fighting with the drivers. Don't do it. And don't ask for any special favors. They will respect you and give you empties as soon as they can."

At dinner time, they had the remainder of the food in their lunch pails and the last of the tea.

"What were you and Dada promising to tell me about the mules?" Owen asked as they relaxed.

"You said something about an obedient mule. I don't believe I ever saw one," Evan said. "They generally move when they decide to. If they move on command, it's just because their own minds are made up at that precise moment, and it just looks as though they are responding. People say they are stubborn. I think they are more smart than stubborn. You'll hear many stories about just how smart they are. Drivers hate to be caught with a full load of cars at quitting time because his mule might stop dead. They know it is quitting time. Dynamite will hardly get them to move. And if you start beating them, watch out. They'll rear and kick—or worse yet, get you between them and the side walls of coal and squeeze you to death."

"I know you heard Scotty sounding as though he were killing his mule," said Dada, "but they are very good friends. Trusts him like a pet, feeds him a couple of apples every day. Believe it or not, his mule—Jim, he calls him—likes tobacco. You'll see Scotty taking a bite of plug and giving Jim a hunk too."

"Do they ever take the mules out of here?" Owen asked.

"Hardly ever. The stable is near the foot of the shaft. They are well fed and cared for, but they seldom see green fields, the sunshine, and daylight. When they do take them out for some reason, to heal a serious injury or to recover from sickness, they explode in running and jumping, like any caged creature," Dada explained.

Owen did not reply. He knew how those mules must feel. He had been in the mines less than a day, but he could ignore the darkness and the choking confinement only when he was working, active, following instruction, occupied with a challenge at hand. Owen jumped to his feet to rid himself of the sense of oppression.

"Where are you going?" Dada asked him.

"Nowhere," he replied nervously. "Isn't it time to end our lunch?" What do I do next?"

❧

CHAPTER 11

THE EDUCATION OF A TEACHER

R hondda Hall returned in two weeks as she had promised. She had taken the work train from Avondale late Friday and now sat with Owen in the Roderick's kitchen eager to hear of his first days of mining. Dada and Mam had gone to see the family of Ben Davis, his widow and four children left with little income after Ben was killed at Fellows Square. Since his death, the Rodericks had helped to organize a fellowship church group to supply some kind of small weekly income to the family. Rhondda eyed the small, clean room and said, "If I didn't know better, I'd think I was in Avondale."

"Yes, it's very much the same," said Owen.

Rhondda, admiring the design and keepsakes of the neat kitchen, said, "There are the two Welsh porcelain dogs exactly as your mother had them, the wooden love-spoons, and the towels. And, of course, that beautiful Welsh clock fits in perfectly, as it always will. It's amazing to me how your parents and so many others were able to carry these beautiful hand-made clocks to America. Look at it, the face is at least thirty inches wide."

Rhondda got up and walked to the clock to admire it once again, as she had often done in Avondale, and read again on the face of the clock *Aberaeron.*

"I'm going to visit Aberaeron some day," she continued. "I love the sound of it, and I know it is just below Aberystwyth, right on Cardigan Bay. I'm sure it's beautiful!"

"If you'll wait, I'll go with you," Owen heard himself saying, "That is, if you and Mr. Burr don't leave me behind."

Rhondda laughed and said, "Maybe we can all go together, a regular excursion."

Two or three steps from the clock, just beside one of the porcelain dogs, Mam had placed the clean and sparkling brass safety lamp belonging to Taid. He had never used it in America, but it was a reminder of his mining days in Wales. Touching the little lamp reminded Rhondda that she was much more concerned about Owen's work than she revealed to anyone.

She was eager to get from him a complete understanding of his work, and especially his attitude toward it. That he was in a life-threatening dismal darkness every day was one thing; to have him depressed and disoriented was another. Fortunately, she found that Owen was well adjusted after two weeks with his father and cousin Evan. To Rhondda, he did not admit that he enjoyed his work, but already he had come to understand the point of view of hundreds of miners who would not work at any other job. He had met a few young men who had "graduated" from other occupations.

One said, "I'm glad I'm out of that silk mill. I was a bobbin boy. I was run ragged for ten hours a day. Of course, I liked the girls, but they gave you a hard time if you didn't give them their supplies. Anyway, you never had time to talk to them. The straw boss helping the foreman was a pain in the ass, on your back every minute."

Another said, "That factory job? You can keep it. Then I went to the cookie bakery. Packing those cookies was worse than picking slate. Talk about agony, all day, same thing all day, pack, pack, pack, standing in one place, leaning on one foot, then the other. That's a lot of crap. Give me the mines any day."

Owen explained to Rhondda that for some men working in the mines, with all its danger and dirt, was preferable to the excrutiating monotony and constant supervision of other jobs. He described the camaraderie and interdependence existing underground. He told Rhondda that he had seen fifteen miners gather out of nowhere when a rock fall had caught Tudor Morgan and pinned him, covering him up to his shoulders. Tudor, working about seven hundred feet from their breast, let out a scream. In minutes, every miner within hearing was at his place, some shoring the roof, others shoveling and lifting rock. Even a mine foreman and a fire boss, who heard his cry, were indistinguishable from the miners and laborers as they worked furiously to free him. Owen saw the care with which Tudor, a leg and an arm both broken, was taken to the shaft, placed on the cage, then hauled up to the care of others for hospitalization. After Tudor was safely on his way, the men returned to his breast, cleaned his workplace, and replaced the props, making it safe for the next miner to work there.

The common dangers of miners, the shared experiences, and the challenges created an atmosphere and bond within the mine that pervaded the mine and mine yard. Coal mining elicited a pride in skills, strengths, intelligence. Every miner had to be something of a carpenter, a mason, and handyman.

Every miner wanted others to respect him for his strength and abilities. He wanted, above all, to be known as "a good miner."

Owen conveyed all this as he shared his first two weeks of work with Rhondda. He still addressed her as Miss Hall. He could not bring himself to do otherwise, nor would Dada or Mam have tolerated it. Once at home, hearing Rhondda's name used in exchange between his mother and father, he had unconsciously slipped and heard himself saying Rhondda. He corrected himself immediately as his mother admonished him, "There is a time and place you know."

"I'm so glad you're not too upset about working with your father and cousin Evan," Rhondda said after Owen had described his first experiences. "I'm glad, too, that you understand and respect those with whom you work."

"I do very much," he said. "But as much as I do, I hope someday to work above ground. I must admit that every morning when I wake I wish I did not have to go down. Or rather, I wish I were going to work above ground. Every morning when I get off the cage, I see and feel that blackness, the darkness. I am not comfortable until I get back to our workplace. There I forget my feelings. Time passes quickly. It is not monotonous."

"I'm so glad," Rhondda said. "Are you still reading Reverend Williams's books at night?"

"No, not really. After I wash and have my supper, I read for an hour or so, then I fall asleep. But I shouldn't say I'm not learning, because I am. I know a lot about mines and mining, about gas and flooding and rats and canaries and mules."

"Rats and canaries? What do you mean?"

"Just joking. There are enough stories about mules and rats to fill an encyclopedia. And while I laugh at them, I'm always on the lookout for packs of running rats. They are a sure warning of a weak roof about to fall. Their hearing is so fine, they hear the faint strains of a weakening wall or roof. I pay no attention to one here or there. As a matter of fact, I think the same one shows up every noon for a bite."

"What about the canaries?" Rhondda asked.

"Well, canaries were used years ago to test for gas. The little birds would quickly die from the smallest amount of gas, long before a man could detect it. We have the detecting lamps today. But once in a while, I see a fire boss with a caged canary."

"I'd be terrified seeing those rats," Rhondda said.

"Sometimes there's good cause to be terrified," Owen explained. "They get much of their food around the mule stables. They love the hay, and they have often—I hate to mention this—bitten the noses of the mules as they feed. And cornered, they will even attack miners."

"Well, be careful Owen, and stay away from them. You are certainly learning many things a school would never teach you."

"Nor even college," Owen bragged just a little.

"Tell me about those things," Rhondda asked.

"At noon, the men who work close to us sometimes gather and eat with us. Much of the talk is about the mines, but very often the talk is of religion, unions, politics, or the depression we are now having. The discussions are very helpful to me trying to understand these matters. For two days this week, I heard a great deal about how men feel about the union. I was glad I met Mr. Powderly. I heard so many good things and bad things about him."

"What bad things did you learn?"

"Well, not really bad, but they say that he is too, well, too refined. He's all right for machinists but not rough and tough enough for miners, many say."

"Do you agree with them?"

"No, I don't. But remember, I saw and heard him only once. He expressed many of the thoughts that you and Dada believe in. He believes the miners and owners want the same thing. The miners want fair wages. The owners want a fair profit. He believes that the miners and owners talking with each other can come to a fair understanding for the benefit of both. I listened to him, and I believe he has a great vision for Northeastern Pennsylvania, especially for Scranton."

"You mentioned religion. You mean they discussed, or did they argue? I hope they don't attack each other's faith."

"Oh no, it's mostly the Welsh. I asked Dada about their arguments, and he said they were just spouting off the way they did in Wales. He said the men, like their fathers before them, knew the Bible inside and out, so wherever they were, in the mines, the slate quarries, the farms, yes, even in taverns, they talked and argued. You might say—and I'm saying what Dada said—that the Bible was the rage. Evey young man bragged about being a deacon. The family who had the minister for dinner was the proudest of the week."

"I'm very surprised, Owen."

"Dada said he never ran into it at Avondale. But these Welsh in Scranton are really fascinated by the Bible. As I said before, Dada says most of the Welsh miners here come from families who would not wind a clock on Sundays in Wales. And it's amazing, none of them here in Scranton will buy or read a Sunday newspaper."

"My mother must have known about these practices in Wales, but as a Quaker, she never spoke about them." Rhondda was both curious and skeptical.

"During the week, as we ate at lunchtime, I heard Tom Tyrell say you could never get a promotion 'back 'ome', as he put it, unless you were known as a fervent regular Sunday worshipper.

"Bill Button said there was an underground chapel cut out of solid coal in Glamorganshire where services were held at six every morning. He also said you couldn't play in the town band if you were a drinker. Drinkers could only join the Baco and Beer Band, which they were proud to do! Do you think that these miners were really that religious? I've asked my father that question."

"What did he say?"

"He said some were, and some were not. According to him, there were many really humble and religious men, and many who just made a show of their pious actions."

"I agree with your father. I believe most miners are good, unassuming men. But we Quakers know from history that when men and women get involved in rituals, observances, and a cringing catalog of thou shalt nots, they lose the inner spirituality of religion."

Owen shook his head in understanding. "In Bethesda, the slate quarry workers certainly got into it. Dick Bevan, who was a quarryman before he came to Scranton, said his mother told him that when she was a little girl she had to go to prayer meeting Monday, study class on Tuesday, literary class on Wednesday, prayer meeting on Thursday, and Band of Hope on Friday. On Sunday, she attended two church services, one morning and one evening. In between, she had singing practice and Sunday School, attending church four times."

"I'm sure Dick Bevan's mother turned out to be a fine person," Rhondda said. "At the same time–unfortunately–there were many who emerged from that same discipline stultified by the routine or Christian in name only. But for the most part, I believe those hard working people found the chapel the only relief from the mines, quarries, and child rearing. Best of all, they thrived on music and poetry. They revelled in their adjuncts of the church, their Cymanfaoedd and Eisteddfodau, their song festivals and competitive celebrations. Nowhere in the world, Owen, will you find a people so engrossed in music and poetry."

"Don't forget the rugby and American baseball," Owen interjected, "and there were worse games, but on the sly. In Wales and here in Scranton, some Welsh prefer cock-fighting, card-playing, and boxing, but they are a small group."

"I'm sure some do, Owen, but tell me, what do the men talk about most?"

"Well, right now it's the pay, the conditions, everything that brings up the union question. And it's strange how these subjects get us back to religion."

"Not so strange, Owen. It's a natural application of religion in this world. And for miners, the world is the here and now, where they are working and living. These miners of Scranton know their fathers and grandfathers prayed at the shaft before going down, they know some of the first voices for justice and safety were ministers, so it is natural for them to look to men like Mr. Williams, your friend and pastor, to speak out for them, as does The Reverend Ellis, who had the funeral services here at Washburn Street for the Avondale men. Most important, they know their Bible. They know the prophets like Amos and Micah. They know especially the ministry of Jesus. For them, they are the standards, and not what a Mr. Scranton or a Mr. Dickson or a Mr. Markle or a Mr. Pardee says."

Owen looked confused, "Don't you think Mr. Scranton and the others are religious men?"

"Yes," she said. "But like all people, religious or not, they are not perfect. They divide their lives into separate compartments, corporate and religious. In contrast, your father, Mr. Powderly, and Reverend Williams see no such division. I'm sure the operators are serious—if wrong—when they say over and over, 'Don't mix politics and religion and don't mix religion and business.' They believe it."

As she was talking, the door opened and the Rodericks entered. As they walked into the kitchen, Dada spoke, "My, my, what a serious sight. Another lesson for Owen is it, Rhondda?"

"No, no, not a lesson for Owen. One for me. Owen has really been educating me about his work."

Mam asked rhetorically, "Talking your head off, is he? He can do that you know, especially after he's read something."

Owen, embarrassed, started to say, "I was only . . ."

Rhondda interrupted, "Indeed not, we had a very interesting talk."

"You must be worn out then, both of you," said Mam. "Time now for te bach."

❧　　❧　　❧

This visit was the last time the family saw Rhondda for two years. The depression of 1873 almost drove her father's iron business into bankruptcy. Rhondda had to give up her teaching in Avondale and return to do his secretarial and bookkeeping work. Actually, she enabled her father to reduce his staff by two. Rhondda and her mother working together saved the family firm.

During the next two years, Rhondda did not return to Wyoming Valley or Scranton. The depression continued.

CHAPTER 12

෪

A NATION IN FLAMES

The next three years were difficult for the Rodericks in Scranton, for Rhondda and her parents in Philadelphia, and indeed for the whole country. All the economic problems and deprivations of the nation came to a head in 1877, a year of turmoil in the United States, a year of tragedy in Scranton.

A series of labor protests climaxed in the hot July of that eventful year. A mountain of labor grievances, built during the tumultuous seventies, reached its peak when the Baltimore and Ohio Railroad informed its employees of a pay reduction. In May, the Pennsylvania Railroad had discontinued its fast line from New York to Chicago and announced a ten percent cut in wages. The actions on the part of the owners of the great railroad corporations, which had benefited from extensive grants of land for rights of way, incensed many editorial writers across the nation. Working men and women cried for fair play.

The Baltimore and Ohio workers, victims of an earlier slash in wages from $1.75 a day to $1.58, appointed a committee to see the officers of the Baltimore and Ohio. The company refused them an audience, which precipitated a series of violent events throughout the nation. These actions in turn evoked mixed responses. For every favorable speech or editorial calling for labor justice there was a hysterical opinion warning that America faced the subversion of the Paris Commune. They remembered that in 1871, after France fell before Bismarck's German invaders, the radicals of Paris—in the midst of a devastated, rat-infested city with a starving population—had formed the Paris Commune. The specter of Communism invading America was conjured up and promoted by extremists opposing the working men and women.

American workers in 1877 did not know and did not care about the Paris Commune. What they sought was a way to defend themselves against further wage cuts. The national depression, which had begun in 1871, intensified in the mid-seventies and threatened to become even worse as the decade came to an end. Railroads and other corporations eyed the labor potential of European immigrants, a seemingly endless supply of cheap labor. As profits declined, the first cost to be cut was labor. Laboring men and women were primed for a defensive battle.

On July 16, 1877, the date the Baltimore and Ohio cuts were to take effect, forty firemen abandoned their engines. All along the line, other firemen and brakemen responded in the same way. Other workers in Baltimore, non-union as well as union, joined the strike.

A chain reaction moved across America. In Martinsburg, West Virginia, railroad cars were uncoupled and traffic stopped. Shots were exchanged between strikers and the militia. But the militiamen, realizing they were shooting at neighbors, put down their rifles and joined the strikers.

The telegraph lines buzzed as they carried messages of labor protests. The president of the Baltimore and Ohio appealed to President Hayes for federal troops. President Hayes diplomatically refused. A reporter explained why: The lower ranks of society . . . had been wronged and oppressed beyond endurance."

Demonstrations and labor protests exploded in Philadelphia, Columbus, Chicago, Cincinnati, and St. Louis. The major American cities were in an uproar. The property damage and violence spread. Law and order were gone. Fears of socialism petrified the establishment. "The Commune had found a place in America," one writer said.

In Baltimore, where the strike had started, many blamed the women, wives of railroad workers. They were in the forefront of a rally of ten thousand, shouting their willingness to starve outright rather than slowly. President Hayes decided not to send troops to Baltimore, but to encircle Washington with them to protect the Capitol and the United States Treasury buildings. In Washington, the troops were hissed by strikers.

In Pittsburgh, the violence came to a climax. There, the announced ten percent cut in wages was exacerbated by the railroad policy of demanding "double headers," requiring trainmen to double their work. The strikers followed the same tactics as those used in Martinsburg. No freight could move. When the Pennsylvania National Guard moved in, the strikers, their wives, and their friends met them with cries of "We want bread."

The commanding officer of the Pennsylvania National Guard tried to get the trains moving. However, warned that he would be shot, he backed down. In a short time, railroad cars were standing immobilized for twenty miles. When the

Pittsburgh soldiers became reluctant to move against their neighbors, a contingent of Philadelphia soldiers, along with the Allegheny County sheriff's men, moved against the crowd of ten thousand, by now composed not only of strikers and their families but also of a mix of labor sympathizers, socialists, syndicalists, communists, and ne'er-do-wells. Heated exchanges between the Philadelphia units and strikers ended in bloodshed. Sixteen people were killed in a sickening melee.

In sympathy, the Pittsburgh militiamen joined the strikers. The Philadelphia units contained upper-middle-class men more sympathetic to the company than to the employees, but when the Pittsburgh guardsmen put down their arms, the Philadelphians were outnumbered. They fled to the railroad roundhouse to defend themselves. By this time, the mob went on a rampage, raided stores in town, stole four hundred rifles and an assortment of knives and revolvers, and set out to capture the roundhouse. Unable to overcome the soldiers, entrenched there with three Gatling guns, the mob began to burn railroad properties. Soon they poured oil over a train full of coke and set it afire, then ran it into the roundhouse. Eight hundred Philadelphia soldiers, under cover of their Gatling guns, escaped from the roundhouse to Claremont, twelve miles from Pittsburgh, with the loss of eight lives. By then, much of the mob had moved to another tremendous fire.

By July 23, the strikers had burned more than a hundred locomotives, hundreds of tons of coal and coke, thirty-five hundred railroad cars, two hotels, the Union Depot, the Pittsburgh and St. Louis freight station, and hundreds of smaller buildings. The entire city of Pittsburgh was threatened with flaming extinction. The riot and the looting left the city completely unprotected.

From one border of Pennsylvania to the other, riots and protests scarred Altoona, Meadville, Lehigh, Lebanon, and Summit Hill. In a week, United States regulars killed several protestors in Johnstown. In Reading, the Easton Greys, another unit from Philadelphia, retaliated. Without provocation, they fired on a public meeting and killed thirteen, wounding thirty-three others.

When the strikes spread to New Jersey, the New York *Herald Tribune* blamed the too lenient public for fostering Communism. The *New York Times* bewailed the control of Chicago by Communists. But the Chicago *Daily News* supported the strikers, editorializing that the railroads had corrupted officials, charged gouging fares and freight rates, plundered the public through stock manipulation, and now were raiding their own employees.

While Pittsburgh was going up in flames, President Hayes and his cabinet met three times. Order was finally restored when General Scott was sent in with regular army troops to quell the "insurrection." The Great Strike in Pittsburgh was the most violent and costly in American history.

The strike still spread—to Syracuse, Albany, and Buffalo, and all across the United States to San Francisco. Finally, the two turbulent weeks ended. A review of the events showed that whenever local officials acted with restraint, the strikers did likewise. Whenever a threat of force by soldiers challenged the right to protest, violence exploded. Altogether, nearly two hundred people were killed and a thousand wounded.

Recapitulating, the *New York Times* dropped its charges of Communism and declared "The workmen have here and there compelled compliance with their demands . . . and have attracted popular attention to their grievances. The balance of gain is on the side of the workmen."

The spontaneity of the Great Strikes, resembling that of the French Revolution, convinced millions of the widespread injustices suffered by working men and women. Such a widespread flare-up could not possibly be the work of Communists. The American worker was too intelligent and straightforward to have been controlled by such an alien influence. The truth was that violence and burning were spontaneous combustion in the presence of ill-advised troops, frightened vigilantes, and a few reckless hoodlums.

Thousands saw the Great Strike as the precursor of a socialist society. Millions, on the other hand, interpreted it to mean American labor could not be exploited, that the right of fair wages was part of the American Dream. The violence, the pillaging, the burning were attributed to a minority of hot-heads, bums, or foreign agitators. The pronouncements of labor leaders, especially Terence Powderly, confirmed that view, as time and time again, the Knights of Labor pleaded for peaceful negotiations and nonviolence.

The national railroad strikes, starting in Baltimore and climaxing in Pittsburgh, inflamed the large railroad cities of the nation. The city of Scranton did not escape. The railroad strike fueled and fired the iron workers and miners of the Lackawanna Iron and Coal Company, igniting Scranton in a historic labor conflagration.

CHAPTER 13

༄

THE SCRANTON STRIKE

By the spring of 1877, John, Evan, and Owen were working only a third of the time. In March, they were compelled to take a fifteen percent cut in wages. As miners, John and Evan were managing to make only $1.50 a day, while Owen was earning $1.15. Other workers in the Lackawanna and Wyoming Valleys and in Schuylkill, Carbon, and Columbia counties were similarly reduced. Railroad laborers were making $1 a day; canal workers, 80¢; iron workers, 85¢ for a ten-hour day and $1.02 for a twelve-hour day. The mine owners and iron producers complained about the loss of profits. The workers and their families faced slow starvation. The Scranton *Republican* criticized laboring men for not really appreciating William Scranton's willingness to give the miners and iron workers partial employment.

During the hectic, violent summer of 1877, the noonday talk of the miners turned from warm give and take to a realistic appraisal of wages and survival. Influenced by the economic convulsions in every city of the nation, every miner brought a new, concentrated attention to his own welfare. In this atmosphere, Owen's reading and research often made him the focus of questions. In the years between 1873 and 1877, Owen had set out to know everything it was possible to know about mining. So full of mining history and statistics were his infrequent letters to Rhondda that she once chided him in reply, "Owen, please tell me something about yourself. I am not entertained by the problems of circulating air in the mines. Tell me more of the men and their families. How are you and your parents managing to keep alive? If wages keep going down, I don't know how you'll manage."

Owen immersed himself in study. He understood mining air control, water management, and a little of surveying. He knew his study would qualify him to become a fireboss or an assistant mine foreman, but he never expected such a job. As John Roderick's son, he knew he would never be hired for one of these positions.

The subjects he was most interested in, he had to study and read and ask questions for himself. Labor history was not available in 1877. His sources of knowledge were newspapers, magazines, and books which he devoured.

One day during the summer of 1877, while nine men relaxed having their lunch, Frank Ruane posed a question:

"Owen," he said, "You know, I used to live in St. Clair, and I know in the '60s my father earned $18 a week. That's fifteen years ago. Why hell, I'm not making that much myself."

"I know," Owen said, "Wages never go straight up. And you're right. Your father did make that much."

"Well, what's happening?" Frank asked.

"Lots of things are happening, but we're not having our say in correcting the bad things. The operators and owners have their own engineers and go their own way. They don't pay much attention to the problems of the men."

"Well, how about the years between the time my father worked and now. How about the years in between. How much did wages go up?"

"The day wage of a miner in 1839, when mining was just beginning, was a dollar a day. Ten years later, it was a dollar and a quarter. During the same ten years, his laborer made from seventy cents to eighty cents a day. That comes to about twelve and a half cents for loading a car of coal. Remember, that was before the Civil War.

"During the war, men left for army service. Nobody was coming over from the old countries. Labor was scarce, so wages went up, sometimes one hundred percent or more. Some miners earned almost two hundred dollars a month during the war. But when the war ended, down came the wages. The year the war ended, wages dropped twenty percent. In '67, another cut was close to ten percent."

"Couldn't the W.B.A. stop the cut?" Bill Berry asked.

"Yes, even though the W.B.A. was new then, they did stop it, they even got a raise. But then came the wage slash of thirty percent in 1871. And since then, it's been all downhill. Right now, we are getting wages lower than those of thirteen years ago. It's really unbelievable!"

&. &. &.

At the end of the day, when John, Evan, and Owen got off the cage, they saw Tom Cawley gathered with ten or fifteen men. As they approached him, Cawley said, "There you are, Mr. Roderick. I've been waiting for you. Mr. Powderly asked me to meet you to tell you many things happened today. Can we have the men gather 'round so I can tell them?"

"Yes, yes, of course." Turning to Owen and Evan, he said, "Go by there and gather the men out in the mine yard. There's much to tell of today. Mr. Powderly has sent Tom here to tell us."

About seventy men gathered in the mine yard around Tom Cawley. In a loud voice, Cawley gave his account of the day. "At noon today," he said, "the men at the Lackawanna Iron and Coal quietly left the rolling mill and marched to the machine shops. Mr. Scranton followed them and asked them why they walked out.

"'Can't live on your wages,' they answered.

"Mr. Scranton said he was sorry but that business was bad. He could pay no more. There were about one thousand men in the group. Without any fuss, the men just took off and dispersed. A strike is on! As of right now, there is no iron being made in Scranton!

"One more thing. This all started yesterday. I don't believe you heard, but yesterday, the trainmen of both the DL&W and the D&H asked Mr. Halstead to restore their ten percent cut. The Brotherhood meeting in Scranton today heard the refusal of the railroad heads. At six o'clock tonight, all trains will be peacefully brought back to the yards, their fires put out, and left in their proper places. There will be no destruction of engines or cars. The Brotherhood wants nothing like Pittsburgh or Baltimore. They are all for stopping the ten percent cut in wages. But they'll do it peacefully."

Then coming to the main point of his mission, Cawley

shouted to the group. "Now how about us? Tonight we are all meeting at Fellows Hall to decide what action the miners' unions will take. Get your supper early men. We'll see you later at Fellows! We're with the trainmen. We're with the Rolling Mill men!"

The seventy men in the mine yard let out a yell that was heard in Taylor. They were more than ready to strike. The frustrations of the past years, the lower rates, the days of idleness, the sparse and poor meals, the struggle for clothing and shelter, all wore heavily on them. The image of a positive change led to the shouting explosion.

On the other hand, a few were quiet. Among them were John Roderick and Owen. Like thousands of other Scranton citizens, they remembered the recent days of violence and destruction in Chicago, Baltimore, and Pittsburgh.

As they walked home, the threat of the strike filled them with mixed feelings. Once home, each took his turn washing in the four foot tub. The washing was a working ritual for Mam. She had the tub ready in the center of the kitchen, filled it with water from a pail, than added several kettles of boiling hot water. She laid out clean underwear, socks, shirt and trousers: Dada first; then Owen. After scrubbing Dada's back, she disappeared to other chores. As a breaker boy, Owen had got the back wash as well. Now, as a miner, he did his own with a soaking-wet hand towel. As Owen washed, he heard his mother call out in a pleasant note, "We've had a letter from Rhondda today. Some good news in it."

Owen accelerated his washing, dressed quickly, and devoured Rhondda's letter.

Dear Mr. and Mrs. Roderick and Owen:

I am very happy to report that my father's business has improved to the point that I shall be able to return to Wyoming Valley very soon. I am very eager to resume my teaching. Making bookkeeping entries and paying bills is far less rewarding than teaching, so I'll be very happy to get back working with children.

However, I will not be returning to Avondale in Plymouth. Instead, I will be returning to Wilkes-Barre, where I have been offered a position teaching at the Home for Friendless Children. The home was formed during the Civil War to take care of children orphaned or made homeless by the conflict. I was hired by Miss Mary Bowman whose brother, Bishop Bowman, started a similar home in Lancaster. The home was originally in a small frame house owned by a Mr. William Gildersleeve who made it available, rent free. The money needed came from donations of sixteen men and twenty-four ladies who acted as a board of managers. Every lady contributed one dollar to get the home started, and they all added various household articles for the use of the children. Thereafter, these good people continued to donate.

During the war, the home became so crowded with orphans sent there and paid for by Pennsylvania that a larger building was contributed. The state gave $2,500 for the new building provided $5,000 was raised in Wilkes-Barre. Of course, more than that was raised. A Mr. Hollenback, Mr. Gildersleeve, and a Mr. Ross each gave $1,000 to lead the money raising.

The lot for the new building was sold to the Home by Mr. Parrish and Dr. Mayer. The new building is the one I will be teaching in. It is a fine large brick building with beautiful land around it. Everybody in Wilkes-Barre calls it the "Soldier's Orphanage," but most of the orphans of the war are gone. A new home for war orphans was built in Harford in Susque-hanna County. The children I will be teaching are children who are homeless.

According to Mr. Bowman, there are many community leaders here who think the home is very necessary. I understand from Mrs. Bowman that there are many waifs wandering about the city who might fall into evil hands and be led into lives of crime. Thank goodness for men like Mr. Gildersleeve, the mer-chant Isaac Osterhout, and Mr. William Conyngham. They have contributed thousands of dollars to keep the Home going.

I am so proud to be going to teach these wonderful children.

In the meantime, I look forward to seeing you. I will be back in the "coal regions" again and just miles away. Don't be surprised if I drop in to see you all sooner than you think.

I am

Truly yours,
Rhondda

CHAPTER 14

❧

THE KNIGHTS OF LABOR

B uoyed and exhilarated by Rhondda's letter, Owen relaxed with his father for an hour waiting for Evan to arrive so that they could walk together to Fellows Hall. They knew a strike would be called. They knew it was justified, but they wondered if it could be controlled and successful. They wondered whether Terence Powderly and the knights would participate or just give it moral support. All their discussion was in the perspective of their initiation into the Knights of Labor. They remembered their initiation well. They remembered the night they stood before the Chief Officer of the Assembly of the Knights of Labor as the next ranking officer, the Worthy Foreman had read:

In the beginning God ordained that man should labor, not as a curse, but as a blessing; not as a punishment, but as a means of development, physically, mentally, morally, and has set thereunto his seal of approval in the rich increase and reward. By labor is brought forth the kindly fruits of the earth in rich abundance for our sustenance and comfort; by labor (not exhaustive) is promoted health of body and strength of mind; labor garners the priceless stories of wisdom and knowledge. It is the "Philosopher's Stone," everything it touches turns

to gold. "Labor is noble and holy." To glorify God in its
exercise, to defend it from degradation, to divest it of
the evils to body, mind and estate, which ignorance and
greed have imposed; to rescue the toiler from the grasp
of the selfish is a work worthy of the noblest and best of
our race. Without your seeking, without even your knowledge, you have been selected from among your fellows,
for that exalted purpose. Are you willing to accept the
responsibility and trusting in God and the support of
sworn true * * * * *s, labor with what ability you possess,
for the triumph of these principles among men?

They both recalled the master workman taking them by
the hand and saying:

On behalf of the toiling millions of earth, I welcome you
to this Sanctuary, dedicated to the service of God, by
serving humanity. Open and public associations having
failed, after a struggle of centuries, to protect or advance
the interests of labor, we have lawfully constituted this
Assembly. Hid from public view, covered by an impen-
etrable veil of secrecy, not to promote or shield wrong
doing but to shield ourselves and you, from persecution
and wrong by men in our own sphere and calling as well
as others out of it, by endeavoring to secure the just
reward of our toil. In using this power of organized effort
and cooperation, we but imitate the example of capital
heretofore set in numberless instances. In all the multi-
farious branches of trade, capital has its combinations,

and whether intended or not, it crushes the manly hopes of labor and tramples poor humanity in the dust. We mean no conflict with legitimate enterprise, not antagonism to necessary capital, but men in their haste and greed, blinded by self-interest, overlook the interests of others and sometimes even violate the rights of those they deem helpless. We mean to uphold the dignity of labor, to affirm the nobility of all who live in accordance with the ordinance of God, "in the sweat of thy brow shalt thou eat bread." We mean to create a healthy public opinion on the subject of labor (the only creator of values or capital), and the justice of its receiving a full, just share of the values or capital it has created. We shall with all our strength support laws made to harmonize the interests of labor and capital for laws which tend to lighten the exhaustiveness of toil. We shall use every lawful and honorable means to procure and retain employment for one another, coupled with just and fair remuneration, and should accident or misfortune befall one of our number, render such aid as lies within our power to give without inquiring his country or his creed.

At the conclusion of their initiation, the members of the Assembly in attendance were led by the master workman in this prayer:

Father of all, God of love, we render Thee hearty thanks for Thy goodness. Bless all our acts; may all our work begun, continued and ended, redound to Thy glory and the good of man.

The whole ceremony had inspired them. It gave them pride, even a sense of some elation. The religious overtones gave them a dignity and assurance. They felt they were part of a mission. They had not memorized the oath, but its spirit filled their minds and hearts.

❧   ❧   ❧

As they walked with Evan to Fellows Hall for the meeting, they could not help wonder how they could fulfill their oath if the strike deteriorated into physical combat. Again, they discussed whether the strike could be conducted according to the spirit and by-laws of the Knights of Labor to which the three were devoted.

At Fellows, Terence Powderly was already there, with just one or two other early arrivals. Although the day had been a historic one and the evening's business was to be very serious, Powderly was in a pleasant mood. He shook hands warmly, and good storyteller that he was, regaled them with a story of his early organizing days. He learned very early that trying to conduct meetings using common sense was impossible. One had to have a book of order. His was Cushing's Manual. Cushing's Manual became his bible for all meetings. But it was not always appreciated, as Powderly revealed in his anecdote:

> At a public meeting one night Tom Foley was, much to his dismay, called on to preside over its deliberations. His name wasn't Foley, but he still lives, is moderately healthy, has a string of relatives, all descendants of Irish kings and warlike in disposition, so to spare their feelings

and mine too, I'll call him Foley. Tom took the chair
and after an attempt to thank the meeting for the honor
conferred asked what they wanted to do. Two men were
nominated for secretary of the meeting. Let us call them
McGrath and Rubenstein. When the nominations were
made Foley said: "Come up Rubenstein and be the secretary." Several protests were voiced but Foley silenced
the protestants by saying "Rubenstein will do this business
all right, he won't dare do anything else for he's the only
Jew in the house and anyway there's Irish enough on this
platform now to keep the peace." Exasperated by Foley's
high-handed procedure, a member moved: "that in our
future deliberations we be guided by Cushing's Manual."
Everyone present who thought, or wanted others to think,
that he knew something about parliamentary law shouted:
"I second the motion." It looked unanimous to Foley
who slowly rose to his feet, walked to the edge of the platform, and solemnly announced: "When yez selected me
to be yere president I thought ye meant it, but before
I'm warm in me sate ye make a motion to be guided by
Cushins Manyel. Now I don't know Cushins Manyel, he
may be a rale fine man but I give yez distinctly to understand that the minute Mr. Cushins Manyel steps up on
this platform Mr. Foley steps off."

❧   ❧   ❧

Soon Fellows Hall was churning with members from all
the knights' assemblies in the Scranton area. There were also
many others unaffiliated, who stood out from the others
because they were very boisterous. Hearing the clamor,

Powderly looked at the chairman of the meeting and motioned to him to get started. Amid much turmoil, the chairman opened the meeting, asking Mr. Powderly to address the group.

"Gentlemen," he said, "this nation is on fire with the hopes and aspirations of every working man. The Knights of Labor did not start these strikes, but now that they are started, we cannot turn against our fellow workers. The Knights of Labor were never consulted, but we will have to support the movement. The events of this week have been so exciting and swift that we can hardly measure them. So, tonight we must declare in resolutions how we will approach the strike."

"Never mind the resolutions!" came a cry from the rear of the hall. "I say follow the workers in Baltimore and burn the breakers."

"Right, right!" exclaimed a large number of others. Even some members of the knights, carried away, spontaneously shouted, "We'll burn them down."

"Wait, wait," shouted Powderly. "This cry of 'burn the breaker' is not news to me. I've heard it on the streets many times. Just today, a stranger told me what was going to happen tonight. But listen. Think a little. Isn't that what some of our enemies want? I was informed on the street, by a stranger, that you men were laying plans to burn down a coal breaker tonight; I don't know where you work, but you have no right to do anything like that. If you were employed there, you will not find your places waiting for you when this strike ends. If you don't work there, your act will prevent others from regaining their old places when work has been resumed elsewhere. But there is a reason far higher than that of securing employment which should prevent you from becoming incendiaries. The burning of that breaker would be a crime of such proportions as to earn every man taking part in it a cell in the penitentiary. Surely you don't want to bring misery to your families and shame upon your children by such an uncalled for, fiendish crime. Again, if you will be influenced by no other consideration, reflect that the breaker is a living arsenal and your first step toward its destruction will result in bloodshed. Abandon this undertaking, go to your homes, and maintain your standing as peaceable, law-abiding men."

Powderly's words had no effect. Instead, they seemed to infuriate a large contingent. The noise grew louder as someone cried out, "I move we adjourn and burn the breaker," as they ran toward the front to get out.

Powderly was there first, and spreading his arms, pleaded with the men to wait. But there was no waiting! One burly fellow grabbed a wooden bench and hurled it against the door, above Powderly's head. It fell on Powderly and knocked him out cold.

By the time Powderly came to, the hall was deathly quiet. The sight of Powderly bleeding and unconscious had shaken even the recalcitrants, who were afraid the blow might have killed him.

The chairman asked Powderly if he were strong enough to continue. Shaken and wanting above all to see a doctor, Powderly nevertheless agreed.

While he was still making his way to the podium, the stalwart who had wielded the bench croaked, just loud enough to be heard, "I move we forget the breaker and adjourn." Frightened that he might have committed a criminal act, he was eager to absolve himself.

Powderly stood rather wobbly, and without waiting for a second to the motion, he said, "We will adjourn, but will you authorize the officers to prepare resolutions of peace and support?"

A thundering affirmative came from the group.

"Meeting's adjourned," Powderly said. He handed a paper of prepared resolutions to the chairman and then left hurriedly, saying, "I'll see you later. I must see a doctor."

The resolution contained five paragraphs. The main one stipulated:

We extend our moral aid to those engaged in struggle. We pledge to them our best efforts to bring the strike to a successful close. The strike is not being conducted under our auspices and we will not in any way hold responsibility for injury, violence, property loss or any other damage. We counsel moderation in speech and action that will assist in maintaining peace and prosperity in our community.

When Powderly left the hall, John, Owen, and Evan slipped out on his heels.

Outside, John Roderick called out, "Terry, wait a minute. I want Owen here to go with you. Where is the doctor you hope to see?"

Powderly turned, still holding a handkerchief on top of his head. Recognizing the three, he said, "Oh, thank you, Mr. Roderick. I think I'll be all right. It's not the cut. I just hope I don't have a bad concussion. I'm going over to see Dr. Evans in Hyde Park, near Taylor. He's on Main Street."

"I'll be glad to walk over with you, Mr. Powderly," Owen volunteered.

"Well, thank you, Owen, I'd really like you to come along. I don't want to keel over without anyone near me. Anyway, Owen, you're the right size to lean on if I get dizzy. Come along then."

As they walked, they were soon engrossed in conversation. "As I remember, you were just a youngster when I first visited your home. You were about fifteen, weren't you?" Powderly said.

"Just about," Owen said. "I'm nineteen now."

"And taller and heavier, quite a young man."

"Loading coal isn't exactly light work, so I'm lucky to be five feet eleven and one hundred sixty-five pounds," Owen said.

"As a youngster, you were a great reader. Are you able to give your mind some exercise after a hard day's work?" Powderly asked.

"At first, that is, when I first began working down under, I didn't. I'd fall asleep. But I got used to it, and now, I really enjoy my evenings."

"Good," said Powderly, "If you're ever interested in any subject and can't find a book about it, let me know. Maybe I can help."

"Well, I'm stuck right now," said Owen. "I'm interested in the way Wyoming Valley and Lackawanna Valley grew, but every book I have is about the Colonial and Revolutionary times. I'm interested in coal. Coal seems to be the gold of the valleys. Our future is coal, and I'd like to know the history of the cities it has made."

"You'll have to read the old newspapers to satisfy you there, Owen. No books will contain that information," Powderly said, shaking his head and handkerchief as he walked along.

When they arrived at Dr. Evans's house, they found him tending a small tomato patch in his backyard. He hailed Mr. Powderly warmly, and Owen realized they were warm friends.

"What happened, Terry?" was his greeting. "Did you let one of Mr. Scranton's heavy wrenches fall on your head?"

"Not at all, Dr. Evans. I'll tell you about it when you tell me how serious it is. Owen, this is the DL&W company doctor, Dr. Evans. Doctor, this is Owen Roderick."

"John Roderick's family?" the doctor asked.

"Yes, I'm his son."

"Met your father and mother at the Ben Davis funeral. Fine family people. Come on in, Terry. Come in, Owen."

Powderly and Dr. Evans went into the doctor's office while Owen sat down in the waiting room. Before long, Dr. Evans called Owen into the office. Powderly had a square bandage on his head and appeared relaxed and comfortable.

Dr. Evans, seated in his swivel chair, removed his stethoscope, placed it on his desk, crossed his knees, and relaxed. Powderly was at ease in the patient's chair. Owen leaned forward in a pull-up chair, wondering why Dr. Evans seemed to want to talk.

He began to speak very thoughtfully. "Owen, my friend here, Terry Powderly, is the most mature twenty-seven-year-old I know. He told me what happened tonight at Fellows and he also told me what you two talked about walking to my office. You sound like the oldest nineteen-year-old I am about to know. Frankly, we need some old heads in Scranton, regardless of age. I mean mature thinkers, because the city of Scranton has me worried."

Neither Powderly nor Owen interrupted. They sensed Dr. Evans had been thinking about the national railroad strikes, the violence of 1871, and now the rising labor passions in Scranton in 1877.

"I can't do much about Pittsburgh or Baltimore or any other big city, but here I am in Scranton, where I have practiced for twenty years, except for the two years I tried to ease the pain of those poor southern boys in the camp in Elmira where they were prisoners. Before that, I practiced briefly in Lansford, among the miners of Panther Valley. Now, as I said, Scranton has me worried. There are good people here – hardworking, church-going. Most of them are miners, railroad workers, on the road or in the shops, or iron workers in the mills. They have children, and most of them go to work at fourteen to help support the families. The boys go to the breakers, the girls to the silk mills. That describes most of the people of Scranton, whether they are Welsh, Irish, English, Scotch, or like some of the new immigrants, Polish, Italian, Lithuanian, or whatever. They are all good people.

"As the Scranton Iron and Coal doctor, I've come to know Mr. Scranton, the officials, and some of the board members. These men remind me – in what they say and do – that there are other good, hard-working, church-going people as well. They are the industrialists; others are running businesses – insurance companies, law offices, banks. They always go to work neat and clean, and they would not be caught in overalls or greasy pants. They work in high celluloid collars like mine.

Most of them go to the Episcopal or Presbyterian church. There is a sprinkling of Irish Catholics in the group, but not many. Most of them came down from Carbondale. They are all contributing to the growth of Scranton.

"What concerns me is that each one of these groups wants the same thing—a better Scranton. For each of them, a better Scranton means a place to make a good living, where they can raise a family in a peaceful, religious town. Yet—and this is a big yet—they are constantly at odds, not only one group opposing another, but within their own groups, there is mistrust and alienation."

Looking at Powderly, he said, "I know you very well, Terry, and I think I know Owen's father slightly. I agree that you and the miners are not getting what you deserve. I also know William Scranton. He's not a bad man."

Powderly interrupted, "I remember saying the same thing to the Rodericks. I agree with you about Mr. Scranton."

Dr. Evans continued, "Yes, but after I've said that he is not a bad man, I must add that I think he is capable of doing bad things."

"What do you mean?" Owen asked.

"Let me put it this way. All of us are human. We jump to retaliate whenever we are hurt. The hurt may be real or imagined. Nevertheless we put up our mental fists and are ready to defend ourselves. Some turn into aggressors, and a fight is on. William Scranton is human. He sees and hears of turmoil in Europe. I know from talking to him (and he will tell anyone), he believes that Communism and Socialism are spreading to America. He has many contacts among bankers and industrialists in New York and Philadelphia. He is impressed by their thinking. He imagines himself the defender of Scranton against foreign agitators and ideas. I asked him once about you, Terry. His answer was that you were an outstanding machinist, but that you have been misled, that he wished you would forget union and become a company man, that with your talent for speaking and writing, you could have your own company and be a millionaire. He genuinely admires and likes you."

"I like Mr. Scranton myself," said Powderly, "but his fondness for me didn't prevent his dropping me in 1871 and sending me, hat in hand, walking all over the state, looking for work. He feared that as a union man I wanted to ruin his business. Only two weeks ago, he called me into his office and told me that unless I resigned my position in the union, he would fire me again."

"You prove my point, Terry. And Mr. Scranton is capable of using guns against working men if he sees them doing what he perceives as a Communist action, even if the men he faces are men who work for him and belong to the same Christian community he lives in."

Dr. Evans paused; looking first at Owen and then directly at Terence Powderly, he uttered some words that disturbed both Powderly and Owen very much. "Of course, you Terry, are not blameless. I hate to say this, but you are capable of leading men to their deaths."

"Me?" asked Powderly incredulously. "I spend as much time speaking against strikes and violence as I do pleading the just cause of men."

"I know you do," Dr. Evans said, "but unfortunately, you cannot control the violence by saying no to violence. Your words of warning are forgotten. Men, frustrated by economic deprivation, afire to correct these evils you so eloquently describe to them, men do not hear your pacifistic words."

Powderly was quiet. He understood the point Dr. Evans was making. He knew it was true. History was full of examples of peaceful reform detonating into riot and war. In his mind's eye, he was John Brown running riot at Harper's Ferry, shouting the slogans of peaceful New England abolitionists.

Powderly arose from his chair. Owen looked up at him, uncertain of his action or reply, waiting.

Powderly looked at Evans and nodded his head. "I will have to plead guilty to your charge, even though I abhor violence. I know that I cannot discipline every man who hears my documented cases for labor. Even Lincoln could not do that. In fact, Jesus himself could not do it. So I have no choice but to make my case to them as best I can."

"I hope you will," Evans said, "because I have no formula to offer you or William Scranton. I wish I could create a way for you both to sit to talk and to agree, but the time is not at hand. Perhaps in twenty-five years . . ." his voice trailed off. Turning to Owen, he said, "Owen, you are not yet twenty years of age. Perhaps you can do—or perhaps you will see it done— something that will bring peace to Scranton and these other large cities which saw bloodshed this summer."

Owen wanted to reply, but before these articulate, experienced men, he hesitated. Evans and Powderly both observed him and said simultaneously, "Go on, Owen, say it."

"Well," Owen said, "I don't know a way to bring Mr. Scranton and Mr. Powderly together. But I feel we must do something before they can ever achieve an understanding."

"And what is that?" Dr. Evans asked.

Owen answered, "We—all of us in Scranton—must know each other better. The German railroad workers of Cedar Street do not know the Welsh coal miners of Hyde Park. The Polish and others live alone in scattered patches. The Irish laborers live on the hill pretty much to themselves. In the central city, all the way to Providence, the people think of themselves as the pure Americans, when all of us are Americans."

"Very true, very true, a good observation," Powderly agreed.

"But look here," Dr. Evans said, "Owen, you and I are Welsh. Do we not add to this misunderstanding by retaining Welsh sermons, enjoying our Cymanfaoedd, reading our Welsh newspapers?"

"No, no." Powderly interrupted. "Every people should preserve its own heritage. I believe it makes them better Americans. In time, the Polish and Welsh newspapers will disappear. We will grow together, but for now let all of us keep some of our customs we love. You're not going to deny me St. Patrick's Day, are you?"

"But don't you agree that the nationalities must come closer together, Doctor?" asked Owen.

"I believe they must," Dr. Evans agreed. "It is a problem as it is in all the great cities where immigrants flood in. The barriers will come down in time. The schools will do it. The workplaces will do it. Even baseball will do it."

Powderly posed another question. "Are the nationalities more of a problem than the jealousies and suspicions of occupations?" Answering himself, he said, "I don't think so. That is why I believe in the program of the Knights of Labor which brings all workers together. We believe in an industrial union, not crafts or trades where each little union protects its own welfare at any cost. I mentioned to Owen on the way over that we—Scranton—are a city of forty-seven thousand people. You, Dr. Evans, started this discussion saying you were troubled about our future."

"Yes, I take that responsibility. I said that. I raised questions about the implications of leadership. Owen has added concerns of divisiveness."

Dr. Evans rose as he spoke. "I am optimistic about some aspects of the future, but I am anxious about tomorrow and the months to come. Now, let me bid you good night. This has been a meaningful discussion for me."

"Good night, Dr. Evans. I shall send you a check for your services tomorrow," Powderly promised.

"Thank you, and good night Terrance." Dr. Evans called out as they left the walkway, "Remember me to your parents, Owen," he added. "Nos da, machgen y."

ᵺ　　ᵺ　　ᵺ

His concern for the peace of Scranton was well taken. While Terence Powderly and the Rodericks were holding their meeting, the railway unions were meeting at Washington Hall. The miners affiliated with the National Union, the union that had grown out of the failed Workers' Benevolent Association, also held a meeting the next day at Fellows. There they heard that Mayor McKune, who at first refused to deputize special police, was now having second thoughts. The miners passed a resolution condemning the creation of special police.

The news of the National Strike disasters spread like fire through Scranton.

Specifically, a crisis was developing around the Lacka-wanna Station. The mail train, carrying some passengers coming down from New York State, was due to arrive in Scranton at eight o'clock in the morning. It had already been attacked in Great Bend, where railroad men attempted to detach the passenger cars but allow the mail train to proceed. This attempt failed, but when the train got to Hyde Park, strikers uncoupled these cars. Only the engine and the mail car proceeded across town to the Lackawanna Station. A huge crowd met the train. Among them were travelers trying to buy tickets for trips out of Scranton. W. A. Fuller, the ticket agent, realized that no passenger cars would be allowed to leave the station and wisely refused to sell any tickets. The postmaster, E. L. Buck, appealed to Superintendent Hallstead to let the mail go through since the strikers would permit it. Hallstead refused, saying that the railroad contract included both passengers and mail and decreeing that both would go or nothing would go. He maintained that the strikers would have to take responsibility for interfering with the United States mail. Frantic telegrams flew back and forth between Scranton and the governor. The Brotherhood of Railroad Workers tried to uphold their responsibility, offering to run the mail without pay and saying they had no grievances against the state or the nation. Their offer was refused.

The city of Scranton was now isolated. There was no rail service for coal, passengers, or mail.

The working men and women and their families now waited for their employers to respond. The brotherhood made it clear that they would not accept a cut in wages. They stood fast with the national railroad workers, but they had not burned engines or cars. They had placed them properly in the railroad yards.

The coal miners had burned no breakers, destroyed no mine property. They wanted restoration of the wage cuts they had endured since 1871. They believed a twenty-five percent increase would do this.

The city establishment, supported by the middle and upper classes, had some appreciation and sympathy for these demands, but they were repelled by the inconveniences the strikes made them endure. The Scranton *Republican* ran a cautionary headline: "Strange Faces and Suspicious Characters Walk the Streets of Scranton," and fear spread through their neighborhoods. Just who these strange faces were was never revealed.

CHAPTER 15

≈

COLLECTING THE GUNS

On the day after the Lackawanna Station disorder, Mayor McKune published a call to businessmen seeking to establish law and order in Scranton. At the same time, he appointed a group to advise any volunteers who would respond. It included Colonel Frederick Hitchcock, Austin Desha, Henry B. Rockwell, B. G. Morgan, J. A. Price, M. W. Clark, C. Du Pont Breck, and Edward Merrifield.

The response was disappointing. Many felt that volunteers would exacerbate the violence. Others wanted to serve, but not under Mayor McKune. Two young men who felt this way decided to organize their own independent Scranton Citizens Corps. They were Charles R. Smith and Arthur Logan, and when they posted an enlistment paper in Phelps's Drugstore, they attracted one hundred sixteen volunteers. The organizers cautioned secrecy and quiet. That night, twenty-eight of them illegally entered the Forest and Stream Club, over the Lackawanna Valley Bank on Lackawanna Avenue, where they set up a structure and elected officers. As captain, they chose a local Civil War officer, Colonel Ezra Ripple, who was not present and knew nothing of the organization. When informed of his election, he was happy to accept.

Colonel Ripple took James Ruthvan and Charles Smith to Wilkes-Barre with him to obtain authority from General

Osborne, commander of the National Guard, to collect any arms belonging to the state. With this power, they combed Providence and Abington. In three days, they collected three hundred fifty guns.

They tried to get the banks and railroads to put them in their safes. They were refused. William Scranton accepted them without hesitation and hid them in the company store of the Scranton Iron and Coal Company.

Ammunition was obtained by William Watts, William Paterson, and William Henwood. They drove a two-seated buggy to Kingston, where they got permission from General Osborne to obtain spare ammunition from the militia in Pittston. At daybreak on the twenty-seventh of July, they added the ammunition to the guns in the company store.

With fifty additional rifles, William Scranton, just as he had done in 1871, offered protection to any men who wanted to return to work. This time, none responded.

While the railroad men and the miners continued to meet, the company officers and corporation heads did so also. Communication between the railroad workers and owners led to rumors of a settlement, but none came.

The owners and managers remained on edge as rumors persisted that strange meetings were being held in the coal patches. Word spread that there was to be an uprising and an organized looting expedition.

Finding no place to prepare and drill, the Scranton Citizens Corps turned to William Scranton who let them have the top floor of the company store. The lights there shone through the night as men fixed ammunition or polished guns. Some of the older rifles were repaired in a makeshift shop in the store.

Every day some new lawlessness occurred. The Lacka-wanna and Bloomsburg division of the Lehigh and Susque-hanna Railroad was especially vulnerable. Scrantonians were aghast to hear about an engineer who saw a woman lying across the tracks, and stopped his train to help her. Dismounting from his cabin, he found a lifeless scarecrow. Just then a bullet knocked off his hat. He scrambled back to his post and set the train in motion again. Such violence had to be ended. Many merchants and managers believed that the only way to do it was to create a permanent military organization for the protection of the city. Those who urged this action most vehemently usually pointed to the heroic efforts of the fabulous Franklin Gowen of the Pottsville area.

While Americans at large were fascinated by the names of Vanderbilt, Carnegie, Gould, and Morgan, Pennsylvanians were more impressed by the name of Gowen. For them, Gowen represented law and order. Just a year earlier, he had personally ended the terrorism of the Molly Maguires throughout Schuylkill, Carbon, and Columbia counties. Addressing the jury of Pennsylvania Dutchmen chosen to hear the case against the Mollies, Gowen described conditions with which the Scrantonians could identify.

These coal fields for twenty years, I may say, have been the theatre of the commission of crimes such as our very nature revolts at. This very organization that we are now, for the first time, exposing to the light of day, has hung like a pall over the people of this county. Before it fear and terror fled cowering to homes which afforded no sanctuary against the vengeance of their pursuers. Behind it stalked darkness and despair, brooding like grim shadows over the desolated hearth and the ruined home, and throughout the length and breadth of this fair land there was heard the voice of wailing and of lamentation, of "Rachel weeping for her children and refusing to be comforted, because they were not." Nor is it alone those whose names I have mentioned—not alone the prominent, the upright, and the good citizen whose remains have been interred with pious care in the tombs of his fathers; but it is the hundreds of unknown victims, whose bones now lie mouldering over the face of this county. In hidden places and by silent paths in the dark ravines of the mountains, and in secret ledges of the rocks, who shall say how many bodies of the victims of this order now await the final trump of God? And from those lonely sepulchres, there will go up to the God who gave them the spirits of these murdered victims, to take their places among the innumerable throng of witnesses at the last day, and to confront with their presence the members of this ghastly tribunal, when their solemn accusation is read from the plain command of the Decalogue, "Thou shalt not kill." . . .

Now that the light of day is thrown upon the secret workings of this association, human life is as safe in Schuylkill County as it is in any other part of this Commonwealth; that as this association is broken down and trampled into the dust, its leaders either in jail or fugitives from the just vengeance of the law, the administration of justice in this court will be as certain as human life is safe throughout the whole length and breadth of the county.

The time has gone by when the murderer, the incendiary, and the assasin can go home reeking from the commission of crimes, confident in the fact that he can appear before a jury and have an alibi proved for him to allow him to escape punishment. There will be no more false alibis in this county; the time for them has gone forever.

Franklin Gowen, an Irish Protestant – handsome, highly educated, dramatic, and forceful – was indeed one to admire. A skillful lawyer, he had the entrepreneural vision to become president of the Philadelphia and Reading Railroad at thirty-three years of age and to steer the company into the purchase of one hundred thousand acres of coal for forty million dollars. His one-man crusade against the Molly Maguires, adding luster to his managerial genius, set his name above even those of Vanderbilt and Gould, among many Scrantonians. They agreed wholeheartedly with *The American Law Review*, which characterized his prosecution of the Mollies as "one of the greatest works for public good that has been achieved in this country and in this generation."

Even as the distinguished law journal lauded him and Scrantonians revered him, the secret financial maneuverings of Franklin Gowen, his manipulations and land speculations inevitably threatened both the Philadelphia and Reading and Gowen himself.

Ironically, Franklin Gowen had been a progressive manager early in his career. He was one of the first employers to sign a union contract and to try to keep coal prices down. He fought the rail-rebate systems and discouraged the indiscriminate free-pass system through which railroads obtained good will and special treatment. He once even supported a plan for cooperation between the company and workers to pay death and accident benefits to employees. The union was skeptical. He then set up the first company-supported plan in anthracite history. Another point in his favor was that he never would permit the operation of company stores. But by 1875, Gowen's name had become anathema to the miners.

When all else about Franklin Gowen was forgotten, he was remembered as the prosecutor who sent ten men known as Molly Maguires to the gallows on a single day, June 2, 1877, six in Pottsville and four in Mauch Chunk. The *Philadelphia Times* headlined it:

JUSTICE AT LAST
TEN MOLLY MURDERERS HANGED

Few in the coal regions of Pennsylvania did not know these facts. They were indeed still fresh on the minds of those in Scranton who saw the need for law and order in their own community in 1877. Those who thought about any parallels between the Mollies and the Knights of Labor usually remembered that Terence Powderly had condemned the Molly Maguires, that he was well educated, even a friend of William Scranton; but he was still condemned as a labor leader.

Actually Powderly had never faulted William Scranton. When he returned from Erie after his first firing, he was rehired because Scranton recognized him as a superb mechanic. One day while Powderly was working on an engine, Dawson, his old nemesis, saw him and promptly fired him again. Powderly appealed to Scranton, and told him Dawson had fired him because he was secretary of the union. Scranton asked if he would resign that office if Scranton reinstated him. Powderly replied that the only insurance he had, a one-thousand-dollar policy, was paid by the union. He asked Scranton, "If I resign and I am killed while an employee of the company, will the company pay my wife one thousand dollars?" Scranton told him to go back to work.

Despite any respect William Scranton may personally have felt for Powderly, in his eyes and in the view of the moneyed people of the community any labor leader was dangerous, more than likely an incipient Socialist.

❧   ❧   ❧

On Monday, July thirtieth, a break came in the tense Scranton atmosphere. The strike of the Railroad Brotherhood was settled. Mayor McKune, using his good offices and speaking for the railroad companies, informed the firemen and brakemen that if they went back to work, the railroads would rescind the announced ten percent reduction in pay. The unions accepted, and the strike was over.

As the trains began running again, their white puffs of smoke announced that Scranton was once again in communication with the world. The people of Scranton relaxed, but not completely. The miners and iron workers were adamant in trying to restore the wages they had lost. Their demand for a twenty-five percent increase still stood.

Encouraged by his success in settling the railroad strike, Mayor McKune sent John Brislin to meet with the miners. As a mediator, he informed the miners that the company would make a concession and grant them some grievance procedures, giving them more power in settling disputes in and around the mines, but would not pay the increase. Since the pay was the paramount issue, the offer was refused.

The end of the railroad strike led to the reopening of many businesses. But one man not ready to accept these indications of peace was William Scranton. He appeared disappointed, and he wrote to New York saying, "I trust when the troops come—if they ever get here—that we may have a conflict in which the mob shall be completely worsted. In no other way will this thing end with any security of property. . . . It was a ticklish time and it is not yet over in my opinion."

William Scranton later declared that he had no faith in any compromise with the mill workers and miners. As one of his admirers noted, Scranton preferred a "trial of strength with the law breakers."

William Scranton was to have his wish.

CHAPTER 16

੩ঌ

THE GUNS OF SCRANTON

A t seven o'clock on the morning of August first, Owen, his father, and his cousin prepared for a mass meeting of miners at Round Woods in Hyde Park. The settlement of the railroad strike had weakened the resolve of a small segment of the miners who were now willing to accept another defeat and return to work. But thousands of miners who belonged to the Knights of Labor or the new National Union were as strong and as unified as ever. They wanted to bring back the rates and wages they had lost between 1871 and 1877. Their goal of a twenty-five percent increase was intended to accomplish this restoration. The public generally deemed a twenty-five percent increase excessive, forgetting the earlier wage cuts.

Two meetings had been called for this day, one at Round Woods and one at the Silk Mill, a factory standing on a high knoll southeast of central city. The Silk Mill was the designated spot, but in the August weather a large, open, high field adjoining the Silk Mill became the meeting place.

As Owen, John, and Evan opened the kitchen door to go to Round Woods, they almost collided with Rhondda Hall. All three let out a combination of gasps, greetings, and welcoming words. They had not seen her in at least three years. Although they knew she had accepted a position in the Children's Home they had not expected to see her so soon. It took them some minutes of disconnected conversation to orient each other. Taking Rhondda inside, the men saw Rhondda and Mam hug and kiss in a joyful reunion.

Owen smiled from ear to ear. Now twenty, he had largely outgrown the conflicts of adolescence, and his exuberance poured out freely and openly. In his eyes, his teacher was younger and more beautiful than she had been when he slyly watched her walking up and down the aisles of the little Avondale school room.

In turn, Rhondda, while giving full attention to Mam, was not unmindful of this tall, slim, young man. He still had something in his countenance that reminded her of the twelve-year-old boy she had known who, despite her kindly probing, insisted on writing with his head and nose almost touching his paper as though he were going to devour it.

Learning that the men were hurrying for Round Woods, Rhondda asked if she would be intruding if she went along. "I've been reading the Philadelphia papers every day," she said. "Everybody there believes Scranton is under siege. They think Scranton is hostage to iron workers and miners who are being misled by foreign socialists."

"Sounds like they're reading the dispatches from the *Republican*," Owen said. "We're beginning to get a better representation from *The Scranton Times*, quite a bit of truth, in fact."

"Sure you want to come, are you?" Dada asked. "We'd love to have you."

"Yes, we would," Evan added, "And you will have plenty of company. Some of our men are weakening, but I don't think their wives are. They'll be there at Round Woods."

"Of course, of course, I want to—if just to hear my pupil speak. Will you be speaking, Owen?" Rhondda asked.

"If I need to," Owen answered. "But come along, please."

"We're on our way," Dada said, as he took Rhondda by the arm. "Tell me about this iron business."

Owen and his cousin followed Rhondda and Dada who were walking energetically before them, with Rhondda doing most of the animated talking.

When they arrived at Round Woods, they saw only a handful of miners there. A large contingent, led by Trevor James, who was wearing a tan duster, could be seen walking away from the site.

A dozen of those remaining called out, "This meeting's broken up, Mr. Roderick."

"What do you mean?"

"Someone came here very early and said everyone should go over to the Silk Mill," came the reply.

"I can't understand," Owen said. "My father and I were on the committee that called this meeting. Every colliery had a notice from Mr. Powderly to meet here."

"Well, we can't argue among ourselves about that. We'll go over to the Silk Mill. We'll find out," Dada said.

As they walked up Lackawanna Avenue, they saw people pointing to the mob up on the knoll near the Silk Mill. At least three thousand were milling around.

They also became aware of dozens of well-dressed young men, who should have been working in stores or banks, running around as though there were some emergency.

❧   ❧   ❧

Early in the day, Charles Smith and Arthur Logan, who had slept in the company store all night with a dozen others of the Scranton Citizens Corps, were mesmerized by the sight of the thousands gathering on the Silk Mill hill. What should they do? They had orders to run to the First Presbyterian Church and ring the bell if there were a riot or an emergency. The bell would call all members of the corps immediately to the company store for rifles.

As the men in the store watched the swarming mass of humanity on the Silk Mill hill, they were astounded by the number. The mob might be merely another mass meeting. Or they might be gathering there to send out a message of their great numbers and strength.

When members of the corps saw men like Mr. Roderick and members of the knights walking up toward the hill, they were relieved. They knew that these men had made many pledges of peace. But the newspaper accounts of strange faces in Scranton made them uncertain about the growing size of the mob on the hill.

When Owen, John, Evan, and Rhondda reached the hill, they were stunned. By now, more than five thousand were there. The mob included ironworkers from both the DL&W and D&H shops, as well as miners and laborers from sixteen or more collieries. The ironworkers were a large segment still dissatisfied with their status. That the Brotherhood of Railroad Workers had settled, satisfied that they would not be cut ten percent in wages, meant nothing to the ironworkers. The miners were here to give a definite no to a settlement giving them only grievance representation without wage restoration.

Several speakers at the Silk Mill rally had already attacked these points. As successive speakers became more vociferous, one or two more calming voices were also heard, including John Roderick's. Following him, a young Polish lad inspired the crowd in broken English. At this point, Dada motioned to Owen to speak and try to pour some cooling water on the rumbling thousands growing more and more fractious.

Owen was nervous, especially since Rhondda was just beneath the small platform he had mounted. As he looked out on the enormous group, he knew he could only reach about a quarter of them. The challenge of his message and his determination to make them hear made him forget Rhondda and his nervousness.

"Ladies and gentlemen," he yelled with all his lung power, "please, ladies and gentlemen." The sight of the tall young man and the power of his voice stopped half the noise and chaotic talking. Owen began to speak.

"As we walked up Lackawanna Avenue, many of us saw some signs of danger. The Scranton Citizens Corps is arming itself. Mayor McKune believes the corps will help to keep order. But I do not trust them. They are afraid of us. If we go downtown, these thousands of us here are going to scare them to death. They will get panicky and start shooting."

"Let them shoot," came several cries from unthinking sources.

"Wait a minute, please," Owen pleaded. "That's not what we want. You really don't know how many rifles and how much ammunition they have in the company store. I don't either, but if I know Mr. Scranton, he has hundreds of guns. And listen, these guns and bullets will kill us, just as they killed strikers in Pittsburgh, Philadelphia, Chicago, and Reading."

That statement, plus Owen's fervor, produced silence. Over the quieting crowd, Owen's voice rang out.

"Mayor McKune doesn't want to kill any of us, but if that signal bell at the Presbyterian Church starts ringing and they think we're going to loot the stores or burn the railroad shops, they're going to shoot us down. So let's cool off. Go back to union meetings and deal with the companies. I know we can win if we do it peacefully. Remember Briggs Shaft. We had two workers murdered, and when they died, the union died too."

Believing he had made his point, Owen left the platform. Before his feet touched the ground, Trevor James was on the platform shouting. "What Owen Roderick says is right. We have to keep the peace, but let's not miss the chance to show them down in the city we mean business. We'll march down Lackawanna Avenue and show them that Scranton is a working-man's town. They're not going to push us around anymore . . ."

Before Trevor could say another word, someone pulled frantically at his leg. He looked down and saw someone thrusting an envelope at him. He leaned down and took it. Quickly noting its contents, he hesitated to read the letter inside. He handed it down to Owen, who was still standing at the base of the platform. Owen read it and shook his head. He returned it to Trevor shouting, "Don't read it. I think it's a fake."

Owen leaped back up to the platform. Sensing that the fake message would excite the crowd, he cupped his hands around his mouth yelling, "Every miner here is asked to go behind the Silk Mill where we will hold the meeting we planned this morning at Round Woods. We have several resolutions to pass."

Hundreds of miners started up the hill heading toward the rear of the Silk Mill as Owen had pleaded with them to do.

Trevor was about to pocket the note when a small group, including the man who had handed it to him, insisted he read it. "Read it! Read the letter!" they screamed.

Trevor hesitated, but more pleas followed, made as threatening cries.

"All right," said Trevor. "Someone has just handed me a letter written by William Scranton–I can't read it all. But listen to this," he said. "This letter says, 'We will never give in. They'll never get the twenty-five percent increase out of me. If they don't come back to work soon, I'll have them working for thirty-five cents a day.' "

At the last words, pandemonium erupted. Three thousand ironworkers and miners screamed in a cacophony of anger. Trevor, who had been hesitant about reading the letter, now shouted loud enough to be heard in Hyde Park, "If that's what Scranton thinks of us, let's go." As he leaped from the platform, his tan duster flew in the wind like a flag flying in battle, and he led the more excitable down the hill toward Lackawanna Avenue. The workers now were divided into two groups, one walking up to the Silk Mill, the other pouring into town.

In a moment, Owen grabbed Rhondda's hand. "Come on," he said. "We still can try to stop this madness."

"Your father! Evan!" she cried.

"Let them go up to the Silk Mill. The miners will follow."

By now, more than a thousand miners were walking quietly toward the mill while the mob of two thousand led by

Trevor marched downtown. Pulling Rhondda by the hand, Owen shouted above the noise, "We must get to the front to talk to the leaders. We've got to stop them!"

At the head of the mob, Trevor James and a dozen others strode forward. Owen and Rhondda ran as fast as they could to go around the mob and catch up with the leaders.

Before they could reach him they heard Trevor, now the unchallenged leader, shouting, "Go for the shops. Clear out the dirty blacklegs!"

The mass of marchers suddenly broke like a turbulent river into two branches, one heading for the Lackawanna Iron and Coal Company on Roaring Brook, the other turning to the Delaware and Lackawanna Shops on Washington Avenue. A third group continued to follow Mr. Roderick and others to the Silk Mill.

Melvin Corbett, a clerk at the DL&W office in downtown Scranton, saw the stream heading toward them through a field glass. Mr. Storrs sent him to warn the mayor, who in turn ordered him to the company store where the citizens corps would gather.

The city of Scranton was now teeming with spectators on the streets and on railroad tracks. Intersections were jammed with wagons and carriages.

During the meeting at the Silk Mill and the frenzy downtown, William Scranton was at the family-owned First National Bank. When he heard that his mills and shops were endangered, he went to the military headquarters in the company store. Seeing none of his corps there, he gave orders to ring the Presbyterian Church bell, but confusion held up the alarm. One man stood beside the bell holding the rope in one hand and a pistol in the other.

In the meantime, one of the waves of strikers had driven workers from the foundry and were now at the furnaces, a short distance away.

William Scranton, now in command at the store, exhorted the men who had gathered to "fear nothing and to shoot to kill." He was convinced the marchers would attack the store after they left the furnaces and began to move to meet them head-on. Colonel Hitchcock pointed out that they should await the mayor's order or they would have no more authority than the marchers. As Scranton and Hitchcock conferred, a policeman arrived with Mayor McKune's instructions.

Until that point, Scranton and Hitchcock were unaware that Daniel Bartholomew, first sergeant of the citizens corps, had been on the roof of the store building for some time, keeping watch for his comrades on the third floor. When they saw the policeman, they came down and joined the others. Two separate groups were formed, with Scranton in command of one and Deputy Sheriff Bortree of the other. Each had command of about twenty-five men—fifty men to stop a crowd of thousands. Only half of these men were authorized policemen under the mayor. The others were employees of the Lackawanna Iron and Coal Company. All were armed with guns and ammunition owned by the Lackawanna Iron and Coal Company and the DL&W Railroad. Thus armed, they headed for the mayor's office.

❧   ❧   ❧

Quite sure that order would prevail, Mayor McKune had started to walk toward Washington Street where the shops were located. Accompanying him was Father M. H. Dunn.

On the street they met Mr. Needham, the timekeeper at the shops. Pale and excited, Mr. Needham urged them to follow him to Superintendent McKenna's office. When they got there, they found McKenna holding his daughter-in-law in his arms. She was his secretary, and she had fainted at the sight of the violence in the shop. From the office the mayor saw Harlon Little, lumberyard and car superintendent, fighting with some marchers.

The mayor dashed outside, followed by Father Dunn, pleading with the crowd, who had been watching the melee, to calm down. They responded until Trevor James, his tan duster still very conspicuous, pushed to the front demanding, "Who stops the people? Forward!" As the crowd surged, the mayor was knocked down, although Trevor later denied it, witnesses said he hit the mayor and fractured his jaw. Trevor maintained that he was pushed forward and put up his arm to keep from bumping the mayor. With the help of Father Dunn, the mayor regained his feet, and with blood streaming from his mouth reached the corner of Lackawanna and Wyoming Avenues. There, Mr. Scranton found him in a dazed condition and began to escort him back to his office. The crowd parted to let him pass, but at the Lackawanna Crossing, the crowd closed in on them. The mayor, Scranton, and the escort of corps members were now surrounded.

By now, three thousand people were massed around the armed guards. The sight of the guns and the company police and the citizens corps infuriated the strikers. They were incensed that they—workers and taxpayers—should be treated like street rabble. Most of all, they wondered who this man Scranton thought he was, treating them like criminals while he assumed the posture of a military authority. How did his rights supersede theirs? He got away with shooting Ben Davis and Daniel Jones, but he'd better not try it again.

Owen and Rhondda were only a few feet from the leading marchers. All the way down from the Silk Mill, walking sometimes just feet away from Trevor James, Owen and Rhondda poured cooling words and sentences over the persistent, excited marchers, pleading for peace and caution, but to little avail. In their hearts, like Mayor McKune and the others, they believed there might be pushing, shoving, name calling—but no real violence. They were unaware that some iron furnaces had been destroyed.

Two of Trevor James's compatriots, infuriated by a company employee who pointed his rifle directly at them, maneuvered themselves into position while two others distracted their enemy. At a signal, they lunged forward and disarmed him. In seconds, two or three similar fights had started. In the confusion, the mayor, wounded and exhausted, allegedly gave the order no one wanted or expected:

"Fire!"

At the first shot, Rhondda grasped Owen in fright. He threw his arms around her and half-dragged, half-carried her through the mass of human obstruction. Like frightened animals, the marchers bumped and struggled, surging against each other as they ran in different directions.

Owen and Rhondda finally reached the edge of the crowd, now scattering in all directions. They were not yet safe. A large band of marchers had armed themselves with stones to throw at company and corps men. These missiles were flying in all directions. Owen sank to his knees and covered Rhondda with his body, hugging her tight. In the midst of terror, dodging the rocks, watching the fighting, he knew in a flash that his relationship with Rhondda had been transformed. At that very moment, he saw a shot from a company rifle all but blow Trevor's head off! Trevor's body was lifted from the ground and his linen tunic flew in the air. Then he collapsed. In seconds, Owen saw another fall, and many others wounded, hobbling and screaming as they scrambled away.

In minutes, Lackawanna Avenue was completely cleared of marchers. Standing white and frightened but holding their rifles as though they were somehow going to be met by opposing fire, stood the transfixed gunmen.

Owen and Rhondda stood up, still terrified, and quickly walked away, half expecting that one of the deputies would fire upon them. They reached a storefront, where a kindly merchant unlocked his door and let them in. Rhondda had lost her hat; her hair was awry and her skirt was covered with dirt. Owen's shirt was ripped down the back. Rhondda gasped. Owen's back had been cut, evidently by someone's large stick as they milled in the crowd. The cut was not deep and the bleeding had clotted, but the ripped shirt was smeared with the red-black stain.

Rhondda and Owen rested and accepted a drink of water from the merchant. Then they started the long trek back to Hyde Park. As they left the store, they saw little except a straggler here and there. The gunfire had cleared the area. The quiet, naked street burned in the early August sun. They walked with their arms around each other.

For the first block or two, both were unsteady and shaken by their experience. For Rhondda, the confrontation was so shocking that she had to fight off hysteria. Owen's revulsion filled him with a sense of futility, loss, anger, and defeat.

By the time they reached the west end of Lackawanna Avenue, they began to recover their composure. As they walked uphill toward Hyde Park, a new feeling, an internal exhilaration began to sweep through them. For Owen, the emotion told him his youthful years of longing for Rhondda were answered. His preoccupation with overcoming their age difference was solved. The fantasized conversations in which he declared his love would not be necessary. Time and time again he visualized his declaration to Rhondda, only to imagine her ending the scene with, "But you're so young, Owen," or "I'm old enough to be your auntie, Owen," or "I'm sorry, Owen, but Reverend Burr and I are engaged."

Now as they walked arm in arm, they merged. For Rhondda, the precocious boy she had cherished was gone. In his place was a strong man, admittedly five years younger than she, but with a maturity to match hers and a compassionate visionary nature, a man with whom she wanted to build a family and a future.

Without a word between them, they climbed toward Main Street, holding tightly to each other. As they looked back toward the city, they could see the wholesale district, the business area, the Lackawanna Station, the iron furnaces, and the smoke-stained shops of the Scranton Iron and Coal Company. On the outskirts of the town, they could see the silhouettes of a half-dozen coal breakers standing black and stark, smokeless, cold, and unmoved in the summer heat.

In this most unromantic setting, in the blazing August sun, they embraced.

CHAPTER 17

NEW COMMITMENTS

A rms entwined, Owen and Rhondda walked slowly homeward after the midtown melee. They did not know the number of casualties, but from the blaze of gunfire, they believed many had been killed. Exhausted from their walk—from Hyde Park across town to the Silk Mill, then back to midtown, and finally home—and expending all their physical and emotional energy to calm the leaders of three thousand working men and women was challenge enough. Added to all this were the minutes climaxing the day when they were caught in the center of a face-to-face confrontation between the workers and the Scranton Citizens Corps. They were completely drained, but somehow their experience had brought them to a loving, cohesive unity.

They walked toward the Roderick home, but as they passed the small manse of the Reverend R. J. Williams, Owen realized he was actually taking Rhondda to that light of hope and security. For the past five years, Owen had spent many hours in the company of Mr. Williams. His advice and counsel, like his books and sermons, had been Owen's university. Owen asked, "Would you mind if we stopped to see Mr. Williams for a few minutes before we go home?"

"Do you really want to? You know, we are really a sight. Look at me. And your shirt is covered with blood."

"I know, but I think I'd feel better. The afternoon has been an awful failure, so terrible. Maybe if we could share it, Mr. Williams could help us clear our minds, give us some sort of perspective and hope. We can clean ourselves in an hour, but it's going to take much more to clean out my thoughts."

"I do understand," Rhondda said, "But let's go home first and get cooled off. Then, refreshed, we can come back and have a good long time to talk with him."

Owen agreed.

"But," she added, "and this is a gigantic *but,* there is something else we must talk about with your parents, much more important than anything else in the world. We must let them know what has happened to us."

"Of course, yes, yes. I have been so unnerved about the shootings and the tragedy of it all that I'm forgetting this joy of the day. I really am mixed up." Taking her in his arms, a most preposterous action on Washburn Street, Scranton, in 1877, he kissed her with impassioned fervor.

Mam greeted them at the house with relieved astonishment. "What in the world! What happened to you two? A wreck you are—both looking like a bad rugby team." Running to the back door, she cried out, "John, here they are!" She turned, "Your father has been home for almost half an hour. He's been at wit's end, sure you had been shot."

Dada explained he had met for just five minutes with the miners above the Silk Mill. They had hurriedly passed a resolution to continue the strike. Then many of them ran back to join the march downtown. Dada himself did not like the prospect of untoward violence and took a longer route home, bypassing the demonstration.

"How much do you know about what happened?" Owen inquired.

"Very little. I saw nothing, but I heard the guns. Tell me about it." His usually placid father was really agitated.

Owen and Rhondda gave him a description of the rioting as they had observed it. When they finished, they felt almost as exhausted as they had in mid-afternoon. Discussing the casualties, Owen repeated his lack of accurate numbers.

Dada said, "We'll know tonight, I'm sure. Some of the men will go to the newspaper offices. They'll let us know. The word will go round Hyde Park like wildfire."

"Mam," said Owen, "Will you help Rhondda? I think I ruined her clothes trying to get her out of that mass of humanity."

"Yes, indeed," Mam replied quickly. "Oh, Rhondda, it must have been terrible," she said, leading the way to her bedroom.

In an hour, Rhondda and Owen were both clean and refreshed. After supper the family gathered outside in the dusk of the hot summer evening.

The supper conversation had covered every aspect of the historic day, including speculation about accountability, the future of the strike, and the casualties. In the calm of the outdoors, Owen ventured to say, "This day has been a momentous one in more ways than one. In the midst of all this tragedy, one beautiful thing has happened."

Mam and Dada looked quizically at Owen and waited expectantly.

"Rhondda is to be my wife."

Both Dada and Mam gasped and mumbled. There was no news more welcome and exciting, but it was astounding also. They knew Rhondda was a teacher, professional and mature. She was five years older than Owen, who was not yet twenty-one. They were incredulous.

As Mam and Dada expressed both their surprise and their strong approval, Owen, who had been seated across from Rhondda, arose and walked toward her. Side by side, arms encircling each other, they stood before his parents. Mam and Dada gave them a series of loquacious blessings. Mam jumped up and almost crushed Rhondda with a hug. Dada pounded Owen's shoulder and then kissed Rhondda. "Along with Mam, I've always wanted a beautiful daughter. Now when will you come into the family?" he asked enthusiastically.

Rhondda replied, "Perhaps we'll pick the date later tonight. Owen and I will have to make that decision. I just started my position at the children's home, so I think I should work there for at least six months, perhaps a year."

"Yes," Owen said, "we will decide tonight. Rhondda and I would like to take a walk down to see Mr. Williams. While we're discussing other things, maybe we will set a date for the wedding as well. Right, Rhondda?"

"Right," she answered. "And since I don't know a Quaker within a hundred miles of here, I'd be delighted to have Mr. Williams marry us. From what Owen tells me about his beliefs and preaching, he has a Quaker spirit."

"A wonderful man," Dada said.

"Welsh to the core," Mam said, implying his ethnicity automatically made him a scholar, bard, teacher, and preacher.

"Do you mind if we take a walk down to see him now?" Owen asked.

"Might be in the midst of preparing his Sunday sermon," Mam said.

"Hardly," said Dada. "More than likely he's in the midst of reading the Welsh *Baner*."

Owen added, "Yes, or checking the column he writes for it. Drives the pressmen crazy when they make a typographical error, especially if they misspell the name of some remote Welsh village."

"What really upsets him," Mam stressed, "is the use of Llanfair p.g. He wants it in full—Llanfairpwllgwyngyllgogery-chwyrndrobwllllantysiliogogogoch."

"Well, whatever he's doing, we'll have a welcome, I'm sure. Ready, Rhondda?"

"Any time."

"We'll see you Mam, Dada."

"Ta, ta."

There was still daylight as they walked from the Roderick home down to the manse. As they approached, they could see Mr. Williams talking to a middle-aged man. When they were close enough, Owen recognized him as Rhys Thomas, one of the elders of the church, who was an outside foreman at Briggs Shaft. Holding one of the best jobs to be had, since he seldom if ever had to go down into the mines, he reflected the abject attitude of many of the privileged employees. He was, nevertheless, a very serious and religious functionary. By the time Owen and Rhondda reached the manse, Rhys Thomas was leaving. As he passed them, he nodded, said "Owen," pleasantly, smiled weakly, and went on.

Mr. Williams, in contrast, was profuse. "Rhondda, how are you? I haven't seen you in at least three or four years. Come in, come in! When last I saw you, I had a feeling you were bringing Owen to chapel. Now, it looks as though he is bringing you here. And it's not only his size, but the way he is holding your arm."

Owen and Rhondda both laughed. "Yes, I am holding her arm rather tightly. I want to make sure she doesn't get away before you can marry us."

"What? Well! Well! Well now! Interesting indeed it is . . . come in, come in."

In the house, The Reverend Williams asked the same question as the Rodericks about the wedding date. Both Owen and Rhondda remained vague about the date. Owen explained that while they were excited about their impending marriage, they came because of the horrible afternoon they had witnessed. The Reverend Williams had not known they had actually been in the demonstration. He bombarded them with staccato questions for some minutes, one inquiry topping another. Then he paused. "Do you know why Rhys Thomas was on the porch when you arrived?"

Before they could answer, he said, "There were four killed this afternoon. When you heard those guns and scurried away in fear, four men lay dead. Rhys got the names of the men from Mr. Cadwallader who went to Mr. Scranton's home. Mr. Cadwallader is the inside foreman at Briggs, as you know. Rhys didn't know how many were injured by shots, but he believes there were at least thirty or forty hurt."

Then The Reverend Williams mentioned Trevor's name and Owen and Rhondda took each other's hands, pressing hard as they remembered Trevor flying forward, leading the marchers. Although Trevor obviously had responded to Owen's calming words, had himself detected something questionable in the letter alleged to be from Mr. Scranton, he had quickly fallen victim to the temper of the more radical firebrands and himself rushed headlong to his own death. Owen closed his eyes, recalling the bullet crashing Trevor's skull.

"I can't understand it," Owen said. "Here we are, trying desperately to keep the men together in peace, hoping that at last we might win a strike and establish fair rates and fair pay . . . then everything blows up. What can we do now? That's why we're here, Mr. Williams. I so need your counsel that I would have been here this afternoon. Rhondda prevailed upon me to wait until tonight."

"Well, now, Owen," said Mr. Williams, "it is an awful tragedy, but let us talk about it. First, let me get you and Rhondda some cool lemonade." He went into the kitchen and returned with three filled glasses. Sitting down, he began to speak.

"There is no denying the city of Scranton will suffer for this for a long time. The differences between the owners and employees will be greater than ever. There will be more mutual suspicion than before. Yet, as there was after the Briggs killings, there will be a calming, eventually."

"Unfortunately," Owen interjected, "it will be more than calming; it will be another surrender. A plague of defeatism will smother us again."

"I know what you mean, Owen. It proves again the futility of violence. When will men understand?"

Rhondda, who had been listening closely, said, "How

can we expect the men to understand that violence is unproductive when all around the world, the leaders of nations rely on it. The Franco–Prussian War is only the latest example. Even Napoleon observed that force cannot create anything."

"Yes," said Reverend Williams. "Christ said that he who lives by the sword will perish by it, but this is ignored by both men and nations."

"I know," Owen interposed, "but what Mr. Scranton and all his good friends do not seem to recognize is that hunger, poverty, squalor, and despair are in themselves forms of violence. A miner's uprising is, in their eyes, violence. But the forces crushing people are not violence. Isn't it an act of violence to seek personal gain by crushing fellow human beings, by expecting them to live and grovel in inhuman conditions?"

"Yes," said Reverend Williams. "It is violence. Ecclesiastes tells us of the rich man who destroys many bushels of wheat so that he can get a higher price for two bushels. That is violence. Dairy farmers have been known to throw gallons of milk away to get higher prices. That is violence. We could go on. But people will not think the matter through. I remember once preaching a sermon about the violence of prisons, keeping men in cages like animals. As I delivered my sermon, I could read the eyes of my parishioners saying, 'What else should a prisoner expect?' You mark my words, Owen and Rhondda, those men killed today will not be grieved. They will get no pity." And then he reassured them. "Do not blame yourselves. You did not do wrong today. You tried to stop them, and you must go on doing that. You are both young. You have at least forty years to work for fairness in the workplace. Some day, fairness will be achieved."

"But at what cost?" Rhondda asked. "Antagonism breeds like vicious bacteria. There is the violence of the aggressor, the violence of the defender, and the violence of those caught in between. I was brought up by my parents believing that the Quaker way was the common-sense way. Now I realize what an infinitesimal group the Quakers are. When I was taught the pacifist reply of George Fox to Oliver Cromwell, when Fox was accused of planning to kill him, I thought that his Christian reply was the common-sense one anyone might write. How naive I was."

"Don't despair, Rhondda. I cannot explain the disposition of men who use physical force. But you can do all in your power to curtail it. You must remember, though, that those who would curtail it sometimes are, ironically, the instigators. Whenever we use nonviolent means—strikes, boycotts, protest marches, actions we deem peaceful—these same actions are deemed threatening by others. Immediately, up go the defenses—police, or worse, the coal company police, or even as we have seen, the military troops are summoned."

Owen sat disheartened and dismayed. He said, "Reverend Williams, you have given me many books to read. I have loved them. In one of them, Victor Hugo, who believed in universal peace, realizing his enemies and his friends thought him hopelessly Utopian, said, 'I accept this resistance of other minds without being astonished or disheartened.' I wish I could say that. I am spiritually lifted when I read the works of great men with the noblest of ideals. I am really enthralled. However, five minutes among the screaming, cursing mob and the crackle of gunfire today and I am crushed by the insanity, the madness of it all."

"I remember what you read, Owen," said the minister. "It was Hugo's address to the Congress of Peace. Do you remember what he saw as a solution? He saw guns and horses being replaced by a small box, the ballot box. The ballot box has not been the answer. But then again, perhaps we have not used it enough. In the future, the ballot box may do more."

The three continued their discussion for another half hour, exploring the paradox of violence in a democratic Christian nation. Owen and Rhondda, who had visited Mr. Williams looking for some perspective and peace of mind, found themselves rising to leave more perplexed than ever, more confounded than ever, by the collapse of Christian behavior in the labor struggle.

Mr. Williams, who long ago had learned not to put his hope in man, tried to send his young friends away with a pleasant good night. But as they bade him farewell, he could see that the conversation of the night and the tumult and tragedy of the day had left them exhausted and dismayed in body and mind.

❧

CHAPTER 18

THE TRIAL

B y the time Rhondda and Owen had climbed to Hyde
Park, the main streets of Scranton were deserted. The
injured, almost fifty persons in all, had hurried to hospitals,
doctors' offices, or to their homes to seek care for their wounds.
A dozen of them were to die in the weeks ahead. All of them
had lost blood, which stained the streets of Scranton. In the
midst of the blood-marked streets lay the bodies of four killed
instantly: Patrick Langan, Charles Dunleavy, Patrick Lane,
and Trevor James, whose tan tunic, once flapping like a banner
as he ran, lay like a shroud over his body.

The day after the violent confrontation, the streets were
cleaned. An atmosphere of calm sadness, of grief and tragedy,
prevailed. However, underneath there was civic and social
unease, accompanied by a raging legal battle. The two Scranton newspapers, the *Republican* and the *Scranton Times*, reflected the community's division and polarization.

The *Republican*, "echoing up and down the valley from
Carbondale to Nanticoke gave majesty to the law." The hours
of conflict "demonstrated that the monster of communistic
rage, of pillage and murder that had swept through other American cities had been struck down at Lackawanna Avenue. . .
The telegraph had carried the victory from ocean to ocean.
The defense of the city was carried on wings of lightning
around the world."

In contrast, the *Scranton Times*, supported the cause of the laboring citizenry and made such a brilliant defense of the constitutional rights of American free speech that many citizens joined the thousands of working men and women in proclaiming that the shooting and killings were murder. The arrogance of William Scranton and his companies, allocating to themselves the protection of the community, was to them evidence that corporate power was in control in the city. Hiding guns in the company store for use against taxpayers was revolting. The hundreds of Irish immigrants who had witnessed the conviction of the Molly Maguires, not by the government but by Franklin Gowan and the Reading Railroad, cried "foul" with all their individual and collective force.

Within two or three days of the violence, public opinion had definitely begun to side with the workers. The deeds of the citizens corps were no longer called heroic. Members tried to hide or disguise their membership. Colonel Ripple admitted that "the shooting was hasty and uncalled for" because the aim of the crowd was to convince the shopworkers to leave their work until better terms were obtained.

The citizens corps disappeared from the scene as the First Division of the National Guard of Pennsylvania, led by Major General Robert M. Brinton, arrived to police the city. Three thousand soldiers were posted at key points in the city. Their work was eased when Mayor McKune closed all saloons for an indefinite period. The final clamp of security came when Governor Hartranft arrived from Pittsburgh with Major General Huidekoper and eight hundred additional troops.

The city was now peaceful, but the battle for public opinion was not over. Leaders of the establishment, seeing public opinion turning against them, called a meeting pledging their support of the actions of the Citizens Corps. At the same time, pressure was placed on reporters to calm their writings.

In the next week, Scranton was a divided community. Lackawanna Valley, from Moosic on the east and Hyde Park on the west, through the coal towns of Dickson City, Olyphant, and Throop, to Carbondale, Peckville, and Blakely, bristled in opposition to or defense of the Scranton Citizens Corps and William Scranton himself.

The supporters of the corps fumed when Alderman Peter Mahon of the Sixth Ward, acting as coroner, instituted an investigation, aided by an ad hoc committee called the Workingman's Prosecuting Committee.

Among those testifying were John Roderick, Owen, Rhondda and Terence Powderly. Owen recounted their experiences in going from Round Woods to the Silk Mill, the mixed reactions of the crowd, the determination of his father and others to adjourn and to meet nearer the Silk Mill. Owen admitted that he, his father and other miners knew they had to meet to make a decision to continue the strike. He admitted that after the Railroad Brotherhood settled, many miners also wanted to capitulate.

His father told how he urged many of the miners to follow him away from the main crowd. He stated he was prepared to tell the men to stand firm, that the decreases in wages since 1871 had brought the miners to a pathetic wage scale. He explained the logic of the twenty-five percent restoration and emphasized that the miners were not asking for a twenty-five percent increase but rather for a restoration. Finally he said those miners who had not heeded his call had every right to march to central city.

Powderly had not been at either meeting, but he gave the *Scranton Times* pages of copy describing his career as a machinist in Scranton, his experiences in other cities, the causes of the tumultuous events of 1877 throughout the nation. Queried as to the causes of the unrest, Powderly graphically described the whole post-Civil War economy, the creation and growth of corporations and trusts. He saw the organization of labor as the inalienable right of the workingman. Labor organizations, he said, were the logical response to business organization. Americans who had given their sons and brothers just a decade before in the Civil War, had the same rights as corporations. Describing the profitmaking, the skulduggery in high corporate places during the war, he contrasted these manipulations with the sacrifices of laboring families.

Rhondda was an articulate witness, describing the walk from Hyde Park to the Silk Mill, and the tremendous gathering there, saying it remained peaceful even though she heard inflammatory words now and then. She remarked how the mood of the crowd changed when the letter allegedly from William Scranton was read, saying he would have the men working for thirty-five cents a day. She recalled how Trevor James hesitated to read the letter. She believed that Owen also recognized the letter as a plant, an incendiary fake. She admitted, under questioning, that she herself now felt sure it was a forgery.

Under cross-examination, Rhondda described her fright when Owen said they must stay with the marchers to try to keep some order. She admitted their shouts for a peaceful march were futile and unheard, smothered by the noise and power of the marchers. Asked if the crowd were armed, she replied that she saw many signs and placards and many sticks, but nothing that could be called a real weapon.

Asked why she and Owen did not drop out and return with Mr. Roderick to the Silk Mill, she said she believed in the cause of the marchers. But, like Owen, she felt they might get out of hand. What of the marchers going into the iron works and railway shops? Did she approve of that? She replied that she felt they were urging the men who had gone back to work to change their minds and remain loyal to their cause. She said she thought that the sight of the thousands would give those workers new courage and a sense of renewed solidarity and that some of them might even be shamed into rejoining their fellow workmen.

"In view of what happened, would you march again?", came the question.

She answered, "Yes, because marching and protesting are as old as America. The marching did not cause the shooting. It was the response to the marching."

Asked to describe the violence, she described seeing the young men of the citizen corps running about in central city and wondering why they were not at work. She said the citizens corps was so small a group, fifty men at most, that they were suddenly lost in the middle of the thousands of marchers. She described her feeling when the young men with rifles stood just a few yards away, pointing guns at her.

"I was frightened, almost fainting, because I knew that with one accidental slip, I could be killed. At the same time, I felt angry. Why were these guns allowed in the streets of Scranton? Why should I be threatened? But my fear was stronger than my anger, so I scrambled away as soon as I could."

"Before or after the shooting?" was the next question.

"Minutes before the shooting."

"Did you see anyone of the marchers wielding pistols?"

Rhondda said that she saw no one on either side with pistols.

"Would you say that the mood of the marchers was much like yours?"

Rhondda suggested her own fear may have been greater than that of most in the crowd. She speculated that the number of marchers was so overwhelming that some of them thought, "Who are these young show-offs pointing guns at us?" The young men looked as though they would be swallowed up and lost in the crowd, so completely did it surround them. Two young men were so completely encircled that they lifted their guns over their heads, she said, and could have been disarmed in a minute by a couple of men.

Asked to describe the moment of the shooting, she stated that on the march and at the point of the violence, she had never been separated from Owen. They had retreated from gun point and were continuing to move toward the sidewalk when they heard the shots. Owen grabbed her and they scrambled farther away. She described her feeling, saying it was a mixture of horror and fear.

"I thought from the number of shots that people were being shot down at gunpoint. I screamed 'No, No, Please! Please!' and burst into hysterical tears."

As Rhondda talked, her eyes filled, and the examiner himself could do nothing but say "Thank you, Miss Hall," and excuse her.

Eight days after the tragedy, Alderman Mahon brought a formal charge of first degree murder against twenty-two members of the citizens corps.

During the coroner's inquest, the miners of Hyde Park were literally kept alive by the united action of the union. The union men sent wagons out to the countryside where farmers loaded them with vegetables, fruits, milk, and cheese. This tangible and moral support was difficult for many of the town leaders to understand. The supplies gathered from farmers and others were placed in a cooperative store in Hyde Park. There they were sold cheaply, or donated, to needy striking families.

A considerable portion of the professional and business classes of town, on the other hand, were appalled by what they perceived as an insane action, turning heroes into criminals and criminals into victims.

Obsessed with socialist fears, their newspapers warned of intimidations and invoked the spirit of the Molly Maguires. Warnings were never levelled specifically at the miners and shop workers, but rather vaguely at "tramps," "agitators," and "foreigners" who would vengefully kill people and destroy property.

When a detachment of constables was sent to arrest those charged with murder, a series of counter-moves provided the protection of the military and prevented their apprehension. Instead, General Huidekoper took those charged before the mayor who kept them safely protected all night, impressed by the threat that if the prisoners were released to be taken to the county jail in Wilkes-Barre, they would be waylaid by "worthless tramps and bloody-minded men who call themselves strikers."

Alderman Mahon was infuriated at the interference of the military. When he received notice from Mayor McKune that the general would deliver those charged to jail, Mahon fired off this protest:

R. H. McKune, Mayor.
Sir:
I would say that neither General Huidekoper nor any other man in this land has any right to prevent the arrest and commitment of any person found guilty of murder by a coroner's jury, and the constables that have the warrants of commitment for the persons so guilty of murder will not proceed to act under such warrants until the said Huidekoper and the military under him cease to obstruct them in the performance of their duty.

This communication did not bring the prisoners to the coroner. Instead, the mayor saw to it that the prisoners were escorted to court in Wilkes-Barre by the deputy sheriff, D. O. McCollum, assisted by a body of private citizens and two companies of militia. In Wilkes-Barre, the prisoners were formally arrested before Alderman W. S. Parsons.

Hearing that there was a conspiracy by the establishment to free the prisoners, the Workingmen's Prosecuting Committee sent a warning note. The Welshman John E. Evans, chairman of the committee, urged that the prisoners "not be allowed to escape."

A much stronger warning came from the *Scranton Times:*

> God help the Judges in Luzerne County
> that undertake to treat this matter in any
> other manner than the law provides. We
> caution Judges Harding, Dana and Handley
> to have a care how they move in this mat-
> ter. We want them to understand, and the
> corporations too, that there is but one law
> in this country for the rich and the poor.
> Hell on earch would be nothing compared
> to what will take place in this county if
> the Judges fail to do their whole duty in
> this matter.

When the matter came before Judge Harding, he was not affected by the *Times* editorial. He restated the power of a community to protect itself against "violators" of the law, freed the prisoners on three thousand dollars bail each, and warned the coroner and the constables that the prisoners were not to be molested. The fifty-three defendants, described as coming from the "best society and business associations" of Scranton, were free to go.

On November 26, the case came to trial. Cornelius Smith, Esquire, presented the case for the marchers, who were the prosecutors against the citizens corps. He produced fourteen witnesses identifying the crowd as innocent men, women, and children congregating at the corner of Wyoming and Lackawanna Avenues on August 1, 1877.

One witness testified that the only provocation for the shooting was a blow struck by a boy wielding a stick, hitting Lewis C. Boitree. Alderman Mahon testified that he was three feet away from one of the victims who was shot. After all the witnesses testified, they conveyed the total impression of an unprovoked killing of peaceful marching citizens.

The defense produced twenty-four witnesses, all attesting to the violent mob's rampage threatening the very life and property of Scranton. Witnesses were cross-examined by the Honorable Henry W. Palmer for the defense and Attorney Smith, the prosecutor.

After two days, Mr. Stanley Woodward of Wilkes-Barre recapitulated the complete defense in an eloquent presentation, saying in part that the defendants were respectable, of the highest character. Accenting their roles as community leaders, he described the crime of which they were accused.

Leaning heavily on a decision of Judge King in Philadelphia in 1844 after a riot there, Woodward repeated one of the observations of the court:

> When a riot is running through a city, there can be no neutrals; every man must be on one side or the other. In brief, it is even riotous to be found on neither side. He must be willing to shed his blood for law and order.

Describing the national scene and placing Scranton in the national perspective, Woodward noted: "In Pittsburgh, Philadelphia, and other cities, and here in Luzerne County, it needed only a spark to ignite the flame. Revolution was in the air; disorder choked the atmosphere; a tidal wave of lawlessness was sweeping over the whole land. laboring men everywhere had taken the law in their own hands.

"Now what was the purpose of this meeting at the silk

factory on August 1, 1877?" Answering his own question, he replied: "As far as evidence goes, it was to 'clean out the black-legs,' 'to kill Bill Scranton,' and to 'gut the town.'

"These men, this mob, commenced their work by the declaration, 'Come boys, let's gut the town; the day is ours.' Frenzied, armed with clubs, stones, and pistols, they reached the main street prepared to execute their plan."

He described the legality of the citizens corps and the actions of Mayor McKune in using the men of the corps. Concluding, he said, "We, therefore, hold there was a riot and these men here charged were in the full heroic performance of their duties as citizens when this unfortunate result occurred. But the blood of the victims must be upon their own heads."

Judge Harding charged the jury and again repeated the two diverse descriptions of the tragedy. His description of the alleged wildness of the mob and its criminal intents were as long and as incendiary as that of Attorney Woodward. His charge explaining the jury's obligation to find the corps guilty of murder–if they believed the witnesses–was stated in one or two paragraphs. The rest of the charge, including the last paragraph, was an indirect plea for the Scranton Citizens Corps.

"Gentlemen, if you are satisfied that the true history of the day is that described by the defendants' witnesses, there ought *not* to be a conviction." Judge Harding concluded, "If it is true history, the city of Scranton was fortunate that the mayor's posse was composed of such men as W. W. Scranton, Lewis Boitree, and their associates. If it is true history, these defendants, I repeat, are entitled to a general finding of *not* guilty."

In one-half hour, the jury brought back the verdict: Not guilty.

Quickly, the second and third indictments were given the jury. Without leaving their seats, they added not guilty to the additional indictments. Within the hour, the defendants were returned by train to Scranton, free men.

🙂   🙂   🙂

The events of 1877 had been directed by the Lackawanna Iron and Coal Company. William Scranton, who had paid for the organization of the Scranton Citizens Corps, provided it with a building and paid for its legal defense. Gowen and Scranton were both successful.

In the autumn of 1877, a month before the acquittal of the citizens corps, most of the miners returned to work. At a meeting of miners at Round Woods on October 6, twelve hundred miners voted to continue the strike, and only one hundred fifty voted to return to work, but attrition after that day was fast. As autumn advanced, the miners quickly realized that they and their families would suffer too much in the coming months. They suddenly capitulated.

The federal troops left the city, but the city corps was expanded into a larger force, the Scranton City Guard, and a new armory was built to house it.

The strike of 1877, like previous ones from 1871 to 1877, was lost. The decade of the seventies was one of struggle and defeat. Yet seeds were sown. The Knights of Labor under Terence Powderly was still growing and the membership enthusiastic.

CHAPTER 19

ﻬ

THE FIGHT

In the interim between the tragedy of August 1, 1877, and the trial of William Scranton and the citizens corps, Terence Powderly once again called at the home of the Rodericks. John and Owen Roderick, like thousands of other miners in the Lackawanna Valley, were still on strike.

Powderly believed that his views on violence had been completely vindicated by the riots and killings all over the nation, especially in Scranton. He wanted to see Owen. Since the evening Owen had walked with him to Dr. Evans's office to have his head bandaged, he had begun to think of Owen as a very promising young man. Schooled in mining and avidly interested in the Scranton community, Owen was a resource Terence Powderly needed.

Powderly once again sat with John and Owen in their family home. He said, "You know, when I left this living room several years ago, I promised to return to get your commitment to the Knights of Labor. I'm sorry that I did not keep my promise. There is no purpose in rehashing why I did not return. By now you know well, I was fired and had to leave town to work. Fortunately, the city of Erie was a haven. I got work and found my place in the union there. But, you know all that.

"In the past year, both of you have been faithful members

of the Knights of Labor. You both have lived by the principles, especially in promoting peaceful cooperation in settling labor disputes. Had all of labor believed as you believe, the Scranton confrontation would not have taken place. I am here now because we have suffered a devastating defeat. But we must not collapse. I am convinced our only hope is to become involved politically. Will you hear me out?"

"Of course, yes, of course," said Owen and his father almost simultaneously.

Mr. Roderick said, "I am very pessimistic about this. How can we win a political struggle when we can't win a union contest? If we can't keep men together when their lives and families are at stake, how can we do it just to get someone elected?"

"I know you are skeptical, but let me tell you what I have in mind," said Powderly. "And listen closely, Owen, because I really need your help. We need young men who can do the running around, the legwork, if we embark on my plan. Right now the governments of Luzerne County, Scranton, Carbondale, Wilkes-Barre, Pittston, and Hazleton are in the hands of men who are more responsive to the coal and iron companies than they are to the citizens. This control extends to the state and national levels. Corporate and railroad power rule this nation, not the people. If the trend continues, I predict that in ten years the speaker of the Assembly will be addressing the legislature as 'Gentlemen of the Pennsylvania Railroad' instead of 'Gentlemen of the Pennsylvania Assembly.' The speaker of the House in Washington will call the House to order with, 'Gentlemen of Corporate America.' This misused power is destroying the country. The people can get back control of their cities, counties, and states—and even their nation—only through the political system. And we must start right here in Luzerne County. There is to be an election here in November and we must become involved."

"In what way?" Owen asked.

"By putting up a full slate of candidates for every office open in the county."

"In which party?" John Roderick asked, "Republican or Democrat?"

"Neither," replied Powderly. "We'll run our labor candidates under the banner of the Greenback-Labor party. You both have strong labor ties. Will you help me?"

"Help, yes. Help we can and will!" John Roderick replied. "What of Owen, what is it he must do? You said earlier . . ."

"Owen, to start with, must come with me next week to a meeting of District Assembly 5. I cannot bring a political matter up at the meeting, but I can do it after the adjournment." He turned to Owen. "I want you to be there and hear my presentation so you will have all the facts."

"Mr. Powderly, what chance do we have? I agree it's something we must try, but isn't it a little too early for this political campaign?"

"I don't think so, Owen. Putting it as briefly as I can, here's my plan. There are eighteen thousand members of the knights in Luzerne County. If we get them enthusiastic and keep the election honest, we can win the county row offices."

"Which are they?"

"First, an important office for labor to elect, the sheriff. Then there are recorder of deeds, a coroner, a surveyor, and an auditor. But for now, that is all you need to know. After you hear me make my proposal to the Knights of Labor, if you still have any reluctance about the political action, you are not under any obligation to help me. Will you come to the meeting?"

"I have never done anything political," Owen said, with great reservation. "But I will go to the meeting with you."

After Powderly left the house, Owen and his father discussed his suggestion and his enthusiasm. Slowly the concept began to interest Owen, and then its positive potential began to erase the bitterness and dejection he still felt in the wake of the rioting and shootings.

In the meantime, more and more men were returning to the mines. From Moosic to Carbondale, every day brought new capitulations, and reopenings of more slopes or shafts. By October sixteenth, the three-month strike was over. Lives had been lost, families had lived through deprivation, and mine workers had achieved virtually nothing. Men returned to work for less than they had made in 1871.

Owen's return to work began on a sour note. The first morning down, Jack Joseph, the inside foreman, met him at the bottom of the shaft. "Owen," he said, "we need you at the rock dump today. You'll have to . . ."

"Just a minute, Jack," Owen's father interjected. "He's my laborer. Evan and I need him."

"Can't help it. It's orders from the top. We need someone at the dump today, and I was told to use Owen Roderick."

The message was clear. Owen was being punished by the company. If he did not take the assignment, he would be fired. And after three months of idleness, the family could not risk that. So Owen followed Jack Joseph to the rock dump while his father and cousin went to their workplace.

The rock dump was a deep excavation where the refuse from mining was discarded. Most refuse was removed and dumped outside the mines in huge culm banks, familiar eyesores in the coal-country landscapes, but some of it was used to fill underground voids.

The refuse, or *rock* as it was called, even though it was made up of many components, was hauled like coal to the dump site in cars pulled by mules. Once it was dumped, laborers would spread it and pack it evenly so that the void was compactly sealed. In short, the dump filled two purposes. It processed refuse and stabilized the roofs of the mine.

When Owen got to the rock dump, he discovered he would be working alone. Two men working a dump site was safer. As a driver dumped a load, it was possible for a laborer to get caught knee deep in the debris.

Owen handled the first load without any trouble. The mule drivers were young men Owen knew well. After several loads, Owen found it necessary to crawl down thirty feet or more to the base of the pile. Several large chunks were impeding the even spread. While he was there, a young tough, a recent immigrant from Nottingham named Al Bulesh, came in with a load and dumped his cars without checking on Owen's whereabouts. The coal rubbish roared down toward Owen. He barely managed to get out of the way.

"Hey!" Owen screamed. "Watch it up there!"

"You watch yourself," called Bulesh. "I can't hold your

hand for you. You're not at a union meeting, you know. You get to work!" And then he took off.

Owen was astounded, not only by the inconsiderate unloading, but by the last remark. The only way to account for the remark was that the same person responsible for his rock dump assignment had enlisted Bulesh to harass him. If this were true, then he'd better get out of the depths of the hole before Bulesh came back.

Owen climbed back up to the top. However, he could see he had to back down some length to prevent another pile up. Fortunately, the next drivers waited until Owen was clear before they released their rock.

When Bulesh returned, Owen kept clear and to the right of the main body of rock. Pointing to the far left to indicate he wanted the load dumped there, he stood and waited. Bulesh backed up and let the rock go directly at Owen, shouting, "You dumb anarchist, you can't even handle a rock dump and you want to control the company."

Owen was on the alert. As soon as Bulesh started to back up, Owen scrambled to the left, anticipating that Bulesh would ignore him, or even try to hit him with some of the rock.

In terror of the rocks, and furious at Bulesh, Owen bellowed "You crazy lunatic, I'll kill you."

Bulesh whipped his mule away, laughing and yelling, "I'll see you later, you dog-eared Communist."

For the rest of the day, Owen slaved in the rock dump without any help. Fortunately, Bulesh never delivered another load and the other drivers gave Owen plenty of warning and space. At the end of the day, Owen was so drained of energy, he could barely walk to the bottom of the shaft. The shoveling, pushing, straining at the dump in the midst of all the dust was completely enervating.

Owen was so slow in pulling himself together and getting to the cage that he missed his father and Evan. When the cage reached the mine-yard, he took several extra-deep breaths. The cool autumn air filled his lungs but did little for his weariness. He started home slowly. After ten steps, he looked ahead. There were Bulesh and several of his friends. Owen knew they were waiting for him. Seeing Owen, they walked toward him.

"OK," Bulesh challenged, "you're going to kill me, are you? Let's see how much killing you can do?" He threw his jacket to one of his friends and took a fighting stance.

Owen's anger had long since subsided. He was in no mood to lift a finger, let alone fight. Bulesh was two inches shorter than Owen, but fifteen pounds heavier, a ruffian with a bad reputation for fighting.

At that moment, Owen would have given one hundred dollars to postpone the fight for twenty-four hours. All he wanted was to lie down and sleep. On another day, he could face it. He was not a boxer, but playing baseball had given him coordination and confidence. He had seen enough fights in Avondale and Scranton to know there were some things one had to do and others not to do. Flaying out and throwing a whirlwind of punches was useless, leading only to missed targets and short windedness. He had seen many fighters go down from self-induced exhaustion in two or three minutes.

While he was thinking these thoughts, Bulesh's friends were forming a circle for the fight.

Owen mechanically dropped his jacket and dinner bucket and put up his hands. As Owen and Bulesh began to circle, waiting for an opening, Owen thought, "Why am I doing this? I don't have enough energy to throw one punch. I can't believe what I am doing. I must find a way to fight tomorrow to . . ."

At that moment, a flash of lightening split his eyes and head. He knew he had been hit. Mechanically, he started to jab and back-pedal, jab and back-pedal. Each jab hit Bulesh solidly, and the back-pedal made Bulesh miss his blows. Another jab got Bulesh on the nose and blood spurted from his mouth. Bulesh charged wildly, his arms flaying like a berserk windmill. Owen circled round and round as fast as he could, now too weak to use his arms to jab. Then, winded from circling and back-pedaling, ready to drop, he saw that Bulesh was also exhausted, but not ready to quit. Bulesh came slowly toward him and, with all the strength he had remaining, threw a haymaker to Owen's jaw. Owen couldn't move his body, but seeing the blow telegraphed from the moment it started, he turned his head so that it smashed against his shoulder. Bulesh screamed in pain. He had broken his hand on Owen's shoulder bone. Owen felt the pain run from his shoulder down his arm to his fingertips.

Bulesh, his nose bleeding, holding his right wrist with his left hand, writhed in pain. Owen, unmarked, but now on one knee, gulping air as fast as he could, looked up to see Bulesh hobbling away helped by his buddies. He turned back and called, "You son-of-a-bitch, Roderick, I'll get you for this."

Like hundreds of fist fights in Scranton in 1877, whether in mines, factories or barrooms, it lasted no more than three minutes.

When Owen dragged himself through the back door, his mother, took one look at him and cried, "Duw mawr, what happened?"

"I was in a fight."

"A fight? A fight?" she cried, lapsing into Welsh. "Why? Why?" then after running for a cold towel, she applied it to his coal-black face. The cold water streaked his face comically, but it cooled him somewhat.

Owen, resting, began to recount the experience of the day. His father, by now washed and in home clothes, came into the kitchen in time to hear Owen relate his rock-dump experience with Bulesh.

"In all my years of mining in Wales and here, I never heard of such insanity. He could have killed you if a small avalanche of coal filled the dump. I'm going to report this. The union will have something to say about this."

"No, Dada, there are bigger issues. Anyway, I think the whole thing was directed against me. Somebody arranged to send me to the rock dump and put Bulesh up to it."

Then Owen described the nine-year fight. "I suppose I should feel pretty good about it," he said, "but I really don't."

"You had no choice," his mother said. "Of course, you could have kept on walking and ignored Bulesh, but he would have pounced on you. Anyway, I would not have been proud of you if you had walked away in fear."

"Not in fear," Owen said, "but maybe calmly."

"It would not have worked. That's it for now. Take your bath. And take a good nap before supper. You need it."

Later they had a long discussion again about the provocation and its implications. When it was over, Owen went to his bedroom and wrote a long letter to Rhondda describing the fight and his feelings about it, trying to place it against the violence of August 1.

> *I am trying to understand again why so many personal differences, why so many group differences and national differences lead to quarrelling and war. I think my fight was a symbolic one. I was drawn into conflict despite all I've learned from you about the inanity of it. I do believe the Quaker insights and reasons are right, yet, to paraphrase St. Paul, "Men do what they do not want to do." I did not want to fight. Driven by pride and anger, I found myself fighting. If I were true to my own beliefs, I would have refused to fight.*
>
> *Al Bulesh, as stupid and arrogant as he is, actually believes I am some kind of foreign political agent because he has heard this from the pens and mouths of powerful people. He thought he was destroying something bad when he set upon me. Mr. Scranton believes he is heroically defending America when he refuses to sit among union members to discuss wages and working conditions. When he gathered guns in his store, he was, in his own mind, protecting the city of Scranton. That he is responsible in any way for the deaths at Briggs or Scranton central city, is preposterous and unthinkable to him.*
>
> *I do not know what is darkest tonight, the pits of the Briggs Mine Shaft or my own thought and feelings.*
>
> *Tomorrow I shall write to you again and promise that I will write only of our future. I will also tell you of a political plan proposed by Mr. Powderly. He knows we have suffered a*

bad defeat in the strike. He now feels the only hope for us is to gain political power. He has asked me to help him and I will do all I can. Perhaps his vision will give me some badly needed enthusiasm.

> *With love and devotion,*
> *Ever yours,*
> *Owen*

CHAPTER 20

ॐ

THE KNIGHTS CAPTURE
THE COUNTY

The sense of defeat, rejection, and hopelessness Owen felt after the Scranton riots might have worsened after his fight with Bulesh except for the new sense of purpose that came from the visit of Terence Powderly. His buoyant anticipation of Powderly's political campaign turned to outright enthusiasm when he heard Powderly address the District 5 members of the Knights of Labor. The meeting, called following the adjournment of the formal union meeting, attracted every representative there, most of whom were enthusiastic for a county campaign.

Powderly addressed the meeting with a vehemence Owen had never heard from him. His usual tempering tone was gone. He flayed out against the corrupt political machinations of the coal-company-controlled politicians:

If we find the ballot boxes have been stuffed as on previous elections and ascertain the identity of the scoundrels who do it, let us hang every one of them. Murder may be committed in the heat of passion, robbery may be committed because of poverty, other crimes may be committed against the person, but the man who defeats the will of the people at the ballot box is worse than a murderer, burglar, thief and raper combined, for he strikes at the foundations of civil government and is deserving of death once his guilt is established.

Owen was pleased but shocked by Powderly's address. He thrilled to the exposure of criminality at the polls, but he shuddered at the references to hanging. He concluded the usually mild Powderly was carried away and that he must certainly be speaking symbolically.

Powderly's address was emotional and effective. Owen, like every person there, could see the potential power of the eighteen thousand knights in Luzerne County. The challenge was to give them leadership, objectives, and design for a successful campaign.

The specific plan described by Powderly was to have the men at the meeting return to their locals to enlist their help and advice in putting forward a full ticket for the row offices of Luzerne County. The offices they hoped to capture were recorder of deeds, sheriff (a position of vital importance during labor disputes), surveyor, coroner, county surveyor, and one judge.

The informal meeting was thrown open for discussion after Powderly's dynamic appeal.

The first question came from a knight from Dunmore. "What party are we going to run with? Personally, I'm a Democrat and . . ."

"No," interrupted Powderly. "We can't get involved with the Democrats or Republicans. We'll have to go it pretty much alone as Labor candidates. If we have any designation, we'll go along with the Greenback group, call ourselves Greenback-Labor."

"Can we do that?" asked another member.

"Yes, we can, but first you have the job of picking delegates to a convention we will call."

"How shall we pick them? Do we need to follow some special rules?" George Powell of the Briggs Union asked.

"No special way. You can elect them in your locals, or you can decide on another way to choose them. For instance, if you want to designate your officers as delegates to the convention, you can do that."

"Where's the convention going to meet?" was the next question.

"I think we need a central location between Scranton and Wilkes-Barre. That should be Pittston."

A flurry of questions on details followed, but when the meeting ended, everyone was clear about his need to select delegates to the convention.

At the close of the meeting, Owen and Terence walked out together.

"Well, Owen, what do you think?"

"I don't know exactly, but everyone seemed to accept your ideas."

"How about you, Owen?"

"I think it's well worthwhile, but you asked me to come and I just stood by. I couldn't or didn't help you. You did everything yourself."

"Did you hear everything I said?"

"Yes, of course," Owen replied.

"Do you think you could repeat what I said and answer the questions?"

"I believe I could."

"Then you can help," Powderly said. "I want you to quit your job at Briggs and work for the Knights of Labor. Your first job will be to visit all our locals in the anthracite region to educate them in the procedures and tactics of this campaign."

Owen was stunned. "Quit my job at Briggs—I can't do that. My father and mother need my pay envelope. I can't . . ."

Before he finished, Powderly interrupted, "I see you don't understand, Owen, and I'll not go into it further tonight, but I will be at your house tomorrow night to explain to you and your family why and how you can best help the Knights of Labor."

They parted, with Owen in complete confusion.

ɞ   ɞ   ɞ

The next evening, in a more relaxed atmosphere, Powderly addressed the Roderick family.

"I suppose Owen has told you I shocked him last night with the proposal that he leave Briggs and work for the Knights of Labor. Perhaps it was too sudden, so I want to tell you now more of what I propose. First of all, the Knights of Labor is now the best union ever organized in the anthracite region. Because in its first days it was a secret organization of skilled workers, its success has not been seen. Today, it includes thousands of miners, close to twenty thousand. We have not fifty or more locals as the papers guess, but really over one hundred. What we do *not* have is educated and dedicated full-time leadership. The officers at the locals are hard-working miners who do their union business after a day of hard labor. Frequently, the minutes of their meetings are not written, and their financial records look like their wives' grocery records. The knights are now in a position to pay a few full-time workers to help the locals become more businesslike. But we do not want to hire men who do not believe in the cause of labor. We need young men like Owen. He is well read and intelligent. Moreover, he has a great interest in Scranton and the coal region people. Best of all, he is himself one of the miners. These years he has spent at Briggs will make him very acceptable to the people he talks with, whether they be miners from Ashley or miners from Throop. He is himself a miner and one of them. He knows the heartaches and problems. As a youngster, he experienced Avondale, he has lived through the seventies, he was in the Scranton protest tragedy."

Knowing he had given the Rodericks much, perhaps too much, to think about, he paused before continuing. "I have not met anyone more qualified than Owen to help us improve our union as we build it. Mr. and Mrs. Roderick, you have trained Owen well, and it is time for him to leave the mines to do important work."

The Rodericks were patient enough not to interrupt, but they, like Owen, wondered what the conclusion to Powderly's remarks was to be.

Powderly did not keep them waiting.

"The union will pay Owen fifty dollars a month as a full-time employee."

"Fifty dollars a month?" Owen interrupted. "Why that's almost twice as much as I earned before the strike."

"Yes, it is," said his father.

"I know, I know," said Powderly. "But you are worth that much, and you will earn it."

Owen was now intrigued. "What will my duties be?"

"First of all, during these first few months, you will be working full time on the November election. After that, you will meet with union officers. We want to set up a uniform way to keep minutes and financial records. You will have to spend time at each of the locals. You will travel by railroad whenever possible, but sometimes you will have a horse or a horse and buggy. From time to time, unauthorized strikes may break out. I will try to be on hand to mediate them, but in time, you will learn to adjudicate and resolve those problems yourself. Your mining experience will help me and enable you to solve some problems better than I can. And Owen, let me tell you, it will not be easy. The hours will be long, the issues sometimes complicated—not many blacks and whites—and the men sometimes stubborn. You know miners are individualists and in their own way, very opinionated. Nevertheless, most of them are hard working family men like yourself."

The Rodericks were convinced that Mr. Powderly was very serious. Owen's incredulity now turned to enthusiasm. John Roderick saw the plausibility of hiring Owen.

Mam, impressed by Owen's offer, was a step or two ahead of the men. What of Owen's marriage? How would this position affect Rhondda and Owen? How could they build a family, raise children? She was willing to wait and see.

"When shall I start the new work?" Owen asked.

"I'd like you to start this next Saturday afternoon. There

is a meeting in Taylor for the purpose of choosing delegates to our convention. I'm eager to see how they will handle it. You and I shall walk from Hyde Park to Taylor and be there by two o'clock."

Terence Powderly and Owen made arrangements for Saturday, and with the usual friendly parting, Powderly left the Roderick home.

When Powderly departed, Mam observed, "Whenever Mr. Powderly enters and leaves this house, I know our lives will change."

"Well, welcome he'll always be. He is our friend. Think of it, he is just twenty-seven and so knowledgeable."

By this time Owen had grabbed his cap.

"Where are you going?" Mam asked.

"Just to see Mr. Williams a minute to tell him the big news."

The Rodericks knew no one would be more enthusiastic than the Reverend R. J. Williams.

❧　　❧　　❧

The announcement that labor was going to field a full ticket in Luzerne County created little interest among the middle and upper classes. Mass apathy was the response from the three largest cities, Scranton, Wilkes-Barre, and Pittston, as well as from Hazleton and the smaller boroughs.

On the other hand, the coal companies knew that the locals of the Knights of Labor were springing up all over the coal regions. Their informants told them that the dozens or more locals of a few years ago now numbered at least fifty between Carbondale and Pottsville. Most of these were in Luzerne County. To them, the knights were a real threat, and they issued orders from the top to do everything to stifle this mad "communistic" movement. Americans, they said, would vote only for the patriotic Democrats or Republicans.

If the coal companies were frightened, the newspapers were aroused. The lives of their three main supporters were at risk. Financially buoyed by political ads from the two parties and beholden in a dozen ways to the business and coal community, they leveled most of their abuse on Terence Powderly. Calling him an "incendiary" who would burn the city of Scranton in order to promote himself and his ideas, they called on all voters to reject this inflammatory radical. Despite Powderly's opposition to socialism and anarchism, they railed against him. To the growing radical parties in America, Powderly was anathema, yet the Scranton papers never made any acknowledgment of his opposition to them. The papers painted him a violent Red.

The convention was called for September 11, 1877, in Pittston. After the delegates were seated, Powderly again outlined the election-day procedures, and a full slate was nominated: for judge, William H. Stanton; for sheriff, Patrick J. Kinney; for recorder, Thomas R. Peters; for coroner, William Banks; and for county surveyor, John Lawrence.

As planned by Powderly, the Knights of Labor were ready on the election day of November 1877. Every poll had a contingent of knights in addition to the knights who had been officially appointed by the Luzerne County Court to serve as overseers.

Owen's particular job that day, starting in early morning, was to cover every polling place he could from Hyde Park north to see that knights were present at each one and that voting was proceeding.

In one precinct on Rebecca Street, he found that two young knights, one a patcher, the other a mule driver, had been threatened and physically ejected from outside the voting area. When Owen finally located the two, he could not get them to return. Evidently, the physical threats had been so specific they refused to risk themselves. When Owen returned to the polls, everyone syrupy and pleasantly feigned ignorance of any such intimidation, "knew nothing of such behavior." Owen then walked down to Main Street, where at least ten knights were in evidence outside a polling place. He took five of them back to Rebecca Street, finally convinced the driver and patcher that they had physical protection, and got them to resume their places as court-appointed watchers.

At Main Street, near the Taylor border, Owen observed much illegal help being given to illiterate voters. Paper ballots were being passed around helter-skelter. As soon as he mentioned that he was going to the courthouse to report the irregularities, the illegal assistance stopped. He learned later from the knight overseers that as soon as he departed, the illegal assistance resumed. From early morning until the polls closed, Owen was on the move every minute. Although most of the polls were well-managed, there were a dozen or more with problems like those of Rebecca Street and Taylor.

Owen was happy to see the day end. Exhausted from weeks of intensive legwork, he was nevertheless exhilarated.

The loss of the strike, the riot, even the fight were forgotten as he realized a victory would be compensation for the defeats they had experienced.

As planned by Powderly, every ballot box returned to the courthouse on Public Square in Wilkes-Barre was accompanied by a delegate of the knights. He knew, and every man there knew, that many elections were lost between election night and the official counting, usually conducted some days after the elections. County officials elected through coal company influence had their own special way of counting.

By the time the ballot boxes began to arrive, night and a damp drizzle enveloped the old courthouse. Soon the miners from Avondale arrived, jubilantly carrying lighted torches as well as their ballot boxes. The torches of the Plymouth men set off a jubilant note. In some way or another, every contingent entering the city tried to outdo the others. As they poured into the city from Swoyersville, Plains, Luzerne, Pittston, Scranton, and Carbondale, they swarmed around the old building, their torches lighting Public Square with blazing effulgence. The mood matched the lighting as the men celebrated ecstatically, anticipating a victory.

From that Tuesday night until Thursday, a detail of one hundred knights stood guard around the courthouse. From the Wilkes-Barre area, nine hundred men were on call if any unauthorized persons were seen entering the Court House.

CHAPTER 21

·❧·

A POSTPONED MARRIAGE

O n election night, Owen did not sleep much. In the
morning, he was able to slip away and walk several
blocks to the Home for Friendless Children where he met
Rhondda and made arrangements to join her in later afternoon. They met as arranged and in the early November twilight enjoyed a walking tour of Luzerne County's seat of
government. The center city of Wilkes-Barre in 1877 was a
tourist attraction for both of them.

They walked from Public Square over Market Street to
see the new Wyoming Valley Hotel, built just nine years earlier to replace the old Phoenix House. Rhondda, admiring
the new structure, proposed laughingly that it might be just
the right place for their honeymoon. Owen replied he would
prefer going to Mauch Chunk, sometimes called Pennsylvania's
Alps. Apart from the scenery, there was the possibility of taking the Lehigh Valley train and enjoying the scenic ride through
the mountain-pass along the Lehigh River. Both the Lehigh
Valley and the Central Railroad of New Jersey had connected
with Wilkes-Barre in 1867. Two trains came into Wilkes-Barre
each day.

Continuing their walk along the Susquehanna River
common, they marvelled at the Butler, Slocum, and Robinson

homes and, looking westward, saw a pencil-thin streak of day-light sky above the rim of the mountains.

They walked arm-in-arm, as they had not warmed to each other this way since the long trek from the riot on that hot August day. This evening, they were far more relaxed. They were content to walk together, to enjoy the early evening cool hour, and to savor the sights of older Wilkes-Barre, recalling scenes very much the same as they had been before the great war, some of them identical since the days when the old railroad line ran from the river common to Ashley.

Rhondda, having learned the history well, told Owen of the Wyoming Massacre and the Sullivan Expedition which camped along the very river common they were viewing. The Sullivan Expedition typified the retaliatory militarism of the ages as the thirty-five hundred men under John Sullivan viciously and cruelly burned and exterminated sixty Indian settlements. Sullivan proudly reported that "there was not an appearance of an Indian this side of Niagara." Rhondda described the attacks of savages at the Massacre and the corresponding brutality of Sullivan's troops.

"You realize that's the second time you told me that story, don't you?" Owen asked.

"I did?"

"Of course. You told it to us in one of your special Friday afternoon treats at the Avondale school. I guess I was about eleven at the time."

"Sorry," Rhondda said.

"No. No. It's important," Owen assured her.

"The main thing is," Rhondda continued, "we are on a

historic spot. The scene has not changed along the river. And men have not changed. Zebulon Butler, influenced by the Paxtang Boys and Lazarus Stewart, would not surrender as common sense told them. They not only lost, the colony was massacred. Patriotism made them make a stupid decision."

"Was it patriotism?" Owen speculated. "And what of the barbarity of Sullivan's march? Patriotism, too, I suppose."

"It's sad," Rhonda said. "We are not treating the Indians much better today. We push them into reservations, which are really slums. And then if a railroad needs land, we push them out of the way again."

As Rhondda continued to talk, they left the river common, turned left at Northampton Street, and walked north on Franklin Street where they stopped to admire the First Presbyterian Church.

"I want you to take a good look at this church," Rhondda said. "This is the church I have been attending since coming to Wilkes-Barre."

"So you're now a Presbyterian," Owen said, cajoling her. "Mr. Williams will be delighted."

"You know I'm not. I'll always be a Quaker, but I do enjoy the services here. It's quite a church, and before I start telling you about it, I assure you I never told you about it at Avondale because I've just learned a few things about it since coming here."

"It's architecturally beautiful," Owen observed, admiring the building constructed in 1849. "Who designed it?"

"They really don't know. Some think it was done by the great British architect, Richard Upjohn. More than likely, it was done by two local men who may or may not have had plans from James Renwick, who's even more famous than Upjohn."

"The longer I look at it, the more impressive it becomes," Owen said. "Was this the first church the Presbyterians built?"

"No, there were two others before this. I want to tell you about its beginning because it may make you feel less guilty about the Scranton riot and your own mine-yard fight."

"Oh, I don't feel so guilty tonight," he half laughed. "I feel too good."

"I know, I know," Rhondda said, squeezing him about the waist. "But really, it is an interesting bit of history, and it shows how human good Christians can be, or I should say, how unchristian some professing Christians can be. This is unbelievable, really."

Rhondda released Owen, took a deep breath, and began her story: "This church came out of a Congregational Church built on Public Square about 1802 or 1803. It was called Old Ship Zion Church and it was used also by the Episcopalians in the tiny community as well as the Methodists. The quarrel broke out between the Congregationalists and Methodists because the Congregationalists had the keys to the church and regarded themselves as owners. The Methodists, who contributed toward the upkeep, thought of the old church as a union church, not owned and supervised by the Congregationalists but shared by all. During the quarrel, the Congregationalists, owners of the keys, locked the church. The Methodists asked for a meeting to confer. The Congregationalists refused to discuss the matter."

"One Sunday morning, the Methodists broke open the doors. The Reverend Morgan Sherman announced the opening hymn beginning 'Equip me for war and teach my hands to fight.'"

"An unnecessary prayer, if I ever heard one," Owen broke in.

Rhondda laughed saying, "They finished the service all right. However, as Mr. Sherman announced the next Sunday's service, a Congregationalist in the congregation, Oristes Collins (perhaps a spy), called out, 'At that time this church will be occupied by another congregation.' The Reverend Sherman repeated the announcement. Mr. Collins then repeated his reminder.

"I don't know whether it was the following Sunday or later, but the story goes that the next confrontation took place when the Methodists, under their minister, the Reverend Benjamin Bidlach, arrived early. Mr. Bidlach opened the service by announcing Hymn 144. Just then, up the aisle walked Congregationalist Mathias Hollenback with their minister, Mr. Tracy. They both walked toward Mr. Bidlach in the pulpit, and Mr. Hollenback asked, 'What are you doing here?' Ignoring them, Mr. Bidlach announced the opening hymn, 'Page 144, short metre.'

" 'What did you say?' asked Mr. Hollenback."

" 'Page 144, short metre,' replied Rev. Bidlach."

"Mr. Tracy and Mr. Hollenback then retired. The whole episode was very nasty, and it ended only when the Methodists bought out the others and the Congregationalists and Episcopalians each built their own churches.

"So you see," Rhonda concluded, "these holy wars reveal again how quick men and women are to fight. If these good people couldn't get along, how do we expect capital and labor to do so?"

"That's right," Owen said. "And looking back, it does sound unbelievable that these pioneers we admire so much could have behaved that way. We hear of the bravery of their ancestors in coming to America for religious liberty and freedom. It's a little strange—humorous even—to hear of their denominational squabbles."

"As you read it," Rhondda said, "there is another little local difficulty—just keeping the denominations straight. Although most of them of the church were Congregationalists when they originally came from New England, they had some Presbyterian ministers. Finally, one of those convinced the congregation to become Presbyterian, as it is today."

After viewing the First Presbyterian Church, they decided it was time for Rhondda to return to the Home for Friendless Children, just three blocks south of the church.

"But let's just walk over to South Main Street so I can show you the Pickering house," Rhondda said. "It's just one block farther. It was built by Colonel Timothy Pickering of Massachusetts, who became a citizen of Philadelphia. During the Revolutionary War, he was quartermaster general. He came to Wilkes-Barre in 1787 as a Pennsylvania official to organize Luzerne County. He conducted the first elections here. Then he went back to Philadelphia to serve in President Washington's cabinet. He was secretary of war and postmaster general and Secretary of State. Not all at once, of course."

When they reached the white clapboard house, Rhondda added, "This is one of the oldest houses in Wilkes-Barre. Very distinguished."

"Who lives here now?" Owen asked.

"I'm not sure, but when Pickering left, he sold it to General William Ross. I believe his descendants live here now."

"Well, it's time for you to get back. We'd better get back over to Franklin Street," Owen urged.

"Oh, Owen, I almost forgot. We *must,* yes, *you must* see the old Fell Inn. It's just around Northampton Street on Washington on the corner. It's so important to you. It's coal history," she said excitedly. "It's where it all started."

"What do you mean?" Owen asked marvelling at her excitement and interest.

"Let's walk fast," she said. "I must get back to the home, but I must first show you . . ."

"What?"

"Another place I taught you about in school, another Avondale lesson, the place where anthracite was perhaps first burned in an open grate. You see—and I know all this because Jesse Fell's parents were Quakers, and my mother knew all about him—anthracite was only used by the blacksmiths and others because they could use it if they had a bellows to make a forced draft. But Judge Fell broke the coal into small pieces, placed them on an open grate, and just kept adding coal and removing the ashes, proving it could burn continuously with just a natural draft. Soon the word was spread. People experimented, found that anthracite definitely was a great fuel for heating. The demand for anthracite just exploded all over."

In minutes, they were at the old site once called Jesse Fell's Inn at the sign of the Buck. It was still an inn and tavern.

"Was he just the innkeeper?" Owen asked. "Was he a real judge?"

"Yes, indeed. He was the first burgess of Wilkes-Barre and a judge for many years."

"Hmm," said Owen. "So this is where it all began."

"Well," said Rhondda, sheepishly making a slight retraction, "my father disputes some of it—says others did what Judge Fell did. But my mother, always loyal to the Quakers, insists Judge Fell was first. Anyway, it is a great story, and perhaps true. Come on, let's run," she said, grabbing his arm.

"Right," he said. "And don't stop." In seconds they were walking at a fast pace. "We better go down Washington Street," he added. "There may be fewer historic sights. If we see anything else, we won't get back to the home till midnight."

As they hurried, Rhondda said, "Now, I don't want you to stop, but don't miss the beautiful high spire of the new St. Mary's Church. Here it is, just before us. And on the other side the Jewish synagogue built before the great war."

As they hurried, half-walking, half-running the several city blocks to South Franklin Street, they vowed to write to each other every day and that they would definitely postpone their marriage for at least another year. Rhondda was fulfilling a need at the Children's Home and Owen had really not assumed his organizational duties under Powderly. With permission of the knights, Powderly had used him exclusively for the county campaign. Unless diverted again, Owen would be spending all his days and most of his nights traveling from one union local to another helping them with records and procedures. Many of the officers of the locals could neither read nor write. Owen had to find a way to make each local responsible for its own records.

Both Rhondda and Owen needed a year to understand their jobs and goals. For Owen, the year was easy to give, for he was not yet twenty-one. Rhondda, five years older, found the time at the Children's Home so absorbing and challenging that she was also welcoming the period for her work.

As they parted in Wilkes-Barre, it was with stressful pangs of separation, but with the zest and optimism of youth as each saw in his and her life the satisfaction of sacrifice and achievement, the inspiration of high purpose.

🐦   🐦   🐦

The week following the historical walk in Wilkes-Barre, Rhondda and Owen read enthusiastically of the confirmation of the county victory. There had been no stuffing of ballot boxes at the polls, and there was no altering of the returns, thanks to the Knights of Labor guard. The vote was honest. The count was honest. The Greenback-Labor ticket was victorious.

Powderly proclaimed the victory as a Waterloo, perhaps an exaggeration, but a victory nevertheless. Every one of the labor candidates for row offices was elected, including their candidate for judge. Each candidate received between 14,400 and 14,800 votes. As one writer put it, "Labor had at last triumphed; the unity which had failed to win the strike ending three weeks earlier had been successfully transferred to the political arena." The writer predicted, "Luzerne County was won. Scranton is next."

The victory of Judge William Stanton was especially sweet. Judge Stanton, along with the *Scranton Times*, had been the major voice in calling for the trial of William Scranton and the City Guard. The jury had exonerated the accused, but the election of Stanton proved that his actions reflected the opinions of the majority of Luzerne County voters.

CHAPTER 22

ॐ

BEER, RUM, AND VILE CIGARS

The celebrations of the Luzerne County Courthouse victory were over, and the locals of the Scranton Knights of Labor were agog with new political speculation. In February, Scranton was to elect a mayor. Fresh from victory, the union locals couldn't wait for the nominating convention. Their experience in Pittston at the county nominating convention was exhilarating to recall. It invigorated them to anticipate the choice of a candidate for the executive office of Scranton. The convention was scheduled for December 20.

Terence Powderly, who had been the dominant leader of the county campaign, could not be relied on for the approaching mayoralty contest. He had made a commitment to return to western Pennsylvania, this time to Oil City, to work in the railroad shops there. He had regained his position as secretary of District 5 of the knights, and was ready to depart on the night train of December 20, the day of the convention. At three o'clock in the afternoon of that day, Hank Cavanagh, Hugh Murray, and Owen Roderick called at his home to announce that the convention had nominated him for mayor.

Powderly was shocked and unnerved. He knew he had no experience to handle the powers of a civil magistrate. As mayor, he would be required to sit as a police judge. Cavanagh and Murray induced him to return with them and appear before the convention as the nominee. He agreed to go even as he considered rejecting the nomination.

As he entered the convention, he overheard some negative words about his candidacy. The words annoyed and animated him. He was hailed by the convention and accepted the nomination.

After the noise and good fellowship of the convention ended, he sat with Owen on folding chairs on the convention platform.

"Owen," Powderly said, "I got you into this business because I felt that the city of Scranton needed young men like you. Tonight, you and the others brought me back home when my mind was on Oil City."

"The men wanted you. I just did my part," Owen replied.

"Well, it was a big part. When I helped to get you on the payroll of the knights, I told you of my expectations for you. The county elections sidetracked us a little. But the district leaders approved using you in that election. Now I have to ask you if–with their cooperation and approval of course– you will help me in Scranton?"

"I want to very much."

"Fine, but let me tell you, Owen, this is going to be difficult. First, I know that the Democrats and Republicans are going to do something they never did in their history. They are going to join together and nominate a fine man, a Civil War veteran. The two parties are agreed on one thing. They do not want me, as a labor man, to be elected. So the campaign will be rough and tumble."

Not only was the campaign turbulent, but Powderly made it a strange and unorthodox one. At the outset, some ironworkers, following the pattern of all elections, arranged meetings in two saloons in the neighborhood of the mills and one in the Patagonia section of Hyde Park.

Owen and Powderly discussed whether they should go or cancel. Owen prevailed upon Powderly, an avowed temperance advocate, that he must go, that he need not imbibe, that his stay could be short but effective. He owed it to the well-intentioned workers who arranged the meetings, Owen maintained.

Owen and Powderly appeared first at McNally's. Powderly had never been in a saloon in his life. The smell of the beer and the smoke almost ended the campaign then and there. His first speech fell completely flat.

Smarting from the stifling atmosphere, he said, "I am not running in the interest of any persons or party. If I'm elected, my sole duty will be to serve all the people of Scranton."

Right then, he lost his audience, who began to talk and drink instead of listening. Powderly tried to hold them with generalities, but it was over.

At the next saloon, Steinhauer's, they found a predominantly German audience, but Powderly's speech was just as pointless and futile.

Without too much conversation, Powderly and Owen set out for Patagonia. As they left Steinhauer's, Powderly appeared bilious, but the cold winter air restored his color by the time they entered Billy Bevan's Three Bells pub in Patagonia. Owen felt that the night was already lost. He hoped that Powderly, here at Bevan's, would say something positive about the loyalty of Welsh coal miners, or their disdain of black-legs, or anything that would bond them. Even a serious labor speech, inappropriate as it seemed, would be better than the fiascos at McNally's and Steinhauer's.

Strange, Owen thought, that Powderly, who had a good sense of humor, could not or would not yield to the saloon men or atmosphere.

Only later, when he read Powderly's account of the visit to the Three Bells, could he understand. Powderly wrote:

I was in this saloon campaigning when this man approached me. When he talked, or tried to, he squirted liberal quantities of a mixture of beer and tobacco gravy into my face. His clothing, which was unclean, untidy, and unsanitary, looked as if it had been spread over him with a hay fork. I experienced a feeling of loathing, not because of what he said, what he did, or how he looked, but because he called himself a workingman and as such demanded of me to supply beer to him in exchange for his vote. I despised myself for placing it in his power to tender such an insulting offer to me by going there to meet him. Then I made one of my first public speeches in the mayoralty campaign of 1878. It wasn't very long and it won't bore you if I repeat it. I said: "You say I am not a politician; you are mistaken. I am a politician but not the kind you have been accustomed to meeting in such places as this. As a politician, I am a living protest against the beer-swilling, back-biting, hand-wringing, saloon-haunting practices of the old time politicians, and if the men of Scranton demand of me to do as the citizen-debauching politicians of the old parties have done in the past, I don't want to be your mayor; I'll stop running, and you may all go to hell." Of course consternation prevailed. I didn't wait to observe it, for I at once left the place and went home.

I had no supporters among the daily papers. A reporter for one of them overheard my speech and without quoting it all said my language was unfit to print and that "Powderly assured those who offered to vote for him that if elected they might go to hell." Editorially, I was roasted in about a half column of much sympathy for the honest workingmen I had wheedled into nominating me. It was pure demagoguery from end to end.

Having no great moral prop in the shape of a daily paper to lean on, I wrote a circular and had it given out all over the city. The campaign committee tried to choke me off but to no avail. Let me quote from that circular. "I did not want or seek the nomination for mayor. I accepted it not to do as others did before but to do the best I knew how to give Scranton an honest administration. I intend, if elected, to pay every citizen a full equivalent for voting for or against me by doing my duty as mayor fearlessly, faithfully, and as well as I know how. I intend to remain sober all the time so that I shall know what I am doing. No man, whether he votes for or against me, has any right to expect more than that from me.

My work has been and shall be a protest against the practices which reduced that man to, and below, the level of a common beggar. Capable of earning good wages, at his trade (he was a stone mason), he practically offered his vote to me for beer. I can find no language severe enough to properly characterize the habit men have fallen into of going to saloons to offer their ballots, our ballots, in exchange for a drink of beer, rum or a cigar. The right to vote was won for us on many a hard-fought field by our revolutionary fathers and should be held so sacred that conscience alone should direct its course. It should be cast for the man or principles, or both, that appear best for all the people. If you think I am that man and represent such principles, vote for me. Whether you vote for me or not, do not ask me to solicit votes in exchange for beer, rum or vile cigars.

"I am sorry I told that man to go to hell, not so much on his account as my own. I became indignant at the sight of a man with marks of labor on his calloused hands degrading himself and asking me to become a party to his degradation. Perhaps I should have said something else to bring him to a true realization of what he, and those congregated there, were doing to make themselves slaves to liquor and political boss rule. If I pay for a vote in beer or cigars, the man I buy from has no further claim on me. I intend that every citizen of Scranton shall have the right to come to me and demand of me to set the name of Scranton right before the country. I'll do that if elected, but I shall not go to another saloon to buy votes or debauch voters."

Owen understood Powderly's convictions. But he knew from witnessing the meeting that Powderly came off as pompous and self-righteous. So there were no saloon political rallies after that.

For the most part, Owen and Powderly divided their

engagements, each working separately. Once or twice a week, they would compare notes and confer.

One night in Green Ridge, Owen addressed a large middle-class gathering. The audience was skeptical—for the previous week they had heard Powderly viciously condemned in the Scranton *Republican* as a socialist saboteur, one who would destroy the American worker and workmanship. Owen, remembering Powderly's pride in the workmanship of a good mechanic, answered the charge by telling the audience a story Powderly had told him, accenting the responsibilities of a worker.

Owen recalled that 1876 was the year of the great Centennial Exposition in Philadelphia. For that great exposition, the Dickson Manufacturing Company built three locomotives at the Cliff Locomotive Works. One was a small mine engine, the second a large freight one, and a third, a beautiful large locomotive designed for pulling passenger cars. Picked to start and put the finishing touches on these engines was the best mechanic in the shops, Terence Powderly.

Owen described the loving attention Powderly gave his job. Thrilled to be chosen for the task, Powderly worked from December 1875 to June 1876 to make the machines mechanical, functional beauties. He worked many nights to complete tasks started in early morning. Never once did he ask for overtime pay. To Powderly, the labor was a labor of love. He felt these engines were his very own. "He polished the guides and rods with the cushion of his right hand." And when the engines won a prize at the exposition, he felt as though he personally had won.

And then Owen attacked the problem of the responsibility of workingmen head-on, a problem that would crop up perennially for generations. He said, "I would like to read to you what Mr. Powderly has written about the obligation of a working man."

During my Knights of Labor days, I struggled to get fewer hours of toil and larger pay for workmen. I think I was right in doing that. If I am correctly informed, you men think it is right to do as little in the short-hour day as possible while contending for still higher pay. I am told that workingmen think it right to "loaf on the job" now in order to curtail production. I have also been informed—and by workingmen too—that to slight the work, to turn out the inferior in order to have it wear out or give out quickly, is not regarded as reprehensible. I hope I have been misinformed, but if not, let me say to you as earnestly and as emphatically as I know how, that the workingman who resorts to such practices is as guilty of theft as if he put his hand in the pocket of his employer and took therefrom in money the equivalent of the time he steals. He is a double thief, for in turning out the inferior in workmanship he helps to rob the consuming public which embraces workingmen and women, as well as others.

I am somewhat conversant with the history of labor and know that laboring men and women were treated as slaves, as beasts, for centuries and that many old-time employers were heartless oppressors . . .

I have heard workingmen say: "Well they robbed us once, now it is our turn to rob them." No, men, it is not your turn to rob now or at any other time. It was wrong for the old-time employer to degrade, oppress, and rob your fathers, and it cannot be right for you to rob or oppress anyone.

Besides, you owe a duty to yourselves, you owe it to your children to let them look upon the face of an honest man when you enter your home, and you cannot do that if you purposely slight your work. The work you do is part of yourself, you should do it well and as faithfully as you know how.

The audience at Green Ridge responded with friendly questions, ending the newspaper charges of "socialist saboteur."

In another campaign appearance, Owen, addressing a rambunctious political rally in the hill section, found himself caught in the middle of an Irish problem. While Powderly's power lay in the presence of thousands of Knights of Labor in Scranton, he had won the loyalty of thousands of Irish immigrants by his strong support in raising eighty-seven thousand dollars for the defense of an American, Captain Edward O'Meagher Condon. Condon was born in Cork in 1835, came to the United States and served bravely for the Union Army in the Civil War. After the Civil War, he went back to Ireland on a visit as a representative of the Fenian Brotherhood, formed to win Ireland's freedom from England. There he was arrested for his activities.

When Owen started to detail Powderly's Irish sympathies, spiteful remarks echoed across the room. Then a booming voice exploded:

"What does a cheese-eat'n Welshman know about Ireland?"

Owen held his composure and answered, "There's no doubt I'm a cheese-eater. I love it. My favorite cheese comes from Castlebar in Mayo."

"Mayo, God Bless Us!" rang out from five young huskies in the rear of the hall.

"Furthermore," Owen replied, "if anyone knows English landlords, it's the Welsh. There's a body of water between the Irish and English, but we have no water to keep them out. We have them right on our backs."

The crowd began to listen, and Owen renewed his reply to the Irish question.

"It may come as a surprise to you," Owen explained, "but the poor Welsh land-renters have the same problem as the Irish. The rural Welsh have the same hopes as people in Michael Davitt's Land League. The Welsh poor have protested just like the Irish poor. The Welsh have their Tom Ellis, the Irish have their Michael Davitt. One of the strongest protestors in Wales is the Reverend E. Pan Jones of Mostyn. He follows our American Henry George, demanding the large landowners be taxed on land."

A thoughtful older Irish immigrant stood and quietly inquired, "Is there a Welsh movement then to win political freedom for Wales? And if there is, can Ireland and Wales join together?"

"I'm afraid not," Owen explained. "Ireland wants political

separation. The Welsh want religious separation. You see, the Welsh pay a tithe to the Church of England, the Episcopal Church. They hate it because they are Congregationalists, Methodists, Baptists, and Quakers. Now the government did pass a law making the landlords pay a tax, but that was just a trick. The landlords pass the tithe on to the poor, and they still pay the tax to the English Anglican Church, but they pay it indirectly."

Several questions followed that revealed Owen's knowledge of the land question in Ireland. Then a man to whom this question was paramount asked, "If Powderly becomes mayor, will he quit his support to Ireland? I know he has helped raise thousands of dollars. Even as a boy, he tells how he emptied his savings cup for Ireland . . ."

Before the speaker could finish his thought, a man in his working clothes having come directly from the iron mill, jumped up and loudly proclaimed, "That's right, that's right. I saw him do it. It was at a meeting we held in Carbondale. I saw this boy, no more than twelve, come in the meeting and put five dollars in the collection we were raising for Ireland's freedom. Joe Mulhern who was conducting the meeting, grabbed him and asked 'What's your name?'

"'Terence Powderly,' the boy said.

"'And tell me, Terence, where did you get the money?' Mulhern asked.

"'From me own savin's,' said the boy.

"'And why would a boy your size want to give away his own five dollars?'

"'Because,' said Terence, 'I was passing by, overheard the man speaking, and I listened. When I heard of them poor

Irish and the cruel English, I wanted to help. So I went to me home, emptied me tins and brought 'em here.'

"'And are you sure your parents won't punish you?'

"'Punish me? Of course not. They love Ireland more 'n me.'"

The man in working clothes ended his story with, "That's the true story. I was there."

"Thank you," said the Irish patriot, slightly annoyed that he had been interrupted. He countered, "But what I'm getting at is this. If Powderly is mayor of Scranton, Ireland will be forgotten. He won't have the time to give to the cause."

Owen took time to recall Powderly's work for the Irish Cause, his support of the movement to free the American-born Captain Edward Condon from prison. Condon had been condemned to life imprisonment for participating in a raid on Manchester, a raid designed to free two Irish prisoners. Powderly and two others petitioned with twenty-one thousand signatures for Condon's release. The petition, with the help of Congressman Hendrick B. Wright of Wilkes-Barre, led to the release of Condon, who returned to the United States.

Owen ended his speech in Dunmore, speaking with fervor, promising the group that Terence Powderly as mayor of Scranton, could do much more for the cause than he could do as labor leader and private citizen. His promises came true as Powderly worked indefatigably for Irish Independence, once going so far as to invite Charles Parnell to appear in Scranton.

Owen was at once eager and, at the same time, hesitant to campaign in Providence, hesitant because these people of Providence had a strong independent history. The oldest section of Scranton, it was one of the original townships developed by the Susquehanna Company of Connecticut in northeast Pennsylvania. Ira Tripp, the proprietor of one thousand acres along the west bank of the Lackawanna River came as early as 1774. Twenty years later, the whole of Providence Township, which included Hyde Park, Slocum Hollow, and Dunmore, as well as Providence itself, was all a farming area containing only fifty-six taxable persons and their dependents. Of these sections, Providence grew fastest because it was on the main highway between Philadelphia and New York state. It was also on the main route between Carbondale and Wilkes-Barre. Consequently, by 1849, it became a borough with a population greater than the other areas. The borough was self-sufficient and independent.

In the meantime, the smallest area, Slocum Hollow, exploded in population when the Scranton family's coal and iron industry stimulated this neglected section. Leaders from the area took the initiative before the Pennsylvania legislature in 1866 and had a law passed creating the city of Scranton, uniting Providence borough and township, Hyde Park, and Scranton, the old Slocum Hollow. In short, the sleepy Slocum Hollow, later called Harrison, then re-christened Scranton, became the hub of the new consolidated city.

Everyone was happy except Providence. They protested. Their fight for independence went on for ten years claiming only fifteen residents wanted the jointure and that most of the citizens were hoodwinked by these fifteen. The Pennsylvania legislature sympathetically granted Providence the right to secede, but secession never took place.

When Owen arrived in Providence to campaign for Powderly as mayor, there was still a discontented minority in the audience. They figured the Scranton acquisition of Providence had cost Providence taxpayers over ninety-six thousand dollars. Others in the audience were pacified, since Scranton was now the third-largest city in the commonwealth, with close to forty thousand people. They enjoyed the distinction.

However, the dissatisfied and the contented were now joined together in one objective, and that was to break away from Luzerne County and to form their own county. They felt that there were enough people between Old Forge and the mid-valley, with Scranton as the hub, to make a new county called Lackawanna.

Owen addressed the group by pointing to the successes of Powderly in winning the political contest for the Luzerne County row offices. He argued that the same combination of leadership: Powderly, labor, and the Greenback Party could guarantee the creation of a new county with its seat in Scranton. Owen pointed out that since 1835 every previous attempt had been thwarted.

"Now," he pleaded, "is the time to bring this idea to full flower." Embarrassed within himself at his own oratory, he nevertheless continued to promise and plead.

A wiry Irishman spoke: "They tell me Powderly has control of the courthouse now and doesn't care whether the county seat is in Wilkes-Barre. Is that right?"

"No, it's not," Owen was aroused. "Powderly is the strongest man for Lackawanna County. He always was and will be. Powderly predicted in 1870 that the Lackawanna Valley would boom and Scranton would be greater than Wilkes-Barre. And today it is. He wants Lackawanna County more than anyone."

An older man slowly rose to his feet and warned, "Let's not be in a big hurry to ask for our own county. The bigger our county, the better for every taxpayer. More people to share the expenses . . ."

"No, No!" came a chorus. "We want our independence. We want our own county!"

A well-dressed Englishman from Taylor held up his hands. "Don't be carried away. The old man may be right. Furthermore, I'm from Taylor. I'd just as soon have the seat in Wilkes-Barre. Powderly might use his influence to put the seat in Carbondale or Dundaff. I don't think he will, but let's keep the county together and in Wilkes-Barre!"

"Sit down, we've heard all that bull before," was heard over the hall.

The Englishman did not sit down but persisted. "Listen, you're throwing our power away. Luzerne County is one great county with its population increasing every day. We have great strength in Harrisburg. If we divide, we're going to weaken our influence."

A negative roar revealed that few in the crowd shared the Englishman's opinion.

A young man got Owen's attention. His face and arms were marked with blue spots of imbedded coal, testifying to his fifteen years of mining, including one explosion and one roof fall. His precise speech revealed his self-education.

"We've deserved our own county now for several years. But I doubt we will ever get it. Why? Because those men in control want to keep control. Even if the state approved and we get the question on the ballot, we might not win. Look at what happened here. Providence did not want to be a part of Scranton. We wanted our own borough government. The state approved it. But we were taken into Scranton despite our own protest. What makes you think it will be different. What makes you think you can get a county when Tilden last year won the presidency and had it stolen by President Hayes's friends in Congress and on the Supreme Court. Listen, my friends, don't get your hopes up."

The meeting lasted an hour and a half. Owen answered every speaker who had a statement or question. He closed the evening with a strong statement for Powderly and for American democracy. He heard all the truths spoken, all the reservations, all the disillusionments, but nevertheless he had faith in Powderly and the system. At the end, he said,

"My friends, listen, please. Terence Powderly is an honest man. He has made a promise. When he is mayor, he will work to give us our own Lackawanna County. He has many reasons for wanting independence. He will never forget that justice was smothered when six persons died and twenty-six others were injured by bullets fired from guns which came out of the Lackawanna Iron and Coal Company store. He knows that if the trial were held in Scranton with a jury of workingmen hearing the case, justice would have prevailed.

"Furthermore, he knows that the tail cannot wag the dog. The Lackawanna Valley and Scranton are growing faster than the Wyoming Valley and Wilkes-Barre. It's just common sense."

The strength of Powderly among Welsh and other ethnic miners and laborers and his strong Irish support was overwhelming. His unorthodox campaigning was effective. Ignoring the saloon circuit was not damaging. His use of Owen and others in the labor movement intimidated the opposition.

The popularity of Powderly with labor and the Greenback Labor party frightened the Republicans and Democrats into an unprecedented action. They joined forces and nominated the Honorable Daniel M. Jones as the citizens' candidate. The Scranton newspapers immediately endorsed Jones to no avail. On February 19, 1878, Terence Powderly was elected. He became the fifth mayor of Scranton.

As Owen and his father analyzed the election, they realized that the Knights of Labor had carried the day for Powderly. The other results were less than triumphant. Two Greenback Labor candidates, Godfrey van Storch and Nicholas Kiefer, became treasurer and comptroller respectively. Both branches of the city council, the select and the common, were captured by large majorities by the Citizens' Party. Obviously, the tactic of the Democrats and Republicans in joining to form the Citizens' Party had kept the Greenback Labor Party from gaining control of the city council.

On election night, Owen, whose political and philosophical depression engendered by the riots of 1877 had been partially erased by the row-offices election, now exulted in exciting aspirations for Scranton with a pro-labor man as mayor.

Before going to bed on election night, Owen wrote a long letter to Rhondda expressing his jubilation over the election of Terence Powderly. He reported on the beer consumed by the joyous partisans and the calmness of Powderly who, instead of celebrating with the others, was content to share the victory with his friend Hughie Jennings, in Scranton.

Powderly insisted Owen accompany him. Owen's letter described the serious conversation they had as they walked to the Jennings home. The upshot was that Owen was to leave his employment with the knights to become the secretary to the Mayor. Owen saw the new position as an opportunity for him to see Rhondda each weekend and closed the letter on that positive note.

The conversation in which Powderly asked Owen to serve as his secretary took place as they both walked to the Jennings home.

"Owen," Powderly began, "your speeches did much to bring us our victory. The reports I received from Hyde Park, Green Ridge, and Providence were all very complimentary to you."

"It was the work you assigned me to do."

"I know it was, but you did it in a way justifying my hopes for you."

"Thank you, but I still haven't started my real work with the local union of the knights."

"And I don't think you will for a while. If you are willing, I would like you to come into the city government with me. How do you feel about that?"

"You once convinced me," said Owen, "that because of my years in mining, I could help in the union. But I have no knowledge of Scranton government."

"Neither do I, really," said Powderly. "As I said often, I have much to learn. You can too."

"Why exactly do you want me?"

"First of all, I need someone of ability to handle much of my contracts and correspondence. You have the temperament and writing ability. Your reading and intelligence are more important than precise qualifications."

"But how about the work we planned with the Knights of Labor?"

"That will have to wait until I take office and get the affairs of the city going smoothly. I have not forgotten the needs of the union. Later on you can do the job I designed for you. As a matter of fact, I am sure there will be time, especially in the evenings, for you to attend union meetings and give them help, especially in the Scranton area."

"Are you going to resign from your position in the knights now that you are mayor?"

"Indeed not. The city of Scranton will have my best efforts and attention. But the Knights of Labor, the union, is my consuming passion and life's work. I would not be mayor of Scranton tonight if it had not been for the Knights of Labor, but such an election may never happen again."

"What do you mean?"

"Uriah Stevens, our master workman, does not believe that the knights is a political party. It is a union. And the fact is he is right. I believe that, too. This election in Scranton and the one before it in the county were exceptional. We may never be involved again."

"How can labor achieve its goals without political action?" Owen asked.

"Labor can support any party that supports our issues. We should support the parties that stand with us. Union members belong to different parties. We don't want to coerce them, but we do educate them to know their friends. What

I'm saying is that even though we became involved with the Greenback Party and won, we should never do that again. The Greenback Party will not survive. The two main parties, Democrats and Republicans, still offer the best hope for progressive labor measures. We will have to work with them and support the party that supports us."

When they arrived at the home of Hughie Jennings, they were welcomed. The small gathering was a warm, congenial one. The conversation was thoughtful and responsible. Over a cup of tea, Powderly, Owen, and the Jennings family relaxed, talking primarily of the possible new county of Lackawanna, sprinkled with other topics and with anecdotes about recent Irish-British matters. It was hardly a victory celebration.

On their way from the Jennings home, Powderly reopened the question of Owen's work. "Talk to your parents, Owen, about my needing you in city government."

Owen, still unable to picture his job, said, "If I were to walk into your office tomorrow, I would not know the first thing I should do."

"Neither would I," said Powderly. "But we will walk in together. We'll take our place each day and confront the issues as they come to us. In the meantime, we will together go to the municipal building before we take office and gather all we can about ordinances, procedures, and obligations. Mayor McKune is not an enemy of ours. He was a good man doing the best he could. He will help us. Most of all, we'll help each other."

❧

CHAPTER 23

MAYOR POWDERLY

When Terence Powderly, with Owen Roderick as his
secretary, took office in April 1878, they were immediately absorbed in the creation of Lackawanna County. In
June, a legislative commission recommended to Governor
John F. Hartranft that organization be started. The governor
ordered a referendum on the question.

In July, a citizens' committee to promote a yes vote was
formed. They elected Mayor Terence Powderly as corresponding secretary.

As expected, over nine thousand voted for the new
county, only two thousand voted against it. Lackawanna
County, with Scranton as the county seat, became a dynamic
center of Northeastern Pennsylvania with a population of about
forty-three thousand. Wilkes-Barre, the former county seat,
had only about twenty thousand. The cities of Pittston and
Carbondale, which in 1850 had been four times the size of
Scranton, were still tiny cities of about seven thousand people.

After the overwhelming vote for the creation of Lackawanna County, Powderly called Owen into his office.

"Well, Owen, I remember the great meeting you had in
Providence when I ran, you implied strongly we would have
our own county. Did you expect it all to happen so quickly?"

"No, never," Owen said. "And did you ever think during the bloody summer of 1877 that only eight months later you would be mayor of the city?"

"No, I didn't. We lost almost every strike in the '70s, including the long strike of '75 and the riotous one of '77. But here we are. We must prove now that we can govern the city in a responsible way."

Owen, reflecting about the recent desperate months and the paroxysm within the community, confessed, "I was emotionally drained and morally defeated after the riot. You had a longer view than I."

Powderly smiled, "You see, Owen, it was experience. You are only twenty-one. I have lived all of twenty-nine years." They both laughed.

"And I thought the Scranton Iron and Coal Company would be running this town," Owen laughed.

"No, they are not," Powderly became serious. "But they are still our constituents. So is the DL&W Railroad. They have as much to say in Scranton as Mrs. Pat Murphy, but no more."

In the first days of office, Owen marvelled at Powderly's capacity for work. He frequently wrote forty letters a day. Every aspect of the city was his concern. He presided at police court with humor and dignity. He understood large issues but loved to know individual people. The economic development of Scranton was almost a fetish. He sent Owen to every civic and booster-club meeting in the county. Owen, in turn, delighted in the enthusiasm of the efforts. Powderly's physical and mental capacity for work was not restricted to his office. He became more involved than ever in Irish affairs. The

Knights of Labor, always first in his life, drew him more and more into national prominence. The national officers, recognizing his prestige as a large-city mayor, elected him grand master workman, succeeding Uriah Stephens, the founder, in 1879.

Terence Powderly, as mayor of Scranton, was conservative and impeccably honest. The epithets hurled at him before and during the campaign, explosive words like socialist, syndicalist, and anarchist were silenced.

He was on the job every day and conducted his interests in Ireland and the Knights of Labor through correspondence. However, when required by these concerns, he would travel great distances. With all his outside concerns, he dedicated his strongest efforts toward the improvement of the city of Scranton.

One day, three months into the new administration, Owen walked into Powderly's office and said, "These nights, I have been reading a book by an Englishman. His name is James Bryce, and he is intrigued by the American government system. He has much praise for our democracy. But do you know what he sees as our weakest unit of government?"

"Let me guess. I'd say Congress," said Powderly.

"Wrong. The cities," Owen said.

With a twinkle in his eye, Powderly said, "I hope he didn't mean Scranton."

"No, but he says flat out—and I copied this down—'Poor administration in American cities has become the one conspicuous failure in the United States.' "

"Well, I hope we are going to improve things in Scranton. The other cities will have to row their own boats."

"I think we are," Owen said. "But do you know the city was almost bankrupt when we came into office?"

"I should know. I was behind in my first paychecks a couple of times," Powderly complained.

"If we are going to be better than other cities, we need to make some important decisions," Owen said.

"Lay them before me," Powderly challenged quietly. "Not the details, but what we need to do to get our financial picture in order. How can we do it?"

"After reading Bryce, I listed the essential things we have to do. Number one, we've got to get the city debt down. We inherited some, but we are adding to it. Next, we have to increase our income."

Powderly interrupted, "You mean we have to raise taxes? The property owner is already overburdened."

"Well," Owen said, "we'll have to find another source. We just have to have more income."

"All right, we'll think about that. What else?" Powderly asked.

"If we get the debt down and find some new source of money, then we can make a budget for servicing the people better. We can go ahead with our board of health, food inspectors, and the other needs you and I have talked about."

From that day forward, Powderly and Owen Roderick had a mission. They did not accomplish the mission immediately. It took six years, three terms of office. Powderly was reelected in 1880 and again in 1882. He served as mayor of Scranton from 1878 to 1884.

During those years, the city of Scranton moved steadily forward. When Powderly took office, things were so bad that some city lights remained dark because the utility was unpaid. A court injunction forbade further borrowing and city debt. By 1884, Powderly had reduced the debt modestly.

Property owners screamed about inequitable assessments and free riders. Powderly compelled the city engineers to give accurate maps to the assessors showing new buildings and businesses. The city clerk and assessors closed many loopholes. With the population increasing rapidly, new income was added each year.

In 1881, a new tax, a license tax on all businesses, was created. A mercantile appraiser was hired to set the fees, based on volume of business.

During his administration, Powderly regulated contractors and utilities in their use of city streets. For a small fee, contractors could get permission to excavate, providing they made a substantial deposit to guarantee they would restore the pavement to its original state within a specified time. In addition, street-car companies were compelled to use flat rails, like those "used in Philadelphia." Other regulations stipulated the weight and types of pipes that might be laid within the city limits.

Ordinances were revised, clarified, and digested with appropriate indices.

During Powderly's tenure, the police department increased its manpower from twelve to sixteen. The volunteer fire departments were reorganized and disciplined according to city ordinances. The standards of the companies improved. The city benefited tremendously from these volunteer fire services.

In 1878, an ordinance creating the board of health and an

inspector of meats and food was signed. Following a mandate of the state, Scranton's sewage system was constructed. The city of Scranton, in a single action changed from a sprawling cesspool-oppressed, disease-endangered city to a healthy, waste-controlled municipality. Like the other cities of the nation, Scranton was moving toward the new century with city lighting, sewage disposal, paved streets, and city ordinances to design some semblance of order and growth. In other cities of the nation, it was a period rife with corruption between city officials, utilities, and contractors. In Scranton, the scene was different. Lincoln Steffens described Scranton under Powderly well in his book *The Shame of Cities:* "The puritanical, anti-saloon league, Irish labor leader could not be approached. No manipulator could risk Powderly's pen or oratory."

All in all, Terence Powderly's three terms as mayor of Scranton were most creditable. Owen felt very proud of what Powderly had done for Scranton. In a Labor Day address before three thousand people in the Mid-Valley, he concluded, "Terence Powderly as mayor of Scranton has shown that labor is responsible, that labor believes in good government, efficient government. Labor believes in serving people, giving them protection and service. Labor believes in sound business practices. Most of all, labor believes in industrial peace and stands ready always to settle all disputes in peaceful negotiation."

Owen, proud of the speech, sent a copy to Rhondda. Her reply was realistic: "Yes, a fine speech, but just a little too much salt of Irish blarney and too much pepper of Welsh *hwyl.*"

Owen's reply agreed: "Guilty . . . but seasoning is hard

to control when food is before you." And then realizing he had been carried away by his own words, he added his own self-criticism, "I'll have to remember the adjudicator, George Powell, admonishing that tenor from Mahanoy City last year. After awarding him the first prize, he deflated him, saying, 'But sir, remember . . . enthusiasm and embellishments are, like good seasoning, to be used with gourmet discretion.' "

CHAPTER 24

❧

A QUAKER MARRIAGE

In January 1879, Owen had written Rhondda describing his first year in the city government of Scranton. He summarized the achievements of the first year, the friends he had made, and the joy of helping to make Scranton a better place in which to live. He hailed the labor peace that prevailed. He confessed to his admiration for Terence Powderly, which grew with greater contact and familiarity.

Dear Rhondda:

My admiration for Mr. Powderly continues to grow . . . . In my case, familiarity does not breed contempt for Mr. Powderly; familiarity breeds respect and admiration for his character and for the breadth of his knowledge. I cannot believe that at seventeen years of age he could neither read nor write. However, it is not his learning that impresses me as much as his balanced judgments. For a man who has been in so much controversy, he remains kind and considerate to everyone. I am very happy to be working with him, so happy that there remains only one thing to fulfill my life at present. That is, of course, our wedding.

The year we allowed ourselves to get settled in our jobs is over. I am ready if you are. I know the children at the Chil-

*dren's Home are very dear to you, and, from my own memory,
I know how much they must love you and depend on you, but I
see in my mind's eye children who will love you even more (a
smaller number of course). I know from your last letter that,
generally speaking, you have been thinking about a late spring
or early summer wedding. My preference is for early April.
Let us plan to meet this coming weekend to make specific plans.
I believe an early April date will still enable you to remain at
the Home to complete the school year and help the staff there
prepare for next year.*

> *With much love,*
> *Owen*

The next weekend, Owen took the DL&W train, alighted
in Kingston, and walked across the Susquehanna River bridge
to Wilkes-Barre where he met Rhondda. During their weekend
together, they decided to be married at the Old Friends' Meeting House on Montgomery Avenue in Merion, a suburb of
Philadelphia. Their admiration for Reverend Williams had
not lessened, but they gave up the idea of his marrying them
only because of Owen's growing admiration for the teachings
of the Friends.

The meeting house they chose had first been built of
logs in 1683 then rebuilt of stone in 1695. The old structure
was at a convenient location in the late seventeenth and early
eighteenth centuries. The Welsh Friends living in what was
called the Welsh Tract or Welsh Barony were settled in
Merion, Haverford, Radnor, Libertyville, Bryn Mawr, and

Gulph Mills. Montgomery Avenue was once known as Lancaster Road, and earlier was identified as the Conestoga Road. The Welsh Quakers who built the meeting house had purchased the large tract of land on the western side of the Schuylkill River from William Penn and settled there in 1682.

Despite Owen's love of learning, he knew very few specific details of the practices of the Friends. From Rhondda, he knew the pacifism and dedicated services of the Friends over the world. He knew very little of the discipline of the Quakers. Nor did he know the complete history of the great movement.

Over the weekend, Rhondda described for Owen some of the history of the movement. Owen was surprised to hear that the birth and growth of the Quaker movement paralleled that of other religions. First, there was the creative stage when they brought to the world their promise that life spent seeking and following divine revelation was exhilarating and productive for both society and the individual. The next stage, from the beginning of the eighteenth century to mid-century, was one of lost enthusiasm and containment. Like many other great movements, it succumbed to routine ritual. Rhondda compared the change in Quakerism to the change that occurred in the early days of Christianity and the changes which took place among the followers of Luther and Calvin after their deaths.

Rhondda pointed out that from her own reading, ideas and truths discovered by others never drove persons as did their own discovery. Nevertheless, even as Quakers moved

into the second stage, Rhondda pointed out, there were individuals who continued to be creative in the applications of its
principles.

"You know," Rhondda stated, "Quakers are mystics. You
find what Quakers do by studying their lives, not by studying
their history. You see a quiet inward force moving individuals
to do something." Quoting a Quaker writer, she added, "Mysti-
cal religion is elusive, hard to catch."

Owen, who was fascinated by Rhondda's explanation,
asked, "Do you mind if I say that despite my great admiration
and conviction that I want to be a Quaker, I . . . well . . . I
find the whole worship service . . . I hate to say it, uninspir-
ing, even . . . dull."

"Don't be afraid to say dull. Of course, you are right. Compared to the rich, emotional, musical services you have experienced, it is often dull. But what happens after the service is
what counts. If you find Quaker services dull, you are in good
company. One of our most honored figures, John Griffiths,
born in Wales, who came to Pennsylvania as a boy, complained
often that dullness and lethargy abounded. He said meetings
were often 'heavy and painful.' Yet, John Griffiths was a typical
Quaker saint, a quiet, child-like man risking peril on many
seas to serve as a Friend. Once, captured by pirates, he endured harsh imprisonment and used the experience to display
his convictions and service to others.

"As for myself," Rhondda continued, "I can enjoy an Episcopal or Presbyterian service or, especially, a beautiful, quiet
Catholic Mass accompanied by the music of medieval masters.
And by the way, at some point in Quaker history, there were
those who found spiritual strength in music and dancing, as

well. But, conditioned as I am, I must revert to the quiet of my own inner light, seeking answers and responses. For me, the piety and emotion of a church experience pales when I recall the holy experiences I have had in the quiet moments at Friends' meetings. Those words, 'inner light,' describe an explosive incandescence, not a boring, meaningless phrase."

Owen responded, "But reliance on an inner light can be shallow and seductive sometimes, don't you think?"

"Inner light is personal, never meant as a specific insight into theological or social answers," Rhondda explained. "But the Quaker movement has not been free of controversy. Many Quaker writers have argued that the scriptures are fundamental. Inner light cannot exist in a vacuum."

"Where did the whole Quaker idea of quietism come from?" Owen asked.

"I don't know, but it is not just a Quaker concept. Some things I have read point to the influence of the Catholic saints of the sixteenth century, Loyola and the Jesuits, St. John of the Cross, St. Teresa, St. Vincent de Paul. Thomas à Kempis earlier used the language often used by Quakers for contemplation."

"Well, I see I have a lot to learn. And I want to very much because I know no other group has done more for freedom, peace, and justice in the world than the Friends."

"You're right, Owen, but still . . . remember . . . Quakers are human beings, and even though they are more aware of their own weaknesses than others, they have differed through the centuries. They have failed to live up to their own precepts and they have often differed in interpretations."

"Yes, I understand, but through it all, their history is one I admire; their principles are mine."

"Well, if you are willing to say that before a regular meeting, then I'm sure we can be married."

"Of course, we will, why do you say that?"

"Well, we have been discussing some of the major religious views of Quakers. Now it's time to note that the Quakers have some memorable customs. One of them is very specific about marriage. And since we are to have a Quaker wedding, we need to discuss it."

Rhondda continued, "First of all, the marriage ceremony itself has not changed much through the years. We must announce our intention to marry, and my parents must declare their consent. The meeting will have two men and two women who will investigate to determine if you and I are free from any other courtships or marriage engagements."

"I'm free myself, but how about you, Rhondda?"

"Me, why do you say that?"

"You know, they may discover Mr. Barr."

"Oh, go on with you, Owen, be serious," And then, appreciating his teasing, she picked it up and said, "If any problem develops, it will be you."

"Never."

"You are really not a Quaker, you know. And the custom is to discourage outside marriages."

"But I thought . . ."

"Of course, now it is you who is becoming too serious," Rhondda said. "You shall be a stronger Quaker than any of us."

"Fine. In the meantime, between now and the spring, I must use my money carefully so that we can treat our families to a Philadelphia celebration."

"I'm sorry, Owen, but that will have to wait until we get

back to Scranton. Costly entertainment and sumptuous dining is frowned upon. The Quakers believe money spent fool-
ishly might better be used to relieve suffering or poverty.
And incidentally, Owen, do not buy a ring," Rhondda continued. "Quakers, we, you and I, do not use rings."

On April 8, 1879, Owen and Rhondda were married in
the Merion Meeting House. The marriage took place after a
regular weekday meeting. They both stood, and taking each
other by the hand, they made a declaration.

Owen, speaking first, said:

*Friends, I take this, my friend, Rhondda Hall, to be my wife,
promising through divine assistance to be unto her a loving
and faithful husband until it shall please the Lord by death to
separate us.*

Rhondda, holding Owen's hand, said:

*Friends, I take this, my friend, Owen Roderick, to be my hus-
band, promising through divine assistance to be unto him a
loving and faithful wife until it shall please the Lord by death
to separate us.*

They both then signed a certificate, as did witnesses.
They were apprised through the *Book of Christian Discipline* of
their obligations to each other.

*. . . that such friends as have with serious advice, due delib-
eration and free and mutual consent, absolutely agree, espoused
or contracted upon the account of marriage, shall not be al-*

lowed, or owned amongst us, in any unfaithfulness or injustice one to another, to break or violate any such contract or engagement: which is to the reproach of truth or injury one to another. And where any such injury breach or violation of such solemn contract is known or violation of such solemn contract is known or complained of . . . we advise and counsel that a few faithful friends, both men and women, in their respective meetings to which the parties belong, be appointed to inquire into the cause thereof, and to report to a succeeding monthly meeting the result of their inquiry, that it may use its discretion as to the due exercise of the discipline of the case.

After the brief ceremony was over, there was no other ceremony or celebration. The only visible demonstration was found in the faces and character of Rhondda and Owen, whose features reflected the triumphant elation of two bonded Friends.

For Owen, there was the excitement of a boy who had been in love with a woman since childhood. His adoration was physical and spiritual. His admiration was for her learning and inspiration. That he was to have her near him always, to live with her, to join with her, to have children and a family together was the highest exultation.

For Rhondda, the child she had adored had become the fascinating inquisitive boy and then, spontaneously, became a strong man, driven by honesty and ideals to work for his fellow man. This hard-working laborer through his own initiative, his own reading and study, could speak, write, and lead. She found in him a real friend with acres of common ground they could live on and with whom she was ready to build a life and change the world.

Rhondda and Owen remained with Rhondda's parents for three days. Their honeymoon was spent sightseeing in the area. A pleasant day was spent walking the campuses at Haverford and Swarthmore. The beautiful grounds, now touched by the first green of spring, welcomed the two walkers in the springtime of their lives.

On the second day, they visited Penn's Landing and recalled the landing of the Welsh Quakers there in 1682. Finally, they visited Independence Hall and walked the narrow streets, the first laid out in old Philadelphia.

Fulfilling their earliest honeymoon plans, they stopped for one night in Mauch Chunk, the home of Rhondda's father's friend, Asa Packer. The mountain-locked town that Owen and Rhondda saw was not much different from the Mauch Chunk of the Civil War period. Its population of five thousand or less had been stagnant since 1860. The expansion of population as well as industry was thwarted by the beautiful but cruelly impinging mountains. Rhondda's father was once invited by Asa Packer to locate his iron company in Mauch Chunk. Mr. Hall remembered, perhaps, that Welshman David Thomas of the Ynyscedwen Iron Works of South Wales had rejected Mauch Chunk as a site, and chose Catasauqua near Allentown instead. The mountainous terrain may have discouraged Rhondda's father as well. But the very feature of Mauch Chunk inhibiting industry and growth gave it the charm the honeymooners expected. The Lehigh River, winding through the scenic mountains viewed from the high lookout above the town, captured their emotions.

When they returned home, Rhondda finished her employment at the Children's Home in Wilkes-Barre, and Owen returned to his office in Scranton. In June, Owen and Rhondda purchased a small house in Hyde Park, not far from the Rodericks, and began their life together there. They obtained a mortgage from the Workingman's Building and Loan Society of Hyde Park, which had been chartered in 1869. Their house cost six hundred dollars. Their mortgage payments were eleven dollars a month, principal and interest included. They were proud of their new home, one of hundreds being built in Scranton, most of them company houses built to rent for six to twelve dollars a month.

ða

WOMEN AND ETHNICITY

O wen and Rhondda bought their first furniture on an installment plan, paying fifty cents a week. For Owen, who had lived through adolescence with his mind and emotions fixed in fantasy on the Rhondda of his dreams, the reality was joyous. For Rhondda, who had migrated to Avondale as a seventeen-year-old and spent most of the past decade teaching, first in Avondale then at the children's home, the change was exhilarating. Not only were they excited about their adventure together, but they shared a love for the people and community of Scranton. Specifically, they loved Hyde Park. This close-knit section—with street after street of compact houses occupied by miners, ironworkers, and their families, alive with common goals and problems, filled with strong religious influence, and redolent of their joys, sadness, tragedy, triumphs, and a strong strain of humor—was exactly where they wanted to live.

No one was more pleased to have the young couple in Scranton than Terence Powderly. He immediately recognized the ability and charismatic presence of Rhondda, and he quickly included her in his administration by giving her the opportunity to extend his strong belief in the recognition of women's rights.

During Rhondda's first year in Scranton, Powderly invited one of the proponents of women's rights to speak in Scranton. He gave Frances H. Willard a platform from which to speak and then initiated her into the Knights of Labor. Rhondda had the task of accompanying her during her visit. Like Frances Willard and Terence Powderly, Rhondda saw the devastating effect of alcohol on many working-class families. Although Frances Willard was president of the Women's Christian Temperance Union, her talk was far from just a prohibitionist speech. Rhondda thrilled to her appeal for kindergartens in the public schools and for the elimination of child labor. Rhondda was more than aware that every morning children, boys eight and nine years old, were trekking to coal breakers all over the anthracite area. She keenly remembered Owen leaving her classroom to go into the Avondale breaker.

Frances Willard called for "the enthronment of Christ in the world." In her broad ecumenical plea, she called upon Protestants, Jews, Catholics, and Unitarians to build a nation with a "protected home," the pulse of a redeemed America. In her address, she lashed out at "the love of money" as the rival of liquor, warping the great nation. The speech had evidently been delivered in many places at many times, and her audience accepted it wholeheartedly up to the point where she began attacking money and business. At that point, many began to disagree.

❧   ❧   ❧

As the Knights of Labor grew larger and larger, Terence Powderly was spending more and more time away from Scranton. After these trips, he often visited Rhondda and

Owen to bring them up to date on his contacts. He spoke frequently with Susan B. Anthony and Elizabeth Cady Stanton. Rhondda became more and more aware of women in America. Her own reading told her about the new colleges just for women, Smith College founded in 1875 and Wellesly College the same year. She liked "the simple living and high thinking" of Smith College founded with a bequest from Sophia Smith. She pondered the earlier founding of Vassar by the English brewer, Matthew Vassar, and puzzled over it, since she did not quite understand that kind of philanthropy.

Rhondda began to read all she could on the disintegration of the American home. Brought up in a strong, confident Quaker home, she was eager that their home be as solid and as happy as her family's. Her reading told her that both homes and male–female relationships were undergoing vast changes. The pulpits of the great cities in the eighties were ringing with calls for preservation of the home, or, on the other hand, calls for the dismantling of their contradictions, hypocrisies, and barbarisms.

While conservative voices pleaded for the old-time "true family life," progressive women who analyzed these matters described housewives as nervous dyspeptics yearning for affection.

Some writers described the American home as a place where men and women lived in "suppressed madness." One woman writer wrote "All the fervent discussion of present day woman only proves that there is something wholly wrong with her as she is. . . . It can never be set right until she is released from the tutelage she is so fast outgrowing, and led by man to take her place at his side as an honored campanion and equal in every way."

When Rhondda read that paragraph she thought, "I'm glad I am." At the same time, she found some truth in the broad generalizations. Rhondda had read Catherine Beecher's book *The American Woman's Home.* The sister of Harriet Beecher Stowe had written the book the year of the Avondale disaster. Rhondda, having read the book, was interested in a survey done by Catherine Beecher. The survey revealed a nation of sickly or delicate women, reporting headaches, coughs, chills, convulsions. The survey purported to be national, with city after city reflecting ineffectual, sickly, immobile women. In her own family, Catherine Beecher reported nine married sisters and sisters-in-law and fourteen married cousins, most of them "ailing, invalid or delicate."

As Rhondda read and tried to understand what was happening in America, she also found much sense in reading Jane Addams who observed that, "the mass of immigrant women coming into the nation had no choice but to work to keep body and soul together." As Rhondda saw the women of Avondale and Hyde Park, they were courageous, sacrificing, and devoted. In a new land, often separated from family and friends, they coveted neighbors of the same nation. They often found refuge in the sound of their national tongue, their own church and old customs. And yet, Rhondda thought, what do I really know of what is in their hearts? Nevertheless, their courage in surviving strikes, illness, accidents, and death was unchallengeable.

Half of the people in Scranton were immigrants. In the Hyde Park neighborhood, the percentage was even higher. The largest number were Welsh. The Irish were next; then came Germans, English, and Scots. Rhondda and Owen were entranced by the variety of accents and customs. The atmosphere was charged. The world had entered Hyde Park. Their ears became attuned to the tones and melodies of languages enabling them to spot a speaker's homeland from his first words.

Most of the Irish were bilingual, but some elderly women spoke only Irish. The Germans sprinkled their German with English words as they spoke their Pennsylvania Dutch. The Welsh from the soft-coal pits of South Wales either dropped their *h*s like some of their English neighbors ("'e can go to 'ell, mind!") or added an *h* ("It was a hawful haccident.") Both South Wales and England went to the mountains to pick "'uckleberries."

The North Walians clung to their Welsh longer than the South Walians who had been Anglicized by their English neighbors over a longer period. The Welsh from North Wales spoke more slowly in sing-song. If they were asked if they came from Bangor, they replied "Bangor, aye." North Walians started their answers to questions with "Well, now . . ." The South Walians were constantly amazed or nonplussed, using "Dear to goodness!" as a common expression.

The Welsh, both North and South, belonged to Congregational, Calvinist, Methodist, or Baptist churches. All sermons were in Welsh.

Regardless of nationality, the folklore and superstitions of Hyde Park were pervasive. Owen heard versions overlapping every national group. The Irish told of miners locked in and lost by cave-ins. Each night, the ghosts of the men could be heard tapping. The Welsh and Scots told the same tales.

Owen saw the German miners planting their gardens after

work in the early summer, always planting by "the signs." Tomatoes, beans, and radishes had right times for planting. Beans should never be planted during a waning moon. The Germans, with their dogs and hunting, their tall fishing stories, and their beer-drinking, were great entertainment.

Owen heard the Scots praise the Irish for the "best bury-ings" but criticize them for wasting money on funeral carriages. Once Owen heard of a family hiring one hundred forty rigs for their poor grandmother. Once he came upon a group of Irishmen sitting on a porch near a store defending their family from criticism from the Scots. Most in the group agreed that the Scots were the "tightest" race in the world. One Irishman disagreed, saying, "There's one thing tighter than a Scotchman and that's a free-spending Welshman." The Irishmen roared.

When Rhondda and Owen visited their neighbors in Welsh homes, they saw copies of a book *Ofergoelion-y Cymry* meaning *Superstitions of the Welsh* by Robert Ellis, the popular Baptist minister. The Reverend Ellis, whose sermon at the grave-site of the Avondale victims made him the most revered minister in Hyde Park, nevertheless had only a slight impact in destroy-ing superstition among his parish members.

The life of the Rodericks was for the most part saturated with Welsh culture. The Welsh brought with them from Wales their main source of entertainment and culture, the Eisteddfod, generally held at Christmas or New Year's and always on March first, St. David's Day. These Eisteddfodau featured compet-itive singing for individuals and choirs and competition in poetry writing and recitations.

Each Welsh church sponsored at least one Gymanfa Ganu during the year. These general hymn-singing gatherings brought out the Welsh in droves. For the older Rodericks, the Eisteddfodau and Gymanfa were life-sustaining. For Owen and Rhondda they were exciting recreation.

In June 1880, Owen, Rhondda, and most of their neighbors in Hyde Park were excited to be part of the Welsh National Eisteddfod held there on June 23 and 24. An article in the national publication, *Frank Leslie's Illustrated* newspaper, described the competition:

The Welsh National Eisteddvod was held at Hyde Park, near Scranton, Pa., on June 23rd and 24th. The opening exercises were attended by large audiences, no fewer than five thousand persons being present at the afternoon and evening sessions. Hyde Park, the scene of the great musical and literary tournament, was gay with banners and bunting, and all business in mines and stores was stopped at noon to give the masses an opportunity of attending and taking part in the festival. The mammoth pavilion erected for the Eisteddvod was gayly adorned with flags and flowers, while numerous mottoes adorned the walls and clustered around the extensive platform on which the exercises were held. The opening session was conducted by H. M. Edwards, of Scranton, and the exercises were preceded by a choice bit of favorite airs played by a full military band. The feature of the forenoon, however, was the choral competition on Handel's "Round about the Starry Throne," by four choirs, of about fifty voices each, namely the Bellevue, Taylorville, Fourth Ward and Wilkes-Barre Choirs. Carlyle Petersilea, of Boston, awarded the palm and the prize to the Taylorville Choir.

The conductor then invited Mrs. Davis, wife of David S. Davis, of the Philadelphia Custom House, on the platform, and she presented Reese Price, the conductor of the Taylorville choir, with the prize, a purse containing seventy five dollars in gold. For the metrical poem, in Welsh, the feature of which was its alliterative qualities, the adjudicator awarded the prize of twenty dollars in gold to Rev. G. H. Humphreys, A.M. of New York City. There were a number of competitors entered under noms de plume, that of Mr. Humphrey's being "Saroney," and the subject of the poem was "The Artist."

The afternoon session was presided over by Senator Horatio Gates Jones, of Philadelphia, Rev. Fred. Evans of Franklin, Pa., acting as conductor of the exercises. Senator Jones delivered a happy speech in which he claimed a pride in his Welsh lineage, and expressed his great pleasure at meeting such a vast and intellectual gathering of his kinsmen. Bardic addresses, in which several participated, came next, followed by competitive English speeches on the subject of "National Characteristics of the Welsh People." The prize was awarded to John E. Richards of Hyde Park. Miss Lizzie Harris, of Hyde Park, took the prize for a Welsh recitation, "The Drowning of a Pharoah," participated in by a large number, and Benjamin Thomas, of Taylorsville, a miner who had been working all the forenoon in the mines, took the prize of forty dollars for an essay, entitled, "The Influence of the Greatest Scientific Discovery on Theology." Miss Josephine Rogers won the prize for a soprano solo.

The feature of the afternoon was the

band competition for a prize of one hundred dollars, offered for the best rendition of "The Heavens are Telling." Four organizations competed and the prize was awarded to to Bauer's Band, of Hyde Park. Dudley Buck then led the four bands of one hundred pieces, and elicited great enthusiasm in the performance of the prize piece. The pavilion was again crowded in the evening and many were unable to gain admittance. The united choir of 300 voices rang "Yr Haf" ("The Summer") with fine effect, and George Simpson, the well-known New York tenor, gave a recitative and air from "The Creation"; also Brahms's ballad, "The Anchor's Weighed," and was enthusiastically received. Carlyle Petersilea, of Boston, and Dudley Buck and J. Parsons Price, of New York, also took part in the performance. The piano playing of Petersilea created perfect furore.

On the 24th the choral prizes were awarded. The No. 3, or the winning choir, is the Hyde Park Choral Society, and takes a prize of $300, while No. 2, or the Wilkes-Barre Choir, takes a second prize of $125. The proceeds of the Eisteddvod will be applied, by the Welsh Philosophical Society, to the founding of a free library in Hyde Park.

The Eisteddfod of 1880 was a highlight in the lives of Owen and Rhondda. Owen, like the later Welsh labor leader William Abraham, whose bardic name was Mabon, was a music fanatic. However, Owen never had Mabon's skills. In the midst of a hopelessly divided and violent miners' meeting, Mabon once suddenly started to sing a Welsh hymn. At first the miners stood in shock. Then slowly they started to join in the song. In minutes, a full-scale Gymanfa was in session. Four-part harmony swelled from miners who had been at each other's throats moments ago. After fifteen minutes of singing, the miners miraculously resolved their differences.

CHAPTER 26

ॐ

ANTHRACITE IN THE EIGHTIES

A s mayor of Scranton, Terence Powderly brought national attention to the city. His involvements in Irish freedom, women's rights, and above all, the Knights of Labor, made a Scranton by-line in New York and Philadelphia papers a weekly occurrence.

Under the presidency of Terence Powderly, the Knights of Labor, once a secret society of working men had become by 1885 a union of seven hundred thousand workers. The tremendous leap in membership from eighty thousand came from a labor victory in the wake of a strike of the Missouri Pacific Railroad, owned by the notorious Jay Gould. The knights, who represented most of the workers on the railroad protesting a cut in wages, called the strike. The strikers won the support of the governors of Missouri and Kansas. Through the intervention of these executives, the knights won the strike. The victory brought new members into the union by the thousands, fickle members (in the eyes of Powderly), as likely to leave the union as quickly as they had joined. His opinion was verified in the very next year when Martin Irons led a second strike against the Missouri Pacific, much against the advice of Powderly. The result was a disastrous defeat and the loss of thousands of unreliable union members.

These years, the last ones of Powderly's Scranton administration and the years immediately following, were crucial for Powderly. His positions were attacked by both conservatives and extremists.

Returning to Scranton from Richmond, Virginia, where he had presided at a union assembly, he visited Rhondda and Owen, as he frequently did. After dinner, he sat praising their new home. "It's beautiful, Rhondda. You should be proud of your very own first home."

"Thank you, Mr. Powderly," Rhondda said, "but what we want to hear about is Richmond. We understand you were not made very welcome there."

"Oh, I was, I was! The red carpet was out, that is, until I introduced my good friend Frank Farrell to the audience. When his name appeared in the newspapers and on the program, I'm sure they all thought Frank was another Irishman from Scranton or New York. I introduced him saying, 'One of the objects of the knights is to abolish distinctions of color. I believe I present to you a man above the superstitions which are involved in these distinctions.' When Frank, who is a brilliant black leader, got up, I knew the unCivil War was not over. But that was not the worst. There was so much hatred in the papers the next day that I felt I had precipitated a racial riot. Fortunately, peace prevailed. I was able to get some of my thoughts in print. I pointed out that our union is committed to personal liberty and social equality.

"And I think I made a more telling argument by pointing out to the southern members of our union that cheap southern labor is a greater threat to them than the Chinese or any other competitive cheap labor. And I made a strong statement to the white people, too. Whether they heard it or believe it I can't say, but I said it to them and I believe it strongly. 'Southern labor, white and black, must learn to read and write.' Perhaps I feel so strongly about literacy because, as you may be tired of hearing, I know how illiteracy handicapped me until I was in my late teens. We send missionaries to Africa and Asia to help those people, but the missionaries can't do it because the people can't read. They don't even have a written language. Yet right here in our own country, with a great tradition of literature and language, there are millions who cannot read. We must change that. Anyway, that should answer your question about my reception in Richmond, Virginia. I don't suppose I will be invited back there for a while. And that's too bad. I've always admired Richmond, especially the Richmond of Jefferson Davis. The courage and conviction of the people in defending Richmond against all odds can never be equalled. Their cause could never be mine or yours, I'm sure. But courage, sacrifice, and convictions are always to be admired."

As the three relaxed over tea and dessert, Blodwen and John Roderick knocked gently on the door and walked in. Greetings, commotion, and warmth pervaded the dining room. Rhondda was quick to supply two more cups of tea and a plate of Welsh cookies. After some small-talk, John Roderick said, "Terence, you are taking the city of Scranton around the world. I hope someday people will know us and what we stand for."

"I'm sure they do already, John. If they burn anthracite coal, they know us and don't need me to tell them about Scranton."

"I disagree with you, Terry. I had a letter from a cousin

in Utica, New York, last week, and he said he's seen your name and Scranton in the paper oftener than the governor of New York."

"Another Welsh exaggeration, John, but thank you anyway."

"Mr. Powderly has just been telling us about his trip to Richmond," Rhondda announced.

"Yes, and I will let Rhondda and Owen give it to you second-hand because I was about to bring up something that all of us can help to decide, and that is Owen's future. And, of course, it is related to what we have been talking about. My duties as master workman of the Knights of Labor are national rather than local. I hope as we work to improve the lot of labor everywhere, the miners of Scranton will benefit. However, that cannot be taken for granted. Therefore, I want Owen to concentrate more and more on the anthracite coal miners. Production of anthracite goes up every year. Anthracite is going to be a major industry in this country, but it will be a troublesome one. The bigger the companies get, the less attention they give to the miners. So we must have more and more men like Owen to study the industry, to know about the companies, the railroads, and the bankers. Just a few years ago, getting a fair wage was an ordeal, and all we had to deal with was one company. Here in Scranton, it was the Lackawanna Iron and Coal."

Turning to Owen he said, "Owen, you should be talking here, not me. You've had your eyes on the industry, even as you worked for my administration. This is your idea as well as mine. Maybe more so."

"Yes," Owen said. "I've been trying to keep up with the growth of the anthracite. It is fascinating to me as it was to my grandfather and my father here. Ever since I was a boy working in the Avondale breaker, miners, their families, and these little coal boroughs have drawn me to them. Here in Scranton, we have a larger city, but it still is made up of small mining communities. And, of course, all around us are Minooka, Moosic, Jessup, Dickson City, Throop. Every borough along the Lackawanna or Susquehanna holds a bond for me. These towns and their people live and die with anthracite. Their living is not too comfortable and their dying comes much too soon. The mine owner does not come right out and say, 'I am going to enslave, cripple, and kill people.' He says, 'I will produce tons and tons of coal as cheaply as I can so that I can make my mine pay.' He does not consciously starve, maim, or kill. Starving, maiming, and killing are simply by-products. As mining expands, as the industry grows, the killing, maiming, and starving increase. As the industry grows and the corporation replaces the individual owner, the responsibility for the cruelty becomes more and more dispersed. In time, the miner and laborer and their families become no one's responsibility.

"When Mr. Powderly asks me to give more and more time to the anthracite industry, I am very happy, because I want to help end the irresponsibility. I want to care about mining families. Someone must care. The way the industry is developing, it won't be long before the ten largest railroads in the country—all controlled by one or two large banks—will own the whole anthracite industry. These monopolies will control the production, the prices, the freight rates, the pay rates—everything. The miner and his labor will be forgotten. He will be a lost statistic labeled labor supply. With the corporations importing millions of immigrants every year, these workers will become pawns played off against each other as the corporations seek cheaper and cheaper labor. Those of us who believe people and families deserve fair wages, safe working conditions, and fair play all around must not let these impersonal corporations ruin a great American industry. All that miners of the anthracite want are fair profits for the owners, fair wages for workers, and safer working conditions."

Owen's mother expressed her feelings in Welsh, saying "Chwara teg, Owen bach."

His father, trying to prove Owen's point, said, "Every year it gets harder and harder."

"Managing the food and the house is harder than it was when we lived at Avondale," his mother complained.

"And I'll tell you why," his father said. "Right before the Avondale disaster, I was getting $1.31 for a car of coal. Furthermore, because of our leader, John Siney, our wages were on a sliding scale. Our wages went up if the price of coal did. But we've lost the sliding scale. When I started to work at Briggs Shaft, the car rate had dropped to 83 cents a car. That drop from $1.31 to 83 cents was like getting hit with a rock fall. So we went on strike. When Ben Davis and Dan Jones were killed, everybody gave in. But we can't look back, can we?"

"No, we can't," Owen said. "This great anthracite industry has a tremendous future," Owen looked at his father. He knew that for almost a decade John Roderick had earned less and less as the industry grew. "But it can grow stronger and faster if the companies and railroads decide some basic questions. Are they going to be satisfied with a good profit after they have paid a good wage? Or are they going to ask for all the profit they can get by paying as little as they can give? They are going to have to decide what's more important, the wages of workers or dividends for stockholders. When bad times come, are the corporations going to do what the smaller owners always do, that is, cut wages right off? Or will they first cut dividends to their stockholders?"

Terence Powderly answered the question, "That will be one of your big jobs, Owen. You and other leaders of the miners, myself included, must show these leaders that a great anthracite industry can be built only on a fair labor policy. I hope, Owen, you make it your life's work."

"I hope so too, Owen," his father said, "because fairness is the big question. Not far behind is the safety of the miners. It's a tragedy that the same kinds of accidents that happened in Wales and England a hundred years ago are still happening here. Poor ventilation causes too many accidents. Worst of all is the idea that accidents have to happen in coal mining. When we have accidents, we just clean up the mess as fast as we can, and then we get back to production."

"Tell me," Rhondda inquired, "what are some of the things that can be done to cut the accidents?"

"Better ventilation for one thing," Owen said. "And better lighting."

"Rock dusting," said Powderly. "that is, driving the combustible matter from the dust."

"And don't forget," said John Roderick, "the main cause

for fear in the mines is explosions from gas. This gas comes from decomposition within a mine. Any open light or spark can set it off. This gas cannot be seen or smelled and it certainly is tasteless. But this fire damp—methane—is deadly. We must have inspections more often."

"We are putting a heavy load on your shoulder, Owen," said Powderly. "But the unions will have to lead the way for improvement in safety. We'll have to convince the state and the national government that they have a duty to protect lives. In time, the companies will have to obey the laws. The day will soon be here when we will have over one hundred thousand men working in the anthracite. Two hundred or more will be killed every year; another six hundred will be injured. Look ahead twenty-five to thirty years, we could see a thousand men out of one hundred fifty thousand killed every year."

"And that brings up another matter," Owen said. "How many of the survivors will die just a few years after they are too old to mine coal, racking and coughing their lives away from miners' asthma?"

"Aye," said Blodwen Roderick. "And that comes right home. Your own father frightens me some mornings with his coughing."

"Oh, go on," said John.

"Mind you, I won't go on. That cough frightens me!"

Eager to change the subject, John Roderick turned to Powderly and said, "Well, Terence, now that we have given Owen a coal-car load of problems for the future, how about you? What are your strongest hopes?"

"Well, I want Owen to work on the anthracite to give me time to work on problems within the Knights of Labor. I've served as mayor for six years, and I'm ready to move on. Anyway, I think the Democrats are strong enough to elect their own man and will not choose to support me. I believe they will elect Mr. Beamish, and that's fine with me.

"To get back to your question, there are two major problems facing the knights. First, there is the threat of anarchism and socialism. These two concepts are cancerous in the labor movement. Strange that I, who have been so often castigated as an anarchist must spend my time opposing anarchism. But the anarchist's use of conspiracy and violence is abhorrent to me. It is ironic, isn't it? However, I have come to learn that the number of anarchists in the labor movement is a small number, even if it is vocal and vengeful.

"As for socialists, I love many of them and believe in some of their objectives, but I do believe that our job in the labor movement is to reform democracy and make it work. In the long run, I do not see problems with the socialists.

"The second and most important challenge for me is within the ranks of labor. Many leaders, including Samuel Gompers of the cigar makers and many in our own Knights of Labor, are trying to get the miners into their own union, a union for miners only. I believe that is a weak step. I believe our concept of uniting any and all workers in a single union is the only way we will be strong enough to stand up to the large railroads, mine owners, and other corporations.

"Free of my duties as mayor, I will devote my next years to keeping the Knights of Labor free of anarchistic violence and keeping it as a strong industrial union, not a small craft body. And I will be able to do it with a free mind knowing that young men like Owen will give the anthracite miners good leadership."

CHAPTER 27

ॐ

THE BIRTH OF THE
UNITED MINE WORKERS

I n the winter of 1885–86, shortly after he ended his third
term as mayor of Scranton, Terence Powderly found himself caught up in the maelstrom of unrest in the United States.
All over the nation, bread lines and soup kitchens reflected
the high unemployment. In Chicago, a parade of the ragged
and impoverished, carrying anarchist signs, marched up Prairie
Avenue on Christmas Day. The parade went on unmolested,
even though John Bonfield, the chief of police, was considered
a brutal opponent of strikers or pickets. Not only Powderly,
but even the radical leader Mother Jones, opposed the parade,
believing such a display would frighten the industrialists and
businessmen and lead to violent suppression.

The unrest continued to grow. By May 1, 1886, Chicago
was in turmoil. A major strike was on at the McCormick Har-
vester Company. Pinkerton detectives, scabs, strikebreakers,
anarchists, socialists, capitalists, and every shade of editorial
writing inflamed the great Midwestern city.

Powderly, who had had trouble controlling a small ele-
ment of extremists in Scranton, now saw that the refusal of
the business community to grapple with the needs and demands of the poor was giving the violent anarchists the ammunition they sought.

Several labor rallies led to exchanges of gunfire between

strikers and policemen. A call for a meeting to be held May fourth at Haymarket Square was circulated. The purpose was to protest police brutality. The meeting was broken up by about two hundred policemen, but not before someone threw a bomb into their midst. One policeman was killed and sixty were injured. One man in the crowd of protestors was killed and twelve were hurt. "The event was the inevitable accidental result of the proximity of opposing forces," said one writer. However, the newspapers described the confrontation as a battle led by the anarchists, August Spies, A. R. Parsons, and Sam Freeler, "throwing a bomb and mowing men down like cattle." The *New York Tribune* said, "the mob seemed crazed with a frantic desire for blood." Another journal said the city was "at the mercy of long-haired, wild-eyed, bad-smelling, atheistic, reckless, foreign wretches who never did an honest day's work in their lives." Most of those participating in the rally were Germans, many recent immigrants. They bore heavy abuse.

When six more policemen died from injuries sustained in the bombing, the press—including the Knights of Labor's official organ—railed against the anarchists. A few newspapers pleaded both for severe judgments and for improvement of conditions which precipitated the violence. Thirty-one people were indicted as accessories and eight were accused of murder. Albert Parsons was the only native American among the indicted. In time, many public leaders expressed concern over the specific evidence, averring that no one knew who threw the bomb.

Terence Powderly said the bomb "did more injury to the

good name of labor than all the strikes of the year and turned public sentiment against labor organizations." He was right. The labor movement was weakened tremendously. More important, the bomb split labor because leaders like Samuel Gompers sided with world intellectuals like Bernard Shaw and William Morris, pleading for acquittal or mercy. Even fifty Chicago businessmen and bankers were on the verge of supporting clemency for the eight accused. They changed their minds when Marshall Field, Chicago's department store millionaire, opposed it.

Terence Powderly saw the Knights of Labor demoralized and split apart by Haymarket. Ever a foe of violence, Powderly appealed to the national convention of the Knights of Labor in 1886 to forget Haymarket, pleading that the monopoly of industry was the chief enemy of labor. Seeing the developments in the anthracite region, where New York railroads controlled by the banking wealth of Wall Street were creating an economic stranglehold, he flayed out, saying "anarchy is the legitimate child of monopoly. The true Knight of Labor clutches anarchy by the throat with one hand and with the other strangles monopoly." The speech was unconvincing to other labor leaders. The resulting debate was acrimonious. Powderly, presiding, ruled a motion to support the eight accused men was out of order. He was accused of being authoritarian. In the end, the convention opposed the execution of the eight defendants on the grounds that capital punishment was "barbarism."

Powderly was now master workman of a divided and unsettled union. After the convention, he wrote to Owen:

Dear Owen,

 The Haymarket bomb and the destructive antagonism of the anarchists have torn our union, but the Haymarket wounds will heal. The real threat to the life of the Knights of Labor is the new National Federation. Really, it is not new. It is the Miners' National revived. Until this week, I saw no threat from them. We are stronger in membership than ever. Our membership is far over a half million. We get more press mention than Congress. One paper predicted we will elect the next president. Remembering our Luzerne County and Scranton elections, we have moved up, haven't we?

 My concern this week arises out of the fact that William Lewis is deserting us. God forbid that we return to trade or craft unionism. Lewis, hearing of my concern, accuses me of interfering in his area. Because our union is open to all labor, he says the affairs of miners are being decided by shoe and clothing salesmen not miners. When I come to Wilkes-Barre for the National District 135 Convention in September, I shall sit down with you to resolve this matter.

       Fraternally yours,
       Terence Powderly.

 In the next months, the rivalry between the National Federation and the Knights of Labor became bitter. The national turned its money over to a new body, new in name only, called the National Progressive Union.

 When Powderly arrived in Wilkes-Barre for the September convention of National District Assembly 135, Owen met him. Drawing on his last years of experience, concentrated in the anthracite area, he took Powderly to the Hotel Hart where he convinced Powderly to change his mind and tactics for miners. He received Powderly's permission to speak before the gathered group.

The next day, Owen rose to the convention floor, and addressed the knights in the delegation. "Gentlemen," he said, "I rise to make a very important statement to you. I ask you to pay strict attention because it reflects the opinion of our general master workman, Terence Powderly. For the past two or three years, the coal mines of the anthracite region have labored under the usual hardships of coal mining. But in addition, they have had to bear the burden of bitter fighting between the new national federation and the knights. While this fighting has been going on, the coal operators and all those who oppose us have been laughing behind our backs. The time has come for the miners of America to unite. We have one opponent, the companies. And that is not of our choosing. We would rather cooperate, but they choose not to recognize us. The fighting between the national and knights must end. As Benjamin Franklin said, 'If we don't hang together, we will hang separately.'

"It's up to us here in the anthracite area. We must show our national leaders that the miners of America in Pennsylvania, West Virginia, Illinois, Colorado, wherever they are, must stand and help each other or coal miners everywhere will be choked, not by the dust of coal, but by their own short-sightedness and envy of each other.

"Now I do not know everything we must do to bring us together, but I do know we cannot get together unless we try. Therefore, I offer you this resolution—that we instruct our executive officers to call a meeting of *all organized or unorganized miners in the United States to plan one and only one consolidated union for all miners.* In the name of Terence Powderly, unity, and power, I move this resolution."

Without dissent, in acclamation, the resolution carried.

In a separate action, tired of the conflict and knowing of the knights' resolution, the National Progressive Union took similar action.

Both organizations met in Columbus, Ohio, in January, 1890 and agreed to amalgamate, stating, "This organization shall be known as the United Mine Workers of America, composed of National Trade Assembly 135, Knights of Labor, and the National Progressive Union." When the resolution passed, the delegates of both unions exploded in joyous celebration.

When Owen returned from Columbus, he sat down with Terence Powderly, full of enthusiasm about the future. The rivalry between the knights and the other miners' unions had depressed and annoyed him, and he was glad it was over. Powderly gave Owen much credit for the amalgamation. "I'm glad, Owen, you sat down with me in Wilkes-Barre and impressed upon me the need to end all the fighting. I'll have to admit, I believed industrial unionism would prevail. I thought that the miners would gain by being part of a gigantic union that contained thousands in other occupations, but you helped me see that the miners saw it differently. They were going to go their own way. The main thing you convinced me of was to end the fighting to form the United Mine Workers. When the history of labor is written, Wilkes-Barre, Pennsylvania, in

September 1889 may be forgotten. People will say that miners united in Columbus in January 1890, but your resolution in September at the District 135 meeting of the knights paved the way."

"No matter. There's really unity possible now," Owen said.

"That's right, Owen, but I'm glad you didn't say unity is here. There are dissenting and ambitious men. Furthermore, there are among us real differences in methods and tactics. So unity is possible, but it is not guaranteed."

To many, the jointure was one of desperation. The membership had slipped to seventeen thousand miners. Powderly's influence diminished, and finally, in 1893, he was defeated for national office in the Knights of Labor. ·

Perhaps the sad state of labor was due to the desperate American scene of 1893. The treasury of the United States had fallen below ninety million dollars, creating a panic. Grover Cleveland had returned to power, defeating Benjamin Harrison. The cool Harrison had lost valuable aides, including Pennsylvania's boss, Matt Quay. Quay didn't want the White House "iceberg" again. Harrison said that God, not Quay or the other politicians, elected him. Quay's reply was, "Let God reelect you then." Quay reportedly stormed out of the White House. Harrison was also hurt by the Homestead Steel Strike. Labor supported Cleveland, whose advocacy of gold and the repeal of the Silver Purchase Act was condemned as an unfair way to pay labor and farmers for their support.

During this economically depressed period, few sang a new song composed by Katheryn Lee Bates, called *America the Beautiful.* The nation's "alabaster cities" did not "gleam undimmed by human tears." The year 1893 was one of many heartbreaks. There were many tears.

In labor circles, it was especially tearful. The United Mine Workers was established, but the next ten years were difficult ones for the unions. Not until 1900 was the union to achieve its first great victory. Too, the Lehigh Valley, the great railroad, admired and used by so many in the anthracite region, fell from the Packer ownership and landed in the control of J. P. Morgan. When Asa Packer died, his nephew Elisha Wilbur took over. Asa Packer had pursued enlightened labor policies, founding one of the first railroad pension systems. Fighting the union, Wilbur hired scabs to run his railroad. The unskilled scabs caused one million dollars of damages and caused some loss of life. To save the railroad from bankruptcy, Wilbur borrowed from J. P. Morgan, who gradually took over the line. Elisha Wilbur resigned in four years. The great coal-carrying railroad controlling the collieries of the Lehigh Valley Coal Company was now part of an interlocking New York financial combine controlling the entire anthracite industry. Ten companies, most of them part of the J. P. Morgan Trust, owned 75.8 percent of all anthracite operations. Labor faced a most formidable foe.

CHAPTER 28

 ♥

MINING SUBSIDENCE

At five o'clock one morning, Owen and Rhondda were awakened by a thunderous explosive sound, like the roar of a tornado. They jumped out of bed and ran downstairs as their house reeled from the earthquake. Owen unlocked the front door but could not open it. The door was jammed tight. He ran to the back and found that door just as frozen. He ran to the cellar, but halfway down the stairs he had to stop. The cellar was a pool of water, and he could hear more gushing from a broken main. Returning to the living room, he saw that the front window was already shattered. He grabbed a chair and smashed out the shards of glass to make an opening through which he and Rhondda could escape. The street light revealed a gaping hole, fifteen feet wide, extending from his front porch across the sidewalk into the street. All up and down the street, their neighbors were emerging from their homes in night clothes, most of them carrying oil lamps. Owen and Rhondda, their initial panic over, realized at once that they had been hit by a massive surface caving, known throughout the region as mining subsidence.

In minutes, the whole area filled with people. By now, the sinking had ceased, and people were assessing the damages done to their houses and to those of their neighbors. The subsidence was centered near the Roderick's home. Up and down the street, the earth had moved like a wave, lifting the roadbed in some places ten feet high, as it heaved and dipped through the neighborhood.

Owen returned to the house by way of the window, found outerwear and shoes for them both, picked up some valuables, and returned to the street. He urged Rhondda to get to his parents' home as quickly as possible.

"Look, Rhondda, the subsidence is localized along our street. Get up to Mam and Dada's before they hear, and stay there. Tell them I'm all right. I'll stay and see if I can help along the street. We've got to get the water shut off and watch out for fires."

"I'd rather stay, but . . ."

"No, no," Owen interrupted, "I've been through this. There's nothing we can do now. It'll take weeks for us to get straightened out. Just assure Mam and Dada we're safe."

Such traumatic experiences were becoming more and more frequent among the people of the whole mining area. When anthracite was mined, precautions had to be taken to allow enough coal to remain as pillars to support the roof of the mine and the surface above. In addition, artificial supports in the mine were built as reinforcements for the surface. Unfortunately, these precautions were often neglected, for anthracite was mined as quickly and cheaply as possible. As a result, unsupported areas within a mine often sagged, shifted, or caved. This caused a man-made earthquake with two catastrophic results: Above ground, it destroyed land, houses, public buildings, and human life; underground, it isolated thousands of tons of unmined coal, removing it from the marketplace.

As Owen walked up and down his neighborhood, his first concern was injury to people. By now, the streets were filled with neighbors from blocks away, all eager to help. The key question on everyone's lips was: Is the coal company going to compensate the homeowners? Owen knew from his early morning trauma that the damage to his mortgaged home was extensive. When he assured himself that he could be of no help to others, he returned to the house, now sitting on the edge of the crater.

From his experience in city government, he knew that as early as 1871 the Pennsylvania Supreme Court ruled that a coal operator was liable for damages, confirming old English law. In the meantime, the large coal companies, owners of surface land as well as subsurface property, found a way to evade their responsibility. As they sold surface land above their mines, they inserted waivers in the deeds, known as "cut-throat waivers," which gave the new owners only surface rights, excluding mineral rights, and exempting the owner of the mineral rights from any liability resulting from extraction of the coal.

The Calvinistic Methodist Church in Hyde Park, damaged by a cave-in, took its case to the Pennsylvania Supreme Court. When the court found the church deed contained a cut-throat waiver, it found the waiver valid. The church could not recover damages. From then on in Scranton, the mine companies were free to mine without any responsibility. Time after time, destruction of homes, schools, streets, and hospitals was condoned. The will and welfare of people were sacrificed for the prosperity of the great new industry. As the corporations grew, they became bolder and bolder.

After inspecting the damage to their home, Owen resumed visiting with his affected neighbors. Wherever he went, he heard the same sentiments expressed. Thomas Lloyd, a particular friend of his father, cried out in disgust, "Owen, this has got to stop! These companies are not content to hold back a living wage. They won't even let us try to live. For another one hundred tons of coal, they'll ruin a city street and knock down every house on it.

"Come on next door, Owen, I want you to see what happened to Mrs. James's dining room."

Next door, they found Mrs. James, her eyes red from hours of crying, clutching and wringing a dish towel close to her face as she trembled. Her dining room was a shambles. A huge old Welsh grandfather's clock lay face down on the floor, its mechanism splayed beside it. A Welsh cupboard built by her aging husband was toppled also. The side wall of the room had a crack running from ceiling to floor, two inches in width. Plaster dust covered everything.

Owen could not lie to Mrs. James, but he did manage to say, "Don't worry, Mrs. James. We're going to help you."

As he said these words, he wondered why. He had implied that the coal company would be held accountable. He knew from experience that was impossible. Every city councilman or school director was beholden in some way to the companies. The company controlled jobs, appointments, promotions. Let some independent spirit speak out and the next day his brother and other relatives would be threatened with dismissal if their "big-mouth brother or cousin did not keep his mouth shut." The growth of the companies in the preceding years had been phenomenal, and their power and influence were found in the courts, legislative halls, and city councils. Furthermore, it was considered unpatriotic to attack this great industry which brought prosperity to Scranton. Heard time and time again was, "If the coal is to be mined, everyone must put up with inconveniences. Everyone must sacrifice something in a great coal community."

As Owen pondered the impasse, he looked back on Powderly's tenure as a miracle, free of coal company control. The coal economy had taken over once more and again dictated the economic and political life of Scranton completely.

Owen made his way to his parents' home at the end of a long day. There he found that Rhondda had been able to keep his parents from going to the subsidence area. But now his father was not to be contained any further.

"Owen," he said. "We must get down to your house to start to repair it. We must get that water out, and we must get the doors working and the windows fixed."

"There's much more than that to do, Dada. We'll have to shore some walls and do other major work. But not tonight. Are your working tomorrow?"

"No, we worked four days and there's no work until next Monday."

"Right, then—we'll start tomorrow. Perhaps Evan will come along and help us."

"Fine."

And then Owen collapsed into a chair saying, "We can fix the house in a couple of weeks. But there's a much bigger job."

"What do you mean?" his mother asked.

"If the union is the only possible way to win the rights of labor, then all of us in Hyde Park must join together the same way to stop surface subsidence." And then quickly arising from the chair, he said, "That's it. We'll organize the Hyde Park Surface Protectors. We'll raise money. We'll hire a lawyer. We'll go to court and we'll get an injunction to stop them from mining in a reckless manner. We'll make them liable just as they once were. Dada, quickly, where is your deed?"

"I'll get it."

Owen took it and quickly spotted the paragraph he sought. There at the end of the deed was the waiver of responsibility giving the company the mineral rights underneath the home and the right to mine without any liability.

"See this?" Owen said, pointing to the waiver. "Well, my deed has no such waiver. We must find out tomorrow for sure, but I believe every house on our street is free of these waivers."

The next morning, Owen, John, and Evan got an early start repairing the house. They worked from eight until eleven. At that point, Owen said, "Dada, I hope you and Evan can get along without me for a couple of hours. I'm going to check some deeds and invite my neighbors to a meeting."

For the next two hours, Owen checked almost every deed on the street. The renters promised to check with their landlords. The third house he visited was the home of Miss Mulhern, the principal of the No. 116 elementary school. Miss Mulhern lived with her parents. Like most teachers in

Scranton, she remained single to protect her position. When a female teacher married, she automatically lost her position. As Owen told her he planned to hold a meeting, Miss Mulhern said, "Why don't we meet tomorrow night in 116? The school is used by every other organization. If you wish, I'll call the superintendent. He will clear it with the board. You go ahead, check the deeds and get everyone there for 7:30 tomorrow night. I'll guarantee the auditorium will be available."

Miss Mulhern proved to be an exacting planner. The next evening, School 116 was open and over one hundred persons jammed the small auditorium.

Like most public meetings, it ranged from controlled to chaotic. It was easy to elicit incensed protest but more difficult to design specific legal procedure. Owen acted as self-appointed chairman, and Miss Mulhern acted as secretary. Both were drafted as permanent officers. John Burke was elected treasurer. These three became the executive committee along with Charles Schultz, Edward Phillips, and Howell Williams.

With so many miners in attendance, it was easy to figure out that the caving came from the Eton Colliery, now being mined by the Citizens Coal Company under a lease from the Delaware and Lackawanna Coal Company. The group decided to launch a fundraising effort in order to hire the best lawyer in the country to enjoin the Citizens Coal Company from mining so as to ruin the properties of the citizens. Funds came in from just about everyone in Hyde Park, from prosperous businessmen to the poorest families. They were all amazed when William Scranton himself presented a check for ten thousand dollars which guaranteed the hiring of a top lawyer. The committee retained a Philadelphia attorney who later became a United States senator.

William Scranton's gift stimulated almost as much discussion in the churches and taverns of Hyde Park as the subsidence itself. Why would a coal magnate make such a liberal contribution? Did he do it out of conscience or self-preservation? While he was reaping profits out of his sub-lease to Citizens, he was also owner of the Scranton Water Company whose right of way and piping were being constantly wrecked by surface subsidence. The cynical said, "What's ten thousand dollars to a man worth five million anyway?" Others said, "Bill Scranton has changed. He's no smark-aleck youngster. He's a mature, good citizen."

The court appearance was made quickly, but the committee's plea for an injunction was refused. The court said the company had a lease to mine and that the employment of too many men was at stake. "Mining coal," the court said, "is the industry of Scranton and it is, by its nature, dangerous both to the miner and the community. The industry must prevail for the good of the community as a whole."

Owen called a meeting of his executive committee for 3:30, just after school, at No. 116 in order to decide their next move. The denial of the injunction was a devastating defeat, and it was impossible to believe that the interest of the Hyde Park community could be sustained. Defeatism would permeate the area once again.

Miss Mulhern was standing at the doorway as the last of her charges left school for the day. Owen and the other committee members were walking into the building for the meeting. Suddenly, the building began to shake and crumble. The children who were on the steps near the sidewalk screamed and scattered in terror. Miss Mulhern automatically turned as if to return to her office. Owen grabbed her and pulled her along down the steps with the others. They caught up with some of the frightened children and tried to calm them. A few children, yards away, looked back, and returned to cling to Miss Mulhern. A huge broken water main fifty feet from the school entrance was spouting a geyser, spraying the buckling streets and sidewalks. The rank smell of a broken gas main saturated the area, a warning of fires or explosion.

A block away from the school, Miss Mulhern, Owen, and the others were able to calm the children and get them to walk directly to their homes. In the meantime, parents were running toward them to pick them up.

Believing that the subsidence had affected Main Street, they hurried to the central business area, where they found devastation everywhere. Doorways were jammed, windows were broken, and several buildings leaned crazily, neither as stable nor as picturesque as the Tower of Pisa. The street was filled with shoppers and clerks who had escaped during the subsidence. The air was filled with cries.

"Are you all right? Were you hurt?"

"Those bastards have to go. They'll blow up the whole town!"

"Where's the law? There's no law. Only the coal companies!"

In an hour, the area was filled with thousands of people from all over Lackawanna County.

"We could have had children killed!"

"Something has to be done right now!" was heard over and over.

The very next day, the school board and city council jointly petitioned the court and received an injunction. The public was so shocked and incensed by the collapse of the public school and the idea of the tragedy that would have occurred if the subsidence had taken place fifteen minutes earlier that the court could no longer evade its responsibility. The injunction did not stop mining, but it provided that mining was to be supervised to keep the companies from mining in prohibited areas. City engineers were to make monthly inspections underground. However, the court ruled the companies had to be given advance notice.

❧   ❧   ❧

The injunction helped—up to a point—and the number and severity of subsidences began to diminish. Corruption was widespread, however, and many operators remained on the windy side of the law by making payoffs in the right quarters. The most outrageous offender was clearly the Citizens Coal Company, which was suspected of using every ruse and every form of duplicity in the book to evade its responsibility and haul coal out regardless of damage to life or property.

The requirement that companies be given advance notice of inspections, of course, gave the owners of Citizens plenty of time to make sure the inspectors saw only what they were supposed to see. Owen Roderick became convinced the inspectors were being duped, and his efforts to do something about this led to an event that would go down in Hyde Park history as the Battle of Eton Colliery.

Eton was one of the dubious Citizens' operations where city inspectors could not achieve a proper inspection. Owen, along with his father and State Senator Davis, decided to get into the mine to find out how Citizens Coal was still disobeying the law. Owen and his father knew there was an abandoned air slope near the Taylor line. The slope was long, but they had worked at Briggs with men who knew Eton, and they learned that it led back to the Citizens' operation within the Eton.

Late one night, donning mining clothes, they set out for the slope and started toward the Eton. As skilled as Owen and his father were in walking gangways, they found the old slope a treacherous challenge. Senator Davis, who had not been in a mine in fifteen years, barely managed to keep up with them.

In half an hour, they heard the sound of voices and of picks and shovels being plied. When they could see the open lights on the caps of the miners, they extinguished their own lamps.

Owen softly told his father that he would proceed alone. He hugged the side of the coal wall and got within a hundred feet of the men working. What he saw he could scarcely believe. The miners had constructed a fake wall to hide their mining, so that any inspectors approaching from the regular gangways would not be aware of the illegal mining going on behind the wall. Satisfied at his discovery, he made his way back to his father and Senator Davis, and the three found their way back up the old slope.

When they got outside, Senator Davis said, "First thing in the morning, I'm going to see the mayor about this. Can you come with me, Owen?"

"Yes, yes of course, but do you think he will take action?"

"We'll see."

The next morning, the mayor took decisive action. With a half dozen police in tow and accompanied by Owen, he marched to the Eton mine.

At the top of the shaft, the mayor and his force were met by the soft-spoken superintendent.

"Take us down," demanded the Mayor. "We believe you're in violation of the court order."

In a very humble and disappointed tone, the superintendent apologized, "I'm sorry, your honor, just before you came, the cage stopped down at the first level, and it's not working."

"What's wrong? Get it fixed. We must go down at once." The mayor was heated and nervous.

"I'm sorry, your honor. We just don't know what's wrong. I'm afraid it will be half a day at least before we get it going. We're short of help, too. It could take a long time."

The mayor hemmed and hawed in frustration, then turned to his men and said, "Let's go."

Outside the mine yard, he said to Owen. "Take us into the slope you entered last night." The mayor and the armed police followed Owen to the Taylor air shaft. On the way, Owen made several calls at miners' homes on Luzerne Street, and provided lamps for the mayor and his policemen.

They entered the slope with Owen leading the way. As they approached the working area, it was obvious that the number of men mining there was three times the number em-

ployed during the night-shift when Owen had first observed
the illegal mining. Owen reached the work area first, about
fifty feet ahead of the others. As he emerged from the slope,
he headed straight for the workers. A man with a rifle rose
and barred his way. "Where the hell did you come from? And
where the hell do you think you're going?"

Owen saw the rifle pointed at him and stopped. He saw
that the false wall was still standing. A half-dozen miners and
laborers were eyeing him.

Owen knew the mayor and police were just behind him,
but they seemed to be taking a long time.

"I'm Owen Roderick," he said. "The mayor of Scranton
and his officers want to inspect this mine. We couldn't get
down the shaft because the cage was out of order, so we walked
down the old air slope."

By now, the guard could see the approaching police.
When he saw the mayor, he dropped his gun and stood
motionless.

"Looks to me as though you're doing some illegal mining," the mayor said. "If we came down the shaft, do you think
that false wall would have hidden you? You or your bosses are
pretty conniving, but also dumb. Now, if you men want to
spend the next thirty days in jail, keep working. If you don't,
then get to work knocking down that wall." Turning to the
guard, he asked, "Do you have a permit for that weapon?"

The guard produced a paper.

The mayor looked at it. "Coal and Iron Police, eh? Well,
it's a good permit, but an illegal use of it. You'd better come
along with us. We'll book you. Now, let's all get out of here."

They all walked to the cage. "Now," the mayor said,

"Let's see if the broken cage will come down. Owen, ring for the cage." In seconds, the empty cage came rattling down and stopped.

The mayor said, "Let's see now, we'd better make two trips. I'll go up first with two policemen and three miners and the coal and iron policeman. We'll make sure the cage doesn't break down again."

When the mayor emerged leading the miners with the police guarding the rear, he walked directly into the superintendent's office. The superintendent was speechless.

The mayor wasted no words. "These men were mining coal in a restricted area behind a false wall as a cover. I'm shutting down the whole Eton Colliery. Now you, as superintendent, clear out the mine. Get everyone out. We're arresting the owners of this company. If you don't want to go to jail with them, move quickly."

The mayor proceeded as he promised. The arrests were made. After trials, conviction, and appeals, the case went to the Pennsylvania Supreme Court. The ruling that the Citizens Coal Company pay a fine of $250,000 was upheld. Two of the three owners of the Citizens Coal Company served short sentences in jail. One escaped from the area and was never apprehended.

Surface caving in Scranton did not end. Despite the eradication of the Citizens Coal Company, the problem was to plague Scranton for fifty more years.

CHAPTER 29

❧

A NEW CENTURY

I n 1885, Rhondda and Owen had their first child, Blodwen, named after Owen's mother upon the insistence of Rhondda. In 1889, their second child, Hugh Wynne, was named after several early Philadelphia Welsh Quakers. They continued to live in Hyde Park, as did the senior Rodericks. Both children were born as Scranton moved into a new era.

Electric streetcars, replacing horse-drawn cars, began connecting all sections of Scranton to the central city. Soon streetcars would be traveling to Taylor and Old Forge, all the way to Duryea, where a line would connect with the Wilkes-Barre streetcars—thus enabling passengers to travel almost twenty miles south. Streetcars even extended north to Dunmore, Dickson City, Olyphant, Blakely, Peckville, Throop, Mayfield, all the way to Carbondale. Scranton, in fact, built the first completely electric-powered system in the United States, making it operational on November 30, 1886. The first trip carried passengers home to Green Ridge from the Academy of Music downtown, where they heard a lecture by Henry M. Stanley, describing how he found the African explorer David Livingstone.

Paved streets and electric lights were also introduced. The old city of acetylene gas lights and horse-drawn cars was gone. The iron slag heaps of the Lackawanna Iron and Coal slowly disappeared. Culm banks on the edges of Scranton and in the coal boroughs grew higher and broader.

During this explosive decade, the anthracite industry boomed. When the Roderick family moved to Scranton, there had been about thirty-five thousand men employed in the entire anthracite region. The industry produced about fourteen million tons of hard coal. In twenty years, Lackawanna County alone was mining as much coal as the entire anthracite once produced.

In the same years, Owen saw the demise of the Knights of Labor following the creation of the United Mine Workers of America. Owen became an officer and organizer for the new UMW. In the hundreds of collieries throughout Northeastern Pennsylvania, he became the leading union official, personally acquainted with most of the operations. In the great collieries of the Lehigh and Wilkes-Barre, the Glen Alden, the Susquehanna Coal Company, the Delaware and Hudson, and the Pennsylvania Coal Company, Owen was respected by management as well as labor.

In 1889, when John Mitchell became the fifth president of the UMW, he found Owen a veritable encyclopedia of knowledge about the anthracite region. Owen had grown with the industry. He had been a laborer and miner. He had firsthand knowledge of the Lattimer Massacre and the great disaster at the Twin Shaft in Pittston. He knew the politics of Luzerne and Lackawanna counties, and from his continuing self-education, had developed a passion for national history as well.

With John Mitchell, Owen participated in the first great victory of American miners. Using the political leverage of the national election of 1900, the miners struck for a ten percent increase in wages. There was no doubt that Senator Mark Hanna, chairman of the Republican party, pressured the mine operators to make a settlement in order to assure McKinley's election. The miners were jubilant. October 29, the day the strike was settled, became the miners' national holiday, known as Johnny Mitchell Day. When President McKinley was assassinated and the headlines "PRESIDENT SHOT" appeared, many miners believed Johnny Mitchell had been murdered.

Two years later, the anthracite region was once again in turmoil. The victory of 1900 had left the operators resentful. They felt they had been "taken" by Mark Hanna and forced to make a bad settlement for the sake of a Republican victory. The miners too were dissatisfied, as many wildcat strikes attested. A company miner might earn six dollars a day, but by the time he paid his laborer and bought powder and other supplies, he averaged between sixty and one hundred dollars a month, depending on the number of days he worked. The laborer earned about two dollars a day; the breaker boys, seventy-five cents.

In 1902, when the operators used the press to proclaim that they had given the miners a twenty percent increase in 1900, the miners replied "twenty percent of what?" The miners felt underpaid. They felt that the danger of mining coal had diminished little since 1871. In truth, the industry had changed little. Breaker boys, children really, were still lying about their age and working in coal breakers despite state laws to the contrary. Boys as young as eight were still getting up at six to be at the breakers at seven. When the screaming breaker whistle blew, they took their places over the chutes on narrow planks. As the heavy breaker machines groaned to a start then exploded into a cacophony of deafening noises, the children crouched to separate coal from refuse in back-breaking, monotonous labor, just as their counterparts had thirty years earlier.

In the mines, the threat of roof falls and gas explosions was as great as ever. In 1902, one of the main grievances was the docking practices of the owners. The company had the right to reduce the payment for a car of coal if its own docking boss arbitrarily decided the coal contained too much rock or slate. Furthermore, miners had no alternative but wildcat strikes to settle their grievances. The miners wanted docking representation and grievance committees. Furthermore, the company stores were still in operation, and company houses were still rented for exorbitant rates, and evictions were still a threat.

All in all, by 1902, the coal miners of the anthracite had still not improved their lot perceptibly since the Civil War. By 1900, the anthracite region, producing fifty million tons of coal a year, had only nine thousand members in the United Mine Workers Union, out of a total workforce of nearly one hundred fifty thousand. Nevertheless, more than a hundred thousand miners had responded to Mitchell's strike call of 1900. Now, nearly all of the one hundred fifty thousand were primed to move ahead. John Mitchell himself, however, did not believe the time was right. He was more than aware of all the injustices, but he was opposed to another strike so soon after the success of 1900. He therefore moved cautiously.

He called upon the operators for a wage conference. They refused. Mitchell kept the men working four weeks beyond the expiration of the old contract. When operators refused to budge, the delegates of the miners voted 461 to 394 to strike. Obviously, the vote of 67 delegates decided the action. Mitchell followed the dictates of the majority and called the men out on strike. It was to be one of the most momentous in American history.

❧   ❧   ❧

When John Mitchell arrived in the anthracite region, he met with Owen in the building of the Welsh Philosophic Society and *The Baner America*, the Welsh newspaper. For Owen, it was an unusual experience. He had worked with Mitchell during the 1900 strike, but now Mitchell was drafting him as a friend, advisor, and political and economic authority on the region. Having worked with Powderly (about ten years his senior), Owen found it strange to hear Mitchell address him as Mr. Roderick. Mitchell was just thirty-two years of age; Owen was now forty-five. After the initial meeting, they dropped the formality.

Although Mitchell had won the support of the anthracite mine workers, he wanted them all as dues-paying members. He felt that an integrated membership would eliminate the ethnic differences and rivalries. Mitchell was fond of paraphrasing Daniel Weaver's phrase by implying there were no Polish, Italian, or Slovak distinctions in mining coal: All were miners.

"Owen," Mitchell said after their first meeting in Scranton, "you know, I was not too enthusiastic about walking out at this time."

"I know."

"But you seemed to be one of the leaders insistent on a strike."

"That's right."

"Why?"

"Because America is changing. The time is ripe."

"Explain what you mean."

"In the last twenty years, there has been a consistent voice in America, a voice for economic justice. We heard about it from the Farmers' Alliance, from the populists, from the socialists, even from the anarchists. Because they were minority voices, people did not pay too much attention to them. Sometimes, people were afraid of them—sometimes they had a right to be. Haymarket, Homestead, and the Pullman strike frightened many, but at the same time, they made people see that our nation had some fixing to do. These violent outbreaks molded the opinion of economists, writers, playwrights. Newspapers and magazines carried a message. And that message was 'Make capitalism fair or it's not going to survive.' Trusts, monopolies, and syndicates are dangerous. Their power spawns retaliatory violence. It's bad for the country. Instead, the new message is 'Let's get back to the vision of our forefathers and build a great republic.' This is a sound appeal. But a much more realistic appeal is 'Let's make capitalism work. Pay a living wage to increase purchasing power.' "

"Owen, I agree with you one hundred percent. I'm a confirmed believer in this system."

"I know you are. And so was and is Terence Powderly. But neither of you has conveyed that message clearly enough. I know the organizational problems, your bread and butter, have taken your time. My whole point is not to look back but to say this loud and strong now. I said the time is ripe because, as I said before, the history of the last twenty years has brought us to *now*. The newspapers, the writers, the public are ready. The only ones who are not ready are the industrial magnates, who do not understand the capitalist picture. They believe low wages and big profits can sustain a system. Such short-sightedness and greed are a prescription for disaster."

"And," said Mitchell, "they are the very ones we have to deal with. How can we deal with a George Baer of the Reading Coal Company who is just as prehistoric an animal as his old boss, George Gowen?"

"If we get our support from our friends in the press, we can do it," Owen replied. "In the meantime, we must be able to give our miners hope while at the same time we keep them from either surrendering or becoming violent."

"I don't think they will surrender," Mitchell said. "that is not for the summer months anyway. I think the danger of violence will come in the first days."

"You are absolutely right. Terence Powderly used to say that if you could keep the miners from burning down the breakers in the first week of the strike, the chance of an early settlement was absolutely possible."

CHAPTER 30

&

THEODORE ROOSEVELT
INTERVENES

A s the strike went on and summer turned into autumn, the national coal crisis preyed on the mind of President Theodore Roosevelt. Violence was spreading. The shortage of coal threatened the East and Midwest with cold and deprivation. The coal operators would not budge, saying there was no shortage. They declared indirectly that starvation would make the miners more sensible and end the strike. The governor of Pennsylvania had sent two thousand troops into critical areas. They could not quell the growing violence.

The governor of Massachusetts and the mayor of New York City asked the president to intervene, saying the coal famine and subsequent misery would be devastating. The president responded by talking to senators, cabinet members, representatives of the operators, and John Mitchell himself. Beyond this, he was very reluctant to move. He expressed his attitude in a letter to Senator Lodge of Massachusetts:

There is literally nothing . . . which the National Government has any power to do in this matter. One of the great troubles in dealing with the operators is their avowed determination . . . to do away with what they regard as the damage done to them by submitting to the interference for political reasons in 1900. . . . The sum of this is I can make no private or special appeal to them, and I am at my wit's end how to proceed.

Later he wrote to Senator Hanna:

What gives me the greatest concern at the moment, is the coal strike. . . . The public at large will tend to visit upon our heads responsibility for the shortage of coal as Kansas and Nebraska visited upon our heads their failure to raise good crops in the arid belt . . . . a dozen years ago. I do most earnestly feel that from every consideration of public policy and of good morale, they [the operators] should make some slight concession.

Senator Hanna replied on September 29, 1902:

Confidentially, I saw Mr. Mitchell (the public knows nothing about that). I got from Mr. J. P. Morgan a proposition as to what to do in the matter. I got Mr. Mitchell to agree to accept it if the operators would abide by the decision. I went to Philadelphia and saw Mr. Baer, and to my surprise, he absolutely refused to entertain it. You can see how determined they are.

Despite the recalcitrance of the operators, President Roosevelt decided to send Secretary of State Elihu Root to see J. P. Morgan to tell him that he, the president, was inviting the operators and Mr. Mitchell, with other union representatives, to the White House. Roosevelt planned to use his good offices to generate a settlement by arbitration.

On October 1, John Mitchell asked Owen to accompany him to the White House for the joint meeting of the operators and union officials. Owen agreed immediately. He couldn't wait to tell Rhondda, the children, and his parents. There was much excitement, joshing, and speculation.

When John Mitchell and Owen walked into the conference room in the White House, only President Roosevelt greeted them. The coal operators sat stiff and defensive, making no acknowledgment of their arrival. Owen was shocked to see Theodore Roosevelt in a wheelchair. He had been injured in Massachusetts when his carriage was struck by a trolley car. The president looked much more youthful than his pictures. In person, Owen saw a man one year younger than he, forty-four years of age. His heavy mustache dominated his face. From the side and rear, with the mustache less conspicuous, he looked thirty-five.

Without preliminaries and in a serious, friendly, but assertive way, the president told the group that he had no authority for his invitation. Owen heard him say: "The urgency of the situation, however, and the terrible catastrophe impending this winter impel me to use whatever influence, personally, I can bring to end this situation. I appeal to your patriotism that sinks personal consideration and makes individual sacrifices for the general good."

Owen looked at the faces of the operators, expecting to see somewhere a nod of assent or an eye of attention. Instead, he saw belligerence.

He looked back to Mitchell and the faces of the other two United Mine Worker officials with him. Tom Duffy was an old-time organizer, listening intently to the president.

John Fahy had won his spurs during the Lattimer Massacre. A fine speaker himself, he was entranced by Roosevelt.

After the president's appeal, John Mitchell answered by saying that the miners would be willing to settle the strike by having an impartial tribunal consider the issues and make a decision. The miners, he said, would accept the decision even if it refused their claims.

The operators asked for time to put their reply in writing. A recess was called. When they reconvened, the operators replied with a direct attack on the union and an indirect attack upon the president. George Baer, of the Reading Company, read the statement, part of which said they would not negotiate with terrorists, guilty of crime. "Criminals have dynamited breakers and bridges. These criminals are led by one Mitchell whom you have invited to the same room with us," he accused.

Owen and the others were shocked, not so much by their statement about Mitchell as by their effrontery in speaking to the president of the United States in such a disrespectful tone. Just as Owen expected Baer to calm down, Baer sneered, "Your government, Mr. President, is a contemptible failure." He finally ended his attack by suggesting that Roosevelt compel the men to return to their work at the wages they had been receiving, with the possibility of "some adjustments at each colliery." Unsettled disputes might be referred to the local courts.

"That is a very impractical suggestion," Mitchell pointed out. "There are scores of collieries in each of the three anthracite districts. Settling disputes this way will leave little time for mining coal. If you want labor peace as we do, we urge you to avoid a chaotic wage policy."

Mr. Markle of Hazleton addressed the president, "Sir, perform your duties as president and squelch these anarchistic conditions."

Owen grew more nervous. He wondered how long Roosevelt could contain himself.

Encouraged by the insulting remarks of Markle and Baer, the others—W. H. Truesdale, T. D. Fowler, and David Wilcox—took the same approach. Accenting the violence, one of them accused, "The United Mine Workers have committed twenty murders."

Mitchell responded vehemently, "If you can prove that statement, I will resign this minute. There has been violence and lawlessness, but no little has been provoked by your own coal and iron police."

The meeting continued with more and more invectives until Roosevelt saw the futility of it all and retired from the room. One of his aides dismissed the participants.

Roosevelt was more than dejected. He wrote to Senator Mark Hanna, who had been responsible for the 1900 settlement and was using his efforts to bring about a permanent labor peace. Confiding in him the details of the meeting, he wrote, "The only gentleman in the whole group was John Mitchell."

❧   ❧   ❧

The four union men left Washington. Mitchell returned to the Hotel Hart in Wilkes-Barre, his headquarters there. Owen stopped at Wilkes-Barre with him before going on to Scranton.

They sat together in Mitchell's room. In Washington,

Mitchell had appeared very taciturn and withdrawn, but now he appeared completely relaxed and eager to talk.

"You know, Owen, I've had much relaxation in this room during the strike, playing cards with some of my cronies. When you have Johnny Loftus, Walt McDougall, Frank Ward O'Malley, and Dan Hart punning and verbally jabbing each other, winning a two-bit pot is forgotten. I've also had some great discussions with Father Curran here. Without his support, I don't think we could have survived these months. I've also argued here with old Mother Jones, a labor saint if I ever saw one—except she's no saint at all, I'll tell you. Tell me, Owen, you saw the operators. You heard them. Can we win?"

"I don't think so. Not unless it comes indirectly. Roosevelt could take over the mines and have the government run them."

"He won't do that. He doesn't want to be called a socialist."

"Well, President Cleveland did it in the Pullman Strike. He moved against the strike rioters," Owen recalled.

"I know, but don't forget Roosevelt's party is still the party of corporations and money. He won't risk it. There's no denying, that the president is as concerned about the hardships this strike causes people and the economy as anyone else. But he will stop short of nationalization." Changing his train of thought, he said, "Owen, you know the region. What's going to happen here in the anthrcite?"

Owen thought a minute and said, "Governor Stone will send more and more troops into the area, but not a miner will go back to work."

"I hope you are right. And what about Sam Gompers?"

"He will keep hands off," Owen said. "He will not interfere with you. He might even send you money for the strike fund."

Owen then asked his own question, "I can tell you what I think will happen here in the coal regions, but your ear is tuned to the whole country. How bad can conditions become?"

"Much worse. I read a report yesterday of people digging up wooden pavement bricks in Chicago to use for fuel. We're going to have some rioting, no doubt about it."

Mitchell described more details about conditions in New York and Philadelphia and Boston. He and Owen conversed for another fifteen minutes, exchanging views and speculating about the future weeks. Then Owen arose to leave.

"Well, I must get back to Scranton."

"Keep in touch with me," Mitchell said, rising to extend a parting handshake. "Don't get discouraged. The nation's eyes are on the strike. The president will not be diverted. This strike is the main thing on his mind. I don't believe he is going to forget the coal operators. He'll pressure Morgan and Hanna to talk some sense into them."

As Owen left, Mitchell called out to him, "When you write to Powderly, give him my best. Tell him I think of him often."

❧   ❧   ❧

As Mitchell predicted, President Roosevelt persisted and maneuvered until he was able to persuade the capitalist tycoon, J. P. Morgan, to receive Elihu Root on his yacht, the *Corsair*. After a five-hour conference, Morgan agreed to see the president at the White House. On October 13, just ten days after the meeting with the coal operators, Morgan told Roosevelt that the coal operators would submit the strike dispute to arbitration.

There was no jubilation. Everyone knew there would be a squabble over the persons appointed to the arbitration commission, and it developed almost immediately. The coal operators vehemently opposed appointing a labor man. They wanted only different types of men, including an "eminent sociologist." After some delay, Roosevelt found a way to appoint a labor representative that he and the miners both wanted although he couldn't quite believe how easily it was done. He wrote: "It took me about two hours before I grasped the fact that the mighty brains of industry . . . had not the slightest objection to my appointing a labor man if I called him an 'eminent sociologist.' They saw nothing ridiculous in the proposition."

Later, he wrote to the great humorist Peter Finley Dunne (Mr. Dooley), "Nothing that you have written can begin to approach in screaming comedy, the inside of the last few conferences before I appointed the strike commission. I finally succeeded in reconciling an appointment of the president of a labor union by calling him an 'eminent sociologist.' The appointment referred to was E. E. Clark, Chief of the Order of Railway Conductors, designated as sociologist."

Mitchell's agreement to accept arbitration was confirmed by a convention of miners. They supported him. However, several labor leaders, Mother Jones included, believed Mitchell had been seduced by the capitalists.

The commissioners chosen to hear the testimony of the operators and miners and to settle the strike were these notables: Judge George Gray of Wilmington, Chairman; Carroll D. Wright, United States Commissioner of Labor; General John M. Wilson, an engineer; Bishop John L. Spaulding, a

Catholic prelate; Edgar E. Clark, "sociologist," a union official; Edward Parker, a writer, later an editor of a coal operator's journal; and, Thomas H. Watkins, an independent coal operator from Scranton.

Mitchell was the first to testify. For four days, he underwent grueling questioning. America was astounded by the objectivity and coolness of his testimony. Wayne McVeigh, former attorney general of Pennsylvania, representing the operators, could not shake him. McVeigh, a legal professional, said to Mitchell as he left the stand, "Mr. Mitchell, you are the best witness for yourself I have ever faced in my life."

The miners were represented by the greatest trial lawyer in the nation at the time, Clarence Darrow. The hearings were held in Philadelphia, Wilkes-Barre, Scranton, and Hazleton. Darrow gave the world a picture of anthracite coal mining. Because the daily wage of a contract miner might often be five dollars, the public identified that high figure as the wage of a miner in 1902. Darrow, using statistics presented by Baer himself, established that half the coal miners in the anthracite region earned less than two hundred dollars a year and that only five percent earned more than eight hundred dollars a year. After establishing the pay earned, he dwelt on child labor, accidents, and deaths, concluding:

> If the civilization of this country rests on the necessity . . . of starving wages . . . if it rests on these poor little boys . . . picking their way through dirt, clouds and dust of anthracite coal . . . it is time for these captains of industry to resign their commission.

In Scranton, Darrow called on Owen to testify. After Owen took his oath, he asked: "State your name, please."

"Owen Roderick."

"What is your occupation?"

"A local union official."

"Have you ever worked in a mine or breaker?"

"Yes, sir, both."

"When and where?"

"I worked in the Avondale Breaker in Plymouth."

A gasp sounded throughout the hearing room. Everyone remembered the Avondale fire where over fifty Scranton men and boys had lost their lives even though it had happened thirty-four earlier. Those in the hearing room found the presence of an Avondale miner incredible.

"Avondale? You mean . . ."

"Yes, sir."

"Before or after the tragedy?"

"At the time of the tragedy."

"How old were you?"

"Twelve years of age."

"Tell us what you remember of that day."

Owen described the day, including his fright, the burning breaker, and the death of his grandfather.

"How many were killed that day?"

"One hundred and ten men and boys, in all."

"Why did those men die?"

"Because the breaker was built right over the shaft. When it caught fire, there was no way for the men to get out. There was only one way to get in and out of the Avondale.

That was down or up the one shaft."

"Could the same kind of accident occur today?"

"No, sir. The law provides that a breaker cannot be built over a shaft, and there must be a second opening."

"Was that the first law of its kind?"

"In America, yes. But a similar law was passed in Northumberland, England, in 1852, after more than two hundred men lost their lives in the Hartley Colliery there."

"Is it true to say that in the past thirty years, mining is much safer?"

"Not at all. Avondale did correct one situation, but inside, down under, the mines are just as dangerous as ever."

"How do you know this, Mr. Roderick?"

"Because I worked in the Briggs Shaft in the early 1870s. I saw conditions there. Today, because of my work in the union, I have been in almost every mine between Forest City and Lykens, below Pottsville."

"And what is your observation?"

"The anthracite collieries are as dangerous a place to work today as they were in the 1870s."

"That's your observation. Can you prove it?"

"The reports of the Pennsylvania State Bureau of Mines contain all the accidents and deaths."

"What are some of the causes?"

"The same ones as always: roof falls, explosions, squeezes, floods, and many others."

"You are saying then, that the anthracite industry is as dangerous as ever."

"Definitely—if not more dangerous."

"More dangerous? Why is that?"

"Because in the past fifteen years, the mining threatens the public as well as the workers within the mines."

"Will you explain that statement to the commissioners?"

Owen then described the subsidence problem in Scranton, revealing the destruction of streets, public buildings, schools, churches, and especially the incident at School No. 116.

"What is being done about the problem?"

"Very little. Individuals and public officials are powerless against the mammoth coal companies and their control of the community and courts."

Darrow turned to the commissioners and said, "Gentlemen, I shall not pursue this mine subsidence problem further, but before we leave Scranton, I hope we might see the sections of the city threatened by this devastation." Then, again facing Owen, he asked:

"Is there any way or ways that anthracite coal mining has improved in the thirty years you have experienced?"

"Certainly the production has increased. Profits and dividends have grown."

"How about labor relations? Is there an improvement in the way workingmen and their grievances are handled?"

"I'm sorry to say, no. There is no better procedure for settling disputes in 1902 or 1903 than there was in 1870 or 1877. There is little cooperation between labor and management. It is a constant struggle."

"Elaborate, Mr. Roderick."

"The individual miner is always at the mercy of his employer. Since the Civil War, he has seen many unions started that would give him a voice and protection. In my own lifetime, I have seen unions destroyed by violence and killings."

Darrow interrupted, saying, "But today, you have a strong union. Are you now satisfied?"

"No, the union is not satisfied. We are happy with the union, but the union must be recognized. The union as a collective voice for workers is a good thing. But what is needed is cooperation between the companies and unions. Specifically, we need arbitration boards and conciliation boards to correct problems of labor. The union wants to find a way to prevent strikes and to avoid work stoppages, and especially, to promote peace so that we can produce coal."

Darrow pressed forward and asked, "How important is this matter of establishing a procedure for settling differences between labor and the companies?"

Owen paused and said deliberately: "In my estimation, it is the single most important recommendation this commission can make. If we have a board of conciliation and a decision-making body or member, then all differences can be settled, whether they be about pay rates, working conditions, or any other matters, including the misunderstanding or interpretation of contracts."

❧   ❧   ❧

The hearings continued for four months. Two hundred witnesses testified. Workers, their wives, children, and maimed men (victims of mine accidents) poured out thousands of words, many of them heart rending. Andrew Chappie, twelve years of age, told of earning forty cents a day. However, the money was not paid to him. Instead, the money was applied to a debt owed by his father, who had been killed in the mines four years earlier. Henry Coll, a miner, testified that he, his wife, his four children, and his one-hundred-year-old mother were evicted from a Markle Coal Company house because he was on a strike-relief committee. The testimony was so moving that one historian wrote:

> The special commission listening to the testimony begged that the moving spectacles of horrors be stopped. It is doubtful whether ever before or since, so striking a living picture has been presented of the death toll of industry and of the misery of the men and children who toiled and lived in darkness and cold.

The testimony of the coal operators then began. George Baer testified last for the operators. Baer had written the notorious letter saying "the rights and interests of the laboring man will be protected and cared for—not by labor agitators, but by the Christian men to whom God in His infinite wisdom has given control of the property rights of the country, and upon the successful management of which so much depends." The audacity and presumption that the coal operators ruled by divine right had shocked the public.

Now making the final statement for the operators, Baer described the inflamed passion of the poor workingmen misdirected by labor leaders. He said most miners wanted to work rather than strike, but they were intimidated by Mitchell.

The miners were giving up American rights by joining a union. Only the law of supply and demand could determine wages, and the wages in the anthracite were good, pointing to the available supply of labor in the area. Finally, he stated that the coal operators owned and had a right to run their own business without interference from anyone.

The miners had gone back to work on October 23, 1902. The final decisions of the Anthracite Coal Commission were made public on March 22, 1903.

Owen was in Ashley at the No. 20 Colliery of the Lehigh and Wilkes-Barre Coal Company when he heard that the commission announced its decision. He could not determine whether the miners had won a victory from the hodge-podge of verbal reports repeating what had been on the telegraph wires.

When he arrived home in Scranton, he found a full report in the evening papers. That night, after the children were in bed, he and Rhondda sat down and analyzed the commission's decisions. The miners received about a ten percent increase in pay, not the twenty percent they asked for. The eight-hour day was denied, but a reduction in work hours still left them with a nine-hour work day. For Owen, the most rewarding provision was the creation of machinery for settling disputes.

It was an answer to the plea in his testimony. A board of conciliation made up of three representatives of the miners and three from the operators was to settle disputes. Unresolved disputes were to be referred to an umpire. This machinery was to handle any dispute not resolved directly between the miners and the company.

The United Mine Workers as a union was not yet recognized by the companies and John Mitchell was not permitted to sign the final agreement as president of the United Mine Workers. He signed only with his name, no title given.

As Owen and Rhondda perceived the settlement, it was a victory.

"I know that many of the national labor leaders will not be satisfied," he said. Yet, for me, it's a victory. When I think back to the 1870s to Avondale, to Briggs Shaft, to the riots of 1877, and when I recall the animosities and sufferings in the past, I see great progress. We were defeated time after time. We were divided in the three districts. We were alone. Miners had few national figures who were friends and very few friends among the newspapers. Then we got big help from the *Scranton Times*. Today, we have many national papers and great magazines supporting our cause. John Mitchell has economists and college professors and national politicians who have taken up our cause. Great papers like the *New York World* speak out for us. The coal miners of northeastern Pennsylvania have been in the news around the world for half the year. Our problems are known the world over."

"Another thing," said Rhondda, "the thousands of men who have been coming from Poland, Austria, Hungary, and Italy are now part of us. They were invited like cattle to come and slave. I really believe the owners thought they could get them to work for nothing. Now they're the best union members. They were faithful to John Mitchell to this day."

"Yes, and they will always be. Whenever I visit a mine, I'm sure to hear some Polish or Slovak miner say to me, 'Me Johnny Mitchell man.' "

"There's one big disappointment in the settlement," Owen said.

"What's that?"

"The miners still have to produce a ton of coal measured as twenty-four hundred pounds. When the company sells a ton, they only give the customer two thousand pounds. The union asked for a uniform agreement on the pounds in a ton."

"Well, I'm most disappointed in the hours," Rhondda said. "I thought some of the miners would get the eight-hour day considering its been a national campaign in every industry."

"I am too," Owen admitted. "But we won an important point in having the union hire a check weighman at the head. We just won't have the docking boss rejecting our coal after some poor miner has been breaking his back mining and loading his cars. The union representatives will be right there to guarantee a fair deal. The main thing is that we now have brought the labor problems of the industry to the public. Farmers and small businessmen and yes, even housewives in Chicago, know how a miner and his wife and family live. For us here, our greatest victory is having the conciliation board and umpire. I see labor peace and prosperous times. Believe it or not, the ones who stand to win most from the settlement are those who fought the hardest against the recognition of John Mitchell and the mine workers. I mean the coal companies."

CHAPTER 31

CRUSADERS

Rhondda and Owen talked late into the night. Their conversation turned at the late hour to a comparison of Terence Powderly and John Mitchell. Owen had developed a strong and loyal admiration for young John Mitchell. He felt Mitchell was mature far beyond his years, similar in that respect to Terence Powderly. Mitchell had mined coal early in his teens. Powderly worked in the Carbondale railroad shops at fourteen. By nineteen, Mitchell was a seasoned coal miner, Powderly a master mechanic. Powderly was a visionary committed at nineteen to improving the lot of labor. Mitchell's eyes were on one worker, the miner.

"Of these two," Rhondda asked, "who was the better leader?"

"I can't say," Owen replied. "Powderly, in his time, changed the Knights of Labor from a small, secret organization to a highly respectable national industrial union, with seven to eight hundred thousand members. Mitchell's accomplishment seems much less. Yet, he has leadership qualities among the immigrant European miners that Powderly could not match. He has organized Polish, Italian, Slovak, Hungarian, Lithuanian, and Russian miners—all coming from different cultures—into a united body. Everyone thought that unity was impossible. The earlier Welsh, Irish, and Scots leaders thought that ethnic miners could never be joined together. Language and cultures were so different and antagonistic that cooperation seemed unattainable."

"Do you find Mitchell the scholar Powderly was?" Rhondda asked.

"Not in the same way," Owen replied. "Mitchell reads every newspaper he can find. He knows what is going on in the world of labor and business. He is not so critical of the wheat markets and stock markets as Powderly. I would say Mitchell is much less bookish than Powderly. Powderly could not read and write until he was in his late teens. When he began to read, he devoured everything. Powderly was a real intellectual, on a mission to change the world and the people in it. Powderly learned from books. Mitchell learns from people. Mitchell can listen to the president himself or some of his advisors and repeat everything they said."

"Like my student Joe Mooney in Avondale," said Rhondda.

"Yes, I remember your telling me about Joe."

"Yes, not much for books, but remembering everything I ever said. Were they alike in negotiations? You observed them both?"

"No, they were quite different. Mitchell is the most patient and best listener I ever saw. He can sit and listen to a boring or antagonistic presentation by an opponent without expressing any annoyance or displeasure. However, when his time to speak arrives, he is ready with an item-by-item rebuttal.

"Powderly, on the other hand, was so full of convictions and information that he dominated every group from the start.

Powderly was not always as serious as Mitchell. He had a good sense of perspective and a good sense of humor."

"Yet, Mitchell with his own friends is pictured as friendly and relaxed," Rhondda contested.

"Yes, in private he is much different. And that highlights a big difference between the two men," Owen said. "Mitchell can relax, play cards, and do his share of drinking. Powderly is not only a tee-totaler, he is strongly opposed to drinking. He held national offices in several temperance organizations. At one point in his career, I think he made more speeches for anti-saloon groups than he did for labor. But that was just one of his many interests. He was always ready for a new challenge. Once he organized a boycott against the high price of coffee. He spotted the conspiracy among the marketers and called for a national boycott. It was successful, too."

"In his heyday," Rhondda mused, "I suppose Powderly was more of a national leader than Mitchell ever was."

"Perhaps so, but don't forget Mitchell rose like a meteor in 1900, and in the last two years, he has received more national recognition than Powderly ever did. Otherwise, you are right. Powderly was a spokesman for so many causes in addition to labor that he was known all over the nation for his interest in child labor, the rights of women, Irish freedom, and every national issue. How did all these interests affect him? Was he a better master workman of the knights because of them? I think he was. He had his finger in so many issues. Yet I must say that I think they were part of his rejection by his own union. The leaders who opposed him concentrated on union issues. They used his other interests internally, within the knights, against him. They implied to the rank and file that he was not interested enough in their bread-and-butter issues. They attacked him for scattering his energy in too many intellectual and moral pursuits."

Rhondda asked, "Do you think he could have been more active in the eight-hour day movement? Why was he so placid about it?"

"The eight-hour day was originally one of the knights' main issues. When the radical anarchists picked it up, Powderly de-emphasized it. He thought the anarchists would give the eight-hour day a bad name."

"Do you think he could have been more compassionate toward the Haymarket condemned men?"

"Perhaps, but he hated violence. Undoubtedly, he was influenced by the great newspapers who wrote the details of Haymarket. He was convinced the men were guilty. He not only hated violence, he had utter contempt for anarchists who never proposed a single positive idea for reform or improvement. He believed they wanted to annihilate the system. He believed in a capitalist government. He saw all of its weaknesses, contradictions, and abuses, but with them all, he felt a reformed system could work."

"In a sense then," Rhondda suggested, "Mitchell, these past months, has stuck to the beliefs of Terence Powderly. Mitchell has said over and over he does not want to change the system."

"Yes, and it seems logical and right that John Mitchell, who was one of the first young men to take the secret oath of the Knights of Labor when he was a boy of twelve in the mines of Braidwood, Illinois, should lead the miners to their first great victories in 1900 and 1902, fulfilling this basic belief and some of the objectives of Terence Powderly."

"Do you think Mr. Powderly will ever return to the labor cause?" Rhondda asked.

"That's hard to say. I know he was very happy to be appointed commissioner of immigration by President McKinley. He immersed himself in the study of immigration problems when he was appointed. From his experience in Scranton, he had firsthand knowledge of the people of Europe. His own parents came from Ireland. He saw the Welsh, Scots, and Irish immigrants following their dreams to the anthracite region between the Civil War and the late eighties. Don't forget, he was a great observer. He was eleven years old when the Civil War started, the unCivil War, he always calls it. Then he saw the accelerated migration of southern Europeans starting in the late eighties and still bringing vast waves of people here. He was well qualified for any position involving immigration. I was sorry he lost his job when McKinley was shot and Roosevelt took over. The rumor is that President Roosevelt has seen the mistake he made by dismissing Powderly. He may give him a new assignment as a special representative of the Commerce and Labor Department to study immigration problems."

"Owen, we have been so fortunate to have known Terence Powderly."

"Yes,"Owen said. "He has been a great model for me and a great friend. He opened new vistas for us. I remember so well the day I first met him when he sought out my father to ask for his help in organizing miners. I believe I was only about fourteen then."

"I hope he is not forgotten," Rhondda said. "Everyone has John Mitchell's name before him—and rightfully so—but I think we will always feel personally closer to Mr. Powderly."

"Well, let's not look backward. There is still much to be done. First thing tomorrow, I must go up to the Marvin Colliery. There will not be much talk of Powderly there. The name John Mitchell will be on everyone's lips."

CHAPTER 32

ð.

THE PANCOAST FIRE

On Friday morning, April 7, 1911, two days before Palm Sunday, Owen stopped at the Kenwood Lunch in the four-hundred block of Spruce Street before starting for Throop to visit the Pancoast Colliery. As he drank his coffee, the managing editor of the *Scranton Times* and the city editor, Tom Murphy, came in and quickly asked for Ed Boyle, the proprietor of the Kenwood. Boyle emerged from the kitchen and the three were immediately in agitated conversation.

Ed Boyle reopened the kitchen door and called out to his cook, "Charlie, take over. I'm driving some reporters up to Throop. There's a mine fire at Pancoast." Pointing to Owen who was a frequent customer at the Kenwood, he said to the newsman, "We'd better take Owen Roderick along. Most of the men at Pancoast are his union members. Owen, come along. Let's go," he called as he dashed for the door.

At the words "mine fire at Pancoast," Owen had an instantaneous mind flash of Avondale.

Outside, two reporters from *The Times* were awaiting orders from the front desk men. Tom Murphy gestured to them to follow Ed Boyle to the rear of the restaurant where Ed's Packard was parked. "Pile in," Boyle ordered as he started the motor.

In minutes, Ed Boyle, Murphy, Keaton, Owen, and the two reporters were flying to Throop. "Make yourselves known to each other," Ed Boyle sang out as his car, one of the few automobiles in Scranton, wove in and around horse-drawn wagons and Scranton streetcars. "Owen," he continued, "tell us about Pancoast. Is it a deep mine?"

"Deep enough," Owen said. "About seven to eight hundred feet."

Tom Murphy exclaimed, "That's deep enough for sure, about the depth of two football fields one on top of the other. That's deep."

One of the young reporters asked Owen, "If there's a fire in the mine, is there enough fresh air going in to keep the men from suffocating?"

"I don't think so," Owen replied. "I know the Pancoast has two tremendous fans, one about thirty-five feet in diameter and another about twenty feet, and there is a third, about the same size, an exhaust fan, in another shaft apart from the main shaft. But a good supply of air, enough for normal working conditions, is not enough to clear the smoke from a major fire inside."

"Is the Pancoast a new mine?" asked the other young reporter.

"No, it's one of the oldest in Lackawanna County. But it's well-kept. There are many old, worked-out areas in it, in addition to the sections where mining is now being done."

"I don't know a great deal about mining," Tom Murphy said. "But are there many seams of coal in the mine?" using seams instead of veins.

"Yes, some very productive ones," Owen answered. "Of

course, many are the same seams that run throughout the valley and are mined in other mines around Scranton. At Pancoast, they mine the seams, some with strange names: the Diamond; the Fourteen Foot; the Clark; the Dunmore; No. 2; and the China. Out of these seams, they mine over a half-million tons a year."

"How many men work there?" Ed Boyle asked.

Owen thought a minute and described the mine as two separate units. "There are about four hundred men in one section and five hundred in the other. All told, about nine hundred men and boys work the whole mine."

"If a fire breaks out in a mine," one of the young reporters asked, "how do they put it out?"

"Just as they do where you live," Owen said. "There are water pipes in the mine that can be tapped with hoses. Small fires are usually put out quickly."

The managing editor asked, "Mr. Roderick, who owns the Pancoast?"

"The company is Price-Pancoast. I do not know the owners personally. The superintendent is Joseph Birtley, a top mining man. He has been there twenty years."

They rode in silence for a while until a reporter asked, "These mining areas are pretty complex underground. How do they communicate in case of emergencies and accidents?"

Owen answered, "This is a large mine with telephones throughout."

The reporters were surprised that telephone lines were strung throughout the mine, connecting the colliery office with various points underground.

In twenty minutes, Ed Boyle and his passengers arrived

at the colliery yard. Owen quickly identified Birtley, the super-intendent, walking toward the shaft. He left his riding companions and ran toward him.

"Mr. Birtley, can I be of help?" he asked.

"Oh, hello, Owen. I really don't know. I'm just going down. The fire started about an hour ago," he continued to walk toward the shaft.

"If I can help, I'd like to go down with you, Mr. Birtley," Owen said.

"You're not dressed for it, but come along. You're a miner and I can trust you to take care of yourself."

When they got to the bottom of the shaft, Owen could see only wisps of smoke. They were not near the site of the fire. Mr. Birtley was eager to make sure that all the men in the mine, even those working away from the China seam, were aware of the fire. He was informed all were on alert. While Mr. Birtley talked to his foreman, Owen found out the exact site of the fire from two miners who had been working for an hour to control it. They had retreated from the main blaze for a few minutes of relief and recovery.

According to the men, the fire had started in the E room, an engine room, a twenty-by-fifteen-foot chamber cut in the rock and coal and supported by timbers. The room, lighted by a Dietz lantern, contained the hoisting engines for bringing up twenty-five or thirty cars of coal from one level to another. As geared engines they were clean, but well oiled. A residue of oil, however, was splashed on the timbers. The hoisting engineer was thirty-year-old Jim Moran who handled both the engines in the E room and a similar hoisting engine in north slope C. From the men, Owen learned that Moran had left the E room with the lamp burning to go to C. He returned twenty minutes later and found it ablaze. He had tried to extinguish the fire with water available, but the oiled timbers had caught fire and were uncontrollable.

Owen asked the men, "How many men are behind the fire in there working and in danger of suffocation from smoke and carbon monoxide?"

"We heard Mr. Birtley say there were over seventy."

Owen accompanied Superintendent Birtley as they went closer to the fire area. They could see the blazing timbers and the smoke swirling into the work area.

The crew fighting the fire in the engine room was completely ineffective. The fire had spread and was now engulfing fifteen empty coal cars standing on a nearby turnabout. The hope of putting the engine room fire out and getting through to the miners cut off by the blaze was dimmed by the spread of fire to the coal cars.

The ventilating fans were actually pushing the smoke and the carbon monoxide back into the area where the trapped miners were trying desperately to find someplace inside where they could escape the noxious gas and smoke.

A call went out for outside help. The Throop Hose Company responded and got water into the fire. After hours of hosing, they extinguished the fire at four o'clock in the afternoon.

In the meantime, a coterie of coal company officials, state mining inspectors, and personnel from the United States Bureau of Mines descended upon the scene of the tragedy.

The rescue workers arrived and all worked until late Friday evening finding and identifying victims. Owen worked with Superintendent Birtley until the latter became ill and was ordered to leave the mine by a physician. Owen stayed and continued to work with the rescue team.

Owen re-lived Avondale as he saw victims lying in normal, awkward, or strange positions. One miner sat with a piece of bread in his hand as though he were about to eat it. It was obvious that the victims had pursued different avenues of escape. Twelve men were overtaken as they tried to get out through a main air gangway. The opinion of the mine experts was that all the men were dead an hour after the fire started.

In all, seventy-two men who worked in the tunnels of the China seam were killed by carbon monoxide, "white damp," as it was carried with the smoke by the ventilating currents.

The tragedy was perhaps the worst in Lackawanna County's mining history. The seventy-two fatalities were exceeded only by the one hundred ten of Avondale in 1867.

Owen arrived home at midnight. He had spent most of the evening visiting the homes of men with whom he worked on union matters. Most of them lived in Throop and Olyphant. Rhondda was waiting alone. Their daughter Blodwen was now in medical school, and Hugh Wynne at college. They sat for over an hour as Rhondda plied Owen with questions about the tragedy.

"Why did sixteen get out safely, or rather, why didn't the others follow those sixteen?"

"I suppose those who stayed thought the smoke came from a small fire that would be put out. They were in the mine working, and they were not going to go home and miss a day's pay. Of course, the sixteen saved were alert and did the right thing."

"Were there ways out? You know at Avondale the men were trapped. There was only one entrance and exit," Rhondda asked.

"No, at Pancoast there were three. Of course, the fire blocked one. But I believe most of the men were overcome before they knew it," Owen explained.

"Why was the fire so intense?" she asked.

"Because the ventilation that ordinarily is needed for workers fanned the flames."

"Why didn't they shut the ventilation down?"

"Because then the lives of four hundred or more men in the other veins, that is the Clark and Dunmore, would be endangered. So would the lives of all the men fighting the fire. Another thing—and this is most important—Superintendent Birtley knew a quick way to cut the ventilation from the area without jeopardizing the others by using an available air regulator. Unfortunately, the fire was blocking the way to it."

"From what you said, men continued to work in other parts of the mine during the fire."

"Only in the early stages. When the extent and ferocity of the fire were known, every man was ordered out, and all the hauling of coal out of the mine was stopped."

"Well, the whole tragedy is awful," Rhondda said. "I never thought I'd hear of another Avondale. Think of the widows and children again."

"Yes, it is awful," Owen said. "I never expected this could happen in 1911. It is a well-ventilated, well-engineered mine. Superintendent Birtley is one of the best men in the field.

Avondale was a mine of 1869, an accident waiting to happen. I guess Pancoast proves that everything we said about the dangers of mining is still true. Mining will always be a life-threatening occupation. No use denying it. We must just keep working to improve the safety. Safety must be as important an issue as wages and hours."

"When you came out of the mine late tonight, Owen, were women and children there as they were at Avondale?"

"Exactly," Owen said. "There were the screams and cries. And that will go on again tomorrow as they bring the bodies up."

❧   ❧   ❧

Saturday morning, Owen was back at the Pancoast mine. He learned that after he left Friday night, the search for bodies had continued. By three A.M., twenty-nine bodies had been brought to the foot of the shaft. Actually, the first of them could have been brought to the surface late Friday afternoon, but officials decided to hold them underground until the milling crowd in the colliery yard had dispersed. The three or four thousand spectators were already difficult to control. They might have gotten completely out of hand witnessing the cries and moans of women and children identifying husbands and fathers. All through the night, a small group of distraught wives stood in the dark waiting, some with infants wrapped in their shawl-covered arms.

Late in the night, rescue workers began to bring the bodies to the surface, four or five on every cage lift. The identities of the victims were hidden as the silhouettes of the workers revealed only constant activity. Only the open flames of rescuers' lamps could be seen in the dark of the mine yard. Owen found that thirty-five of the dead workers had been brought to the surface and removed to the undertakers. Every undertaker available had been commissioned to help.

The families were confused by the procedure. On Saturday morning, Owen saw families frantically trying to check with those in charge to determine which undertakers had picked up their loved ones.

One of Owen's first actions was to determine the welfare of his friend Joe Evans of Hyde Park. Joe had abandoned his career as a mine boss to join the Federal Bureau of Mines as a safety expert. Taking special equipment, Joe had gone deep into the fire zone with a squad of men. To Owen's dismay, he found that his friend's heroic efforts had cost him his life. Carrying heavy equipment and over-exerting himself by running, he had collapsed and died. At seven o'clock Saturday morning, Owen saw his friend's body lifted to the surface. Four men with helmets, a "fresh air" stretcher, and an oxygen tank carried him. From the mechanical infusion of oxygen, Joe's chest was moving up and down. As Doctor Jacobs walked at the side of the stretcher, Owen heard him explain to a state mining inspector, "I believe he's dead, but we're still trying to get him back."

Throughout Saturday, the crowd gathered again as five thousand people pressed into the colliery yard. All day long, the coal company's Black Maria and the undertakers' hearses and wagons seemed to be the only traffic in Throop. As night came again, the morbid traffic continued, the sounds occasionally broken by a wailing cry of some poor widow or the screams of a child.

Saturday night, the crowd did not thin out. Instead, it grew beyond five thousand as all the residents of the mid-valley poured into the Pancoast mine yard.

By Sunday, the number of known dead was confirmed as seventy-three, and the day was one of countless funerals in Throop. The bells of St. John's and St. Anthony's churches rang throughout the day. The *Tribune Republican* explained:

> Throop Borough on Sunday belonged to the dead. Death's insignia, the crepe, draped doors on every street. From houses sounded the cries of widows and orphans. From centuries came wailings and lamentations.

At breakfast Sunday morning, Rhondda surprised Owen with a request. "Owen, can we skip church this morning and go up to Throop? I don't know what we can do, but I remember Avondale so vividly. I know what those poor mothers and children are going through. I just want to be near them."

Owen was just as eager to go to Throop as Rhondda. When they entered the little coal borough, they encountered all the funeral activity described by the *Tribune Republican*. On Charles Street they stopped before a home with three crepes. They joined a small group on the porch waiting to pay their respects. When they entered the small house, they found four, not three, boxes serving as coffins side by side.

Three brothers and an uncle were being mourned. There was only one mourner—a seven-year-old girl, the daughter of one of the victims. Her father, Emil, had been a widower living in the house with his small daughter. The others, his brothers and uncle, had been boarders in his home.

Rhondda sat down and took the little girl's hand. The gesture calmed her. Having endured enveloping hugs from every woman who came to the viewing, she seemed relieved to sit quietly with her hand in Rhondda's.

As they left the home of the little girl, they met John Conners, one of Owen's friends from the 1902 strike. Conners was on his way to Olyphant to mass and invited Owen and Rhondda to go with him.

"I'd like very much to go," Rhondda said to Owen as he was about to decline with thanks. "You've never attended a Catholic Mass."

"True enough," Owen said. "I'm sure I'll be embarrassed or, more likely, look stupid trying to stumble through the service."

"No, no, you won't," Conners assured them. "And if you want, just sit quietly through it all. But I do want you to go because Father Murphy is going to have something to say about the Pancoast tragedy. I saw him after confession yesterday, and I know from a remark he made that he has something to say. His own grandfather was killed at the Twin Shaft disaster fifteen years ago in Pittston. He knows something of the mines himself. He worked in the mines during the summers when he was home from college."

Without further protest from Owen, they started for St.

Patrick's in Olyphant. They were glad they did for Father P. J. Murphy delivered a moving message. He began his homily without apology or introduction:

> The appalling tragedy of Pancoast has shocked the world. Seventy-two good men and boys, trapped in a blind tunnel, seven hundred feet in the mine, were cruelly suffocated and killed.
>
> Let me say now, these men were not killed because it was an act of God. You cannot assail God and exclaim, "Why did not the Lord avert the calamity and save the lives of these innocent men?" Some people ignore the Creator until some tragedy occurs. Then they accuse God of being unmerciful. Let me remind you, God has created immutable laws of nature and science, and man must obey them. The tragedy of Pancoast was caused because these laws were disobeyed. Nature and her laws will not tolerate ignorance. She is cruel to those who disobey, but she is gentle to those who live in harmony with her laws.
>
> The disaster of Friday morning can be attributed to no other cause than the ignorant indifference of employers. It is man's inhumanity to man. Society and wage earners are to blame for not demanding better protection for those who work in mine and mill.

And then Father Murphy referred to the Triangle Shirtwaist Factory fire at Washington Place in New York City just a week before, saying:

Society must protect miners just as it must poor women working in the sweat shops of New York. There, last week, one hundred fifty women lost their lives. One New York paper said "it rained burning bodies." The building was supposed to be fireproof. Instead, it was a death trap.

The owners of mines and mills must be more responsible. If they were compelled by law to compensate widows and orphans, they would be more concerned with the workplace and safety. The corporations should not oppose new state laws protecting workers. Nor should they challenge them in the courts where irresponsible judges, tools of the trusts, will declare them unconstitutional.

Owen and Rhondda were amazed by the tone, temper, and content of the homily. In his many speeches for safety, Owen had never been as direct and accusatory.

The closing prayer was a plea for the families of victims:

Heavenly Father, look down on us this Palm Sunday. Stir within us the spirit of charity. Move all of us in this valley to give generously to the families of these victims. We must help them to survive.

The mass ended and the parishioners clustered outside buzzing in conversation, most of it controversial. Were there or were there not second and third openings, ways for the victims to have survived? Could the men have been saved if the breaker had been shut down immediately? The colliery had continued to work for two hours after the fire started. While there were telephone lines for communication, there were areas unreachable by phone. If the colliery had been shut down at once, the superintendent could have diverted air flow without any concern for the men in other parts of the mine. As usual, many parishioners parroting coal company officials repeated aloud what officials were not saying publicly, that the victims panicked. After every accident, there were always assertions designed to reduce company liability.

Rhondda and Owen left the church but remained in Olyphant and Throop the remainder of Sunday, moving from one victim's home to another, doing exactly what they had done forty-two years earlier in Avondale.

For the next two weeks, Owen and Rhondda were involved one way or another with Pancoast affairs. The Pancoast Fund to help sustain the families of victims grew to nearly one hundred thousand dollars. Tag days, musicals, theatrical benefits, and many other activities were used to raise funds. From Carbondale, Scranton, Pittston, Wilkes-Barre, and Hazleton, the dollars poured in. Pancoast and the China vein became household words throughout the region. Substantial corporate gifts, including five thousand dollars from the D&H Railroad, swelled the fund. The spontaneous giving was liberal, yet in the long run, it was insufficient for any long-time sustenance for the families. The tragedy highlighted the need for a workmen's compensation law.

Owen attended the coroner's inquest where he heard contradictory testimony along with sound suggestions. D. T. Williams, a mine inspector, argued that no wooden buildings should be permitted within a mine and that communication lines must be complete.

The state's chief inspector of mines said Pancoast would "revolutionize" safety precautions, but did not prescribe how.

The coroner's jury spent three hours inside the mine two weeks after the tragedy. Inside, they found conditions exactly as they had been when the fire was extinguished. They tested water supply, air and communication lines, asking many questions. Unfortunately, no one was sure that the conditions were identical on the day of the fire.

On Tuesday, April 25, almost three weeks after the tragedy, Owen heard the state chief of mine inspectors, James E. Roderick, not related to Owen, undergo severe questioning from the coroner's jury. The state leader and his crew of inspectors blamed state legislators for many unsafe conditions, contending that the state laws were made "for the great industry." They all testified that they lacked the power to compel companies to follow their orders. Roderick also testified that his staff was not large enough to make the inspections required by law.

Inspector D. T. Williams was required to visit all the mines in his district once every sixty days. He testified that with nineteen mines and twenty-four mine openings to inspect, he could not possibly meet this schedule. He shocked the jury by admitting that his last inspection of Pancoast took place five months before the fire.

As a representative of the union men, Owen was invited to testify. He described his fortuitous presence in the Kenwood Lunch the day of the accident and his experiences during the weekend. Under questioning, he supported the view that Pancoast was a relatively well-managed colliery. "But then," he added, "no mine is an immune mine. The antagonistic environment of mining is life-threatening and demands hour-by-hour supervision. Controlling air, water, roofs, breasts, and gangways is an engineering challenge of unbelievable difficulty. Try as men might, they have never built a safe mine."

"Mr. Roderick," one of the investigators asked, "is it possible to dig a safe mine?"

"Not absolutely," Owen replied.

"Well, what are the chief obstacles?"

"There are two. First, there is the limitation of capital. A coal company wants to crimp on capital investment. It wants to get coal out as cheaply as possible, therefore, it will only spend the minimum that will guarantee that coal will be produced. If an enlightened company were willing to spend liberally for safety, it could substantially reduce accidents and fatalities, but given the components of a mine, I'm sure there would still be accidents, but of course, far fewer."

Another questioner, trying to put Pancoast in perspective, asked Owen, "Is this the worst mining tragedy you've ever heard of?"

Owen described Avondale again, and said, "But these tragedies pale before the Albion Colliery explosion at Cilfynydd, South Wales, just seventeen years ago, in 1894."

"Why do you say that?"

"On that fateful Saturday afternoon in June, two hundred ninety men and boys were killed instantly. I do not mean to minimize the awful tragedy we have had here at Pancoast, but on that day, one hundred fifty women were made widows and three hundred fifty children fatherless."

As he had testified in 1902 before the National Anthracite Commission, Owen gave lengthy testimony, all
dutifully recorded.

The Pancoast Mine was cleared and within weeks, the
debris of the fire was removed. Operations were resumed
and once again a mine tragedy became a footnote to anthracite history.

In the years following Pancoast, Owen and Rhondda
witnessed a boom in the anthracite industry. For Scranton,
the years from 1911 to 1920 were a time of enormous prosperity. The years before World War I and the war years themselves, 1914–1918, created an unprecedented demand for
hard coal. And with the demand and the prosperity came the
accompanying cost in life and limb. By the time 1911 ended,
eighty-one million tons of anthracite were produced, but not
without the death of nearly seven hundred men and boys and
the injury of eleven hundred and fifty others.

The disaster at Pancoast reflected the ethnic changes in
the population of the anthracite region. Nearly all the victims
were eastern Europeans. Of all victims killed in 1911, one
hundred eighty-four were Polish. Altogether, close to four
hundred fifty came from Poland, Lithuania, Austria-Hungary,
or Russia, and fifty came from Italy. The ethnic changes in
Scranton between 1890 and World War I were spectacular as
these industrious Eastern Europeans poured into Northeastern
Pennsylvania to enhance the life of Lackawanna, Wayne,
Luzerne, Schuylkill and Carbon counties.

EPILOGUE

O n January 22, 1930, Owen and Rhondda, both septua-
genarians, rode in their Model A Ford to one of their
favorite lookouts above Eynon. It was a bright, warm January
day, with patches of snow melting as though it were March
22. They loved to visit the high point because it gave them a
view of the whole Lackawanna Valley. This morning, the
smoke from the breakers and the steam engines hauling anthracite coal was not as dense as usual. In earlier years, the
Lackawanna Valley had been so overlaid with smoke and steam
and fog that they could not see the city of Scranton. Only
patches of houses in the foreground of Mayfield and Blakely
were visible. But today, just a half-dozen of the collieries
were working because by January 1930, the Great Depression
was well under way. Ironically, the brighter valley denoted
hard times.

Rhondda preferred to visit this high point in the twilight
of the day when the lights could be seen going on, one after
another, sparkling the valley like a vast Christmas display.
The bright lights always reminded her of Scranton's nickname, the Electric City.

Today was physically exhilarating. As they sat comfortably
viewing the great valley, their conversation rambled in rem-
iniscences of people and events: of Avondale, Hyde Park,

The Reverend Williams, and of course, Owen's parents. His father had died just after the 1902 strike. He had lived to meet John Mitchell and to witness the triumphs of 1900 and 1902. Long before his death, his cough, so unnerving to his wife, had turned into the racking convulsive cough of anthrasilicosis— miner's asthma—the occupational disease of anthracite miners.

Owen and Rhondda's child Blodwen was now a staff doctor at the University of Pennsylvania, specializing in the treatment of lung diseases. As a small child, she had watched her grandfather cough his life away. As she grew older, she witnessed the same wheezing many times as she saw the agony of many a retired miner, his lungs unresponsive to the extra exertion of boarding a streetcar or carrying a load of groceries. Many times she saw old Theophilus Morgan climb the church steps, one by one. Theophilus was only fifty-five, but he had started in the breaker at nine and gone inside the Oxford Colliery at fourteen. Forty-six years of breathing contaminants had made him an old man at fifty-five. There were thousands like Theophilus Morgan in the anthracite fields.

Rhondda and Owen were happy that Owen's mother had lived to 1910. She saw her granddaughter, whom she often called Doctor Blodwen, graduate from Bryn Mawr College and Jefferson Medical School, and her grandson, Hugh Wynne, graduate from Haverford. After grandmother Blodwen died, Hugh Wynne received a theological degree from Union Theological Seminary in New York City, and a doctorate from Columbia University. He then went to Russia with the American Friends Service Committee.

While Rhondda and Owen were happy to view the successful and meaningful careers of their children and their cousins, they were concerned about the nation generally and Scranton specifically.

After the Pancoast tragedy, Owen had watched the anthracite coal industry boom. Production increased every year, reaching its peak in 1917 and 1919. The costly strike of 1922–23 cut production in half, but the output was renewed until 1925. Again, production declined during the 1925 strike but recovered to have good years in 1928 and 1929.

By 1920, one hundred fifty thousand men were employed in the northeastern Pennsylvania anthracite industry. In Scranton, thirty thousand men were employed, directly or indirectly, in the industry.

Scranton, in the meantime, survived these ups and downs on the economic roller coaster. During the 1920s, the overall decline in the domination of coal was evident. Coal veins were exhausted. Oil and gas were replacing coal as a fuel throughout the United States. Another great industry, textiles, was also declining. The silk mills, which once employed thousands of women, were disappearing as synthetics were invented. Scranton had been especially proud of the Sauquoit Silk Mill, hailed as the largest in the world, once employing over two thousand persons, mostly young women between fourteen and twenty-one, predominately the daughters of men employed in the anthracite industry. They were truly coal miners' daughters.

Since the 1877 rioting and upheaval, Scranton had grown to a city of 150,000 people, the third-largest in the commonwealth, eclipsed only by Philadelphia and Pittsburgh. The golden age of Scranton took place between 1902 and 1922. Northeast Pennsylvania remained loyal to the industry, but the conversion to the use of gas and oil elsewhere brought depression to the anthracite area at least five years before the stock market crash of October 1929 signaled the collapse of the vulnerable national economy.

The anthracite industry had never operated full time except for the period of World War I and a short aftermath. Now, in the Great Depression, it ran on a three-day work week at most, just as it had in the tumultuous 1870s. The large companies divided the work among the collieries, and miners got their work schedules from the radio, a new factor in American life. Each day at noon, the miners listened to the announcement of the next day's work schedule. Broadcasts like, "Collieries working tomorrow are Marvin, Moffat, and Oxford. All others idle," became familiar throughout the Lackawanna Valley.

In the Wilkes-Barre area, the announcement might list six to ten collieries working. The fact was that the veins of coal under Scranton were nearly exhausted. In Luzerne County, on the other hand, millions of tons of coal remained to be mined, and consequently, the mining schedule there was better.

The havoc and destruction caused by land subsidence had changed the minds of many about coal. They concluded that the sooner mining went, the sooner Scranton would cease to be a one-product town, subject to its devastations and control. The majority of people, however, still thought of Scranton as a coal town with a future, once the elusive prosperity "just around the corner" returned.

Mine caving worsened in the period of World War I. The frenzied mining to keep pace with the market demands of America and Europe during that period led to an exacerbation of the problem. The Board of Trade was successful in establishing cooperation from the major mining companies which were eager to forestall state legislative control. Companies often repaired damaged houses, spending as much as five thousand dollars on a dwelling. When the companies faltered in their cooperation, the famous Kohler-Fowler Act was passed in Harrisburg.

The progressive legislation did not last long. Testing the constitutionality of the law involved battles between legal giants. Owen J. Roberts, later a supreme court justice, represented the Protective Association of Scranton; the Honorable John W. Davis, later to become Democratic candidate for the presidency, represented the coal companies. The Supreme Court of the United States declared the Pennsylvania statute unconstitutional and mine caving continued to plague the city. Unpredictably it was the vote of the great justice, Oliver Wendell Holmes, that killed the law in the 5 to 4 Supreme Court opinion.

They reminisced more about Scranton and the frightful year of 1877 than any other subject, and especially of William Scranton.

William Scranton, who led the forces of the Lackawanna Iron and Coal through the riotous days of 1871 and 1877, became dissatisfied in his managerial role and ambitious to become an entrepreneur himself. He went to Germany, studied the making of steel, came home, and founded the Scranton Steel Company. However, the old Lackawanna Iron and Coal was too strong a competitor and took over the Scranton Steel in 1891. Then, to the consternation of everyone, both entities were removed to Buffalo, New York. The loss to the city of Scranton in 1901 was an economic upheaval, difficult for the public to understand. The company knew well the advantages of Buffalo over Scranton. Rich ores were available, transported over the Great Lakes. The controlling interest in New York decided to move because it was cost-effective to do so.

"As always," Owen observed, "Scranton and its people had no place on a balance sheet."

William Scranton threw his energies into his gas and water company and expanded it to a profitable northeastern Pennsylvania enterprise.

When he died on December 3, 1916, Rhondda, an inveterate scrapbook enthusiast, clipped the short notice of his death from the *New York Times*:

SCRANTON, Penn., Dec. 3—William W. Scranton, President of the Scranton Gas and Water Company, the wealthiest citizen of this place and said to be worth more than $30,000,000, died suddenly this afternoon at his home on Ridge Row, in his seventy-third year. He was a son of the late Joseph H. Scranton, and this city is named after his family, which settled here in 1847.

Mr. Scranton started work in the puddling furnace of the Lackawanna Iron and Coal Company, and in 1881 organized the Scranton Steel Company, which was the first to roll steel rails 120 feet long direct from the ingots. Ten years later Mr. Scranton sold out to the Lackawanna

Company, and since then had devoted his time to developing the Scranton Gas and Water Company, which was founded by his father in 1854.

Just twelve years later his son Worthington sold the Scranton Gas and Water Company to the Federal Water Service Corporation of New York for twenty-eight million dollars, in a timely pre-depression sale.

Rhondda and Owen lived to see the career of William Scranton change its course several times. On one occasion, Owen asked Rhondda what she really thought of William Scranton. She answered by quoting some sage, "No one can know the inner man outside of himself, and he will not tell, even if he knows, and I'm not sure he does. We paint a character, but in selecting and fusing the colors, we use the pigments of our own imagination with the result that the portrait is largely what we wish it to be and not what the man really is or was."

Owen and Rhondda followed the careers of Powderly and Mitchell to their close. Terence Powderly remained a life-long friend. They corresponded through the years, but their meetings were few. Again displaying his intelligence and intellectual drive, Powderly studied law and was admitted to practice as an attorney. As Owen had implied after the 1902 strike, Terence Powderly returned to the Bureau of Immigration and died in office in 1924 as director of information for that federal agency. He was seventy-five years old.

John Mitchell, the hero of the 1902 anthracite strike,

once hailed by six thousand workers and one thousand labor leaders in Chicago singing, "Hail the Conquering Hero," had completed his labor mission by the time he was thirty-three. Never as popular with his labor contemporaries as he was with the rank-and-file miners of the coal towns like Shenandoah, Shamokin, Hazleton, Pittston, Wilkes-Barre, and Scranton, he was only forty-nine years old when he died. His statue stands on Court House Square in Scranton, portraying him as a young man. The marble inscription identifies him as *Champion of Labor – Defender of Human Rights.* A mile or so away, he is buried precisely where he asked to be – close to his dearest friends, coal miners.

In the half-century of their life together in Scranton, Rhondda and Owen found nothing had given them more pleasure than the great Eisteddfodau. As they recalled them, they remembered the great one held in a tent in Hyde Park in 1875, one at which Governor Hartranft himself had presided. Then there were the great Eisteddfodau of 1888 to 1891, dominated by the Welsh composer and director, Dr. Daniel Protheroe, who had gone on from Scranton to become head of public school music in Chicago. Then, ten years later, the world renowned Walter Damrosch had been the adjudicator, as great choirs from Utica, Wilkes-Barre, and Scranton competed on Memorial Day in 1902. These musical events had been for Rhondda and Owen, as they were for all of the Welsh, a tonic in time of tragedy and strikes and a celebration time in periods of peace and progress.

Owen and Rhondda never missed a journey to Edwardsville, near Wilkes-Barre, every March starting in 1889 to attend the great Eisteddfod held, curiously, on St. Patrick's Day.

They attended every year until 1929 when the Eisteddfod marked its fiftieth anniversary.

The trip to Wilkes-Barre became comfortable and convenient in 1902 when a daily schedule of Laurel Line Electric Cars was established. Eisteddfod enthusiasts could leave Cedar Avenue in Scranton, then traveling through Pittston and Plains, arrive at the Market Street station in Wilkes-Barre in less than an hour. An Edwardsville trolley would have them in the T. C. Edwards Memorial Church, the site of the great Eisteddfod, in another fifteen minutes to delight in the convivial musical and literary competition.

Owen and Rhondda remembered the transition of languages in Scranton. As southern Europeans arrived, new sounds and inflections were heard on the streets and market places. By 1930, riding a streetcar from central Scranton to Dickson City, they could hear as much Polish or Slovak as English. Similarly, on a ride to Old Forge, they could hear some of those same tongues mixed with melodious Italian.

Owen and Rhondda knew Scranton in the 1870s as a city of scores of Congregational, Baptist, Presbyterian, and Methodist churches, with several large "Irish" churches, as the Catholic churches were often designated, and a sprinkling of synagogues. By 1930, almost every coal borough in the Lackawanna Valley had its own synagogue. The valley and Scranton resounded from the bells of many more Catholic churches ministering to a variety of ethnic groups. In addition, the high spires of Greek Orthodox, Russian Orthodox, Greek Catholic, and Polish National churches rose in town after town populated by these industrious Europeans.

Rhondda and Owen saw in their minds' eye this beautiful January day the whole of anthracite history. From their own reading and studying, they knew its pioneer days, its canal days, and its Civil War years. All the remainder of anthracite history, Owen and Rhondda had personally experienced and observed themselves. As they looked back, they often asked: Was it worth it? What they meant, was whether adding it all up, all the tonnages of coal, all the wages, profits, dividends, and then deducting all the pain, accidents, deaths, silicosis, land subsidence, burning coal banks, environmental sores, mine fires—well, was it all worth it?

Having enjoyed again this view from above Eynon, and once again looked at all the small houses up and down the valley, it was Rhondda who said, "Look, Owen, in every one of those homes is a wonderful family with a history that goes back to some country in the British Isles or Europe. They came here, they mined coal, they built churches and schools. They educated their children and never asked for much. When I taught in Avondale, I saw something in those children. At the children's center, I saw orphans with the same qualities. Look at those homes. Think of those people. Weren't we lucky to live with them, to know them, often to help them a little, to realize that these people, so many of them immigrants, were the ones who really built a great industry and two great cities, Scranton and Wilkes-Barre. And what great, good fortune to have known so intimately two of their most beloved leaders, Terence Powderly and John Mitchell.

"Look again, Owen, weren't we lucky to have lived with them?"

Unspoken was her memory of that kiss on that hot August day as they climbed the hill to Hyde Park after the horrible riot of 1877. She remembered her fright, the heat, her exhaustion, her wretched appearance as she embraced Owen and saw in that unlikely atmosphere their future in the embers of the day, a future for themselves and for Scranton.

ಶಿ

AUTHOR'S NOTE

The Osterhout Library—through Joan Costello, head librarian; Diane Suffren of the reference department; and Elaine Schall of collections—was crucial to my research. All on the staff assisted me in many ways. The Albright Library of Scranton was equally cooperative, especially in answering the interlibrary loan requests of the Osterhout.

I acknowledge my indebtedness to the pioneer writers of anthracite coal history and to the present scholars doing research and writing. Peter Roberts wrote two classic books at the turn of the century, one on the anthracite economy and the other on the anthracite community. Faulted somewhat by a Protestant pietism, they are nevertheless a fascinating source for the study of problems and people of the anthracite in the decades before 1904.

Other writers who have contributed to my understanding of the anthracite era are Congressman Hendrick Wright, McAlister Coleman, Elsie Glick, George Korson, Eliot Jones, Scott Nearing, Andrew Roy, and the Rev. William J. Walsh. Current writers who have been helpful are Harold Aurand, Benjamin Powell, Burton Folsom, Jr., John Bodnar, Marvin Schlagel, Donald Miller and Richard Sharpless, Charles Petrillo, and Anthony Wallace.

Special articles on anthracite have also been helpful. The authors are Perry Blatz, Melvyn Dubofsky, Bela Vassady, Joseph Makarewicz, James Radechko, George Turner, William Gudelunas, Matthew Magda, Ronald Filippelli, Stephen Couch, Ronald Benson, James Sperry, Alice Hoffman, Tom Juravich, and James Bohning. Their articles are innovative and illuminating, to say the least.

Two excellent novels, *Breaker Boys* by Jan Kubicki and *Patch Boys* by Jay Parini, gave me valuable insight to life in the anthracite region at the turn of the century and in the 1920s.

Mary Ann Landis, director of the Pennsylvania Anthracite Museum Complex, opened doors for me, as she does for any writers doing anthracite research. At the Scranton center of the complex, the Pennsylvania Heritage Museum, the director, Dan Perry; press administrator, Elizabeth Wassel; and curator, Chester Kulesa, as well as several of the volunteers, graciously responded to appeals for research material on Scranton mining.

The writing of anthracite history in any form would be impossible without the annual reports of the Bureau of Mines published by the Department of Internal Affairs. Needless to say, newspapers such as the old *Scranton Republican*, *The Wilkes-Barre Record*, and *The Scranton Times* are excellent sources for day-by-day history of the anthracite mines and communities.

Although I had a very brief experience working as a breaker boy in the Sugar Notch Breaker during the Great Depression, I garnered mining experiences from my father, uncles, neighbors, and from my brother Thomas, my good friend Gerald Hardiman, and my cousin Hugh Williams.

For Wilkes-Barre history, I am indebted to the Proceedings of the Wyoming Historical and Geological Society, the histories of Oscar Jewell Harvey and Ernest G. Smith, of Charles Miner, of Isaac Chapman, the recent works of Edward Hanlon and John Beck, and the biographical history of Sheldon Spear. The children's home material came from the Children's Service Center and was provided by Lois Harvey.

Scranton history is derived from the histories of Horace Hollister, Frederick L. Hitchcock, Thomas Murphy, the Rev. Samuel Logan, Monsignor John Gallagher, Terence Powderly, and from *The Scranton Times* and the *Scranton Republican*.

Rufus Jones, the eminent Quaker theologian, is the source for the customs and religion of the Friends.

Biographies of President Theodore Roosevelt describe his disappointment with the coal operators in the coal strike of 1902.

The thread of ethnicism was stimulated by continuing conversations about the subject with my friends Dr. Jule Ayers, Dr. Roswell Barnes, and the writing of Dr. Edward Hartmann.

Finally and most important was the assistance of my wife Mary, who reread the developing manuscript several times. The professional editing and design of John Beck of The Bookmakers, Incorporated, author of *Never Before in History: The Story of Scranton*, were critical to the content, cohesiveness, and design of the work.

Mrs. Guy Goodman typed the manuscript and graciously called for and delivered copy almost every day.

Dr. Sheldon Spear was good enough to read the first proofs. His knowledge of the post–Civil War era was especially helpful. I am especially grateful to Professor Robert A. Fowkes, Meryl Davis, George Powell, and Leon Wazetter for correcting errors found in the first printing.

To the librarians, the writers, and all others I have mentioned, I express my most profound thanks, hoping they will forgive any flaws in the book, for which I alone am responsible.